"*A Thousand Shall Fall* is an intriguing tale of romance in the midst of a country divided. I've long enjoyed Andrea's work and this book was no exception. I look forward to reading book two."
—Tracie Peterson, best-selling author of over 100 novels, including the Brides of Seattle series and the Heirs of Montana series

"Lovers of Civil War sagas will delight in this historically rich tale. Boeshaar's research shines, making *A Thousand Shall Fall* a sparkling story that leaps from the pages and into the reader's heart."
—Jocelyn Green, award-winning author of the Heroines Behind the Lines Civil War series

"Andrea Boeshaar writes the kind of books I love. They always go to the top of my to-be-read pile. Her settings are authentic, her characters leap off the pages into my heart, and her story lines are interesting. The spiritual threads are not preachy, but show how characters can react to the conflicts of life in a way that leads them to the heart of God."
—Lena Nelson Dooley, award-winning author of *8 Weddings and a Miracle* and *A Texas Christmas*

"A beautifully written novel with characters who are larger than life, conflicted between the loyalty of family or the fondness of a special friend. . . . Civil War buffs and fans of historical novels will rejoice with this latest offering from Andrea Boeshaar."
—Patsy Glans, reader and independent reviewer

"Andrea Boeshaar writes compelling Christian historical romance that is a joy to read. She is one of my favorite go-to authors, with a voice so lovely, the spirit of the Lord is clearly felt in her stories."
—Carrie Fancett Pagels, author of *Lilacs for Juliana* and *Return to Shirley Plantation*

"Andrea Boeshaar does it again. With beautiful description and historical detail, *A Thousand Shall Fall* portrays the gamut of emotions from a turbulent time in our great nation's history. With a story of war, heartache, betrayal, and love, Boeshaar captured my attention from the first page."
—Kimberley Woodhouse, best-selling and award-winning author of *Beyond the Silence* and *All Things Hidden*

A THOUSAND *Shall* FALL

A Civil War Novel

Shenandoah Valley Saga

ANDREA BOESHAAR

Kregel
Publications

A Thousand Shall Fall: A Civil War Novel
© 2015 by Andrea Boeshaar

Published by Kregel Publications, a division of Kregel, Inc., 2450 Oak Industrial
Dr. NE, Grand Rapids, MI 49505.

Scripture quotations are from the King James Version of the Bible.

ISBN 978-0-8254-4381-7

Printed in the United States of America
15 16 17 18 19 20 21 22 23 24 / 5 4 3 2 1

A thousand shall fall at thy side,
And ten thousand at thy right hand;
But it shall not come nigh thee.
Psalm 91:7

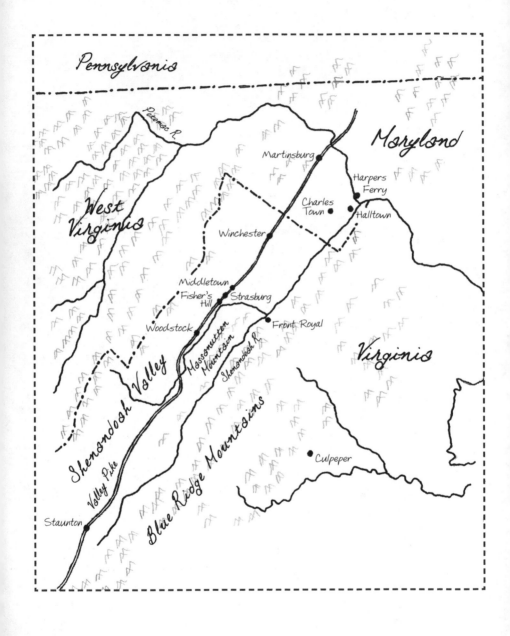

AUTHOR'S NOTE

Although the Shenandoah Valley Saga is fictional, much research has gone into this series.

The Shenandoah Valley

Being a Wisconsin native, I had much to learn about Virginia state history during the time of the Civil War. One of the more interesting facts is that because the southern part of the Shenandoah Valley has a higher elevation than the northern part, the Shenandoah River runs northeast and empties into the Potomac. As a result, when one is traveling north on the Valley Pike, from Woodstock to Winchester, for example, one is going north, *down* the Valley. Traveling south, from Winchester to Staunton, is considered going *up* the Valley. It's opposite the traditional concept of "down south" and "up north."

Whiskey and Cigars

You'll notice that my male characters, although they are Christians, indulge in a swallow or two of whiskey from time to time and smoke cigars. In fact, the Union army sent cases or kegs of whiskey to its troops to keep the men's morale up so they would continue fighting. Furthermore, history shows that whiskey was widely used by Union and Confederate troops alike for medicinal purposes, and the occasional brandy and a good cigar was socially acceptable for men. For example, about a decade after America's Civil War, Charles Spurgeon was reported to have said, "Well, dear friends, you know that some men can do to the glory of God what to other men would be sin. And notwithstanding . . . I intend to smoke a good cigar to the glory of God before I go to bed to-night." While I don't personally condone the practices, I felt it was important that my story be as historically accurate as possible—but without scandalizing my readers.

History Versus Reality

All the dated news reports are authentic from newspapers and telegraphs of that time period. While I did much research, I used my literary license and took great liberties with several prominent historical figures. I added an extra regiment to General Philip Sheridan's cavalry and, specifically, to General Wesley Merritt's division. I added stores and other businesses to Woodstock's Main Street, and I superimposed my characters into Winchester's history, along with Aunt Ruth's home. Even so, I tried to remain accurate to the actual accounts and not diminish either Woodstock's or Winchester's significance during the Civil War. It is fun to note that General Sheridan did ride through Winchester on September 19, 1864. Historical accounts state that the general stopped on the street to speak with a couple of young ladies before he rode to the schoolhouse to thank Miss Rebecca Wright, who passed information to him and aided in the Union's victory that day.

Victorian Love Letters

If you're tempted to think men and women of the Civil War era were too proper to reveal their feelings in a love letter, think again. According to author Karen Lystra in her nonfiction book *Searching the Heart*, "Middle-class Americans believed that intimate communication between individuals disclosed their 'true' self and was an act of good breeding when conducted by the proper participants in private space." These letters were very private, hid away and treasured. One would never consider sharing them even with the closest of friends. A love letter in Victorian times (1837 to 1901 in England and America) was the ultimate in romantic communication.

Helpful Resources

Additionally, I'd like to acknowledge the authors and their nonfiction titles that proved most helpful to me.

The Civil War: Complete Text of the Best Narrative History of the Civil War with over 100 Actual Photographs. Patriot Publishing Co., 1912; Kindle, MonkeyBone Publications, 2014.

Clower, Joseph B., Jr. *Early Woodstock: Facts and Photographs.* Woodstock Museum of Shenandoah County, 1996.

Duncan, Richard R. *Beleaguered Winchester: A Virginia Community at War, 1861–1865.* LSU Press, 2007.

Foote, Shelby. *The Civil War: A Narrative.* Vol. 3. *Red River to Appomattox.* 1974. Knopf Doubleday, 2011.

Gallagher, Gary W., ed. *The Shenandoah Valley Campaign of 1864.* UNC Press, 2006.

Lystra, Karen. *Searching the Heart.* Oxford University Press, 1989.

Mack, Maggie. *Civil War Household Tips.* Vol. 1. Fortuna Publishing, 2011.

Mahon, Michael G., ed. *Winchester Divided: The Civil War Diaries of Julia Chase and Laura Lee.* Stackpole Books, 2002.

McPherson, James. *Battle Cry of Freedom: The Civil War Era.* Oxford University Press, 1988.

McPherson, James M. *What They Fought For, 1861–1865.* LSU Press, 1995.

Quarles, Garland Redd. *Winchester, Virginia: Streets, Churches, Schools.* 1952.

Schroeder-Lein, Glenna R. *The Encyclopedia of Civil War Medicine.* 2008. Routledge, 2015.

Sharpe, Hal F. *Shenandoah County in the Civil War: Four Dark Years.* The History Press, 2012.

Wert, Jeffry D. *From Winchester to Cedar Creek: The Shenandoah Campaign of 1864.* SIU Press, 2010.

ACKNOWLEDGMENTS

Writing and publishing a book is always a collaborative effort, and I had one of the best teams bringing this story-of-my-heart into print.

First and foremost, I'm eternally grateful to Jesus Christ for His gift of salvation and for bestowing me with the gift of words.

Next, a huge THANKS to my husband, Daniel, who doesn't mind being my "logistics guy" whenever I do historical research.

A special thanks goes to my dear friend and literary agent Mary Sue Seymour.

And at Kregel Publications, to Dennis and Steve, who shared my vision for this book—thank you!

Also to Janyre, Lori, Dawn, and the rest of my editorial team—you're awesome!

Finally, to my readers whose hearts are touched by my stories—thank you. You make all my hard work worthwhile!

A
THOUSAND
Shall
FALL

MAJOR-GENERAL CITY POINT

August 12, 1864 — 9 A.M.

Chief of Staff HALLECK:

Inform General Sheridan that it is now certain two (2) divisions of infantry have gone to Confederate General Early, and some cavalry and twenty (20) pieces of artillery. This movement commenced last Saturday night. Sheridan must be cautious, and act now on the defensive until movements here force them to detach to send to Petersburg. Early's force, with this increase, cannot exceed forty thousand men, but this is too much for General Sheridan to attack. Send General Sheridan the remaining brigade of the Nineteenth Corps.

I have ordered to Washington all the one-hundred-day men. Their time will soon be out, but for the present they will do to serve in the defenses.

U. S. Grant, Lieutenant-General

CHAPTER 1

August 15, 1864

Ooh, that Sarah Jane!

Carrie Ann Bell stared at her youngest sister's sloppily scratched note. How could that girl do such a scandalous thing? Running off with a lowlife peddler? Certainly Sarah had threatened to run away numerous times in the past, but who would have thought she'd actually do it? Mama would be heartbroken when she learned the news.

Heartbroken and angry. Carrie could practically hear Mama crying and blaming her for Sarah running off. Mama would say Carrie paid more attention to Papa's newspaper than her sisters . . .

And maybe Mama was right. But her sister Margaret was eighteen and Sarah, fifteen. They weren't that much younger than Carrie herself. And writing for the *Bell Tower* in Papa's absence had been Carrie's refuge, a place of normalcy in a world turned topsy-turvy.

Staring at Sarah's note, Carrie debated whether to withhold this information from Mama. Maybe she'd go looking for her youngest sister and bring her home to the Wayfarers Inn—

What a contradiction. The Wayfarers Inn was no more a home than a damp, dark cave was an elegant mansion. Still, it was a roof over her family's head.

Carrie paced the small newspaper office, paused, and ran one ink-stained fingertip over the smooth service of Papa's desk. Surely she could catch up with Arthur Sims, that no-account speculator with whom Sarah ran off. He couldn't have traveled far in that large, rattling contraption of his. Painted in obnoxious shades of yellow and orange, it resembled a circus wagon.

Carrie's hand shook as sudden fire flowed through her veins. She was tempted to notify the law and file kidnapping charges against the man, except the law had better things to do than go hunting for a fast-talking swindler who rode off with a starry-eyed girl.

Lord Jesus, what should I do?

Praying, thinking, plotting, planning, Carrie resumed her aimless wander, circling the obstinate Washington Iron Hand Press. She halted once more. What would Papa do if he were here?

She'd asked herself that question countless times in the past. With Mama ill and occasionally out of her mind, Margaret behaving like a veritable hussy, and now Sarah Jane running off, Carrie was sure she'd failed miserably at the task of taking care of her family in Papa's absence.

And the *Bell Tower* . . . sales were almost nonexistent for want of supplies. Worse, the old press continually gave her fits.

Her shoulders slumped under the weight of defeat. This newspaper was Papa's purpose for living, and under Carrie's management, the next issue of the *Bell Tower* wouldn't even go to press. But perhaps it was only a temporary setback and the newspaper could be printed regularly again once the War Between the States ended.

If only Papa would return.

Unfortunately, he wasn't here now. It was up to Carrie to find Sarah and bring her back to the Wayfarers Inn.

Stuffing Sarah's note into the pocket of her faded dress, Carrie exited the tiny newspaper office and locked the door behind her. The summer heat had increased since she'd arrived at dawn, and now, as she hurried down Main Street, perspiration moistened her brow and nape. People were out and about, mostly women, as only they, old men, and boys were left in Woodstock these days. They swept their walks and shared information with each other in front of their residences and establishments, but no one seemed to notice Carrie's haste, which was just as well. Mama would have a fit if she saw her unladylike gait.

As she trotted past the printers, then Massanutten Mercantile, Swifts' Seams and Tailoring, and Owens' Bootery, she glanced across the street at the National Hotel and couldn't help recalling the days when this town had seen finer times. Now the brick and wood structures lining Main Street needed paint and repairs. On the next block over, buildings stood riddled with gunshot. Others looked like soulless ghouls, dark and vacant.

Carrie rushed on, into the less prominent part of the town, thinking, worrying, and praying over her sister.

That spoiled Sarah Jane, adding to Mama's worries like this! Lord, what am I going to do now? Imagine running off when her family needed her and just because she wanted a real home. Carrie wanted the same—and more. A family of her own. A husband who adored her.

A pair of brandy-colored eyes surfaced in her memory, eyes that belonged on a Union captain's handsome, bearded face. Wounded and bleeding heavily, he'd come into the Wayfarers Inn more than a year ago. The owner and innkeeper, Mr. Veyschmidt, had ordered her not to aid or assist Yankees. But Carrie, an independent-minded journalist just like her papa, hadn't chosen sides in the conflict, unlike most citizens of Woodstock, who were decidedly Confederate. To Carrie's way of thinking, any man who was wounded, whether grayback or blue, deserved to be helped. So she defied Mr. Veyschmidt and sutured the deep gash on the captain's forearm. Turns out, the captain was the nicest, most charming Yankee officer she'd ever met. Handsome too. Carrie could still feel the warmth of his gaze on her face as she'd stitched the wound. Immediately, she'd sensed something special about the man.

After she'd finished bandaging his arm, she gave him a copy of the *Bell Tower.* The issue contained the article she'd written about several of Lieutenant Colonel John S. Mosby's partisans who stayed at the inn. Drunk one night, Mosby's men bragged about ambushing a Union supply wagon and killing the Yankees accompanying it. The captain read her article as he ate his supper, and afterward he thanked her. He said the information was as helpful as her doctoring. He'd also complimented her writing style, something few people ever did around here. Such a pity the handsome captain got himself killed at Gettysburg—at least that's what she'd heard from a Union sergeant who'd marched through Woodstock last fall.

A sudden clamp on her shoulder, and Carrie missed her next step. She fell forward, the plank walk coming up fast to meet her.

"Whoa, girl." A pair of strong hands brought her upright before she hit face-first.

Her feet planted firmly again, Carrie stared into a familiar sun-bronzed face. Joshua.

Relief turned to irritation. "I almost fell on account of you!"

"Nice to see you again too, Carrie Ann." He regarded her with apparent reprimand. She'd known Joshua Blevens since . . . well, ever since she could remember. "What are you doing, running down the street like the blue-bellies are charging into town?"

She hurled an annoyed glance skyward. "I wouldn't run even if they were charging into town. If you'll recall, Federals have charged into Woodstock before."

"Federals?" Joshua turned and gazed at his comrade. Carrie hadn't seen the other man until just this moment. "This girl ain't always so prim and proper, I assure you. She usually calls the enemy *blue-bellies* or *Yankees* like the rest of us."

"Speak for yourself." Carrie clasped her hands in front of her. "Margaret told me you were back in town." Her sister was far too friendly with soldiers, graybacks and blue. "I'm glad to see you haven't gotten your fool head blown off yet."

"You always were a source of encouragement to me." Joshua's dry tone said he didn't appreciate her teasing. After combing strong fingers through his walnut-brown hair, he plopped his hat back on his head. His cheeks looked hollow and the line of his jaw more narrow than Carrie remembered. No doubt survival proved as difficult for him these last few years as for her.

Carrie dropped her gaze. Like the Bible said, these days life truly was a vapor that vanished away, and she wouldn't want the last words spoken to her longtime friend to be a thoughtless jest.

She peeked at Joshua. "Where'd you get that uniform?" Amazingly, his butternut trousers weren't soiled or tattered. She touched the sleeve of his gray shell jacket. Single-breasted with five shiny pewter buttons going up the front. Black piping along the collar and sleeves added distinction, and the ebony belt circling his trim waist boldly sported the silver letters CSA—the Confederate States of America. He stood tall, his chin held proudly. "Quite impressive, Joshua."

He bowed slightly. "I'm an officer now, Carrie Ann. I've been promoted to major—Major Joshua Blevens."

"My, my. Your folks must be so proud of you." She smiled. "And so am I. Congratulations."

He grinned, his gaze fixed on her face, until his friend cleared his throat.

"Speakin' of folks," the other man said, "didn't your mama teach you any manners, Blevens?"

He whirled around and faced his cohort.

"Introduce us," the man prompted.

"Of course. Excuse my rudeness." Joshua took a step back. "Miss Carrie Ann Bell, meet Major John Rodingham. Likewise, Major, allow me to present the sassiest girl this side of the Alleghenies."

Rodingham strode forward with an air of confidence. His eyes resembled two lead balls set into deep sockets. Oddly, the major's suntanned skin and brown hair were a perfect match, and the exact color of Papa's pipe tobacco. "A pleasure, Miss Bell."

She froze beneath his weighty gaze. His cold, flat eyes reminded her of the reptiles Joshua had teased her with as a child, not all of which were harmless. She blinked, wondering which type he was.

"Carrie Ann?" Joshua jabbed her with his elbow.

She swallowed her misgivings. "The pleasure is all mine, sir."

"Carrie Ann's been working hard, operating her father's newspaper in his absence," Joshua explained, and she detected a note of pride in his voice. "Mr. Bell marched off with General Jackson, taking it upon himself to document the war in hopes a publisher will purchase his writings. Ain't that right, Carrie Ann?"

"Yes, that's correct." But would she ever cure Joshua of using the word *ain't*? Probably not.

"Heard from him lately? Your papa?"

"Not for a while. His last letter arrived some three months ago." Carrie didn't add that it was postmarked from Washington, that Papa must be doing research about the Union army now. She didn't even want to think what Joshua and his friend would do if they found out her father was working inside a blue-belly camp.

"I wouldn't fret if I were you, Carrie Ann." The consolation in Joshua's voice did little to comfort her.

"Folks here in Woodstock say Papa's dead." Carrie's chin quivered in spite of her best efforts to appear as brave as the Rebel officers who blocked the walkway. "But I refuse to give up hope."

Joshua reached for her hand and gave it a brotherly squeeze.

"Quite the honor to be endorsed by General Jackson, may he rest in peace." Rodingham slapped his leather gauntlets against one palm. He too wore a gray shell jacket. "You must be very proud."

"Indeed I am, sir."

The major stepped toward her, and Carrie backed away.

Joshua set his hand on her shoulder and she felt a measure of protection. "In her spare time, Carrie Ann works at the Wayfarers Inn up the block with her sisters." His gaze met hers. "What's for breakfast this morning, Carrie Ann?"

"Porridge, same as every other day this week. It's been so hot that the chickens won't lay their eggs. Then again, I left before anyone else was awake, and Margaret is the one who gathers eggs each morning."

"Were you at the newspaper office?"

She nodded. "I'm having trouble with the printing press again."

"That dilapidated ol' thing." Joshua wagged his head. "Wish I could help you with repairs like I usually do, Carrie Ann, but I've got more important things on my mind."

"Understandable. Besides, I managed to get it working." She glimpsed her stained fingertips and quickly stuffed her hands into her apron pockets. She'd been so distracted when she left Papa's office that she'd forgotten about washing up and putting on gloves and her bonnet. She must appear a disgrace to Rodingham, although she wasn't bent on impressing him as much as she hoped she hadn't embarrassed Joshua.

Sarah Jane's note brushed against her bare palm, and Carrie's gaze bounced back to her childhood friend. Would he help her—just like he used to when they were children?

"You back home for a while now, Joshua?"

"No. Awaiting orders is all—and trying to show everyone in Woodstock that continued support of the Confederacy will bring prosperity."

Carrie's hopes deflated like one of the Union Balloon Corps's aerostats that she'd read about.

"These new uniforms and our victory at Cold Harbor a couple of months ago prove it." A look of pride spread across Joshua's face. "About two thousand Yankees dead, and we didn't even lose a hundred men."

Carrie knew the details. She'd printed them in the *Bell Tower*. "And so far, you've been able to protect Petersburg from falling into Union hands."

"The Yankees'll never get Petersburg," Joshua muttered.

Rodingham cleared his throat. "Tell us, Miss . . . what are you doing in town this fine morning, galloping down the street such as you were?"

Joshua stared at her from beneath an arched brow.

Carrie's cheeks burned with a rush of indignation. "I have an important message to deliver to my mother." *Not that it's any concern of yours.*

She turned to her friend. "Joshua?" There had to be a way he could help her, especially now that he was an officer. "May I speak to you privately?"

He cast a brief look toward Rodingham. "I'm a busy man, Carrie Ann."

"It's important." She gave him a pleading stare.

Meeting her gaze, his blue eyes turned steely-gray, revealing a hardness that Carrie had never seen in Joshua before. Obviously he'd witnessed more on battlefields than human beings ought to see—things Carrie only heard about when soldiers were well into their cups at the Wayfarers Inn.

Joshua clasped her upper arm and led her down the walk several paces. "All right, what is it?" Impatience clipped his every word. "I don't want to keep Rodingham waiting."

"It's Sarah Jane." Carrie got right to the point. "She's run off with that peddler who was here in town. He and his big fancy painted wagon rolled in a couple of days ago."

"I know who you mean." Joshua narrowed his gaze. "He's quite a bit older than Sarah Jane. How do you know they ran off together?"

Carrie thrust her sister's note at him. "Sarah left this."

He read it.

"Might you know where that no-account was headed?" Carrie asked.

"Well, if it's the same fellow who tried to sell me a cheap pocket watch last night, then he's likely continuing down the Valley. He mentioned having kin somewhere near Front Royal."

"I've got to go after him and bring Sarah back."

"I knew you'd say that. But get the fool idea out of your head. There's a new army just formed, and it includes some of the most ruthless cavalrymen the Union's got to offer. From what I hear they'll give Ol' Jube a run for his money," he said, referring to General Jubal Early. "But the Confederacy will prevail. Even so, I can't imagine what those devil cavalrymen would do to a naïve Southern girl like yourself if they found you outside of town on your own."

"But Sarah is—"

"No! You hear me?" With his hand around her arm again, Joshua gave Carrie a shake.

"Stop it. You're hurting me!"

"What do you think those Yankee invaders will do to you?"

Carrie pulled free from Joshua's grasp.

"Having difficulties over there, Blevens?" Rodingham's mocking voice sailed over on a slight breeze.

"Nothing I can't handle." Joshua rubbed tanned fingers along his clean-shaven jaw. "I'll inform Rodingham of the situation and between the two of us we'll—"

"Don't bother." Carrie peeked at the man from around Joshua's left arm. "I get the feeling that your friend won't be much help. Besides, I don't trust him."

"You never trusted anyone, Carrie Ann. Why would you start now?"

"I trusted you." Maybe she shouldn't have. "The war has changed you."

"It's changed everyone."

"Well, pardon me," Carrie huffed. "I thought you were my friend."

"I am your friend." Joshua set his palms on her shoulders. "And you'll always be like my little sister." He expelled a breath. "Don't worry, all right? Sarah Jane is probably homesick by now. She'll be back soon enough. And we'll keep our eye out for her. But, Carrie Ann, you can't go after her. There's blue-bellies camped all around Woodstock."

"If it's too dangerous for me, imagine Sarah out there alone. She's just a child. What's more, she's in the company of a man who will likely ruin her by nightfall." She grabbed hold of the front of his shell jacket. "I can't stand the thought, Joshua, and I'll confront the entire Union army—the devil himself if I have to—in order to find my sister."

He grasped her hands. "Carrie Ann, you're scarin' me because I know that determined look in your eyes."

Carrie's mind reeled through possibilities of how to reach her sister on the other side of the battleground. She suddenly remembered a Union deserter's uniform in her trunk. She'd found it last spring while cleaning the guest rooms. The Federal soldier had been on leave, or so he said, except he'd left his uniform and never came back for it. After some hemming, it'd fit her. At least passably. All she needed was a pair of boots to ensure her passage past Yankee pickets.

"Joshua, please? I know where I can get a Yankee uniform. All I need is a pair of boots and that's where you can help me."

"Are you touched in the head, girl?" Joshua looked skyward. "Dressing up like a Yankee?"

"Just to get past their guards."

"That's the most harebrained idea you've come up with in all your born days!"

"But if I looked like one of them, then—"

"Then Confederates'll shoot you. What's more, if they think you're a spy, they'll hang you."

"You're just trying to scare me, like when we were children." She folded her arms. "There's got to be a way."

"Maybe, but that plan of yours ain't it. Now you'd best go tell your mama about what Sarah Jane did and leave the rest up to God Almighty."

She took a step back, unwilling to concede defeat. Not yet, anyway. "I could wear one of Margaret's gowns over the uniform while I get out of town. She's larger than I am."

"The scrawniest chicken in the barnyard's larger than you."

Carrie ignored the biting retort and accompanying scowl. After all, her idea was a good one. "I could cut my hair and wear the Yankee deserter's uniform—"

"Cut your hair?"

"Since the no-account peddler's got that heavy wagon and the sorriest-looking mules pulling it, I should be able to catch up easy enough." She imagined his punishment for running off with Sarah Jane. "When I find him, that man is as good as dead."

"Now you're talkin' cold-blooded murder. Sarah Jane went with him willingly. You've got her note in your hand and I'm witness to that fact." Joshua's frown deepened. "Carrie Ann, the truth is, if you do this thing, you're the only one who'll get killed."

That threat wasn't enough to instill the fear of God into her. Rather, it seemed as if God fanned the spark that now burned within her breast, because telling Mama—now that idea terrified her! The angry rants, the curses, the insults and humiliation. Carrie didn't think she could bear another of Mama's episodes.

But if she had a plan, and promised Mama that she'd find Sarah Jane . . .

"You'd best know that both Union and Confederate armies are heavily armed." Joshua's voice penetrated her thoughts. "Carrie Ann, you don't understand what's going on outside of town right now."

She didn't care. All that mattered was finding Sarah Jane. "Please, Joshua?" She gave him the expression that usually made him crumble and relent. "You've known Sarah since the day she was born. She's like your sister too." Holding her next breath, Carrie waited, hoping, praying. "Please?"

"A pair of black boots, huh?" His features softened. "I'll see what I can do."

"Oh, thank you!"

"I said, *I'll see*. That doesn't guarantee anything."

Standing on tiptoe, she pressed a sisterly kiss on his cheek. Maybe some things hadn't changed between them after all.

CHAPTER 2

"Look alive, men!" Colonel Peyton Collier sat astride his black charger and eyed the sorry-looking horsemen of Company D. Thankfully it was the only one of twelve in his newly formed regiment that lacked both discipline and dash. Soon, however, these troopers would realize what an honor they'd received, being mustered into the service of General Wesley Merritt's 1st Division Cavalry.

Peyton continued to survey the eighty men. Their appearances were as rough as he'd expected, considering their riotous living last night. While Peyton wasn't a man to partake of strong drink—not anymore—he could understand his men's desire to celebrate another day of life. He knew the impulse to mask the pain of reality with whiskey—government-issued whiskey at that. But drunkenness wouldn't be tolerated under his command. Death lurked around each corner of this war. His men needed to be sober.

Peyton expelled a weary sigh at the bearded faces, shaggy hair, and bloodshot eyes that returned his stare. Shirts hung over their blue trousers. Suspenders dangled at their hips. Most hadn't had time to don their blue sack coats before the impromptu formation. Peyton was tempted to fine them, which he could do under army regulations. But he wouldn't. Not this time.

He filled his lungs then slowly released a breath. This poorly managed company would surely challenge his leadership skills. Still, the men needed to hear from their commanding officer. After that, his subordinates would take charge of them.

Peyton had only been promoted to the rank of colonel at the beginning of this month, shortly after General Philip Sheridan, a comrade from years past, took command of the Middle Military Division, now the recently christened the Army of the Shenandoah. Peyton often wondered if migrating armies had been such a good idea, and it wasn't the first time he questioned one of General Grant's decisions. Even so, Peyton followed orders, and as a newly appointed colonel, he needed to win his men's loyalty.

"First things first." He sat high in his saddle. "I won't tolerate imbibing while we're in camp. What you do on your own time is your business, but while you're under my command, you'll be sober. We could come under enemy fire at any time so you'll need to have your wits about you." He sent a hard stare to his bleary-eyed captain. "Do I make myself clear?"

"Yes, sir." The captain's reply was accompanied by rumbling unity from the men.

Peyton leaned forward and crossed his hands atop his saddle. "As you are aware, it is imperative that the Union control the Shenandoah Valley. If this campaign is successful, which General Sheridan believes it will be, then we could soon see a Confederate surrender and a swift end to this war."

The men cheered and Peyton felt like joining them. This war had lasted far too long and had taken too many lives.

He pulled back his shoulders. "We'll remain here, camped by the Shenandoah River, until we receive further instruction from General Merritt. Understood?"

"Yes, sir!"

Peyton glanced at his captain. "I'll be reconnoitering with four other cavalry officers later. You're in charge." He raised an eyebrow. "Don't make me regret that decision."

"No sir, Colonel, I won't."

Satisfied, Peyton dismissed the captain and his men and urged his horse, Brogan, onward. He stopped and delivered the same message until his entire regiment of nearly one thousand men had heard directly from him. As General Sheridan said, this campaign was too important to lose due to miscommunication at the onset.

Weariness pervaded Peyton's limbs. Without a doubt another battle loomed, bloody and deadly. Many of the men he spoke to today might not be alive to recount the tale tomorrow. That realization sliced through him with the swiftness of an enemy's saber.

The men he passed stopped playing cards, stood, and respectfully saluted. He rode toward the camp's corral. He'd worked hard for the rank of colonel, fought hard. Dear Aunt Ruth had made sure he'd met the right people. It'd be a lie if he said he didn't enjoy the power and privileges of being an officer. Nevertheless, he understood that the rank bore much responsibility—responsibility that, after Gettysburg, he promised God he'd take seriously. And he did.

"I'll take Brogan's reins, sir."

Peyton dismounted. "Here you go, Tommy." He tossed the leather straps at the boy who longed to be a Federal soldier. Would to God that Tommy lived another year so he could legally enlist—better yet that the war would be won so Tommy could attend school and make something of himself. However, the lad seemed to have soldiering on his heart and always on his mind.

"Did you get all your talking in today, Colonel?"

"I did." Peyton pulled off his gauntlets.

"I wouldn't mind practicing some shooting again, sir, after I get your horse tended to. My chores are done."

Peyton smiled at the eagerness shining on the lad's round face. "Very well." He retrieved the revolver from the pocket inside his coat. "Go on. Just remember my instructions and warnings."

"Yes, sir, I will." Tommy eyed the '55 Colt Sidehammer reverently, which warmed Peyton's heart. The weapon had been Peyton's eighteenth birthday present from Aunt Ruth.

"Don't shoot your foot off."

Tommy grinned at the jest. "No, sir, I won't."

"And once we march out of camp, later today or tomorrow, you stay out of the way. Understand?"

"I will, sir."

Peyton inclined his head as the young man led the black gelding toward the makeshift corral. Bad enough that the number of men he'd lost since Gettysburg could have populated a small city. No sense in more children losing their lives. In his opinion, the army shouldn't allow men under eighteen to enlist. On the other hand, Peyton didn't know what he'd do without boys like

Tommy who tended to the horses, helped the saddler, assisted the surgeon, and served as drummer boys as well as occasional couriers on the battlefield. Still, Peyton felt compelled to keep the boys who fell under his command as safe as possible in the middle of a war.

A horrid memory flashed across Peyton's mind as he strode to his tent. Cold Harbor. It had been a grisly disaster for the Union army. So had most of the battles this summer. However, with Phil Sheridan leading this new army, things were definitely looking up.

⸺◌◌⸺

By nightfall, Carrie Ann was trudging down the rutted Valley Pike toward Strasburg, wearing the deserter's uniform beneath Margaret's dress. She prayed each step of the way, trusting God's hand to guide her and use her to rescue Sarah Jane. And to protect Margaret's dress. *Dear God, please do that.* She promised to do Margaret's chores for a month in exchange for borrowing it. And Carrie felt confident that her plan would work. It had to work. She wouldn't be allowed back home if it didn't—and Mama made good on all her threats.

She moved closer to the side of the uneven road so she wouldn't turn an ankle in her ill-fitting boots. Joshua had come through for her, providing the boots, and she was grateful to him.

With only a sliver of moonlight, she easily made out the way. She'd been this way before, but always with either Joshua or Papa. Known for its tanneries and pottery, Strasburg was nicknamed "Pot Town." Since the war, it had become a dilapidated place. The Yanks and Rebs alike usually marched right through it, so Carrie didn't anticipate being bothered.

Her mind came back around to Papa. If only he were home to advise her . . .

But he wasn't. She supposed the Lord was still with her, though. He had protected her from the devastating fire that destroyed the farm. He'd shielded her from drunken soldiers at the Wayfarers Inn. He was able to take care of her now and direct her path to Sarah Jane.

But would He?

Carrie decided to occupy her thoughts with fond memories instead of her mounting doubts. She recalled some of Papa's tales about the area. The native Indians named the Shenandoah Valley "Daughter of the Stars," and Carrie had always appreciated the unique topography. The land was lush and fertile, and if it weren't nighttime, she'd see the green pastures, golden cornfields, and shimmering wheat fields that stretched out across the Valley like a patchwork quilt. The hills of Massanutten Mountain lay beyond to the east. To the west, the jagged peaks of the Alleghenies were the Valley's backdrop. Carrie had overheard farmers talking together inside the Wayfarers Inn, saying this summer's crops had done well. Soon the bountiful grain harvests would be taken to the Valley's many mills. Little wonder why the Shenandoah Valley earned the nickname "The Breadbasket of the Confederacy."

And little wonder why Rebels and Yankees were ready to kill each other in order to control it.

But fighting wasn't anything new to this area of Virginia—not since this war began. General "Stonewall" Jackson had successfully defended it back in 1862. A shame old Stonewall had been accidentally shot by one of his own men and then succumbed to pneumonia later. Residents in the Valley mourned the loss to this day. Carrie wrote a number of stories about General Jackson, and the *Bell Tower* had sold numerous copies when she'd printed them. Another hero in these parts was General Ashby Turner, known as the Black Knight of the Confederacy because of his expert horsemanship, bravery, and dash. Sad it was when he fell in June of that year. Nowadays, Lieutenant Colonel John Mosby was the living legend around here because of his daring raids against the Union army.

The long grass rustled beside her, and Carrie slowed her pace, listening. She shivered despite the night's thick, oppressive heat. Was she being followed?

She'd cut her curly tresses to her shoulders, hoping to resemble an ordinary shabby-looking soldier. Beneath her bonnet she wore the deserter's blue forage cap that she'd pinned into place.

Carrie inhaled deeply. The scent of an oncoming rainstorm promised to soak her within the hour. That might cool her.

But that persistent stirring in the grass . . .

Her hand curled around the butt of the gun inside the pocket of Margaret's dress and she sent up a prayer. She couldn't afford to waste ammunition.

She waited, holding her breath until her lungs threatened to burst. Nothing moved except the long grass. Carrie exhaled. Her imagination had fooled her again.

The night grew darker as the clouds moved in. More than once since leaving Woodstock, Carrie wondered if she should have waited until dawn to set off after Sarah. But, as anticipated, Mama flew into a rage at the news of her "baby girl" running off. She wailed and blamed Carrie for neglecting her duties and allowing Sarah Jane to leave. Then Mama said Carrie shouldn't bother returning unless she brought her youngest sister home with her.

So, after helping Margaret serve supper at the Wayfarers Inn, Carrie took off, taking a gamble based on hearsay and Joshua's hunch that the scoundrel-peddler ventured down the Valley Pike. The sun had just set when Carrie left, and the chances of slipping by Union troops were better in the dark.

Weren't they?

A shadow crossed the road and Carrie jumped back. She lifted the weapon from her pocket, despising the way her hand shook. Her heart beat fast, but as the clouds briefly parted, Carrie saw nothing and no one except the empty rutted pike. She glanced up at the shadowy mountain ridges. Whose eyes were fixed on her? The devil Union cavalrymen?

Don't think about them. She reined in her thoughts. Jesus would protect her. She was, after all, on a mission of mercy to save her youngest sister from that no-account peddler.

Would she find her baby sister before it's too late?

A howling in the distance caused Carrie to grip the gun more tightly. She knew how to use her weapon, and she could shoot better than some men, thanks to Joshua. He'd given her the Walker revolver in her hand after his father gifted him with a newer model when Joshua enlisted in the Confederate army. Of course, Joshua required that she prove her proficiency with the pistol before he allowed her to keep it in her possession, so she learned quickly. After all, a girl never knew when she'd need to protect herself and her family.

A pity she hadn't been armed at suppertime. She had a mind to shoot that philandering Confederate officer to teach him a lesson. How dare Rodingham behave so inappropriately toward Margaret—and how dare Margaret allow him to do so! Carrie had voiced her protest, only to be silenced by

Mr. Veyschmidt's threats of eviction. Apparently, Joshua's friend had money to spend—and not Confederate currency either, which seemed rather hypocritical of him considering his message of loyalty to The Cause equaling prosperity. Mr. Veyschmidt let the rogue do as he pleased. Worse, Joshua sat by idly while it happened. Carrie begged him to stop his comrade, but he refused, citing the fact that Margaret neither protested nor asked for help. While true, Joshua should have intervened.

He would have before the war. He had changed over the years, and not for the better. Truth was, Joshua wasn't the only one who had changed. Carrie had been mistaken to think otherwise. This war affected everyone.

Quickening her steps, Carrie forced herself to shift her thoughts and mulled over her plan. Once the threat of running into Confederate troops lessened, she would remove Margaret's dress and bonnet so she could pass Union pickets. She would stuff the gown into the haversack she'd discovered along with the Yankee uniform. Then, after she found Sarah Jane, she'd put Margaret's dress back on and return to the Wayfarers Inn with no one being the wiser and Sarah back where she belonged.

Five hours later, and soaked to the bone by a rainstorm, Carrie reached the town of Strasburg only to find it teeming with Confederate troops. She couldn't take a chance at being discovered—a female out at this hour. If they searched her and discovered her disguise, she'd likely get herself hanged.

She detoured east.

As the predawn hours wore on, she glimpsed the occasional lone, intoxicated Confederate soldier, and she hid behind rocks, trees, or shrubs until each passed. Only then did she continue her trek.

The early morning air weighed on her, even heavier now than before the downpour. The lined jacket she wore beneath Margaret's dress only added to her discomfort. The bonnet she wore over the forage cap contained her body heat and furthered her exhaustion. Should she shed the jacket and hide it in the haversack? No. She couldn't risk it. Not yet.

She walked on and minutes later she encountered a man. Older, maybe. A farmer, she assumed, although she couldn't see him clearly at this distance. Up ahead, he crossed the road and strode toward his barn. Carrie neared the structure, concealing her weapon, and worked up the courage to approach him.

"Excuse me, sir."

He whirled around and Carrie could tell she'd taken him by surprise. Darkness shrouded his face.

"I don't mean any harm. I'm just looking for my sister."

He slowly neared. "Young lady, you ought not be out and about this time of day. It ain't safe."

"As I said, I'm searching for my baby sister who took off yesterday with a peddler. She's only fifteen—too young to understand the consequences."

"But old enough to know better, I reckon." The man hiked up his drooping suspenders and slid them onto his broad shoulders.

Odd that this fellow wasn't off fighting for the Confederacy. Few men were left in Woodstock, and Carrie assumed it was the same throughout most of Virginia. She slipped her right hand into her dress pocket and gripped the pistol.

"Did you see a peddler's wagon come by here yesterday?"

"I might have." He cocked his head to one side.

"If you want money, I don't have any."

"Then I didn't see a thing."

"All right, then. Thank you anyhow, sir."

Carrie resisted the urge to stomp her foot and yell. Exhaustion nipped at her every muscle, but she wouldn't stop. She couldn't, not after what Mama said. What's more, Carrie figured that even being a day behind that scoundrel-peddler she could cover more ground on foot than he could cover with his rattling, ostentatious wagon.

"Does this road—" She pointed to the one running between the house and barn. "Does it go into Front Royal?"

"Yep, but you'd best not head in that direction, missy. There's dirty rotten Yankees camped on the other side of the Shenandoah."

"Well"—Carrie squared her shoulders—"Yankees are the ones with the money, so I imagine a peddler would head that way."

"Go on imagining then." There was an edge to his tone, and a second later Carrie noticed the man's light-colored trousers. Maybe butternut, but probably gray.

A Confederate. Nervous flutters filled her insides. She'd best make a hasty departure.

"What you got in that bag you're carryin'?"

"Nothing much. A few biscuits and sliced ham." Carrie plunged her hand into the haversack and pulled out the food, wrapped in a checkered napkin. "You're welcome to them." She prayed he wouldn't confiscate the rest of her belongings.

"Nice of you. Thanks."

Carrie took a step backward. "I always do my part for The Cause, little as it might be."

"Good. Now you'd best run along home."

She released the breath she'd been holding.

"Me and my men are getting ready to take on them Billy Yanks, and you don't want to get caught in the fray."

"No, sir, I don't."

"Incidentally"—he paused before entering the barn—"a peddler did come through here late yesterday afternoon. He had a girl with him, although she didn't seem too unhappy. Last I heard they were headin' for Culpeper."

"Culpeper?" Surprise ricocheted through her. "But that's some fifty miles away."

"Listen, missy, that's all I know."

"Thank you for the information." Carrie glanced up the road. That peddler traveled with a burdensome load. Maybe it wouldn't be too hard to catch up.

The soldier opened the barn door. As soon as he disappeared inside, Carrie sprinted in the direction of Front Royal, a five-hour trek. Exhausted, hot, and still wet from the earlier rainfall, Carrie doubted she'd make it by dawn. Even so, she had to try. Surely Confederate troops wouldn't attack their enemy until after the sun came up . . .

CHAPTER 3

For the next several hours Carrie stayed on the pike as much as possible. She stood little chance of achieving her goal, but perhaps that miserable peddler and Sarah Jane had stopped for the night and she'd happen upon them. Besides, there was always hope she would avoid the impending conflict—that is, if the Confederate soldier at the barn was correct.

As her mind gnawed on the thought, the earth began to quake beneath her feet. The rumbling grew louder with each passing second. She glanced over her left shoulder and her heart jumped into her throat. Horses thundered toward her.

Carrie scampered into a thicket of trees and crawled beneath the long branches of a fir to watch the Confederate troops ride by. After they'd passed, she scampered up a tree-studded slope. By the time she reached the top, guttural cries of agony like she'd never heard split the stillness of the morning. Had General Early's army taken the Yanks by surprise at the north fork of the Shenandoah? Had the Yanks surprised the Rebs when they forded the river? What a story it would make. An eyewitness account! Papa would be so proud.

Carrie found a place between the trunks of two maples from which she could watch the action, but she soon wished she hadn't.

As the fighting intensified, the river ran red with the blood from men clad in both blue and gray. A shell exploded. Carrie felt a wave of the blast. Below, horses and their riders flew into the air like wooden toys. Cavalrymen clashed. A Confederate lost his head to his enemy's saber. Carrie sucked in a breath, horrified. The soldier's lifeless body remained on its mount for several seconds before slumping to one side and dropping to the ground.

Carrie tore her gaze away and fought the rising nausea. War was a despicable waste of human life. Still, if she wanted to be a respected journalist she ought to force herself to observe. Shouldn't she?

Slowly, she lifted her gaze in time to see another shell blow a Yankee's arm clear off his body. The man's high-pitched shriek reached her ears and melded with the guttural cries of other wounded soldiers. Carrie covered her ears.

Gradually the Union army reclaimed its ground. Steel blades glinted in the rising sunshine. Gunfire cracked and a smoky fog developed around the warring men. A heart-wrenching scene, and yet Carrie couldn't work up the gumption to run away. How did the illustrators of Frank Leslie's newspapers abide viewing such devastation? Did they become numb to it?

Carrie's heart broke for the wounded and fallen men on the battlefield. She wiped away the moisture off her cheeks, although it did nothing to ebb the flow of tears. How infantile. Certainly Papa wouldn't weep. He'd report the action in an objective manner. She needed to follow in his footsteps.

She sniffed and focused on the battle still unfolding before her eyes. A portion of the Yankee army chased some Rebels toward the pike. Meanwhile combat continued on foot and on horseback. She could see the Confederates were outnumbered and outgunned. Plumes of sulfury smoke wafted her way, forcing her to cough every now and again. Oh! If she could only help the wounded somehow. The color of their bloody uniforms mattered little to her. That they lay writhing on the muddy banks of the Shenandoah, helpless and dying, tore at her heart. Carrie had read of the battles and heard accounts from soldiers who stopped at the Wayfarers Inn, but she'd never witnessed the brutality of war firsthand. What a shame the United States and Confederate States couldn't solve their differences without killing each other.

Union troops came and went, and after some time, those Southern soldiers who were still alive were rounded up like cattle. Bodies were fished from the water and lined up on the riverbank. Several Yankees on horseback, cavalrymen, she figured, crossed the Shenandoah and thrashed their sabers through leafy shrubbery. However, the Confederates weren't finished. Like lightning and thunder, artillery boomed and exploded from what had to be Guard Hill. Men's bodies flew in the air like rag dolls as shells struck their targets. Horses lay dead, their massive bodies quickly multiplying in the meadow across the river.

Union men rode along the bank and scanned the hillside. Carrie sat unmoving. Had they seen her? When finally their gazes landed elsewhere, she removed her bonnet, unbuttoned Margaret's dress, and hurriedly pulled it over her head. She stuffed the gown into the haversack. She now wore the blue trousers, coat, and forage cap, but she still felt exposed and vulnerable. She couldn't let insecurities hinder her, however. She'd come this far, and she had to find Sarah Jane.

Cannon fire in the distance shook Carrie to her core. She shifted her focus to the present. Disguised, or at least she hoped so, she eased down the hill on her backside, readying herself for a fast run. She prayed the Yanks wouldn't pay her any attention. Her only hope was to hightail it across the covered bridge and then keep running until she was safely beyond the fight.

Troops galloped past. Once clear, Carrie crossed the road. Reaching the bridge, she looked over her shoulder only to see Confederates on horseback engaging the Union horsemen. Bullets whizzed dangerously close to her head, and fear momentarily rooted Carrie in place.

But then she realized it was either move or die.

Carrie swung one leg and then the other over the side of the bridge and shinnied down a wooden support until she couldn't go any farther. Her feet brushed a thick beam, so she climbed over and stood on it. Looking down, she guessed it was a twenty-foot drop to the riverbank, so a safe jump was out of the question. Besides, she'd land in the middle of warring troops.

Clouds of smoke rolled over her, making her cough, but thankfully hiding her from all the action below. Men's cries before death made her shudder. She must escape.

With her hands on the large post, now above her, she scanned her surroundings for options. The giant sycamore that reached skyward and stood just a few feet away seemed the obvious choice. If she could leap to the closest branch, she could hide in the tree and climb down once the battle was over.

Above her, the bridge shook violently from the weight of men galloping their mounts across its planks. The wooden beams creaked as though they might give way.

Bending at the knees, Carrie pushed off and sailed across the short expanse between bridge and tree. Smoke stung her eyes. She blinked. In that second, she missed her intended target. An odd sense of weightlessness engulfed her before she landed hard in the middle of two thick branches. Her heart hammered as realization dawned. She'd nearly fallen onto the fighting men!

As the world righted, it became apparent that she'd landed in the crux of the sycamore. She wiggled her toes. She appeared unhurt for the most part, although the throbbing in her left wrist indicated an injury. Had she cracked a bone? Perhaps just a sprain. Either way, it would have to be bound somehow. Her wrist was swelling by the moment. She shrugged her haversack's strap off her right shoulder and tried to grab it with her right hand, but the sack dislodged and fell between the branches before she could catch it.

"No! Oh, no!"

The clashing armies below paid no mind to Carrie's cry or the fallen haversack. Helplessly she watched her belongings float away on the swift current of the Shenandoah.

_____

With his senses on high alert after today's surprise meeting with enemy forces, Peyton combed the north fork of the Shenandoah, searching for injured men, fugitives, and Confederate soldiers. The majority of the Rebel army had moved up the pike a ways and now Peyton rode with a few select troops. But every so often a remnant of the enemy lobbed a shell in their direction.

"Let's go, men. Time is of the essence." Peyton's orders called for his brigade to retreat to Nineveh, but he wasn't about to leave any of his troops behind if he could help it. If he knew where the injured lay, he'd send for ambulances to collect them under a white flag of truce.

A strange sound came from somewhere over his head. Peyton reined in Brogan and lifted a hand, slowing the men behind him. He sat, listening. Sure enough. Coughing. And it came from . . . from the treetop?

Peyton lifted his gaze and glimpsed a patch of blue uniform. "What in the world are you doing up there, soldier?" A coward? The man hid in the tree to avoid the fight?

"I—" *Cough. Cough.* "I fell."

"You fell into a tree?"

"Off the bridge." The fellow's voice was raspy, no doubt from choking on the incessant smoke.

Peyton's gaze wandered to the covered bridge on the Front Royal Pike. It was possible, he supposed, but what had the fellow been doing up there in the first place? Running?

"Come down from there at once." If he'd run during a battle, the soldier would be immediately shot. Either way, he'd have to face Peyton. "Do you hear me? Climb down now!"

"I can't." More coughing. "I'm stuck."

Swiveling in his saddle, Peyton motioned for his sergeant to dismount. "Get that man down from the tree."

"Yes, sir." Sergeant Donahue climbed the bank and over the gnarled tree roots. He glanced upward and then walked back toward Peyton. "Sir, I'm afraid I can't get the man. You see . . ."

"Get to the point, man." Peyton's temples began to throb.

"I'm timid of heights, sir."

"For crying out loud!" He swung down from his saddle and walked to the base of the tree. Upon closer inspection, he noted that the barking soldier sat between two thick branches that were fairly high up indeed.

"I can get him down, Colonel." Corporal Bob Tompkins approached with a confident swagger and a coil of thick rope over one broad shoulder.

"Good—and be quick about it."

Peyton visually scoured the area. He and his men were easy targets here for enemy sharpshooters. The last thing he wanted was to go on the defensive again. They were all weary from today's fight, but it'd be worse to wind up in Confederate hands.

Tompkins climbed the tree and Peyton ordered the other men to continue their scouting along the riverbank. A shell whistled in the air and exploded too close for Peyton's comfort. A pity his orders were to retreat, not fight. "Hurry up, Corporal."

"Um . . . Colonel?"

Peyton stared up into the tree. "What is it?"

"This here ain't no man. It's a boy. No more than fifteen, I s'pect."

Thank God. Then he's not a fugitive.

"And he's wearing sergeants' stripes. No way he outranks me."

Peyton groaned. The corporal was forever complaining about the unfairness of his lowly rank. "Bring him down. We'll discuss the details later."

An intense rustling ensued. "Ow!"

"What's going on, Corporal?"

"The ingrate bit me!" Tompkins climbed down. After jumping from the lowest hanging branch, he faced Peyton and extended his bare palm where bite marks were evident. "That boy can stay up there forever as far as I'm concerned."

"No, he has to come down."

Cough. Cough. Cough. The tree-bound lad's hacking persisted. If it continued, he might cough his way out of the tree and fall to his death. Peyton had seen enough of that today.

"Lend me your rope, will you?" He'd get that kid down if it killed him. And it just might at that.

The corporal complied and Peyton began his ascent. Smaller branches snapped beneath his boots and a barrage of twigs fell as he climbed. When at last he reached the boy, he could smell the fog of war, lingering in the sticky vegetation. And sure enough. The lad sat with his back against the trunk while his lower body was pinned between two thick branches. He'd certainly got himself wedged in tightly.

Peyton found sure footing. "What's your name, son?" He arched a brow. "And don't say Zacchaeus because I'm in no mood for fun and games."

"My name's . . ." It came out wheezy. "'ary."

"Harry? Is that what you said?" Hard to hear the name clearly with the boy's hoarseness. Peyton tried to get a good look at him, but the kid's features were concealed beneath a layer of soot. Amazingly, though, he hadn't lost his blue forage cap in the fall. "What's your last name?"

"Bell."

"Well, all right, Harry Bell, allow me to introduce myself. I'm Colonel Collier. I mean you no harm. No need to bite, scratch, or claw, understand?"

A slight nod.

Peyton noted the sergeants' stripes that his corporal had been quick to point out. The coat obviously didn't belong to this boy. It appeared four sizes too big, although its sleeves along with the trousers had undoubtedly been hemmed.

So where'd he get it?

"I'm here to get you out of this predicament. Do I have your full cooperation?"

The boy regarded him with a glassy-eyed stare that suggested shock but returned another slight nod.

"Good. We understand each other." Peyton tugged off his gauntlets and tucked them into his belt before securing one end of the rope around the boy's waist. "Where's your weapon?" he asked, finding none as he tightened the knot.

No reply.

Definitely shock. Peyton had seen it before, especially on soldiers who had just fought their first battle. The sight of rolling heads and severed limbs wasn't soon forgotten. "Where's your gear?"

"River." The boy began coughing hard again. Branches shook beneath them.

"Easy now." Peyton considered the kid's slim form and decided the best way to get him down—them down—safely was to tie the other end of the rope around his own waist. If the boy fell, Peyton could support his slight weight and likely prevent his demise.

"What are you doing? Are you going to hang me?" *Cough. Cough.*

Peyton waited for the fit to subside. "On the contrary, *Sergeant* Bell"—he couldn't help the sarcasm—"I'm trying to save your life and get you out of this tree."

Bracing himself first, Peyton cupped the boy's upper right arm. His hand nearly fit around its circumference. A weakling? Except he felt some muscle beneath his palm. Something didn't add up, but there was no time to figure it out now.

He gave the boy a hard yank and freed him from the sycamore's grip.

"Don't let me fall!"

"I won't. Just don't look down. We'll work together, one branch at a time. Got it?"

"My wrist . . ."

"Injured?"

The boy nodded.

"Let's have a quick look." With his own arm slung around a branch, Peyton reached for Bell's injured one. Pushing up the coat's sleeve, he spied black stains on the boy's rather delicate-looking hands.

"What's that?"

"Ink."

"Ink?" *What on earth?*

Something hauntingly familiar passed through Peyton, but before he could give it more thought or force the boy to explain, another round of hacking ensued. Peyton's own lungs were becoming irritated by another onslaught of dark plumes moving into the treetop.

"You all right up there, Colonel?"

Peyton knew the voice. "I'm fine, Major Johnston." He regarded the boy once again. "It doesn't appear broken, but I'll examine it again once we're on the ground. For now, do the best you can. The main thing is we get down safely."

Peyton descended one branch at a time, gaining a sure footing before the boy followed after. When he reached the lower crux of the tree, Peyton jumped easily to the ground. A second later, a weight crashed into him. He lost his balance and slid on his back over bumpy tree roots and into the Shenandoah. He opened his mouth to yell, but got a mouthful of murky river water instead.

A brief tussle ensued, but he managed to toss the ballast off his chest. Sitting, Peyton gulped his next breath. The imitation sergeant stared back at him with wide eyes.

"Boy, are you trying to drown me?"

"No, sir."

Major Vernon Johnston, Peyton's most trusted friend and aide-de-camp, had the audacity to smile from atop his horse. "The rope between you two was short, Colonel. You jumped, the lad didn't, and—"

"I get it." Obviously the mishap hadn't been intentional. "Corporal," he said to the trooper standing nearby, "help this boy to his feet. Watch his left arm. It may be broken."

"At least he's got two arms, sir. Some ain't been so lucky today." Tompkins jerked the boy upright before giving Peyton a hand up.

Dripping with river water, Peyton pushed his hair off his forehead and glared at the kid. At least he had the good sense to appear frightened—well, maybe not frightened exactly.

"Have we met before?"

Bell lifted his slender shoulders.

"Hmm . . ." Peyton could swear their paths had crossed at some point. "If we have, it means you're a persistent troublemaker for the Union army."

"No, sir." *Cough. Cough.* "I'm no troublemaker, especially where you're concerned."

Peyton drew his chin back. What was that supposed to mean?

"What do you want me to do with him, sir?" Tompkins gave the boy a shake.

"I'll think of an appropriate punishment while we ride back to camp."

"Colonel, he's obviously impersonating an officer," Tompkins insisted.

"I'm aware of that and I'll deal with it accordingly once we're out of the line of fire."

Tompkins puffed out his chest. "I'll tie his hands. He can walk behind the horses."

"No." Peyton regarded him and their fellow cavalrymen. Hardened expressions said they wouldn't be pleased to share their saddles with a younger man who illegitimately outranked half of them. Peyton wasn't exactly thrilled to be encumbered on his mount either, for that matter, but Harry Bell was just a lad, perhaps Tommy's age. "He can ride with me."

"No! Let me go!" The boy squirmed, coughed, and squirmed some more. "I'm looking for my sister. She ran off yesterday morning with a no-account peddler." He croaked out each word. "All I wanted to do was get past . . ." *Wheeze.* " . . . past Union lines." Bell coughed again.

"You'd best learn right now—" Tompkins gave the boy a cuff upside his head. Bell fell to the ground. "No one talks to the colonel like that."

"That'll be enough." Peyton stepped between the two.

Bell cradled his left arm. That dazed look had reentered his eyes—deep blue eyes that Peyton knew he'd seen somewhere else.

He'd have time to mull it over as they rode toward White Post.

"Don't bother with the boy, Corporal." Peyton helped the lad to his feet. "I'll deal with this one—personally."

CHAPTER 4

His voice certainly sounded like Captain Collier's. Carrie had heard it plenty of times in her dreams. It was the same bass timbre with that perfect blend of silk and steel. And this man looked like the same captain to whom Carrie gave aid nearly a year and a half ago, although from her place behind him, she couldn't be absolutely sure.

She didn't dare try to catch a glimpse lest she slide off the saddle and get trampled. Instead, she clung to him a little tighter, trying desperately not to gag from the stench of wet wool and raw humanity.

She busied her thoughts and continued pondering her captor's identity. True, last fall she learned the captain had fallen at Gettysburg. An inexplicable sorrow filled her—sorrow for a man she'd met only once. How foolish. Yet, that dashing, charming officer had occupied a lot of room in her mind until she learned of his tragic demise. On the other hand, the soldier who passed the information to her might have been mistaken.

So then, did she only imagine this Union cavalryman, a colonel, resembled the captain whose forearm she'd sutured? Perhaps. But, if it were him, she felt fairly confident she could trust him.

Then again, if this wasn't the same man, God only knew what fate awaited her. Would these Yankees torture her as Joshua implied?

Maybe for once she should have listened to him.

One fact remained, whether or not this was Captain Collier, holding onto a dirty, wet, and smelly man on a torrid August day was punishment enough!

The colonel urged his mount up a small hill. Carrie held on even tighter for fear she'd fall backward off the horse.

"Ease up, boy. You're liable to crack one of my ribs."

"Sorry." Her voice was returning, although her throat felt raw and parched. She adjusted her tone to mimic a male's. "Sorry." She loosened her hold around him and forced herself to lean back an inch or so. She eyed the man's thick, tawny hair and the way it curled slightly over the collar of his dark blue coat.

He turned slightly in his saddle. Despite the fact they could use a trim, his mustache and beard weren't at all scraggy like some whiskers she'd seen on soldiers. Instead, the colonel looked fairly well groomed, sooty face and all. However, his brow puckered and an unmistakable curiosity sparked in his golden-brown gaze. "Does your wrist hurt?"

"Yes, sir." She used the deepest pitch possible, praying she wouldn't give away her gender. "My jaw hurts more, thanks to your corporal."

"You shouldn't have sassed him." The colonel turned frontward again.

Outrage struck her nearly as hard as the corporal had. "So you think it's all right for a man to hit a—" She quickly swallowed the word *female* and lowered her voice again. "Never mind." Of course a soldier would feel justified striking a juvenile boy. The pity was that the corporal rendered Carrie senseless for a time so she couldn't fight back. Next thing she knew, she'd been stuffed onto the back of the colonel's saddle.

"You also bit him," he stated over his shoulder.

"I did?" Carrie didn't recall.

The Yankee horsemen steered their horses across a stream then along the water's gently sloping bank. The powerful muscles in the colonel's legs seemed to match his charger's sinew, working beneath them.

At last they reached a clump of trees, and Carrie yanked on his coat.

"What is it now?"

"May I have some water? I read somewhere that even Rebel prisoners at Camp Chase are given water."

With a low growl, the colonel halted his large steed and handed back his canteen. He ordered his men to move onward, indicating he'd catch up with them later.

Carrie fumbled with the canteen then dropped it. "Sorry, sir."

He swiveled half around and took hold of Carrie's upper arm. With his support she swung out of the saddle. Then he lowered her to the ground with nary a grunt. She felt unsteady on her feet for a moment, but managed to retrieve the canteen from the grass. After removing its cork, she drank from it. The water, though warm, tasted sweet. She couldn't get enough.

"Easy, boy." The colonel dismounted and loosely tethered his horse to a low tree branch nearby. Facing Carrie again, he said, "No sense in drinking your fill only to have it come back up." The colonel stepped toward her slowly and removed his gold gauntlets. No doubt he expected her to run—and she considered the idea. But she wouldn't get far.

Carrie coughed. Her lungs felt clearer now that she'd gotten out of the smoky haze of war.

"Finished?" He tucked his leather gloves into one of the belts around his trim waist.

She took another long drink before handing back his canteen. "Thank you." She considered him closely. A fine figure of a man to be sure.

She'd thought so more than a year ago. Yes, it was indeed Captain Collier . . . or, rather, Colonel Collier.

"Something on your mind?" He scrutinized her until she blushed.

"Nice to see you again, sir." She looked down at her boots.

"See me . . . *again?*"

"Yes." She gazed up at him. "I know I can trust you, so . . ."

"You have information for me?" He folded his arms.

"Yes, but perhaps not the kind you might think." Carrie reached up with her right hand and removed the forage cap. "I'm not a boy, sir."

The colonel's eyes widened.

"And you were right. We have met before. I'm from Woodstock."

"Woodstock . . ." He squinted as if searching his memory.

"I work at the Wayfarers Inn and operate the local newspaper in my father's absence."

Recognition flashed in his gaze. He snapped his fingers. "Miss Bell, the aspiring journalist."

"Yes, sir." He remembered her name! "And you're the captain whose arm I stitched."

"The very one." Doffing his blue slouch hat with its golden cord and emblem of two crossed sabers, he bowed in a formal greeting. "My wound healed perfectly, although that ale you cleansed it with proved nearly fatal."

Carrie recalled his moaning. He said it stung like a swarm of hornets. "As I told you that day, the inn's owner, Mr. Veyschmidt, makes the ale himself with raw alcohol, black pepper, and gunpowder, just to name a few ingredients. But I learned his concoction fights off infection . . . and it works fine for polishing metal too."

The colonel chuckled. It was one of the most pleasant sounds she'd heard in a long while. What's more, she was pleased to hear that her doctoring was successful and happier still that he'd survived Gettysburg.

"I see you're a colonel now."

"That's right. Colonel Peyton Collier, First Division Cavalry of the newly christened Army of the Shenandoah."

"That's quite a mouthful."

He smiled. He hadn't lost a bit of his charm.

"Last autumn I heard you fell at Gettysburg. I thought you were dead."

"Gettysburg." A peculiar emotion stole into his gaze—one of great sorrow, perhaps. He blinked and it vanished. "Not killed, obviously, but I was severely injured. I made a miraculous recovery and . . . here I am."

"With a higher rank too."

"I received a promotion after acting on the information I gleaned from your newspaper, Miss Bell. Another promotion was awarded me after Gettysburg. Then, after I helped to explode a mine beneath a Confederate fort last month near Petersburg, I was promoted to colonel."

"Congratulations, although I read that the Yankees suffered enormous casualties in that battle."

"We did, unfortunately, and the siege continues."

"But I'm pleased to see you're still one of the living."

"Me too." Another smile. "So let me guess . . ." He set his hat on his head and clasped his hands behind his back. "You're out chasing a story for your newspaper?"

"That is incorrect, sir." Carrie rather enjoyed refuting him. "As I said earlier, I'm chasing after my baby sister. She ran off with some loathsome peddler yesterday. My mission is to find her and bring her home."

"Baby sister?" He frowned and his soot-stained brows met above the bridge of his nose. "Do you mean the blond girl with a low opinion of Union soldiers?"

"Yes, sir." He had a very good memory. "I would have caught up to them by now if I'd made the jump off the bridge and onto the tree branch as I'd planned. But my foot slipped and I fell into the sycamore's crux."

Colonel Collier's eyes lit up with amusement. "Now there's a story for you."

"Make fun all you want." Carrie felt scraped and bruised from head to toe. "And while it's nice to see you again, I need to set off for Culpeper. I've been told that's the peddler's destination."

"You can't safely get to Culpeper from here, Miss Bell. It's at least a two-day trek and you have no gear. Besides, the way you're dressed you'll be killed or captured. The Confederates have, for the time being, pushed us northward."

"But I have to find Sarah Jane and get back home." Carrie's chores were probably going undone and Mr. Veyschmidt would soon be apoplectic.

"Reaching Woodstock is an impossibility too, I'm afraid."

"Why?" A sense of panic threatened.

"For the same reasons I just mentioned."

"Colonel, I have to keep moving or I'll never find my sister."

His gaze narrowed and he rubbed his right palm over the left side of his whiskered jaw. "Your insistence concerns me, Miss Bell."

"I mean no disrespect, if that's what you're thinking. But I am determined to stay on that peddler's trail."

A wag of his head. "I can't allow it."

"Can't allow it?" This man had no authority over her!

The colonel brought himself up to his full height and assumed an imposing stance.

Carrie took a step back.

He caught her elbow. "Miss Bell, I'm placing you under arrest for impersonating a Union officer."

The Soldiers' Journal, Alexandria, VA
August 17, 1864

Official War Bulletins.

[second dispatch]

Mobile, August 8 — It is painfully humiliating to announce the shameful surrender of Fort Gaines, at half-past nine o'clock this morning, by Colonel Charles Anderson, of the Twenty-first Alabama Regiment.

CHAPTER 5

August 18, 1864

"Here she comes again, Miss Ruth."

"Frances?"

"Who else?"

Setting aside the socks she'd been knitting for her beloved nephew Peyton, Ruth Collier glanced at Tabitha. The other woman stood at the bay window, gazing out to the street. Although a Negro, Tabitha was more like a sister to Ruth, rather than the house slave whom Pappy purchased at an auction many decades ago. They'd grown up together. Then, after Pappy died, nearly twenty years ago, Ruth freed Tabitha and her brother, Samuel. They both stayed on, Tabitha overseeing the housework and cooking, and Samuel tending the livestock—until Rebels took every pig, cow, horse, and chicken.

And then, horror of horrors, those despicable men hanged Samuel before burning the outbuildings, leaving only the fieldstones as reminders of that terrifying night.

Ruth still thanked God to this day that she'd possessed the wisdom and foresight to hide Tabitha in Pappy's secret cellar below the house. Tabitha survived. Now Ruth was grateful to have her trusted friend here in Winchester, Virginia, in their golden years, especially since they were both unmarried women and abolitionists. They couldn't help but be fast allies in this war. However, their support of the Union cause often created conflict with their

Confederate neighbors, although Winchester had its loyalists too, including a population of Quakers. Still, every now and again neighbors were wont to put Tabitha "in her rightful place."

Their next-door neighbor and old family "friend" Frances Monteague was one of those folks. She and her daughter, Lavinia, were the bane of their existence. But they needed to keep a close eye on their enemy—for their own protection, as well as for Peyton's. Oftentimes Ruth and Tabitha passed information learned from Frances on to the Union army. General Philip Sheridan, Peyton's commanding officer now, was most appreciative.

"You want I should let her in, Miss Ruth?"

"Oh, I suppose so." She sighed audibly. "It is nearing teatime."

"Of course it is. But since most of her slaves done ran off, Miss Frances wants someone serving her, especially this time o' day. And you can bet she'll be braggin' on those wicked children of hers."

"A safe bet to be sure." Those Monteagues were wicked indeed. Ruth and Tabitha both suspected that Frances's sons participated in murdering Samuel. Edward was away, fighting for the Confederacy, while Anthony ran the family business, Monteague Shipping. God only knew what he was doing—but it most likely concerned smuggling slaves into the Confederacy.

Even so, Ruth had vowed to look after Frances . . . besides, they had much to lose by refusing Frances's visit today.

"Mm-mm. I know what you're thinking. You're thinking that if we turn away Miss Frances, she'll tell that no-good son of hers that we were less than cordial, and then he and his ill-mannered Rebel troops will take over our home again."

That's exactly what Ruth had been thinking. "One can never guess what might happen when it comes to the Monteagues."

"Ain't that the truth! And if you ask me, Miss Frances is one of God's strangest creatures." Tabitha grumbled as she limped to the front door. Her gout was obviously acting up again. Ruth would have to insist Tabitha rest after Frances left. "But I'll let her in anyhow."

Ruth arranged the skirt of her favorite brown and ivory lace day gown, noting the worn and faded spots in the fabric. She glanced around the bare parlor. Judging from its meager furnishings, one would never guess that the Colliers were one of Winchester's more prominent families. At least they were before this poor town became the armpit of the lower Shenandoah Valley. But Winchester would arise from the ashes—

And so would the Collier family. Of course it would help if Peyton married so he could inherit his trust that sat in a bank in Washington. The young lady would have to be just the right one—a believer in Christ, a loyalist and abolitionist, mannerly, and well-read. Other than those qualifications, Ruth wasn't particular. What mattered most was that Peyton's future wife loved him for more than his inheritance.

But for now Ruth and Tabitha lived like paupers in a house that had seen better days. Frances, a Confederate supporter, enjoyed reminding them of the fact.

Ruth shook off her gloomy thoughts as her neighbor entered the room. As usual, Frances walked with her chin held high, looking as proud as a peacock.

"A good afternoon to you, Ruth."

"Frances." Ruth inclined her head. "Do come in and make yourself at home. Tabitha is about to serve tea."

"Thank you."

She seated herself in one of the three armchairs whose upholstery required attention. But at least Ruth had rescued them from the Rebels who had burned some of her other furniture—items that had not been hidden away in the secret cellar.

Tabitha lifted the mahogany tilt-top occasional table and carried it across the room, placing it in front of the settee.

"Another torrid day in Winchester." Frances's gloved hands opened her fan, and she waved it in front of her slender neck and long face.

"Mm, yes, hot and sticky."

"It grows worse every year, I believe."

"No, we just grow older." Ruth smiled.

A little frown worked its way across Frances's wrinkled brow. "Speak for yourself."

"I always do."

With a huff, the other woman collapsed her fan and held it in her lap. "I apologize for not sending a calling card earlier." Her thin lips curled at the edges in an attempt at a smile. "But what's a casual visit between two old friends?"

"You're always welcome to call, Frances." After all, they'd once been the dearest of friends . . . that is, until Frances stole Harmon Monteague, the love of Ruth's life.

Tabitha entered the parlor with the silver tea service and poured out. She politely served their guest first.

Ruth collected a teacup and saucer for herself. She glanced into the dark face of her friend. "You're welcome to join us for tea, Tabitha."

"I'd rather get burned at the stake," she muttered.

"Be careful what you wish for." Frances arched a brow.

Ruth's heart beat faster. No. Not Tabitha! She glanced at her faithful friend and found the expression on her narrow face to be as confident as always.

"I'll be back with the biscuits."

Tabitha left the room, stepping gingerly on her left foot. Although a free woman of color, Tabitha chose to stay with Ruth as a companion, house-keeper, and cook. Tabitha especially enjoyed bossing the other servants—that is, when Ruth could afford to hire them. Unfortunately, the last of her dwindling funds sat in a bank in Washington along with Peyton's inheritance. The money was untouchable for now. If Ruth dared make one last transfer, the Confederates would confiscate her money.

She clenched her jaw. Such hypocrites! The Rebel army preferred using Federal currency because theirs was useless. General Ramseur had been quoted as saying that he and his staff could get almost everything they needed for their dining pleasure with Yankee money. But Ruth had no intention of contributing to the secessionists' cause.

"Why do you put up with that insolent slave when you could buy another who would serve you in all humility? Or you could hire a lady's maid and housekeeper from England. Anthony could make the transaction for you. He'll be traveling to London soon, and I've told him to bring back hired help for me."

"How exciting for Anthony," Ruth said, referring to Frances's eldest son. She felt a bit sorry for the future hired help. "Thank you. But I'm happy with the way things are. As you're aware, I consider Tabitha a part of my family."

"You'd do better to get over that notion. She's a Negro slave."

"She's a freed woman of color." Ruth sipped the weak tea from the chipped blue and white cup. "You and I have debated this issue for years. You know where I stand."

"No wonder your neighbors and the whole Army of the Valley despises the Collier family."

Such nonsense, but Ruth didn't argue. Instead she imagined what her neighbor might think if she discovered Ruth occasionally passed information to spies and officers of the Union army. Frances would likely lead the way to Ruth's hanging, but freedom for the slaves was a cause worth dying for.

Frances continued. "I will never understand why you don't move north like the other Yankee supporters."

"This is my home. My grandfather built it in 1781 and I'll not abandon it."

Frances waved a gloved hand in the air. She had, of course, heard the origins of Piccadilly Place many times before. "You're a stubborn woman, Ruth Collier. You could be living in the lap of luxury."

Luxury. That's all Frances cared about—and the reason she stole Harm away, knowing full well that Ruth loved him. The Monteague fortune was all too tempting.

A pity that Frances and Lavinia squandered half of it and invested the other half in the Confederacy.

"In time, Piccadilly Place will return to its former acclaim and so will the Colliers. Watch and see. Winchester has changed its flag from Confederate to Federal and back again more than seventy times over the course of the last three years." Ruth took another sip of tea. "It won't be long before the United States flag flies here again."

"Fiddlesticks. That new commander, General Sheridan, is timid. That's, of course, according to Edward." Frances's voice sang with a note of pride at the mention of her younger son. "He told me that the new Union commander merely engages in a few skirmishes here and there, but never an attack. Sheridan is no match for General Jubal Early and General Robert E. Lee, and he knows it."

"War is coming to Winchester again, Frances. General Early's army will be defeated." Ruth could feel it coming in the thick air she breathed.

"I hope not." Frances set aside her cup and saucer. "But as long as we're speaking of Yankees, have you heard from that no-good nephew of yours?"

"Peyton? Certainly not. I'm sure he's far too busy with the Union cavalry to correspond with his spinster auntie." Ruth grinned at her own sarcasm.

"Well, that's gratitude for you." Frances's brows pinched together. "After all you did for that boy, taking him in when your brother and his wife died, and then seeing his way into West Point, not to mention enduring his rebellious ways for years."

"I'm aware of my family's history, Frances dear." Every nerve in Ruth's body tensed, although what her neighbor stated was true. Still, Ruth had always seen a redemptive quality in Peyton.

"And then you nursed that scoundrel back to health last year," Frances continued, "after he was so dreadfully wounded at Gettysburg." She released a dramatic sigh. "I honestly believed you'd wind up with an invalid on your hands."

"It was a miracle, indeed. Although I would have happily cared for my nephew if God hadn't seen fit to heal him. But thankfully he recovered in our Washington townhouse." Ruth arched a brow.

Frances drew back slightly. "I truly don't know why you don't move to the Union capitol. It would be more convenient for you there." She clucked her tongue. "Besides, Lavinia has attended several parties in Washington and says it is quite lovely for a northern city. In fact, she was there while Peyton recovered, and she would have visited him, honest, Ruth. However, she's like I am when it comes to nursing. We can't abide sickness, blood, or broken bones."

"Yes, I'm aware."

Harmon came to mind and Ruth shuddered. How the man had suffered so in his last days. When Frances couldn't bear the sight of him withering away, Ruth acted as his nurse. Together they recalled fine days—days when Harmon Monteague was a strapping young man.

Days when Ruth loved him so . . .

"Frances, do you remember how dashing Harm looked on that Sunday afternoon at the church picnic?"

"Which one?"

"If my arithmetic is correct, it was the picnic thirty-seven years ago."

"Good heavens! How should I remember that long ago?" Frances's eyes glazed over. "But my husband always looked dashing."

"Indeed."

Despite her neighbor's poor memory, Ruth would never forget that particular church picnic. That was the day she'd fallen in love with Harmon Monteague. Frances knew it, and knew Harm was wealthy. Before Ruth could turn around, Frances and Harm were engaged. They married within a few short weeks, and Frances never failed to remind Ruth of the triumph. Then, adding insult to injury, shortly after their wedding Frances and Harm moved into the Monteague family home next door.

"Thank God you were there to help me care for Harm in his final days." Sincerity pooled in Frances's rheumy, dark eyes. "What would I have done without you?"

"That's what friends do for each other, Frances dear." Ruth couldn't keep the irony out of her voice. She and Ruth weren't friends, but they were the best of enemies. Even so, as he lay dying, Harm begged Ruth to take care of Frances after he was gone. She'd promised . . .

And so it was.

"But, unlike poor Harm, Peyton made a full recovery. And let me remind you, Frances, my nephew is no longer a scoundrel. He made the decision to change his ways last July, right there on that Pennsylvania battlefield."

"Well, as the old adage goes, the proof of the pudding is in the eating." Frances pursed her lips in prim manner. "Most folks in Winchester remember Peyton Collier as a troublemaker and a rogue."

"The same could be said of your sons, Frances."

She glowered.

"And, contrary to your offspring, Peyton has changed. He's a new man in Christ."

"Which brings me to the reason for my visit."

"Oh?" Ruth sat forward on the settee. This couldn't be good.

"As I mentioned, Anthony is sailing for London and Lavinia refuses to remain in Staunton where they've been visiting friends. The summer is winding down and she's bored, so Anthony is sending her home." Frances let go of a long sigh. "What a relief. I've been worried about my baby girl."

"Baby girl? Bah! She's twenty-four, Frances. A woman of the world."

"A babe in the woods."

Ruth filled her lungs, praying for temperance along with some air. She glanced up at the cracked plaster on the ceiling. In her day, reaching the age of twenty-one was considered to be precariously close to spinster status.

"But it is of some consolation that she'll have guards with her. Anthony hired the best money could buy."

"Yankee money?" The quip sailed out of Ruth's mouth.

"I didn't ask. Anthony runs Monteague Shipping, not I."

Ruth bit her lower lip but couldn't control her fury. "He makes his money by illegally smuggling Negros into Confederate ports where they are auctioned off to the highest bidder. That is, if they survive the journey." The only good news was that Monteague Shipping had suffered greatly from the effects of the Union's blockade.

"You will, of course, keep that fact to yourself."

Ruth conceded a nod. As the best of enemies, they kept each other's confidences . . . unless it proved terribly inconvenient.

Frances pulled back her slumping shoulders. "As I was saying, my darling daughter wonders if, while she's here in Winchester, she might keep company with Peyton, now that he's a changed man and all that. Let him prove to Lavinia that he's different."

"Peyton is an officer on duty with the Union army," Ruth needlessly reminded her.

Frances waved her comment away. "Oh, politics should never stand in the way of romance. Won't he get leave any time soon?"

"I doubt it, and unless Winchester flies the United States' flag, Peyton wouldn't come here if he did have time off. It'd be suicide." Ruth marveled at her neighbor's ignorance while everything inside of her screamed against the idea of a reunion between Lavinia and Peyton. "Besides, things are heating up in the Valley. I doubt Peyton can find a moment's leisure."

"A pity." Frances lifted her teacup and brought it to her age-lined pink lips. She sipped from it. "Lavinia still fancies Peyton."

"If that's true, Frances, she could have corresponded with him over the years. And, as you said, she could have come to see him last fall in Washington when he was recovering from his wounds. Good heavens, but she never missed a social event in the city. We saw her name frequently printed on the society page."

"Yes, and I'm so proud of her." Frances sighed, her smile fading. "And now that Peyton has recovered, Lavinia is interested in him again."

"You mean Peyton is good enough for her now that he's not an invalid?"

"Yes." Frances batted her lashes and pushed out a grin. "Not that I completely approve, mind you. I'm a Confederate woman and Peyton is one of those awful Yankees—like you."

Boiling indignation rushed into Ruth's face. She opened her mouth to speak her mind, but Tabitha walked into the parlor carrying a tray of freshly baked biscuits and berry preserves.

"Couldn't help overhearing, ladies, and the way I see it, Miss Lavinia had her chance with our boy, but she decided not to show up at the church on their wedding day." Tabitha's dark eyes sparked with mischief. "Remember, Ruth? She done left our boy waitin' at the altar."

"I remember." And she thanked God Almighty that Lavinia Monteague was not her niece by marriage today.

"Such insolence from a slave! Ruth, I can't believe you tolerate it."

"Oh, she tolerates it, all right. Looks forward to it, I'd say." With a wink and a grin, Tabitha left the room.

Ruth smiled in her wake before glancing back at Frances. "You know as well as anyone that Tabitha is like a sister to me—and so were you. We grew up together—all three of us."

"I'm aware of that . . . that you and I grew up together and that Tabitha was—is—a slave." Frances glared at Ruth. "As for Peyton, can you blame my daughter? That rake spent the night before their wedding in the company of Lavinia's cousin Verna." Frances stood, crossed the room, and helped herself to a biscuit. "Absolutely scandalous! Lavinia wanted to teach him a lesson. She never dreamed he would ride off with the Yankee cavalry instead of seeking her out and begging her forgiveness."

"It worked out for the best, I think." Ruth released a long, slow breath. Peyton had successfully dodged that bullet. "Besides, Lavinia supports the Confederacy like her brothers, Anthony and Edward—and you."

"Oh, but you're wrong, Ruth dear. Lavinia doesn't subscribe to any political viewpoint."

"Really? During her last visit to Winchester, Lavinia was quite friendly with Confederate officers."

"She merely wanted to lift those soldiers' morale is all. She would entertain Union troops too."

"I'm sure she would." Ruth couldn't contain another bout of sarcasm.

"Lavinia is bored with politics and current events. She never reads the newspaper unless, of course, her name appears on the society page."

Claiming a biscuit, Ruth split it and spread berry jam across its soft surface. Was Frances aware of how shallow she made her daughter sound? A truthful description nonetheless.

"But things are different today than they were three and a half years ago." Frances returned to her seat. Her voice sounded calmer. "Peyton is, as you say, a Christian man."

And he's still heir to a small fortune. Ruth bit into warm, doughy goodness and thought of some way to discourage Frances for a while. Perhaps even for good. "There's another reason Peyton can't visit with Lavinia."

"Oh?" Frances tipped her head and leaned forward. "What is it?"

"He has a new romantic interest." The words popped out before Ruth could think better of them. And maybe it wasn't a bald-faced lie. For all she knew, Peyton was corresponding with a nice young lady right now.

"A new romantic interest?" Frances's eyes grew as round as the saucer beneath her teacup. "Do tell."

"I don't know much about the young lady at this point."

"When will you meet her?"

"Soon, I imagine. They're exchanging letters, similar to the manner in which General Custer courted his wife, Libby." The news of the young couple had filled pages of Washington's newspapers. "As you're aware, the Custers were Washington's societal darlings."

"Custer? I hear he's a blood-thirsty thug." Frances snorted. "Lavinia met him and told me so."

"Well, the general is not Peyton's commanding officer, but Custer is a cavalryman too."

"Despicable!"

"Exactly how I thought you'd feel about it, my dear Frances." Ruth couldn't have hoped for a better reaction. "So you see? For many reasons a reunion between your daughter and my nephew is not meant to be."

CHAPTER 6

"You've kept her prisoner for two full days now, Peyt. What do you plan to do with her?"

"Not sure." Peyton glanced at Vern Johnston as they ate beneath the partially cloudy evening sky. "But I certainly wasn't about to set her free and let the Confederates blow her to bits."

"Understood. I would have done the same thing." Vern scratched his stubbly jaw.

"She was that girl we encountered in Woodstock last year, remember? The one who sutured my forearm." Peyton pushed his sleeve up, revealing a neat scar.

"Oh, right . . . and she gave us information about those bushwhackers we were tracking."

"Correct."

"We caught 'em and earned ourselves a nice promotion." The smile in Vern's voice was evident.

"Right again, my friend—thanks to Miss Bell."

Vern let out a slow whistle. "She's a feisty little thing. As I recall, she warned all of us not to lay a hand on that sister of hers—the sister who helped the innkeeper serve ale."

"A poisoned potion. Rotgut."

"I wouldn't have guessed by the way our men drank it up." Vern chuckled.

Smiling, Peyton searched his memory. He had forgotten about Miss Bell's other sister, although he remembered the youngest, foul-mouthed one—the runaway.

"That little brunette enjoyed flirting."

"Were you tempted?" Peyton already knew the answer but enjoyed goading his friend. Built like a hulking brown bear, Vern still demonstrated amazing agility in the saddle.

"Tempted? Me? Are you daft, man? Meredith would skin me alive if I even considered dallying with another female, not that I would."

"Why not? You're human."

"So was Joseph, and I always remember how he answered Potiphar's wife when she tried to seduce him. 'How then can I do this great wickedness, and sin against God?' It's not only Meredith's wrath I'm afraid of—it's God's."

"Good point. But I was thinking more about the fact that you're just not the kind of man who cheats on his wife." Johnston was as faithful as a hound, which was part of the reason Peyton always valued the man's word, not to mention his service. "And if I remember correctly, Miss Bell's flirty sister was far too young for my liking. Of course, that was before Gettysburg."

"Amazing what God can do with a man's life in little more than a year."

Peyton truly was amazed. If he hadn't experienced the spiritual metamorphosis, he wouldn't have believed it possible.

"You know, if we had bivouacked farther east tonight, I'd suggest smuggling Miss Bell off to Meredith in Germantown."

Peyton recognized the note of longing in Vern's voice. No doubt his comrade wished that *he'd* be smuggled off to his wife in Maryland—and not in a pine box either.

"Meredith would know what to do with a scamp like Miss Carrie Ann Bell."

"I'm sure she would." Peyton set aside his tin plate and stretched his legs out in front of him. "Meredith is one of those women who appears meek and soft-spoken and fragile, but who possesses an iron resolve."

"Tenth wedding anniversary coming up in November."

Peyton glanced over in time to see Vern stuff half of a boiled potato into his mouth. Since several of his men had raided a Confederate farmer's storehouse this afternoon, Peyton and his troops would eat well the next couple of days.

"Hard to imagine being married that long." Peyton's relationships with women had been brief encounters, except for his regrettable engagement to Lavinia Monteague. But since Gettysburg, Peyton refrained from both saloon girls and camp followers. Miraculously, they no longer interested him. Vern once said it was a sign that God had indeed taken Peyton up on the bargain he'd made after the first day's bloody battle in Pennsylvania.

"Your time will come to fall in love, Peyt."

"Well, don't get any ideas about matching me up with one of Meredith's unattached girlfriends."

Vern chuckled. "Not to worry. I don't have any tricks up my sleeve." He bit into a piece of dried beef.

"Good." Still, Peyton couldn't deny the loneliness he often felt.

The memory of a particularly low time during his recovery scampered across his mind, a day when Aunt Ruth suggested they pray for God to bring just the right young woman into his life—and hers too. After all, Aunt Ruth and Tabitha were the only family he had. There might never be any pleasing Tabitha, but his aunt's opinion of his future helpmeet greatly mattered to him.

Off in the distance, Peyton surveyed the small clusters of men. They ate their suppers, drank boiled coffee, and conversed. Some played cards, wrote in their diaries, or penned letters to loved ones at home. Some sang. Even now, sweet notes from a harmonica wafted over on a gust of smoky breeze. *There's no place like home . . .*

Peyton drew in a long breath and slowly released it. Why in the world did musicians choose to play this mournful melody? It made mush out of his men.

Movement a ways off caught his eye. Sitting up, he bent his right leg and slung his right arm over his knee. He squinted at the lone shadowy figure hurrying toward them. Soon recognition set in. Tommy.

The younger man swept off his hat. "Evenin', Colonel." He glanced at Vern and inclined his head. "Major Johnston."

"Evening." Peyton stood. "Do you need to speak with me?"

"Yes, sir. Miss Carrie Ann was sore uncomfortable in that uniform she's been wearing, so I scrounged up trousers, a shirt, and a vest. Don't know who the garments belonged to, on account of the laundress, Miss Phoebe, has had them for some time. The owner was smaller-boned than most fellas, so his clothes ought to come close to fittin' her." The grin on his face was obvious even in the faint moonlight. "Found her a bar of nice-smelling soap too. Then we exchanged boots, since hers fit me better and likewise the other way. Miss Carrie Ann was awfully pleased with me."

A grin worked its way across Peyton's mouth. The boy looked a mite besotted. "Did Miss Bell eat tonight?"

"Yes, sir. Three boiled potatoes, a mess of dried beef, and two apples."

"Good work, Tommy."

"Thank you, sir. And Major LaFont wants to see you right away. He says if Miss Carrie Ann is staying in camp awhile, she can help him with the wounded."

"What does she say about that?"

"Don't know, sir. Miss Carrie Ann is bathing in the creek 'fore she puts on them clothes I found her. With the rain we had, she got muddy, and she already come here with a lot of dirt on her."

"She's what? Bathing in the creek!" Peyton's heart beat faster. "We're in a camp full of men here!" Despite the exclamation, he kept his voice lowered. "You can't allow her to bathe—"

"Don't worry, Colonel." Tommy came forward with hands out, as if forestalling further reprimand. "She's hid behind trees, long grass, and bushes. If she doesn't get snake bit, she'll be fine, and Miss Carrie Ann said she ain't afraid of snakes. What's more, Major LaFont promised to keep an eye out for her."

Peyton swallowed the rest of his argument. The Louisiana-born physician had saved his life after he'd been wounded at Gettysburg. Now, Paul-Henri LaFont served as his regiment's surgeon, and Peyton trusted him as much as he trusted Vern and Tommy.

"Tommy, you've got a good head on your shoulders, and I appreciate that you went out of your way to see to Miss Bell's comfort. Good work."

"Thank you, sir." Tommy stood a little taller.

With a grin, Peyton faced Vern. "I'll head in the direction of the field hospital. This might be a good time to begin questioning Miss Bell. I'd like you to be there to take notes, Major Johnston."

"Yes, sir." Vern stood.

"But first, find General Merritt and ask if he has new orders for us. Then meet me at the hospital."

"Will do, Colonel."

When others were within earshot, Peyton and Vern returned to their respective ranks. This was war. They had jobs to do. But, oddly, Peyton's position suddenly included guardianship over a young lady who evidently had a knack for getting herself into dangerous predicaments. *Bathing in the river . . .*

He untied Brogan, who had been grazing several feet away, and tossed the reins over the charger's large head. Then, putting his foot into the stirrup, he mounted and began the ride toward the tented infirmary. In spite of his displeasure at the irksome task, he dared not give the responsibility of protecting the aspiring little journalist to a subordinate. They'd likely either allow her to sneak off or treat her roughly—or worse if it was discovered that she hailed from Woodstock, a Confederate town.

A year ago last April, he believed her when she insisted that she was "independent minded" like her journalist father. Peyton recalled that particular portion of their conversation clearly. He doubted that she was a threat to the United States Army. What's more, Miss Bell didn't strike him as a female who would flaunt herself to garner a man's attention.

So she was either extremely naïve or ignorantly courageous to bathe inside a soldiers' campsite, or, as the Almighty might have it, both!

Vern's question burned in Peyton's mind. What was he going to do with her?

Carrie Ann climbed the hill behind the hospital tent outfitted in some man's forgotten blue dungarees that she'd belted with rope, a cambric shirt that hung to her knees, and a dark blue vest that was equally as long. Mama would have a fit if she saw her in this getup. Carrie had repented for putting on that deserter's uniform. All her life she'd been told it was a sin for women to dress like men. She'd only meant to wear male clothing for a couple of hours, maybe one night, but not two days. Well, it couldn't be helped— and it was over and done now. At least this present outfit was far better than that smelly wool uniform. She was cooler now, and the long shirt provided a bit more modesty than the Union jacket she'd hemmed before leaving Woodstock.

And now, after a long soak, she felt refreshed. She thanked her heavenly Father for the soap Tommy found so she could finally wash away the soot, sweat, and grime. The opportunity hadn't presented itself since she'd arrived in the Union camp. The day she arrived was still foggy, but that evening Dr. LaFont placed her sprained wrist into a sling. Afterward, she'd fallen asleep in the field hospital. The next day, like today, Carrie followed the Union army, staying close to medical personnel in the rear, just as the colonel ordered. From what Carrie gathered, General Sheridan was withdrawing northward, in the direction of Halltown. The rain made travel difficult and often wagon wheels sank into the muddied pike and had to be dug out. Tonight, though, gentle clouds breezed past the moon.

If only the colonel would let her go free. Already it was almost a three-day trek back to Woodstock.

Nearing the hill's top, Carrie became aware of how very exhausted she felt from the day's journey. She reached for a tree branch to pull herself up only to have all her muscles throb in painful unison. She still ached from her fall into that sycamore.

Think about something other than yourself . . .

Mama and Margaret back at the Wayfarers Inn came to mind. She prayed for them both. Was Mama feeling better, or was she worried about her two missing daughters? But maybe Sarah Jane had a change of heart and found her way home. Maybe only Carrie Ann was missing. Did Mama even care? Likely not.

What about Margaret? Was she behaving herself and doing her chores? Would she realize that flirting with the male patrons was a wicked sin just like Reverend Carson said? But knowing Margaret, she was livid about having to do three times the number of chores now that her sisters were gone.

Carrie's foot slipped and she slid backward. Someone caught her elbow before she fell. Beneath the glow from within the field hospital, she glimpsed the figure of a man. He was too tall, too broad-shouldered to be Tommy.

She jerked her arm free.

"You're just the person I've been looking for, Miss Bell."

Recognizing the voice of her rescuer, she expelled a breath of relief. "I'm glad you showed up when you did, Captain Collier—I mean, Colonel." Carrie's face flamed, having misspoken his rank.

Clasping her elbow once more, he effortlessly brought her the rest of the way up the hill.

Funny, she'd dreamed up at least a dozen fairy tales about this man ever since they'd first met nearly a year and a half ago. In her dreams, he was always Captain Collier, the fearless, handsome Union officer whose arm she'd sutured and who, out of gratitude, eventually returned to Woodstock, fell madly in love with her, and rescued her from a life of drudgery at the Way-farers Inn.

But, of course, they had been mere fairy tales. This was reality.

"You and I need to talk." The colonel's stern tone vanquished the last of Carrie's imaginings.

"I know. I've been waiting to speak with you. Are you finally going to let me go?"

"That's what we need to discuss."

"Oh." His tone left her feeling no more hopeful about her release than yesterday or the day before. But what did she really know about this man? Perhaps he was a devil cavalryman like Joshua said.

"I understand from Major LaFont that you sprained your wrist."

"Yes, but it's much better." She wished she could say the same for the rest of her aching joints after today's arduous trek. "I didn't have a single problem with it tonight."

"Which brings us to our first order of business." The colonel halted, forcing Carrie to do the same. The night songs of crickets and katydids filled the space between them. "This is a camp comprised of several thousand men. I can't possibly speak for the integrity of every single one of them. Many have not enjoyed the company of a female in a long while and may not be able to control their . . . manners should they happen upon you alone and in a most vulnerable situation again. Do I make myself clear?"

"Extremely clear." Picturing the consequences wasn't difficult.

"Good."

"I work at the Wayfarers Inn, remember? I am accustomed to men forgetting their . . . manners. But I can sense danger, and I felt safe and well hidden."

"Did you feel safe two days ago when you were found suffocating in that sycamore?"

"Are you going to hold that— that *accident* against me forever?"

"No. I really meant no insult. Forgive me. But I hope you will take my warning to heart."

She softened at his apology. "I will."

"Excellent."

"But I won't be in camp that long, right? I mean, you do intend to release me, don't you?"

"I will decide after your interview."

"What interview?" This man was exasperating! She pulled her elbow from his hold. "I told you why I wore that deserter's uniform—to slip past Union troops and find my sister. I thought you believed me."

"I do, actually, but I must file a report, so we'll discuss the matter in detail. Follow me."

The colonel led the way to the hospital tent, opened one of the flaps, and politely held it for Carrie. Several glowing lamps lighted their way. No men lay writhing in pain on the grassy ground as in the last couple of days. The field hospital had emptied, save for a few attendants coming and going. The remaining wounded from the fight outside of Front Royal had been taken to Harpers Ferry, and there were no badly injured men to tend to today.

"You're back, *petite*." The dark-haired French physician hurried toward her. Carrie found him amiable and gentle. Reaching her, Major LaFont looked her over. "And you are wearing a most interesting outfit, yes?" He worked the tip of his mustache between his thumb and forefinger.

"Not my preference, I assure you. If I had my druthers I'd be in a ladylike frock." She glanced at the colonel. Did he think she ran around all day in men's breeches?

"Please, sit down." The physician moved a wooden stool toward her and extended his hand in an invitation.

Carrie walked farther into the tent and stifled a groan as she lowered herself onto the stool.

"Your muscles still ache, yes?"

"Extremely." She'd hoped bathing in the creek would alleviate the soreness, and it had, to some degree.

"It will be that way for another day or so."

She sighed. "I figured as much."

Colonel Collier spoke up. "Major Johnston and I will be questioning Miss Bell. You believe she is recovered enough to handle an interview?"

"Indeed, she is. I shall leave you to your duties." Major LaFont bowed slightly in Carrie's direction before exiting the tent.

Colonel Collier reached inside his coat and produced a cigar. He bit off the closed end and spit it out. After finding a match, he struck it against the sole of his boot then held the lit end to the tip of his cigar and waited until it glowed red.

"Let's get this over with." He took a puff and exhaled a cloud of bluish-gray smoke. His gaze fell on her and he grunted irritably. "Please forgive me, Miss Bell. I'm aware that in polite society my smoking in front of a lady would be deemed quite rude, and if you object to my habit, I will put out my cigar. It's just that I've had a very long and difficult day and I feel the need for a bit of relaxation as we converse."

"Smoke to your heart's content, Colonel. My father smokes a pipe, and I've always found the rich smell of burning tobacco rather comforting."

After a grateful smile, the colonel glanced toward the tent's entrance. "Major Johnston, I want no interruptions." Another puff on his cigar. "Are you ready?"

"Yes, sir." A large man stepped out of the shadows. Carrie recalled seeing him around camp the past two days. He held up a pen, a small inkwell, and a record book.

Tommy had said that Major Johnston was the colonel's right-hand man. Tommy claimed to be the runner-up.

"Excellent." The colonel's gaze fell on Carrie. "Shall we begin?"

Chapter 7

"I never did hear who won the conflict near Front Royal. The Union or Confederacy?"

"I'll ask the questions, Miss Bell."

"Fine." Carrie's nerves began to fray. "But you can't fault me for being curious. After all, the Union has taken quite a licking this summer."

"Which side do you *hope* lost the Front Royal conflict?" The colonel puffed on his cigar, eyed it speculatively, and then gazed back at her.

"Neither side. I'm independent minded, like any good journalist."

"Since when are journalists independent minded?" The colonel frowned over his cigar. "Have you not read Frank Leslie's *Illustrated Journal, Harper's Weekly*, or the *New York Times*?"

"Yes, I've read issues of those newspapers—that is, whenever a soldier has a mind to leave a copy behind in Woodstock. I've also read copies of the *Daily Progress* and the *Richmond Examiner*."

"None is objective, wouldn't you agree?"

"Yes, I agree, but that doesn't mean the journalists themselves are biased. They may be pandering to their audience—or their editors."

"Perhaps, although I do find it strange that you've kept your objectivity in Confederate Woodstock."

"And how fortunate for you that I've managed to do so or you would have bled to death in the Wayfarers Inn."

"Touché, Miss Bell." He sounded amused.

"The battle near Front Royal was inconclusive from what I've heard." The resounding timbre of Major Johnston's voice made Carrie turn and look his way. His hulking frame remained near the opening of the tent, record book in hand, his pen poised. "We lost less than a hundred men and took almost three hundred prisoners."

"Does that include me?" Carrie looked at the colonel.

"Depends on whether we finish this interview." He emphasized his statement with a wide-eyed stare.

Carrie still hadn't decided how cooperative to be. "What is it that you want to know?"

He blew out a plume of smoke. "You stated your sister ran away. When did you first learn of it?"

"Before breakfast the day before you found me. You see, I went to my father's newspaper office at dawn that day, before I began my chores at the Wayfarers Inn. It was then I discovered the note Sarah Jane left me. It read that she'd run off with a peddler by the name of Arthur Sims." Carrie glanced at Major Johnston. "Do you need help getting this all down?" she asked facetiously. "If so, I'd be happy to write it myself."

He chuckled. "After years of seminary training, I think I can manage."

"Seminary? Are you a priest?"

"Hardly." He chuckled. "I'm a minister in civilian life. I served a church in Germantown, Maryland, until I marched off to war with the Union."

"I didn't know there were loyalists in Maryland."

"More than you'd expect. Abolitionists too."

"Miss Bell." The colonel cleared his throat. "Major Johnston is not the one I'm investigating. You are."

Carrie expelled a long breath.

"Now, as you were saying . . . you set off to find your sister, wearing a Union officer's uniform?"

"Not exactly. First I ran into my childhood friend Joshua Blevens and his ill-mannered comrade, a man by the name of John Rodingham."

The name obviously didn't mean anything to either Yankee officer.

"Go on," the colonel said.

"I hadn't seen Joshua in a long while and we've known each other since the day I was born. So, naturally, I stopped to converse."

Carrie hoped to bore the two men to tears. Maybe they'd fall asleep as she prattled on. Then she'd slip away into the night.

"Continue, please." Having finished his cigar, the colonel dropped it and ground it out with the heel of his boot.

"I showed my sister's letter to Joshua, and about that time I remembered the deserter's uniform. Like I told you before, I found the garments this past spring as I cleaned one of the rooms at the inn. After I found it, I checked Mr. Veyschmidt's register. The man had signed his name *Tom Foolery*. Obviously not his real name."

"Obviously." There was no mistaking the sarcasm in the colonel's tone. "And you never bothered reporting the deserter and turning in his uniform to Federal authorities?" He folded his arms.

Carrie gave a shrug. "No Federals have come to town since then." She couldn't resist goading him just a bit. "They might have dashed down Main Street as if the devil himself chased them, when in actuality it was the Confederate army on their heels."

To his credit, he didn't bite. "And then what happened, Miss Bell?"

She told him and Johnston, using every unnecessary detail that popped into her mind. She recounted how, after completing her daily chores, she'd hemmed the Yankee uniform and concealed it beneath Margaret's dress in case she ran into Confederates—which, indeed, had occurred. She described meeting the Rebel soldier on the way to Front Royal.

"The idea of getting in the middle of two opposing armies wasn't enough to send you back to Woodstock?"

"No. The soldier said he'd seen a peddler and a girl just ten hours earlier. I knew if I hurried, I could catch up. But I was just too tired by then." Exhaustion weighted her limbs now too.

"I imagine so, not having any sleep the night before." The colonel sounded . . . sympathetic.

Carrie felt herself soften. Odd, since she'd never been one to cave into a man's will simply because he showed her some politeness or concern. But the colonel was different somehow.

"The main thing that kept me going was that my mother told me I couldn't return home unless Sarah Jane was with me." Carrie bowed her head. "I'm sure she thinks I'm dead now."

"I'm sure your mother didn't mean those harsh words," Johnston said.

"Oh, she meant them." There wasn't a doubt in Carrie's mind.

"What about your childhood friend, Joshua. Is he a Confederate soldier?" The colonel squatted so he was eye level with Carrie.

She squirmed at his scrutiny. "Yes."

"Do you know where he was headed?"

She did, but should she say?

"Any information would be of help, Miss Bell, and I would be very grateful."

She supposed it wasn't any big secret. "Joshua had just received his orders and he and Rodingham were to set off for Staunton after they finished eating. I served them dinner at the inn the night I left, since I couldn't leave my sister Margaret to serve customers on her own. Mr. Veyschmidt would have gotten suspicious about my absence."

The colonel released a heavy sigh.

"Anyway, I overheard Joshua and Rodingham discussing how Confederate troops were regrouping at Fisher's Hill. Evidently, General Early and his men are waiting for reinforcements from General Richard Anderson and his First Corps, who, you must admit, fought amazingly well at Spotsylvania Court House and Cold Harbor."

"I will admit no such thing, Miss Bell. Many of my friends were killed in those battles."

Carrie immediately regretted her words.

The colonel sprang to his feet and took in a breath through his nose, slowly yet audibly as if he fought to control his anger. Carrie reminded herself that she wasn't among curious patrons at the Wayfarers Inn, anxious to hear the latest news of Confederate victories. She was among officers in the Union army, who might just shoot the messenger.

"Did these men mention the number of Early's forces?"

"No, but it can't be more than thirty or forty thousand and that's including Anderson's troops."

"Based upon what, Miss Bell?"

"Based upon"—Carrie lifted her shoulders—"basic mathematics, sir."

The colonel peered over her head and looked at Johnston.

"I'll tell Tommy to relay this information to General Merritt."

"Thank you, Major." As Johnston left the tent, Colonel Collier glanced back at Carrie. "And thank you, Miss Bell. As I said, I'm grateful for any information."

"Happy to oblige, especially if it means you'll turn me loose." She didn't feel at all like she betrayed Joshua or any Confederates she knew. Like the graybacks, the Yankees had their spies, and soon the colonel would learn the very same things she'd just told him. "Except, I didn't really say anything you wouldn't find out soon enough."

"Sooner rather than later is oftentimes the difference between life and death." The colonel walked to the medicine trunk, closed it, and pulled it across the carpet of soft, trampled grass. He sat on it, close enough to Carrie that his knees nearly touched hers. Strange flutters filled her insides and she wondered over her reaction to this man. The last time she'd felt this way was when she'd sutured his forearm.

"Is there anything else you're willing to share?"

"Well, the only other thing I know is—" She didn't mind betraying that varmint Rodingham one bit. "I overheard Major Rodingham tell Joshua—"

"Your friend—or is he more than a friend?"

"Actually, more than a friend. He's like an annoying older brother."

"I see." His tone was a mix of amusement and perhaps curiosity. "But I interrupted you. Please continue."

Carrie focused on the top brass button of his dark blue coat. If she looked into his handsome face, she'd lose her concentration for sure. "Rodingham told Joshua that General Early likes to hit the Union army's rear because then the Confederates will have less of a fight."

"That's probably true and it's no secret. Both sides employ the tactic." The colonel's voice sounded velvet soft. "Ambulances, supply wagons, and artillery pieces travel with the rear guard."

Carrie knew that; after all, she'd traveled with them for two days. "But Rodingham said he'd gladly meet the Yankees head-on. He wasn't afraid to fight. Joshua agreed. Personally, I think they're fools." Her eyes met the colonel's steady gaze. She could barely think. "I read somewhere that General Sheridan's army is comprised of fifty thousand men."

"You're well informed, Miss Bell." The colonel sounded impressed. "That's quite accurate, and we'll be concentrating our efforts on winning the Shenandoah Valley."

"That's been tried before, sir, back in '62 when General Jackson defended the Valley. The Union had no luck then."

"This time it will be different."

He sounded determined, but Carrie wondered. And whether good news or bad, she couldn't say. Often when Union forces invaded towns they brought with them law and order and curtailed guerrilla activity. But there were other times when Confederate citizens under Federal authority suffered greatly—like when General Milroy invaded Winchester.

She pulled her thoughts together. "Will you show mercy to the citizens in the Valley?"

"By 'mercy,' what do you mean?"

"Will you respect us instead of harassing and threatening us? There's a woman in Woodstock who was brutalized by several Yankees."

"Are you certain they were Union soldiers? Or were they bushwhackers and deserters in Union uniforms?"

Carrie couldn't say for sure.

"Such raids and terrorism have been an enormous problem for residents in Shenandoah Valley, particularly in the lower portion. I have an aunt in Winchester, and the things she's reported to me make my blood boil."

Carrie blinked. "You have an aunt in Winchester?"

He nodded and leaned forward, resting his forearms on his knees, his face alarmingly close. "I actually consider myself to be a Virginian. My parents died when I was twelve and I went to live with my aunt. So, in fact, Winchester is my home."

"Then you're from the Valley too."

"Yes, from the *Daughter of the Stars*, as the Indians called it."

"That's right." Carrie felt an immediate kinship with the colonel. "So you'll be fair-minded to its citizens?"

"I will. You have my word."

Again, Carrie detected the man's sincerity. She smiled. "I knew there was a reason I liked you so much when I sewed up your arm."

"I'm flattered, Miss Bell."

She dropped her gaze, embarrassed about her unintended declaration. Goodness! What was she thinking, saying such a thing out loud? "Forgive me for sounding so forward, Colonel. I'm awfully tired and my mind isn't as sharp as it should be."

"Understandably so. No need for apologies."

She lifted her gaze. Without a doubt, Colonel Collier was the kindest man she'd ever met. "The Army of the Shenandoah outnumbers General Early's army by at least ten thousand—that is if Anderson's troops are really on their way to assist. But the Rebs are fierce and tenacious, and willing to die to preserve their way of life."

"I appreciate the warning, Miss Bell. I will take it to heart." He straightened. "However, I think we should pause here for the night. We'll continue this interview tomorrow."

"What?" Carrie jumped to her feet. She had hoped to be on her way tonight.

"By your own admission you're exhausted and you're obviously still hurting from the fall you took a couple of days ago." The colonel stood also. "I wouldn't want to take advantage of your weakened state. It could reflect badly on me as an officer in the United States Army, and my report may not be taken seriously in Washington."

Washington? "Who will read this interview?"

"All reports go to Washington and are reviewed by the Office of the Chief of Staff."

"I didn't realize that I was in so much trouble."

"You're not, assuming you continue to cooperate."

"I will. I promise."

"However, depriving a detainee of sleep goes against my principles of interrogation."

What a poor time for his noble character to show its face. "Please, Colonel, won't you reconsider? I have to find my sister."

"I'm afraid not."

The tent flap opened and Major Johnston reentered.

The colonel looked his way. "Major, I've decided we'll continue this interview tomorrow."

"Very well, sir."

"No, please, Colonel." Carrie had no intentions of spending another night in a Yankee camp, although the men she'd had contact with were all polite . . . so far. "Finish questioning me so I can be on my way."

"You need a good night's rest, Miss Bell. Tomorrow will come soon enough."

"But that peddler has probably reached Culpeper by now." A yawn threatened and she couldn't fight it off. To her chagrin, she'd just proved his point.

Despite the dwindling lantern light, his wry grin shone through his beard. He gave her a small but gallant bow. "Until tomorrow, Miss Bell."

$$\sim\!\!\infty\,\,\infty\!\!\sim$$

"What do you think?" Peyton glanced at Vern. They stood outside the tented field hospital and watched Tommy lead Miss Bell to a grassy spot where she could sleep a safe distance from his bivouacking regiment. Just as in the last two nights, she'd given her word that she wouldn't run away, and, in turn, he agreed not to shackle her ankles. Besides, he didn't think even Tommy could scrounge up shackles small enough to hold her.

"I think that, not only is Miss Bell spirited, she's astute and well-informed." Vern tucked his log book beneath one arm. "What's more, I believe she is as independent minded as she claims—at least as far as anyone can be. I haven't sensed any animosity from her, and she answered your questions."

"After a bit of sass, yes, she did." Peyton glanced at Vern and grinned. For some odd reason he found her pluckiness amusing, not aggravating.

"She seems desperate to find her sister," Vern remarked.

"Agreed. Her return home seems to depend on it."

"So are you going to let her go in the morning?"

Peyton drew in a breath and released it audibly. He'd volleyed the question in his mind for hours and came up with the same conclusion time and again. "I can't, in all good conscience, let her go, Vern. She'll get herself killed—or worse."

"I'm in agreement, but you can't hold her against her will. You'll either have to charge her with a crime and let her have her day in court, which means sending her on a harrowing journey to either Harpers Ferry or Washington, or you've got to allow her to be on her way."

"I'm aware of my options." Peyton kneaded his whiskered jaw with his thumb and forefinger. "Unless . . ."

"Unless what?"

He stared at Vern. "Unless I send her to Aunt Ruth in Winchester."

Vern fell silent.

"She's no threat to others," Peyton said. "I'm convinced of it. She was kind to my troops and me last year at the Wayfarers Inn, and very cooperative. She's intelligent and determined, and my aunt will admire Miss Bell's tenacity." He grinned. "The alternative is incomprehensible. If I turn her loose, I'm certain she'll fall into the wrong hands, and I hate the thought of her returning to that innkeeper. I found him to be a calculating, quick-tempered lout. I'm afraid he's sorely used Miss Bell and her sisters."

"I'm inclined to agree—from what I remember of the man."

"Yes, well, Carrie Ann Bell has potential." Peyton also guessed she managed to stay innocent. He could tell by her mannerisms when they were alone in the tent minutes ago. "All she needs is an opportunity."

"And you're in a position to give it."

"I am." Peyton further considered his idea. "Aunt Ruth would be in her glory, having a protégé living under her roof. Likewise, Miss Bell would learn proper etiquette from my aunt, which she's obviously not getting at her place of employment. And, staying with my aunt, she'd meet interesting people. She can search for her runaway sister just as well from Winchester—probably better with my aunt's help."

"It's a solid plan, but will Miss Bell go along with it? She doesn't strike me as one to accept charity."

"I agree. But, you heard her—unless she has her runaway sister with her, Miss Bell can't return to Woodstock. She has nowhere to go."

"Another good point." Vern turned and rapped Peyton between the shoulder blades. "My friend, I think you've solved the problem of what to do with Miss Carrie Ann Bell."

HEADQUARTERS MIDDLE
MILITARY DIVISION,
Cedar Creek, Va., August 16, 1864

GENERAL [Torbert]: In compliance with instructions of the Lieutenant-General commanding [Grant], you will make the necessary arrangements and give the necessary orders for the destruction of the wheat and hay south of a line from Millwood to Winchester and Petticoat Gap. You will seize all mules, horses, and cattle that may be useful to our army. Loyal citizens can bring in their claims against the Government for this necessary destruction. No houses will be burned and officers in charge of this delicate but necessary duty must inform the people that the object is to make this Valley untenable for the raiding parties of the rebel army.

Very respectfully,
P. H. SHERIDAN
Major-General Commanding

Chapter 8

Carrie listened as Colonel Collier relayed the orders, written three days ago and handed down through the ranks, to his officers who would then pass on the instructions to men in their commands.

"I will not abide plundering or intentional harming of citizens," the colonel added. "Is that understood?"

His subordinates muttered the affirmative, but Carrie wondered if they meant it. She'd read tales of horror after Yankees descended on unsuspecting farms. Then again, she'd read the same about guerrillas who terrorized loyalists in the Valley as well as Confederate citizens. What's more, Colonel Collier had given his word last night that he'd treat residents of the Shenandoah Valley with respect and show them mercy. The man seemed trustworthy, so she figured he'd deliver harsh punishment to those men who defied his command.

With hands clasped behind his back, the colonel gave a nod. "You are dismissed, men."

His soldiers filed off, talking and murmuring as they went.

Colonel Collier turned to Carrie. "I'd like to speak with you. Come this way." He waved her into the officer's tent.

When she'd awakened this morning she was amazed to see the tents that had been erected for the upper command. This one, Tommy said, was referred to as the "officer's wall" and could sleep eight to ten men comfortably beneath its billowy mass. It looked similar to the field hospital.

"I trust you slept well, Miss Bell." The colonel walked to where a table stood in the center of the tent.

"I guess I did. I don't recall anything once I placed my head on the horse blanket Tommy lent me."

"Well, don't worry. Your snoring didn't disturb my men."

"My . . . what?" She set her hands on her waist. "I do not snore."

The colonel chuckled, a deep rich sound that made Carrie smile in spite of herself.

"Pardon my jest." His brown eyes twinkled.

So he had a sense of humor. Carrie always appreciated a good wit. "I suppose I can overlook it this time."

The man had revived his appearance and wore a clean, white shirt this morning. Carrie wondered if he had located that concealed swimming hole at the edge of the pond, the one she'd availed herself of. Perhaps he'd also indulged in a bath.

"I gather you want to finish interrogating me." She folded her arms.

"There's no need, Miss Bell." He stood with one hand on the table and the other on his hip. "I believe your story."

Relief like the cool, spring-fed water in the pond washed over her. "Thank you, sir."

"However—"

She groaned inwardly. She should have known there'd be some conditions to her release. "I already took the oath, pledging my allegiance to the United States."

"You did?" The colonel's brows drew together. "When?"

"Some time ago. A Yankee, not sure of his rank, barged into the Wayfarers Inn with his rowdy troops and held my sisters and me at gunpoint, threatening to do us bodily harm unless we took the oath. I didn't feel it was wise to call his bluff, so we took it. We promised not to poison their dinners or shoot them while they ate or drank or slept at the Wayfarers Inn." Carrie rolled one shoulder. "I'd never kill another human being unless it was self-defense. I'd rather give aid than kill." She remembered what Papa said one time. "I'm what's known as a *humanitarian*."

The colonel's features relaxed and he smiled. "I believe that too, Miss Bell."

"So"—hope soared inside of her—"I am free to go?"

He drew in a breath, his wide chest expanding. "Yes, but I have an offer to present to you first."

She'd already taken several steps toward the opened flap of the tent. Halting, she turned. "An offer?"

He smoothed the paper covering the tabletop. "Come and look at this."

She strode forward and peered at the map he'd unrolled.

"We're here." He pointed to a place north of Front Royal. "Generals Crook and Wright and their men reached Winchester, but were pushed back. For now, General Sheridan has ordered us to continue probing the enemy. I shall spare you specifics." He moved his finger to the left. "The goal is to have our pickets stationed from Winchester to White Post and then push the enemy south, ultimately out of the Valley. Meanwhile, over here . . ." The colonel moved his finger downward and to the right. "General Grant is battling Lee's troops for Petersburg. There are skirmishes going on all around the area." He straightened. "You can see why it would be quite unsafe to venture off on your own, attired as you are, and without any gear."

"But—"

"I know you want to find your sister, and I may be able to help." He leaned over the map and tapped on a point. "As I told you last night, I have an aunt in Winchester. You'd be doing me a favor if you went to stay with her, as Aunt Ruth is getting up in years."

"So I'd become her housekeeper?"

"No. Tabitha runs the house. I was thinking more along the lines of a . . . companion. The benefit for you is that my aunt has a large home and you'd have your own room, complete with a soft bed."

A soft bed? Carrie never had that luxury before. She'd always shared the loft and a bed with Margaret. Then, once Sarah Jane got older, all three of them shared the bed. After the farm burned down, she and her sisters slept on the wooden floor, as Mr. Veyschmidt only rented a small, corner room to them with a single bed upon which Mama slept.

"Additionally, my aunt has the means to help you find your sister," the colonel said, "without you having to wander the countryside, hoping to catch up with that peddler who may or may not have really gone to Culpeper. In fact"—he tapped the map again—"I think it's likely he headed down the

Valley Pike. My aunt has written to me of how most stores in town closed so residents must travel a long distance to purchase many basic necessities. It's safe to assume a peddler would be aware of the fact and know that he could make some money in Winchester, as many there use Federal currency."

Carrie surveyed the map, running her forefinger along the route. "I hate to admit it, but your logic makes perfect sense. That no-account will likely charge folks one hundred dollars for a bag of flour."

"Would that be Confederate money?" The colonel arched a brow.

She nodded and grinned at his quip. "But I read somewhere that even General Early uses Federal currency to send his telegrams and purchase foodstuffs."

"He's an intelligent man." The colonel wore a hint of a grin. "Confederate currency is worth almost nothing."

Standing beside him now, Carrie caught his fresh but musky scent, an improvement over yesterday to be sure! She stood as tall as his whiskered chin, and my, but he was a handsome man. Straight nose, square jawline . . . What would happen if she reached up and touched his beard? *Was it as soft as it appeared?*

She quickly took a step back, horrified by her wayward thoughts.

The colonel didn't seem to notice. "My aunt is a loyalist, Miss Bell, and she possesses all her faculties. She'll have ideas of how best to locate your sister. Perhaps you can write an article or ad for some local newspapers. That's your area of expertise, is it not?"

"Yes, but—" Carrie would enjoy an opportunity to write for a real newspaper. "It's just that . . . well, I already have a job at the Wayfarers Inn."

"You told me that your mother wouldn't take you back unless your sister was in tow, Miss Bell, and I believed you."

"That's true . . ." And she was sure that Mama had meant every word of it!

"Then wouldn't you agree that my offer provides you with both room and board and an occupation for which I will pay you?"

"Pay me?"

He gave a nod. "Seven dollars a month."

She inhaled quickly. No one she knew earned a whole seven dollars a month. But was there a catch? She narrowed her gaze. "Is that seven dollars Confederate money?"

He chuckled. "No, U.S. currency."

That changed everything. She could send money to her family. Maybe they could collect enough to pay off Mr. Veyschmidt and leave the Wayfarers Inn. Of course, working for a Union officer would be considered treason, but so was the oath she'd been forced to take. Was the money worth the risk of never being able to return to Woodstock?

"So what's your answer, Miss Bell?"

"May I get a message to my sister Margaret and tell her I'm alive? Mama is illiterate, but Margaret can read. I'll let her know I've found paying employment and perhaps my mother won't be so angry with me."

The colonel paused briefly to consider it while rolling up the map. "Yes. I'll take the message and deliver it personally to the Wayfarers Inn if we get as far up the Valley as Woodstock in the next day or so. Should we not be successful, I'll send a telegram from the nearest town."

"Thank you." Selfish as it was, Carrie hoped he wouldn't get himself killed before delivering or dispatching her note. But in reality, she didn't want the colonel to meet the same fate as those poor souls near Front Royal a few days ago. The memory of their maimed, twisted, and bloody bodies haunted her. "Do you think you'll really get that far south without General Early's men stopping you?"

"They'll try to stop us, but they can't win. Not this time."

Carrie pressed her lips together, watching as Colonel Collier stuffed the map into a circular container. Something inside said she should accept this most generous offer and still something else held her back. "What if your aunt doesn't like me? What if we don't get along?"

"I don't believe that will happen." The note of confidence in his tone was unmistakable. "However, if it does, you're free to seek other accommodations."

"Or leave town?"

The colonel hesitated. "Or leave town." His eyes met hers. "I can't very well hold you against your will."

No, he couldn't, and those were the words she'd wanted to hear. She wouldn't be indentured. "I'm glad you believe me, Colonel." She held his gaze, unabashed. "But why are you offering me this position? Truly, it sounds too good to be true."

"It's payback. Plain and simple. You helped me when I needed it so now I'd like to return the kindness. Besides, as I said, you'll be doing me another favor by looking after Aunt Ruth." His features brightened. "I think you'll like her."

Carrie hoped so, prayed so.

And, with God's help, she'd find Sarah Jane. Maybe by then, Papa would be home. He'd have some choice words for Mr. Veyschmidt, that's for sure. Papa's presence would calm Mama and she'd allow Carrie to return home. Soon her family would be reunited. Maybe the farm could be rebuilt with the funds Papa earned from the sale of textbooks along with Carrie's income from her new position.

"So we have a verbal agreement?"

"Yes." A deal with a devil cavalryman. What would Joshua say? Would he call her a traitor?

A shiver of dread trickled down her spine.

There was nothing so glorious for Ruth than to watch the Union army marching past her house . . . except she wished they were marching into town, not retreating. Standing on her front porch, she and Tabitha waved United States flags. Several soldiers nodded their direction. A couple of them shouted, "We'll be back!" while the band played "Battle Cry of Freedom" amidst taunts, boos, and hisses. Secessionist women shook their skirts at the soldiers, a wish of defeat to Union troops.

A horseman, riding alongside the formation, stopped in front of the house, tethered his mount, and then climbed the steep bank of steps that led to the porch.

"Miss Ruth Collier?" He doffed his hat.

"Yes. I'm Ruth Collier." She spied his rank on his coat's sleeve. "What can I do for you, Sergeant?"

"Ma'am, I was ordered to deliver this message to you personally." He retrieved a sealed envelope from his inside pocket.

"Why thank you." Spying the penmanship, which she knew as well as her own, Ruth's heart beat faster. *Peyton! Word from Peyton!* Looking back at the soldier, she noticed the weariness etched into his dirty face. "May I get you anything? Something to eat? A refill of water in your canteen, perhaps?"

"Another time, ma'am, but I have orders to keep my men moving." He gave a small bow before turning and hurrying back to his horse.

"May God go with you, Sergeant."

"Thank you, ma'am," he called from astride his roan. He waved and rode off to catch up with his regiment.

Ruth wasted no time. She reentered the house and made for her writing desk. Tabitha was on her heels.

"Who's that letter from?"

"Peyton."

"Must be important if he's writing. Our boy ain't much for letter writing."

"Quite true." And much to Ruth's great disappointment. "I hope he's not injured." Finding her letter opener, she unsealed the message.

"What is it? What's it say?"

"Give me a moment to read it. For heaven's sake!" As she pulled the letter from its sheath, several dollar bills fluttered to the floor.

Tabitha picked up the bills. "Well, look at this. Our boy sent us money."

"Praise God. The Union wasn't in town long enough for me to make a transfer from our bank in Washington."

The letter unfolded now, she took in each word from her beloved nephew. "We're to expect company in the next few days, although it could be as long as a week from now before Peyton can secure her a safe transport. She's a young lady by the name of Carrie Ann Bell, from Woodstock, but with loyalist sympathies. She's currently assisting Dr. LaFont as a volunteer nurse."

"What's our boy sending her here for?"

"He doesn't say."

"He ain't never sent us a young lady before."

"No, no, he hasn't." Ruth frowned, puzzled.

"This here fell out with the money, Miss Ruth." Tabitha handed her a smaller piece of paper.

"Why, it's the young lady's measurements. The handwriting is not Peyton's, so I'm left to believe it's hers." Ruth was impressed. "It's very neat penmanship too."

"Now, what on earth are we supposed to do with a stranger's measurements?" Tabitha placed her hands on her slender hips.

"Apparently, our guest will be needing clothes."

"This ain't making no sense."

Ruth put the pieces together. "Obviously Miss Bell is a long way from Woodstock, and if she's volunteered to give medical aid at a Union camp, perhaps her belongings were destroyed or had to be left behind in a great hurry."

Tabitha wagged her head of wooly-white hair, neatly combed and swept up in its usual chignon and covered with a snood. "He wouldn't dare send one of them camp followers."

"Indeed not!" Many of those laundresses and nurses by day were prostitutes by night. A year and a half ago, Ruth might have fretted over the possibility, but not now. Peyton was a changed man. "He ends his letter with, 'I believe you'll like her.'"

"What does he care if we like her or not? If she's company, we'll do right by her and he knows it."

"Of course we will." Ruth glanced between Peyton's missive and the more delicate penmanship that appeared on the slip of paper. Then she looked at Tabitha. "I imagine our questions will be answered soon enough. Meanwhile, you and I need to go into town and visit Miss Isles and see about some dresses."

"But, Miss Ruth, it ain't like our boy to send us a young lady and want her outfitted too." Tabitha's brown eyes narrowed suspiciously.

"It is quite extraordinary, isn't it?"

"I'm wondering if . . ."

"The same thing I'm wondering, no doubt."

A grin split Tabitha's dark face. "Maybe we didn't fib to Miss Frances after all."

CHAPTER 9

August 20, 1864

Carrie Ann stood at the edge of a stony hillside and gazed westward. The sun began its descent on this Saturday above a rare parting of storm clouds that cast eerie shafts of light across the lush, green meadow below. Her body ached from bouncing on the hard wagon bench beside Private Owens, a young Ohioan assigned to drive the ambulance.

With hands on her waist, Carrie made several slow neck rotations, hoping to stretch out the kinks. The march today had been long and tedious, and many evidences of the numerous battles were still on sickening display. To Carrie's horror, burned-out wagons, human skeletal remains, and shallow graves of unknown soldiers lined the roadside. Buzzards circled overhead then swooped down to peck at the decaying horseflesh left from a more recent conflict. As the Union army's wagon train neared, the birds scattered, looking like pieces of shot dotting an already mournful sky. Meanwhile, the Yankee cavalrymen commenced setting fire to haystacks, wheat fields, storage barns, and mills. At times, the thick, black smoke blotted out the intermittent sunshine.

If only this war would end.

Carrie looked at the heavens. Why did God allow war? Why didn't He put an end to it?

As if in reply, a single raindrop fell and struck Carrie on the cheek. Perhaps God's heart was breaking as much as hers.

But, of course, a sovereign God wasn't shocked by this war or the weather. It had rained on and off the past five days—ever since the night she left Woodstock. The deluges doused numerous fires and most likely spared the outbuildings of many Shenandoah Valley residents. Still, without livestock and crops, how would people survive? Meanwhile, the Yankees ate well—Carrie included, although she felt pangs of guilt with each bite.

And to think her family might be starving . . .

Carrie whispered a prayer that God would protect and provide for them, just like He had for her.

A slight wind blew against her face as a noisy wagon clattered by. Carrie turned in time to read the bold print on the side: U.S. Mail. She smiled. Letters to the men from friends and loved ones had found their way here from Harpers Ferry. She wondered what it felt like to receive a personal letter, particularly from a sweetheart.

Behind her, a man cleared his throat. Carrie whirled around and the gravel beneath her feet shifted. The earth suddenly gave way. Instinctively her arms sailed upward. Someone clamped onto her forearm and gave a yank. She slammed into something blue and unyielding.

Her gaze moved upward. "Colonel Collier!"

Wide-eyed, he stared at her for several seconds then peered over the edge of the hill. "You certainly do like to tempt the Almighty, don't you?"

"No . . . at least not on purpose."

He guided her to solid ground before releasing her. Then he removed his hat and nodded toward several boulders a safe distance from the edge of the hill. "Let's sit, Miss Bell."

She chose a large rock and waited for her heart to resume a normal rhythm.

"Falling off bridges into trees and now standing on the edge of a steep hill." He gave a wag of his head. "What am I to do with you?"

She detected traces of humor and smiled. "I confess I'm drawn to views overlooking the countryside. I always have been. The panoramic view from the top of Massanutten Mountain, for instance, captivates me every time."

"Hmm . . . you on top of a mountain is a frightening thought. Evidently, you keep your guardian angels busy."

"Or a Union colonel on his toes." Her smile grew.

"Indeed."

She tipped her head, suddenly curious. "Do you believe in guardian angels, Colonel?"

"Yes, because I believe the Bible. It says that God will give His angels charge over us to guide us in all our ways."

"You believe the Bible?"

"Yes." The lines around his eyes creased in display of his amusement. "You ask as though you're surprised, Miss Bell."

"You've given me no reason to doubt your statement."

"Does it surprise you, Miss Bell, that I'm a Christian man?"

She lifted a shoulder, not wanting to admit that she often wondered if Yankee Christian was a contradiction. "My friend Joshua called you and your command 'devil cavalrymen.'"

His expression darkened. "And you agree?"

"No. I don't think so. Everyone in your command has been very courteous to me."

"Good." He punctuated the word with a single nod.

"You've been exceptionally kind, Colonel, although in the past I have met Yankees who fit that devil description."

"I don't doubt it. Some Union soldiers have shamed our army, and those men have either got hatred burning in their souls or they're power-hungry brutes."

"Exactly. I've run into both sorts of miscreants at the Wayfarers Inn."

"On behalf of the Union army, please accept my apologies for their poor manners."

"On behalf of myself, Colonel, I accept your apology." They both laughed lightly.

"Thank you." He inclined his head most graciously before gazing out over the Virginia countryside. "I'm sure you're equally aware of the atrocities committed by deserters and bushwhackers—men masquerading in Union uniforms."

"Yes, in fact, I wrote an article once about those sorts during a time when people in the Valley were frequently being robbed and beaten."

"It's unfortunate." He pulled a cigar and match from his inside vest pocket. "Do you mind?"

She shook her head.

"I didn't think so, but I thought I'd be polite and ask anyway."

She enjoyed their banter, and the man was beguiling to be sure.

"Tell me more about the article you wrote."

"Which article?" She blinked. "Oh . . . the one about the deserters and bushwhackers." Good gravy! She'd taken momentary leave of her senses. "The point of it was that Unionists as well as Confederates suffer at the hands of those scoundrels."

"Quite true." He struck the match and lit the tobacco. "Tell me, Miss Bell, who looks out for you—protects you?"

"Me?"

"Yes. I've gathered from what you've said that you're responsible for your sisters and mother. But what about you? Why couldn't anyone else help you after your farm burned down? Why did you wind up working for room and board at the Wayfarers Inn? And don't tell me it's because your friends and neighbors couldn't manage a few more mouths to feed."

That's exactly what she'd been about to say.

"Anyone can see that you're not only a hard worker, but you're resourceful."

"Thank you." At least she thought he'd complimented her. "The truth is . . . well, it's Mama. Not to be disrespectful, but it's on account of her that no one wanted to take us in. Over the years she has offended most everyone in Woodstock, and then, after the fire, she was touched in the head. However, after a good rest, which she got after I checked into the Wayfarers Inn, she snapped out of her spell. Except, by then, I owed Mr. Veyschmidt a hefty sum and still had nowhere else to go."

The colonel eyed her speculatively for several moments. "You've had the weight of the world on your shoulders for a long while."

"No more than anyone else." Carrie glanced back at the sunset.

"Your Confederate friend, Joshua—he couldn't help you?"

Carrie shook her head. "He was off fighting for liberty against those evil Yankee invaders." She smiled to let him know that she teased him. But truth to tell, she'd rather have him miffed at her than have his pity.

The colonel's cigar's tip turned a reddish-orange as he puffed on it. "I get the feeling that you enjoy goading me, Miss Bell."

"Maybe just a little." She'd admit it.

Another noisy wagon rattled past followed by limbers of artillery.

"All joking aside, Miss Bell, I admire the way you protect your family." The colonel blew out a puff of cigar smoke that matched the distant gathering rain clouds.

"I haven't been very effective lately." Somehow confiding in the colonel lightened that weight he'd mentioned. "My sister Margaret enjoys flirting a bit too much, and Mr. Veyschmidt encourages it. Good for business, he says. Meanwhile Sarah has been unhappy and now she's run away. I try to help them and do everything I can, but they don't listen to me."

"Miss Bell, your sisters are old enough to know right from wrong."

"You're not the first to say so, but I feel responsible for them just the same. As for Mama—"

"You can't mother your mother, Miss Bell. It's disrespectful."

"I never thought of it that way." She did now.

"Look, I don't claim to have all the answers, but I don't believe I'm ill advising you here. Your best option—for you and your family—lies in Winchester with my aunt."

"Thank you, Colonel. You've more than paid me back for the kindness I showed you last year."

"Hardly. And you'll both help your family and search for your sister in a safer, smarter way by working for me—for my aunt."

The idea lifted her spirits.

"Perhaps the position in Winchester will equip you to better handle your home situation. Aunt Ruth will be a good influence on you, and meanwhile, you'll earn a salary . . . which reminds me." He pulled several bills out of the same inside pocket that harbored the cigar. "My men got paid today, which means you do also."

"But I'm not employed by the Union army."

"No, but consider this money a sign-on bonus of sorts." Standing, he leaned forward, took her right hand, and placed the money in her palm. "My hope is that by accepting the sum our agreement will be sealed."

"It already is. I gave you my word."

"And I believe you'll keep it. Nonetheless, you've worked harder these last four days than some of my enlisted men, so take the money."

She counted it. Four dollars! "I don't think I've ever earned this much money before."

His brow furrowed. "Veyschmidt doesn't pay you?"

"Room and board only."

"He's gotten quite a deal, practically slave labor."

"I'll say! A pity I didn't have another choice."

"Now you do."

Carrie stared at the money. Could this really be happening? Arrested by Yankees one day and earning wages for decent work only a few days later? "Thank you."

"You're welcome." The colonel brought his booted foot up on the rock, appearing quite relaxed as he enjoyed the rest of his cigar. "Tell me more about yourself and your family . . ."

_____

Peyton wanted to keep up the small talk with Miss Carrie Ann Bell. Not only did it give him insight into her life, which, in his opinion, sounded more and more like a sad Cinderella tale, but it affirmed his decision to send her to Aunt Ruth. True, Aunt Ruth had a close and trusted friendship with Tabitha, who was as crusty as week-old bread, but Miss Bell would bring a certain energy and excitement that would stimulate both women and keep their minds sharp.

On the other hand, if he was completely honest, Peyton would have to admit that Miss Bell was a bright spot for him in what had been a series of long, dark days, weeks, and months.

"Some time back I read in a newspaper that General Grant is calling for the South's unconditional surrender."

Peyton inclined his head. "That's true."

"But if General McClellan is elected president in a few months, he promises to end the war. Most Confederates pray that McClellan will win, and I understand that many northern folks feel the same way."

"You're right again, Miss Bell." Her hair matched the autumn sunset, as if God had woven strands of orange, gold, and chestnut together in a curly mass and affixed it on top of her small head.

"Colonel?"

"Yes?" He shook himself.

"Is anything wrong?"

"No." He cleared his throat. "My opinion of the upcoming election is this: If McClellan wins and does what he's promising then all the bloodshed will have been for naught." He drew in a breath on his cigar. He'd lost good men and friends in this conflict. "I respect General McClellan. I served under his command during my years in the Army of the Potomac. However, the United States cannot compromise with the Confederacy. The Union must remain intact, and slavery, abolished."

"So you support Lincoln?"

"Yes."

"Hmm . . ." Miss Bell stared off into the distance. "I hate to think what that means."

"It means the war continues. Grant must continue pushing toward Richmond. Sherman must continue his assault on Georgia, and it means we must defeat Early's army here in the Shenandoah Valley."

A challenge glinted in her eyes. "Even though the Union has suffered many defeats this summer?"

He smiled. "Even so."

"But I read somewhere that the people in the north have no more stomach for war."

"I've read—and heard that too, Miss Bell." She'd obviously read every newspaper she could get her hands on just as she'd told him. "Nevertheless, we can't give up—we won't give up." Peyton considered his cigar for a long moment and decided to change the subject lest he increase her anxiety before she had to turn in for the night. "Major LaFont tells me that you've been very helpful to his medical staff."

She lowered her gaze. "I'm happy to help Dr. LaFont, but all I've really done is roll bandages and treat minor wounds."

"LaFont appreciates the fact you don't complain."

"Not aloud." She smiled. "After all, it is my Christian duty to help everyone that I can."

"I seem to recall you saying the same thing almost a year and a half ago after I asked you why you would risk your employer's wrath to suture my arm."

Miss Bell tipped her head to one side. "Did I tell you that it was my Christian duty?"

Peyton nodded. Bits and pieces of details were coming back to him. Like the color of her eyes, for instance. He remembered that as she had stitched his wound and glanced up at him from time to time, her eyes were as blue as the ocean. It had brought back the memory of voyaging as a youth with his parents on the Baltic Sea.

An eternity ago. Another life ago.

A couple of raindrops fell and Peyton tossed his cigar over the sodden hillside. Standing, he stretched, dropped his hat back onto his head, and crossed the distance to Miss Bell. He extended his right hand and she slipped her small palm into his much larger one, causing Peyton to feel an even greater need to protect her.

Several more raindrops fell and Peyton looked at the dreary sky. He took Miss Bell's elbow. "Let's head for the hospital tent. I've been soaked enough times today."

Together, they hurried across the field and over to the tent. Just after they'd ducked under the tent flap, the sky opened up and it began to pour.

"You successfully evaded another soaking, Colonel Collier." Miss Bell laughed.

He swept off his hat, considering her for a long moment. "You need to do that more often."

"Do what?"

"Laugh. Smile. You're really very pretty."

"Me? Pretty?" Her cheeks turned a lovely shade of pink. "No one has ever—and I mean never—called me pretty. Oh, I've been called pretty stubborn, pretty sassy, and pretty skinny, but never pretty in reference to my looks."

He leaned toward her. "I know a pretty face when I see one." He tapped her nose with his index finger. When he straightened, his humor vanished. "Which is why I want you in the company of one of my officers or Tommy at all times. Understand?"

"Yes."

"Good. And tomorrow you'll assist Major LaFont again and ride with the ambulances in the rear."

"Yes, sir."

Judging by her downcast expression, his orders didn't please her, but it was for her own good.

Peyton turned to leave, but Miss Bell caught his shirtsleeve. "Colonel, you know almost everything about me, but I know nothing about you, other than you have an aunt in Winchester."

He folded his arms, regarding her. He wasn't accustomed to imparting personal facts about himself. Yet this sassy young woman evoked his longing to trust someone—someone special. "Just what is it that you'd like to know, Miss Bell?"

"Oh, I don't know. Perhaps some information like . . . Do you have a young lady waiting for you somewhere?"

The forthright question entertained him, although he'd be suspicious if it came from anyone else. Most proper young ladies with whom he was acquainted were interested in his trust fund, not in him. Miss Carrie Ann Bell, on the other hand, hadn't a clue. "Other than Aunt Ruth and Tabitha, no. There are no special females in my life at this time."

"Tabitha? Yes, you've mentioned her before. The housekeeper, correct?"

He inclined his head. "Tabitha is a free woman of color. She and my aunt have been as close as two sisters since they were children. See how large my ears are? It's from Tabitha yanking on them whenever I disobeyed. Finally I grew taller than she, which spared my earlobes."

Her eyes brightened at his jesting, but a thoughtful look settled on her brow. "Could be you do fewer acts that require ear yanking. I mean . . . you've been kind to me. You seem fair-minded. Your officers and enlisted men speak highly of you."

"Thank you for the high praise, Miss Bell."

"Please call me Carrie Ann." Her face flushed at her unintentional forwardness. "That is, if you want to—if it's proper."

Peyton chose to ignore her social blunder. The truth was he felt quite enchanted as evidenced by the sudden warmth pumping through his veins. "As you wish, Carrie Ann. Anything else you'd like to know?"

"How were your parents killed?"

"In a carriage accident in France when I was twelve."

"How tragic."

"Yes, but oddly I wasn't as devastated as you might think. My parents were consumed with their social lives and traveling around the world. There wasn't much room for me."

"The real tragedy, then. It's my belief that children are treasures from heaven."

"Hmm . . ." He glanced around the tent. Enlisted men milled about. Peyton began to grow uncomfortable with the direction of this conversation. His gaze drifted back to hers. "Anything else?"

"What did you do before the war?"

He inhaled, opened his mouth, then clamped it shut. Narrowing his gaze, he carefully considered his next words. "If I told you what I did before the war, you would not think highly of me. It's only by God's grace that I am who I am now. But perhaps I'll share the details another time."

"I'd like that." She stared up at him, adoration shining on her small face, and Peyton felt rather invincible, albeit with a humbling dose of awkward schoolboy thrown in the mix.

Except he was hardly an awkward schoolboy.

"If that's all, I'll take my leave. I'm meeting with General Merritt soon."

"Of course. I've kept you from your duties far too long."

"On the contrary, I have enjoyed our conversation." He set his hat on his head then touched the rim. "Good night, Carrie Ann."

"Good night, Colonel."

As he stepped out from beneath the tent he was met by cold, hard rain. Even so he felt Miss Carrie Ann Bell's gaze burning into his back—

She already seemed to have melted his heart.

CHAPTER 10

August 21, 1864

The Sabbath dawned revealing gloomy skies. A church service was held in one of the officers' tents, but instead of Major Johnston at the foot of the tent, Carrie discovered another chaplain there. He read from the book of Revelation.

"'Behold, I come quickly: hold that fast which thou hast, that no man take thy crown.'" The reverend looked up from the Bible in his hands and scanned the sparse crowd. "No man knows the hour of his death, but it is appointed unto man once to die and after that the judgment. See that there is no sin between you and your God."

Carrie glanced at the troops around her. She'd heard horsemen ride out of camp in the wee hours of the morning. Evidently only foot soldiers and details were left behind. Their somber expressions weren't lost on her. How well they must know that life was a vapor and that theirs might vanish during the next skirmish or battle.

As she finished her bit of introspection, a shell exploded, rocking the ground on which the gathering sat. The men jumped up and ran for their posts. The tent emptied quickly.

Ducking beneath the flap, Carrie barely had time to take in the chaos around her when Tommy appeared and grabbed her wrist.

"We gotta get outa here." He began to run, pulling her along.

"What's happening?" A stupid question. Had she thought about it, she would have figured it out on her own.

"The Rebs are attacking."

A shell burst nearby, sending grass and dirt flying high into the air. Thick, dark smoke blotted out the dawning light. Carrie coughed. Her lungs burned. Tommy, however, was undeterred as he ran through the waking camp, shouting to the men as he tugged Carrie behind him. Gunfire sounded in the distance, echoed by frantic bugling.

"Them dirty rotten graybacks." Tommy spat on the ground and wiped his sleeve across his mouth. "They got a lot of nerve, hittin' us on the Sabbath."

Carrie's thoughts whirred. Memories, horrible memories, marched across her mind. The farm . . . the explosions that knocked pictures off the walls and dishes from the shelf. The barn . . . the fire! Animals, whinnying, baying, lowing in terror. The flames licking high into the sky. The house, soon ablaze. Mama's soul-piercing screams.

"Miss Carrie Ann?"

Her gaze found Tommy. "Where's Colonel Collier?" His presence would be a comfort.

"Fighting! Where'd you think?"

"I . . . well, I can't think at the moment." Remembrances and images of what she witnessed nearly a week ago near Front Royal flashed in her head and melded with the ones that had already resurfaced. "I can't think at all."

Scores of cavalrymen on horseback galloped past her, kicking up dirt. More shelling exploded, although she and Tommy now stood a safe distance from it.

"Sorry to be so hard on ya." Tommy slung his arm around her shoulders. "I know you're a girl and all."

Carrie mustered some backbone. "My gender has nothing to do with it. I'm a very capable female. I'm just"—her shoulders sagged slightly—"inexperienced." She gulped back her fear and confusion then blinked away the moisture collecting in her eyes.

"All you gotta learn is one thing: Run in the opposite direction of the cannonading. We ain't supposed to get in the way, understand?"

She nodded.

"Colonel Collier gave me the duty of making sure we both turn up alive at the end of the day when he gets his evening report on who got killed and who didn't."

Again, she nodded, but her stomach lurched. Putting her hands on her knees, she bent forward to suck in clearer air and catch her breath. Her heart still pounded.

Tommy gave her a smack between the shoulder blades that nearly sent her flying onto her face. "You're smart. You'll learn it real quick."

"I appreciate your encouragement." She couldn't keep the sarcasm from her tone.

Tommy didn't seem to notice. "C'mon, we got to keep moving. Seems like the Rebs are pushing us back."

Again? Carrie's faith in the Union army waned. "Do you think it's safe for me to reenter the hospital tent?"

"Maybe." Seconds passed as Tommy mulled it over. "But I'd best go with you."

They walked back, careful not to get trampled by horses and limbers. By the time they reached the hospital, the wounded were being loaded into ambulances headed for the general hospital in Charles Town while tents and gear were hastily packed into wagons. Carrie did whatever she could to help.

The fighting continued for several hours and so did the withdrawal. They packed up the wounded and continued northwest until they reached Halltown. They camped in the same place the army bivouacked only weeks before.

The next day, there were no marching orders. This gave Dr. LaFont and his medical staff a chance to get the last of the severely wounded into ambulances bound for Harpers Ferry. The conveyances weren't having an easy time of it due to the rain. Worse, Carrie suspected most of those men would never make it to the hospital.

Meanwhile in camp, everyone remained on alert. The enemy was in the area.

Inside the field hospital, Carrie tended to the dying as directed by Dr. LaFont. She was relieved when female camp followers and loyalist women from town arrived to render aid. They administered sips of whiskey to the wounded and, at first, Carrie refused to follow suit. After all, the Bible said "Woe unto them" who did such things. But Dr. LaFont was short on medicines until the next supply wagons came in from Harpers Ferry. Meanwhile men writhed in agony at her feet. Carrie knew she couldn't stand by and do nothing.

Collecting a bottle from out of the medicine trunk, she knelt before a man whose lower torso had been mangled on the battlefield. One of his legs was gone, but amazingly he was still alive. God wouldn't mind if she gave strong drink to a suffering man to ease his pain, would He?

Lifting the bottle to the wounded soldier's lips, she gave him sips of whiskey until he ceased his thrashing.

"Almira . . ."

Was he delirious now, thinking she was his wife?

"Tell Almira . . . I love her. And the children . . . Robert. He must . . . be strong."

Carrie bit back a sob. There was no time for tears. "I will," Carrie agreed. She didn't know the soldier's name, but she'd figure out how to keep that promise.

"Tompkins," he rasped as if reading her thoughts.

"Corporal?" His face was blackened with soot and unrecognizable—until now. He'd hit her upside the head after Colonel Collier rescued her out of the sycamore. "Corporal Tompkins?"

He moved his head slightly, indicating the affirmative. "Sorry . . . cuffed you." A wheezy breath. "Thought you . . . were Rebel boy . . . killed our men."

"Don't talk anymore. Just rest." Carrie gave him another sip of whiskey. "I forgive you." She thought of the chaplain's message yesterday. "Make your peace with God."

She gave him another swallow before making her way to the next patient. Then the next. When she returned to Corporal Tompkins, he lay dead, his sightless gaze staring placidly heavenward.

First icy numbness spread through her body and then fire filled her veins. She ran from the tent, unable to stem her emotion. The blood, the death. She couldn't bear any more of it.

She sprinted toward a cluster of trees with thoughts of disregarding her agreement with Colonel Collier and going . . . going somewhere. Anywhere but staying here. The edge of a tree branch scraped her cheek before she could push it aside. She nearly tumbled over a fat root, but pressed on.

"Hold on there, girl. Where do you think you're running off to?" A shapely woman stepped into her way.

Carrie slowed, then stopped. Her breath came in quick spurts.

"You must have come late to the war." She expelled sweet-smelling breath near Carrie's face. "I can always tell the new nurses by the fright in their eyes. Besides, I haven't seen you around camp before." Her bold eyes took in Carrie's less than flattering attire. "Wouldn't have thunk you was a girl until I got a closer look at you."

"I wish I never came here. Fact is, this wasn't my idea in the first place."

"There, there, no need for bawling and murmuring. Men die all the time in battle. Have been for the last three years, for sure. You best get used to it."

"It's not that. I'm aware of the lives lost in the name of freedom. I even sensed Corporal Tompkins wouldn't make it for long. But I never experienced death so— so personally before."

"Someone you know just breathe his last, honey?" The woman had a comforting manner.

Carrie nodded, although she hadn't known Tompkins very well. They'd never engaged in conversation. She despised him when their paths first crossed. But minutes ago he seemed like a decent fellow . . . before he—

"He left loved ones behind," Carrie croaked. Her throat ached as if she'd swallowed an apple whole and it got stuck on its journey down.

"Don't they all?"

Carrie wiped her cheeks while thunder rumbled in the distance. How fitting.

"You'll be all right. I can tell."

"How?" Carrie longed for a bit of hope.

"You've got fortitude, that's how. My granny used to say she admired women with fortitude and just look at how you stand so straight, even if you are a bitty little thing. Anyhow, you don't have time to feel sorry for yourself." The woman nodded toward the worn road.

Another wagon of wounded was rolling in.

The woman hooked her arm around Carrie's elbow and drew her back to the makeshift hospital. Once inside, Carrie forced herself to tend to the injured and willed herself not to think about the sights and sounds. A strong mind was required of every worthy journalist, after all. Perhaps Papa would let her write of her experiences—if she lived that long.

Fortitude.

She paused near Dr. LaFont who listened patiently to a dying man's last words. When she finally made sense of what he said, a jolt ran through her. While Union troops reconnoitered earlier, Lieutenant Colonel John Mosby and his Rangers ambushed fifteen men, killing them all ". . . without mercy," the cavalryman added, slipping away.

Carrie sucked in a breath. General Merritt's division, which included the colonel's brigade, had gone hunting for the elusive Mosby. Known for his raids against Yankee forces, the man was a hero in the Shenandoah Valley, although Carrie didn't think much of Mosby's antics anymore.

Gradually, dusk settled over the camp, and the wounded—those that survived—were as settled as was possible under these conditions. Dr. LaFont forced her out of the tent to seek respite.

She collapsed to the ground beneath a large willow. Its overhanging branches and feathery leaves made her feel tucked away and secure. Moments later, Colonel Collier rode in her direction. He appeared weary, his shoulders slumped and his uniform mud splattered. But, seeing her, he reined in his black charger.

"Good evening, Miss Bell." Despite his disheveled appearance, his voice carried an air of a noble gentleman.

She tried to reply, but no words came out.

He dismounted and tossed his horse's reins over a tree branch not far from the tented hospital. He walked toward her, halting when he stood only a few feet from where she'd dropped down beneath the tree. The colonel removed his hat. "Are you feeling all right?"

She glimpsed the concern in his golden-brown eyes and wanted to assure him. But how could she? She was hardly fine. But how could she describe the tumult inside of her without sounding cowardly and weak?

The colonel hunkered down. "Pardon my saying so, but you don't look well."

"I'll survive." She recalled her meeting with the mysterious woman earlier. Carrie never did learn her name. "I have fortitude." In an effort to prove it, she pushed out a smile.

"So you do. May I?" Tucking his hat and gauntlets beneath his arm, he indicated the ground beside her.

She replied with a nod.

He sat and stretched his long legs, but his gaze didn't waver from her face. "You look a bit pale—and sad. What happened today?"

"Corporal Tompkins died," she blurted.

The colonel grimaced. "I knew he'd been wounded. What a shame he's gone. He was a good soldier. Loyal. I shall miss him."

"He asked me to tell his wife that he loved her."

"Do you mind?"

Carrie shook her head as fresh tears blurred her vision. She blinked them back, unwilling to let the colonel see her cry. She of all people in this camp had no reason for tears. "Before he died, he apologized for hitting me." She swallowed hard.

Staring straight ahead, his lips pursed in thought, the colonel merely nodded. "Good of him to do that. I know it bothered him when he discovered you weren't the enemy—or a boy."

"Next thing I remember after he hit me, I was riding on the back of your saddle." Funny how she could think fondly on such a thing while simultaneously swatting tears off her cheeks. "Of course, I told Corporal Tompkins I forgave him."

"A good thing."

"I just can't imagine why I'm taking Tompkins's death so hard. In truth, I didn't like the man until the very end. In Woodstock, soldiers came into the Wayfarers Inn wounded, and I did my best to patch them up."

"I'm proof your nursing skills are admirable."

Carrie doubted her skills were even passable. "I know families who have lost loved ones in this conflict. Many were my childhood friends. I mourned their passing, true, but I never witnessed death so . . . so closely." She shook her head, trying to make sense of it all.

"I think I understand." The colonel spoke in compassionate tones. "It may be of some consolation to learn that every man in this army has had to stare death in the face, myself included."

"I'm sure they have."

"Oftentimes soldiers watch helplessly as death's formidable grip saps the life right out of another human being. I've seen grown men put their faces in their hands and sob right there on the battlefield."

"A weakness in their character?"

"Not at all. Grieving is part of being human, don't you think? Even so, we cannot allow our emotions to rule the day. Admirable officers pick themselves up and carry on, and so must we all."

"But I'm not in the army."

"You're in God's army, aren't you? The army of believers? And not a sparrow falls from a tree without the Lord's knowledge."

Fortitude. That word echoed in Carrie's head. Papa would want her to be strong. She finally turned and faced the colonel. He radiated empathy, but not a trace of pity. "I feel better. Thanks."

"I'm glad I could help, even in some small way." He considered her for a few moments more, then rubbed his whiskers with the backs of his fingers. "Have you eaten today?"

Carrie's mind went blank. She couldn't recall. "We've been busy in the hospital . . ."

"Come on, then." The colonel stood and then, reaching for her hands, pulled Carrie to her feet. "I got word that pigs are roasting near the officers' tents and I'm famished."

Confederate pigs, no doubt. "I don't think I could swallow a bite."

"Perhaps you'll be surprised."

Obviously, he wasn't going to take no for an answer. The pressure of his hand around her elbow only affirmed her theory.

The colonel led her to where his horse stood and grabbed hold of the reins. Then they walked as far as the nearest tree stump. The colonel swung up into the saddle. He kicked his booted foot out of the stirrup.

It didn't take Carrie but a few moments to figure out that she was to climb up behind him—which she did gingerly, favoring her wrist. She hadn't thought about her injury as she worked in the hospital, but now it ached. Swinging up into the saddle, she found a relatively comfortable position. She didn't relish being squished, although accepting the ride was more appealing than walking the distance.

When they reached their destination, men had already begun eating. As Carrie dismounted with help from another officer who stepped in to assist, she noticed the festive mood of the troopers. A ways off, a couple of fiddlers, a guitarist, and a clarinetist played a hand-clapping melody. The scene reminded Carrie of Woodstock before the war. Residents would pack picnic baskets and gather together in town each year to celebrate the Fourth of July.

The colonel fetched a couple of plates, filled them with pork and cooked carrots, and topped them with a chunk of buttered bread. Then he collected two forks before leading her to a grassy spot where they sat down to eat.

He handed her one of the plates and utensils.

"What's the occasion?"

"Nothing particular. The cavalry is merely enjoying the spoils of war."

Bestowing a smile on her, he then bowed his head and murmured a prayer of thanks. It seemed rather hypocritical to Carrie, thanking God for the provision of stolen food. However, she was well aware of the fact that the Confederate army did its share of raiding.

She closed her eyes and silently asked God's blessing on both this meal and on those who had unwillingly contributed to it from their storehouses, barnyards, and kitchens.

They ate in silence for a full minute. Finally, Carrie had to know.

"Did you find him?" Carrie nibbled on her bread. "John Mosby?"

"No. The Gray Ghost evaded capture again." The colonel ate a piece of roasted pork. "I suspect he's somewhere up in the mountains, and probably looking down on us right now."

Carrie munched on the boiled carrots. She hadn't realized how famished she'd been. Within minutes, she'd cleaned her plate. As she considered a second helping, Major Johnston and Tommy showed up, Tommy carrying a cherry pie. Unable to resist, she scooped a healthy portion of dessert onto her plate.

"Thank you for sharing your . . . spoils with me."

"It's our pleasure, Miss Bell," Johnston said rather gallantly. He, Tommy, and the colonel finished off the rest of the pie in record time.

Colonel Collier stood, stretched, and then ambled off in search of coffee. Carrie surreptitiously watched him go, feeling grateful that an important man such as he would deign to see after her welfare. If it weren't for him she'd either be stuck in a sycamore, or wandering the countryside in futile search of Sarah and suffering any manner of abuse.

The musical ensemble stopped playing and a flamboyantly dressed officer stood to address the assembly from atop a wagon bed. His shell jacket was shorter in length than most that Carrie had seen and ornamentally decorated in gold braid and brass buttons. He removed his feathered hat, revealing yellow curly hair that hung to his shoulders. He made a dramatic bow and the men cheered wildly.

Carrie's first thought was that the man standing on the wagon was part of a traveling theatrical group. But then Johnston informed her that the officer was none other than General George Custer—Autie, to his closest friends.

"And now I shall recount for you all a most amusing tale," the general said.

Colonel Collier returned and took his place beside Carrie, a tin cup brimming with coffee between his hands.

"It was back in 1862, during the Peninsula Campaign."

Nearly all the other cavalrymen cheered and waved their caps in the air.

"I happened upon a former West Point classmate who'd been taken prisoner. I told him that's what he gets for joining the wrong army."

Chuckles went up from the crowd.

"And then, seeing there was a cameraman on-site, I had the audacity to insist upon getting my photograph taken with the captured Confederate. That's the kind of audacity that wins wars, and each of you has it in him."

More laughing, cheers, and then a round of applause.

Carrie smiled. The man certainly did have charisma about him.

The colonel leaned over to her. "Feeling better?"

"Yes, thank you. I'm grateful for your insistence that I eat."

"You're quite welcome." His blond brows knit together and his gaze darkened. "I prayed for you quite a lot today—for you and Tommy. You can imagine my relief when I rode into camp and saw you sitting beneath that willow tree, alive and unharmed."

"I was relieved to see you'd survived the skirmishes, both yesterday and today. But, to be honest, when the corporal died this afternoon, I wanted to run away from camp and never look back."

He set his hand over hers and gave it a light squeeze. "Death is ugly." A faraway look entered his gaze, but he blinked and it vanished. "In the midst of suffering, physically or emotionally, I've learned there are several things to relieve the pain. Prayer, food, good friends, laughter, and sleep—they're restorative. Spiritually, God lends us the strength to face it all again tomorrow." The colonel reached up and brushed a curl back from Carrie's cheek, tucking it behind her ear. His gentle touch was healing salve for her aching heart. His eyes held hers for several long seconds. Then in seemingly one smooth motion, he dropped his hand and stood. "Good night, Miss Bell—er, Carrie Ann." He gave her a polite little bow, but his eyes held a certain light. He genuinely cared about her.

"Good night, Colonel." Sitting in the damp grass, she watched him walk toward his horse. Beyond General Custer's voice as he tale-told another of his adventures, crickets chirped. Major Johnston and Tommy chuckled at something their commanding officer said, and at that particular moment, Carrie never felt so alive in all her life.

CHAPTER 11

August 25, 1864

At last the hot, humid days of August neared their month's end and, hopefully, the rain as well. Today had been one of marches and countermarches, reconnoiters, and skirmishes as Sheridan's Army of the Shenandoah probed Early's Army of the Valley. But, for Carrie, today's activities meant tending more wounded beneath a suffocating tent.

And still she wasn't any closer to Winchester and her new job with the colonel's aunt. The Union army had been burning all up and down the Valley, but hadn't yet burned their way as far south as Woodstock. One would never guess it though. Billowing black smoke rose in the distance as far as the eye could see. It appeared the entire Valley was aflame.

Finding a dry patch of ground beneath a leafy maple tree, Carrie tossed down the haversack Tommy gave her and sat down. Her heavy limbs screamed for mercy, but they didn't stop her from wondering how Mama and Margaret fared. Had Sarah come home on her own? Papa too?

Digging into the knapsack, Carrie removed the journal and pen which Colonel Collier had gifted her with, and began writing of her experiences in the past ten days. She had penned the requested letter to Corporal Tomkins's wife, informing her of his death, and his affection. The colonel read and approved the missive before promising to mail it. In the hospital, she assisted Dr. LaFont and administered his prescribed treatments. She rolled bandages, fetched buckets of water, and wrote letters home for injured soldiers who were conscious and awaiting transport to the hospital in Harpers Ferry. She cleaned wounds, sutured many of them, and held soldiers' hands as they passed into eternity. Never in all her days of assisting Dr. Rogers in Woodstock did she come upon such severe cases. True, she'd helped deliver babies, she'd stitched wounds—all very minor compared to the many horrors and heartbreaks she'd witnessed here in camp.

Deep in thought, Carrie touched the end of the pen to her bottom lip. She recalled one particularly difficult situation and began writing about it too. This morning, the young private and his comrade were cleaning their rifles when one accidentally discharged, sending a bullet into the private's chest. By the time he entered the field hospital, he was delirious from loss of blood, and believed Carrie was his mother. For his sake, she assumed the role, speaking softly to him and soothing his brow until he died. He'd been no older than she . . .

An errant tear escaped and fell onto her journal, smearing the ink. Carrie blotted it carefully with her fingertip. A pity if later she couldn't read what she'd just written.

Men's voices from a nearby gathering grew louder and claimed her attention. She listened as they talked and laughed. Since the rain abated, troops had been able to build campfires, causing the hilly landscape to resemble a landing for giant fireflies.

"General Sheridan is playing a child's game of war," one soldier said. "He doesn't intend to smash the Rebs at all."

"It's a strategy, you fool," said another.

"I don't care what it is," the shaggy Union man argued. "I'm tired of picket duty and reconnoitering. I want to fight the way our forefathers did when they battled the British. I want to preserve the Union, and them slaves ought to be free to choose their destiny, but that ain't gonna happen if we don't win this war."

Carrie recorded the men's sentiments in her diary, although it was obvious that the soldier who desired to fight hadn't visited the hospital in recent days. He might see things differently once he entered the tented facility. Carrie certainly gleaned a new perspective. She'd tended to wounded Yankees as well as captured Confederates. The color of their uniforms and their skin didn't matter to her. They were human beings in need of physical and emotional care.

As they lay perishing, and some men stated their last wishes or told of their willingness to die for their beliefs, Carrie knew she could no longer record events in an impersonal, practical way, not when she witnessed blood, death, and glory day after day. Going forward, she would write about matters of the heart, courage, sacrifice, and honor. Papa would be proud.

"Enjoying the damp evening, Miss Bell?"

Glancing up from her journal she saw Major Johnston striding toward her. She smiled a greeting. "I didn't realize your brigade had returned." This morning General Sheridan ordered them to the Maryland border to investigate whether Early and his men were plotting to invade that state.

"We returned a couple of hours ago. We had news for General Sheridan and then ended up dining with him." Reaching the tree, Johnston pointed to the place beside her. "May I?"

"Please do. I found one of the few dry places here in camp."

He snorted a chuckle, and then grunted after lowering himself to the ground. "You'd think by now I wouldn't get sore from sitting in the saddle all day, but I am. I must be getting old."

Carrie smiled at what was surely hyperbole. The man couldn't be more than thirty. She'd learned from Tommy that Johnston was married, although he and his wife didn't have children yet. In addition to being the colonel's most trusted friend, Major Johnston served as something of his spiritual advisor. Twice now she'd happened upon the two officers while they were bowed in prayer.

"I trust Colonel Collier returned safely?" She held her breath, praying it was so.

"He's unharmed."

Carrie exhaled. She couldn't imagine what she'd do if the colonel were injured—or worse. He encouraged her. She found his guidance most helpful. And did anyone else know of the agreement she'd made with him? Would another cavalryman see her safely to Winchester and protect her in the meantime? Likely not. In a word, Carrie *needed* him.

"General Torbert's division got whacked today though. After we learned he was pushed back this way by Anderson, General Merritt sent some of our brigade as reinforcements. We made it back to camp here in time to eat a substantial meal. Now Peyt is lingering at the dinner table, debating strategies with both Generals Torbert and Sheridan and a few scouts from Winchester."

"I'd say you Yanks need a new strategy. General Sheridan's approaches are timid at best."

Johnston grunted a laugh. "It's an election year, Miss Bell, and the Union cannot afford another devastating loss. It's been a bad summer for us."

Carrie agreed. "Why aren't you in on the planning?"

"I was. But after the important information was disseminated, I decided not to stick around."

"I hope you stayed long enough to devise a new plan." Her comment had more of a bite to it than she intended. "I apologize for my tone. The skirmish last Sunday morning wasn't even a full-blown battle and yet I've seen hundreds of men die over the last several days."

"You've been an asset to the army, Miss Bell."

She felt anything but proud.

"I overheard LaFont say he wished he had ten more volunteers just like you."

"I appreciate the sentiment, but I wish there wasn't a need for ten more volunteers." An urge to sob lodged in her throat, but she'd expended every last tear on the men in her care. "As for the upcoming elections this November, I rather hope the Democratic candidate, George McClellan, will be victorious over Abraham Lincoln so some compromise can be reached. The fighting has to stop."

"It will . . . eventually." Johnston paused. "When the South surrenders."

Carrie wondered if it ever would.

The reverend-major grew silent for a full minute. "Are you a believer in Jesus Christ, Miss Bell?" he asked at last.

"Yes. I've loved the Lord for as long as I can remember."

"Then you must know that 'to every thing there is a season,' to quote the book of Ecclesiastes. 'A time to love, and a time to hate; a time of war, and a time of peace.'"

Carrie supposed the Bible passage he quoted did present a new—and true—perspective on the subject, but it didn't make her feel much better about the men dying in Dr. LaFont's surgery tent.

"Forgive me for inquiring over your faith, but you realize that when I asked if you know the Lord, I was not referring to simply knowing that Christ existed. I'm speaking of knowing Him personally, the way you know a very good friend or family member."

Annoyed, she turned to face him. "Do you probe everyone's personal beliefs?"

"Every chance I get." The good humor in Major Johnston's voice somehow disarmed Carrie. His grin faded. "Especially with the fragile nature of life in a war zone."

She released a sigh. "The truth is I know God better than I know some friends—and family members. He has been faithful to me in a way that no person can be. Though I question Him sometimes—like when we lost our home. And now, with Sarah Jane missing, and this war . . ."

Major Johnston nodded sympathetically. "You know, I believe everything happens for a reason. Jesus Himself said we'd face tribulation in this world, and that trials were put in our lives by God to make us better, more faithful Christians."

"I would have said tribulation comes from the devil, not God."

"Yes, but Satan cannot touch us without God's permission. Jesus Himself said so."

Carrie thought back on the last week's events, all the suffering, the death . . .

"I don't know, Major Johnston. This war is filled with an awful lot of hell."

"They're only glimpses of a Christless aftermath."

A frightening thought, to be sure!

"It's my belief that because of this war, many souls have and will turn to Christ." After a long pause, the major added, "I've heard many a prayer said on the battlefield."

"I suppose you have." Glancing his way once more, Carrie saw the major's amused expression despite the cloak of darkness quickly descending.

A flash of movement caught her eye. A woman stood several feet away. Carrie thought she recognized the shapely brunette as the mysterious woman who'd persuaded her to have fortitude. Carrie had since learned her name was Phoebe, and she was one of the volunteer nurses who helped with the wounded. Carrie found her to be both caring and trustworthy.

Having captured her attention, Miss Phoebe sashayed forward, her skirts rustling. She nodded curtly to Johnston although she didn't look directly at him. "Evening, Miss Carrie Ann."

"Miss Phoebe." Carrie pushed to her feet. Were they needed at the field hospital?

"If you'll come with me I'll see that you wash up and change into something more fittin' for a female. A friend of mine had a dress that might be your size, and she was willing to part with it."

A dress! "I'd like that. Thank you."

"My apologies, but I can't allow it." Major Johnston was up on his feet in seconds despite his bulky frame. He placed his heavy palm on Carrie's shoulder.

"Your commander told me to fetch her, Major," Miss Phoebe said with hands on hips, "so spare me any of your moral lectures."

Carrie glanced from one to the other. The two obviously had been previously introduced.

"Colonel Collier authorized Miss Bell to go with you?"

"That's right, Peyton sent me."

Carrie felt a twinge of envy that Miss Phoebe was on a first-name basis with the colonel.

Phoebe tossed her head. "Go ask him if you don't believe me. Peyton is dining with General Sheridan."

"I know where he is."

"I just come from there. I was this evening's entertainment."

And Colonel Collier wanted her to go with Miss Phoebe? Carrie began having reservations about his honorable character.

"I sang 'Just Before the Battle, Mother,'" Miss Phoebe explained. "Not a dry eye among the officers."

"Oh . . . you sang." Relief poured over Carrie like a barrel of rainwater.

"The song is one of General Sheridan's favorites."

"You must be very talented." Carrie admired folks who could sing. Joshua used to say that she couldn't even carry a tune in a bucket.

"I'm a woman of many talents. Singing, dancing . . ." Miss Phoebe swung her hips as if she might begin waltzing without a partner. "And lots of other things too."

Major Johnston cleared his throat, and Carrie got the hint that he disapproved of the woman.

So, did she go with Miss Phoebe or not?

"Miss Bell, I think it's best to get verification of this invitation."

"Oh, keep your brass buttons on, Reverend." Miss Phoebe rested her hands on her waist. "Peyton said he'll come for the girl in a couple of hours. He knows where to find me."

Unease seeped into Carrie's being, except she so wanted to wash and the promise of changing her clothes was more temptation than she could withstand.

"I accept your offer, Miss Phoebe." She turned to Johnston. "Please excuse me, Major."

Carrie didn't wait for Johnston's reply but quickly fell into step alongside Miss Phoebe. The woman sashayed on through camp, humming the tune to "Goober Peas."

Within the hour, Carrie soaked in millions of tiny soap bubbles and the most delicious bath she'd taken in a long while. Miss Phoebe, being a laundress by day, had a washtub large enough for a body and kept it inside her tent so there was adequate privacy.

"I imagine you launder an awful lot of soiled garments."

"And that's not the half of it, sister." Miss Phoebe sniggered as she moved about the tent, lighting tapers inside of paper lanterns. A soft glow filled her quarters. "I wash other things too."

Carrie dared not ask for specifics. She already had a good idea of her hostess's additional occupations. The red satin robe that Miss Phoebe now wore only confirmed her suspicions.

Miss Phoebe left to fetch another bucket of heated water. Outside the tent, the sound of men's voices increased, followed by frequent female cackling. Carrie found it odd that the colonel would allow her to be in Miss Phoebe's company and in this part of the camp. The thought occurred to her that, perhaps, he'd gotten the wrong idea about what kind of girl Carrie was. However, that wouldn't make sense, given all their conversations.

Reentering the tent, Miss Phoebe walked to the tub and poured the warmed water over Carrie's soapy head.

"This is the nicest-smelling soap I've ever used."

"Came all the way from Paris, France—at least that's what the salesman told me when I bought it." Miss Phoebe sat on a lone stool in her quarters. "So now for the hundred-dollar question . . ."

Carrie wiped the water off her face and peered at the woman.

"How do you know Peyton?"

In truth, Carrie had wanted to ask Miss Phoebe that same thing. "He arrested me for impersonating an officer, but I was really just looking for my runaway sister."

"He arrested you?" She brought back her chin. "That baboon!"

"No, he's been quite honorable. He believes my story and no charges were ever filed. I'm not a criminal or anything. What's more, the colonel has been looking out for me because he feels responsible for my welfare." She finished washing. "He hired me to be his aunt's companion. I'm to begin my employment as soon as the colonel can safely get me to Winchester." That would explain to Phoebe why he wanted her to bathe and change clothes.

"Nice of him to offer you respectable work, although 'honorable' ain't a word I'd ever use to describe Peyton." She snorted a laugh and poured a swallow of whiskey into a glass. "Want some, honey?"

"No, thank you."

After downing the amber liquid, Miss Phoebe poured another. "I shouldn't have asked. You're just a girl."

"I'll be nineteen soon." Carrie thought about it. "Wait . . . what day is it?"

Miss Phoebe had to think. "It's the twenty-fifth."

"Then I'm already nineteen. My birthday was yesterday."

"Some way to spend a birthday, taking care of broken, bleeding, and dying men."

While all the death broke her heart, Carrie didn't mind nursing. "Birthdays weren't ever special in my home anyway."

Miss Phoebe pulled the pins from her dark hair and it fell to her hips. She brushed it out in long, smooth strokes. Carrie sank farther down into the tub. Her bubbles were dissipating.

Several minutes later, Miss Phoebe pulled the stool over and placed it beside the tub. Next she set several pieces of linen on it. "Here's the best thing

I've got for toweling yourself off, and you'd best come on out of that water now before you look like a dried apple."

Climbing out, Carrie dried off.

"The clothes I scrounged up for you are over there," she said, pointing to garments slung over a trunk. "They ain't much, but they're better than these." Miss Phoebe picked up Carrie's discarded outfit. "I'll launder the items just in case you want to look like a woebegone orphan again." Another snigger as she set them on top of a tall, round wicker basket. "Oh, and since you didn't have a particular affection for them boots you were wearing, I traded them to a peddler for something more your size."

"A peddler?" Carrie perked up. "Was his name Arthur Sims?"

"No, it's Hank Lemke." Miss Phoebe's brows puckered. "Why'd you ask?"

Disappointment, like fog, settled over her. "I thought maybe it was the man my sister ran off with."

"No. I've known Hank a good long while. He's a cobbler, and evidently some female camp follower dropped off these here shoes—" Miss Phoebe held up a pair of black suede, ankle-high boots that had leather toes. "The customer wanted them resoled, but she never picked them up, so you can have them. Hank'll be able to sell those other boots easy."

"Thank you."

"Don't mention it." Miss Phoebe sashayed to the tent flap. "If you need help, just holler. I'll be within earshot."

Watching the woman duck outside, Carrie wrapped one of the linen towels around her thick hair and ambled to the trunk. She inspected her new clothes—new to her, anyway. The underthings, stockings, drawers, a chemise, corset, and petticoat, all appeared to be at least close to her size.

Touching the soft ribbon laces, Carrie realized she hadn't worn a corset in some time as she'd grown out of the only one she owned a long while ago. Her sisters were more shapely than she was, so any extra funds Carrie got her hands on were used to purchase their underclothes or material to sew their dresses. Being so thin, Carrie managed without the stays, and she was willing to alter her younger sisters' castoffs to fit herself. Their dresses weren't ever badly worn.

And neither was the dress Carrie held in her hands, at least from what she could see within the dimly lit tent. Brown and black checked, although it might be a dark blue, it had a pretty fawn-colored crocheted collar. The same colored lace had been sewn around the waistline. Carrie guessed the dress would be large on her slim build, but she welcomed it over the clothes she'd been wearing.

Quickly, she pulled the knee-length chemise over her head then stepped into the drawers. Sitting on the stool, she slipped on the black stockings. Lacing the corset to its tightest, she wrapped the contraption around her midsection and hooked it up in front. Even with some room to spare, she felt encumbered by it. But it wouldn't be respectable not to wear a corset beneath a dress. After all, she resided, albeit temporarily, in a camp of men. This wasn't the Wayfarers Inn where her pinafore-like apron and baggy gown hid the secret of what she didn't wear beneath them.

At least she was more fortunate than most women in that she could still take in a deep breath.

Carrie dropped the flouncy petticoat over her head and then donned the dress, feeling grateful that she didn't have to wear crinoline. She'd read in a newspaper that the Union's Sanitary Commission ruled crinoline to be dangerous in army camps. Therefore, female volunteers were not allowed to wear them. Quite often hooped skirts went up in flames as women cooked or boiled water over campfires, or they allowed inappropriate views of ankles and legs when women leaned over to assist patients.

Miss Phoebe reentered the tent in time to help Carrie button up the back of the dress. "We have to hurry," she said. "Peyton is waiting and he looks mighty impatient."

With her dress fastened, Carrie began parting her hair into three sections for braiding.

"Not so fast, honey." Miss Phoebe picked up her hairbrush. "As long as Peccadillo Peyt is waiting, he can stand out there a few minutes more."

"Peccadillo Peyt?"

"Sure. That's his nickname among those of us who know him best. The man's no saint, that's for sure."

"I beg to differ." Hadn't the apostle Paul written an epistle to believers and called them 'saints'?

"Honey, you just don't know him."

"Yes, I do. He's been spiritually reborn. It happened during the battle in Gettysburg last year."

"Is that what he told you?" Miss Phoebe's laugh had a derisive ring to it. "I don't know who's more stupid, him—or you for believing him."

Carrie wasn't about to argue. Best she finish so the colonel didn't give up on her and leave her here.

At last Miss Phoebe pushed in the last hairpin. "Now, there, you're almost ready for the unveiling."

"I'm grateful. How can I ever repay you, Miss Phoebe?"

"You don't have to. Peyton paid me plenty to girly you up."

"The colonel . . . paid you?" She should have known the woman had an ulterior motive for befriending her. Even so, Carrie believed that beneath Miss Phoebe's buxomness a kind heart steadily beat.

"He paid me—plenty." With a laugh and a toss of her dark, loosely hanging mane, she collected a brown cape, a straw cap adorned with ruffles and ribbons, and a pair of lady's kid gloves. She handed the accessories to Carrie. "You'll need these to complete your ensemble."

"Thank you." She'd accept these terms graciously, but how would she ever repay Colonel Collier?

"Come on, now. Ol' Peccadillo is waiting."

The name grated on Carrie's nerves.

At Miss Phoebe's mild shove, she exited the tent. There was no sign of Colonel Collier. Perhaps he'd been called away.

More men had descended on the area, standing and sitting around campfires, laughing and singing along with fiddles, harmonicas, and guitars. But the unmistakable clinking together of whiskey bottles was what Carrie heard loudest. Her heart picked up its tempo. While she was confident that she could handle herself around inebriates, she disliked the conflict which, experience taught her, usually accompanied their state of intoxication. Without Tommy nearby or an officer escort that the colonel insisted upon, she had best run to the hospital at the far end of camp before he found her unattended.

As Carrie turned to bid Miss Phoebe farewell, the object of her thoughts stepped out of the shadow of a towering hickory tree. Carrie's heartbeat slowed and she expelled the breath she'd been holding. Relief spread through her body.

"Oh, there you are, Peyton," Miss Phoebe said. She took hold of Carrie's shoulders and twirled her around. "You didn't know I could do magic, did you? From waif to young lady." She laughed. "What do you think?"

"I think . . ."

The colonel seemed to struggle with his next sentence as he stared at Carrie. With each passing second, her discomfort increased. Was he angry? Disappointed? She hadn't seen her reflection. Perhaps she looked disgraceful. But she couldn't appear worse than she did before her bath.

Could she?

"Peyton, say something." Miss Phoebe placed her hands on her ample hips.

"Thank you for your help."

"I reckon that's something." She sighed. "Send the girl on her way, Peyt, and stay for a couple of drinks and a few laughs."

"No. Thank you." His dismissive tone coupled with the way he turned his shoulder toward her, earned him a huff from Miss Phoebe before she stomped off. All the while, the colonel's gaze never wavered from Carrie.

"I apologize for taking so long." She dropped her gaze. Perhaps he was miffed that he'd been made to wait.

"It's quite all right. No need for apology." As he neared, tiny crinkles appeared around his eyes. The corners of his lips twitched beneath his beard. "You, Miss Bell, are worth the wait."

CHAPTER 12

If Miss Carrie Ann Bell looked fetching before, pretty whenever she smiled, and delightful when she laughed, then she was positively enchanting now. Aunt Ruth would love her. Peyton was sure of it.

They strolled at a comfortable pace along the worn dirt path lined with tented shelters and sutler wagons. Men's talking, laughing, and singing filled the air, accompanied by several fiddlers playing a variety of different melodies.

"I'm astounded by the way soldiers can put aside all the hatred and fighting of the day and enjoy a night of leisure."

"Some men can put it behind them and some can't." And a woman shouldn't have to consider the option, which was more the reason he felt compelled to get Miss Bell out of camp tonight. According to LaFont's daily report, she could boss commanders until they submitted to prescribed treatments, but she became too involved with the badly injured—men for whom LaFont deemed there was no medical hope. Miss Bell couldn't save the dying—that was Christ's job; and when she failed to accomplish the impossible, she blamed herself. Her heart was in the right place, her emotions were not, and LaFont's concern was that she'd wear herself out and take ill.

Peyton continued to guide Miss Bell along the campfire-lit path. As they neared a pair of enlisted men playing cards, one quickly stood. Shoulders back, he saluted Peyton, who returned the gesture.

"Good evening, Colonel Collier." The second man clambered to his feet. Then both soldiers moved forward to speak to him.

Peyton halted.

The first fellow came toward him with his right hand extended. Peyton gave it a friendly shake as recognition set in. "Dempsey, right?"

"That's right, sir. Corporal Eugene Farnsworth Dempsey. I fought alongside you that first day at Gettysburg. Felt real bad after you got wounded, but I'm glad you're alive and well now."

"Many thanks, Dempsey."

He turned to the other, older man who wore thick spectacles. "Private Derrick Lemke, sir," he said, introducing himself.

"We're cousins," Dempsey interjected.

"Ah . . . good to meet you, Lemke." Peyton glanced around their small campfire and tent shelter. "You men stay dry tonight, you hear?"

"Yes, sir." After parting salutes, Peyton caught up with Carrie, who had continued her amble toward the hospital.

"My apologies, Miss Bell."

"None required." Sincerity laced her reply. "You're an important man."

Her good nature pleased him. Not many women would understand the interruption.

"I must say, Colonel, I had been under the impression that commanding officers don't converse with enlisted men. But you do."

"Depends on the officer, I suppose." After a glance in her direction, Peyton added, "As for me, I need every one of my men. I want them to trust me to the point of following me into battle even if I'm leading a suicide charge."

"You'd never do that . . . lead a suicide charge?"

"Sometimes an officer doesn't have a choice. When my orders come from General Merritt it's my duty as one of his colonels to obey."

"Without question?"

"Again, it depends. I may respectfully inquire or disagree if the situation warrants it, but, ultimately, I must obey orders regardless of what I think the outcome might be."

"I don't know if I could do that."

"You obey God's commands, don't you?"

"Well, yes . . . that is, I try." A bit of a laugh reached his ears. "Although many times my obedience to Him isn't without question or complaint."

Peyton grinned. He appreciated her honesty and wit, not to mention her deep sensitivity toward others. Her courage impressed him, and yes it took courage to nurse wounded and dying men, although Carrie went a step further than that—perhaps a step too far. Even so, Peyton couldn't recall admiring another woman more—with the exception of Aunt Ruth.

They walked in silence for several paces and Peyton became aware of the weight of her thoughts.

"What's on your mind, Miss Bell? I can practically hear the gears grinding."

Another soft laugh. "I asked you once before to please call me Carrie Ann. After all, I'm proud to consider you a friend."

"Very well." The compliment wasn't lost on him either. "Now why don't you tell me what's troubling you?"

"Not troubling, really. Puzzling."

Hands clasped behind his back, he leaned closer in order to hear her better.

"I'm wondering why you allowed a woman like Miss Phoebe to help me tonight."

"Mm, I see." He straightened. "Well, for one thing, despite the poor choices she's made in her life, Phoebe isn't evil. Second, she's resourceful. I knew she'd find you something better to wear than those dungarees and clunky boots."

"She did, and I'm grateful to her—to you. Miss Phoebe said you'd paid her."

"I figured it was only fair, and I wanted you to have ample time to bathe and dress."

"So I can meet your aunt with some dignity?"

"Yes." He needed to tell her that she was leaving tonight. He hated to see her go. She was his bright spot in a very dark war. "You're a perceptive young lady."

"A good journalist must be perceptive."

"Journalist. Of course . . ." Peyton chuckled inwardly. How could he forget? "And I should have asked this beforehand. Forgive my assumption. But can you ride astride a horse wearing skirts?"

"Actually, yes. I do it all the time." She paused. "That is, I used to—before the war." Another pause. "When I was younger and I didn't know better."

"Glad to hear it." Peyton found her prattled explanation amusing. "I have another surprise for you. A cup of coffee or tea and a slice of apple pie."

Carrie came to a dead halt. She placed her hands on her slim waist. "Who told you?"

"Told me what?"

"That it was my birthday yesterday."

Peyton hadn't any idea of it being her birthday, but he decided to raise her opinion of himself a few notches. Reaching the place he'd tethered Brogan, he took hold of the animal's reins and leaned close to Carrie. "I have a way of learning these things."

"So I see."

He swung up into the saddle and then urged his black charger to a nearby tree stump. He reached for Carrie's hand. "Let's see just how well you'll be able to ride later." Kicking his foot out of the stirrup so she could make use of it, he assisted her as she climbed up behind him.

Carrie hoisted herself into the saddle behind him with relative ease. Her next movements indicated a lady's necessary adjustments. At last she sat motionless with her hands on his waist.

"Ready?" he asked.

"Ready."

Nudging Brogan, he started across camp where details had pitched the officers' tents. They had about an hour before General Sheridan's scouts would leave for Winchester, and Peyton planned to spend it with Carrie. He'd miss her. Their conversations revived him after long hours in the saddle, laden with weaponry, beneath the unforgiving summer sun. She had given him something to look forward to, although her presence and his protectiveness of her didn't go unnoticed by his men. Some of the talk that reached his ears was that Carrie was his wife disguised as a boy so she could be encamped with him. It had been known to happen, although not among his troops. The gossip tickled him initially, but such rumors of love and emotional need ruined men's military careers. Most officers knew of CSA General Tom Rosser's struggle in that regard. Rosser, a former graduate of the United States Military Academy at West Point, like Peyton and Union generals Autie Custer, Phil Sheridan, and others, was said to have summoned his bride to Staunton so she could reside closer to him.

Savior of the Valley, indeed! Rosser's behavior was considered that of a lovesick swain and called weakness by several high-ranking officials, even though Union General Ulysses Grant was known to make visits to his wife and children in order to keep himself sane. Nevertheless, as a precaution, Peyton tamped down the hearsay of Carrie and himself whenever he got wind of it—for the sake of her reputation as much as his own. His commanding officers knew the truth regarding their situation which provided a measure of assurance for him. Yet, there was a part of Peyton that didn't mind the talk. Marrying Carrie wouldn't be the worst of fates. Quite the contrary.

The wind picked up slightly as he spotted a place to tie Brogan and reined in. He twisted around in the saddle and took hold of her upper arm, aiding her dismount.

"Not bad for a female in skirts." Smiling, he swung down from his horse and tossed Brogan's reins around a narrow tree. Glancing over his shoulder, he noticed how Carrie rubbed her left wrist. "Are you hurt?"

She shook her head and lowered her arms to her sides. "Every now and again my wrist aches."

"I apologize if I worsened the pain."

"You didn't."

"Good." He couldn't resist teasing her. "Then I won't have to remind you of the circumstances of your injury."

"I appreciate that, Colonel."

He chuckled at her playful tone while ushering her into the mess tent. A lamp still remained lit on the table at which he'd eaten with his commanding officers earlier. "Make yourself comfortable." Peyton pulled out a chair for her. "I'll go fetch the coffee, unless you'd prefer tea."

She whirled around and faced him. "I'd enjoy a cup of tea very much."

The uplift to her voice made him smile. "I rather thought so, but wanted to ask and make sure." Oh, yes . . . she and Aunt Ruth would become fast friends in very little time.

Peyton left the tent to find the boiling kettle and coffee pot. It mattered little to him that he'd been overly solicitous where she was concerned, although it was a curious thing. Miss Carrie Ann Bell wasn't the sort of young lady who usually captured his attention, and yet with her sass and sweetness she'd somehow captivated him to the point where he made unique allowances for her comfort.

At the same time, he didn't want to give her false hopes. Before the war, he had been expected to find a well-bred woman to run his house, bear his children, and, of course, spend his inheritance. His wife's family needed to have strong societal connections to get his name in front of the echelons in Washington who could further his military career. Carrie Ann Bell fit none of those requirements. However, Peyton was no fool. He understood that, since the war, the world had changed. Plantation owners had become paupers, and in the north, women had taken men's places in factories in order to support their families.

Had the war changed the prerequisites for a Collier wife?

Aunt Ruth would know. All Peyton could do now was pray and sort out his own feelings regarding Miss Bell . . . Carrie.

Could he really be considering spending the rest of his life with her?

In truth, she hadn't been far from his thoughts since the day he arrested her. And when she'd slipped her small hand into his just minutes ago, he was overcome by the desire to protect her. As they rode across camp, Peyton could feel her body pressing up against his back. He felt her legs brushing against his. It was nothing short of torment, and more than once he fought the idea of riding off into the night with her.

But marry her? That idea jarred Peyton. He never imagined that he'd actually *want* to get married. All his life he'd viewed marriage as a duty, an act that would eventually produce offspring. However, Carrie made him think of nuptials in a different light—a brighter, warmer light.

Perhaps it was possible for a man like him to fall in love.

Was what he felt for Carrie . . . love? They barely knew each other, although Peyton could honestly say he knew Carrie better than he knew most women. He definitely knew her heart better than he'd ever known his former fiancée, Lavinia Monteague, even though they'd lived next door to each other in Winchester since he was about twelve.

Outside the officers' tent, Peyton found coffee on a grate over a dying campfire and filled a tin cup for himself. Next to it stood the less-than-elegant but highly functional teakettle.

Hearty laughter wafted from the tent. Peyton peered inside and saw several officers playing a friendly game of poker at a table in the far corner. Ducking beneath the flap, he entered and ambled to the table on which several plates of apple pie remained. He claimed two. Balancing his load, he exited and strode back to where Carrie awaited him.

The mess tent stood empty, save for details milling in and out collecting items. Any officers who had lingered after the general's dinner meeting had gone.

Enjoying the respite, Carrie sipped her tea—black tea from China, not sassafras root tea like she and so many Southerners had grown accustomed to drinking since the war began. The colonel had even found a spoonful of sugar, a commodity most residents in the Valley couldn't afford these days. And the apple pie . . . delicious!

"Mmm . . ." She savored the dessert's sweetness and tartness. "This is a real treat. Thank you."

"You're welcome." He lit a cigar and blew out a puff of smoke. "Are you feeling better? Major LaFont said you'd been upset this week."

Carrie managed a nod. "I never imagined a twelve-pounder gun could do so much damage to the human body."

"Napoleon specifically developed those cannon to destroy the enemy."

"The 'enemy' is made up of flesh and blood—just like you and me." Carrie ran her fingertip around the rim of her cup. "Created by God, in His image."

"Try not to dwell on what you saw. Think, instead, of the things you managed to accomplish. You read to the men from the Scriptures, you were at their side so they didn't pass into eternity alone, and you eased their pain and suffering."

She glanced up with what she hoped was a sturdy grin. "Sound advice."

He took a swallow of his coffee.

"Believe it or not, tonight's simple pleasures all conspired to make up one of the best birthdays I've had."

"I'm glad."

Carrie sipped her tea. Sitting beneath the soft glow of the table lamp, one might regard this moment as actually romantic—if one was of that persuasion, which, of course, Carrie was not. Papa always said a good journalist must keep her mind on her vocation and not allow emotions to distract her.

"If I'm not mistaken, you've reached the ripe old age of nineteen."

He remembered! "A lady never tells her age."

The colonel narrowed his gaze in reply to her sass.

Carrie tamped down a giggle. "Yes, you calculated my age correctly, sir."

"Hmm . . . nineteen. When I was that age, I'd just entered the United States Military Academy. I got into every kind of trouble there was. My actions got me expelled my first year. A superintendent, a man named Robert E. Lee, decided I had the gumption and dash to make a fine soldier, and he persuaded the powers that be to reinstate me."

"Robert E. Lee?" Carrie's mind had parked right there. "You know General Lee?"

The colonel gave a nod. "He's a fellow Virginian and one of the finest gentlemen I've ever had the pleasure of meeting."

"But you're fighting against him and his men—against Virginia. Why aren't you a Confederate?"

"Carrie, there comes a time in every man's life when the line must be drawn. For me it's the belief that an entire race of people must be free. Slavery must be abolished. Second, the Union must be preserved at all costs. My great-grandfather fought in the Revolutionary War so that we Americans might never live under oppression again, no matter what our skin color. Those ideals led me to join the United States Army."

"Well, I agree—that slavery should be abolished. However, I've heard the exact argument come out of Confederates' mouths—they're fighting for their freedom and independence too."

"Ah, yes, but freedom for whites only. I believe all men are created equal."

Carrie's lips twitched with a wry grin. "I think I'm more of a Yankee than I ever dreamed."

The colonel's low-pitched chuckle filled the space inside the tent. "I knew it all along. However, you can still remain an independent thinker."

"I will." Several moments passed and Carrie finished her tea. Questions swirled in her mind. She'd heard the talk in camp about the kind of man the colonel had been before his conversion, although she knew he was an honorable man now. "Colonel—"

"I don't suppose I'm out of line to request that you call me Peyton when we're speaking in private."

Her face flushed, and Carrie was glad her dimly lit surroundings wouldn't reveal it. "All right, Peyton." She liked the sound of his name as it sprang from her lips. Swallowing hard, she forged ahead with her question. "You mentioned the trouble you got into as a younger man, and Gettysburg is mentioned quite often too. Will you tell me what it was exactly that changed you? I learned you had a spiritual experience, but I've heard no details."

"Ah, now you sound like a journalist."

Carrie's cheeks warmed from both his jesting and his scrutiny.

"Yes, I certainly did have a spiritual experience." He paused to enjoy another puff of his cigar. "It's a rather grisly tale. Are you up for it?"

"Absolutely." Her curiosity would never be quelled unless she heard the story of his conversion directly from him.

"All right, then." He inclined his head. "It happened after the first day of fighting. I took a big risk and led my men to a place on the battlefield where we successfully held off the enemy until reinforcements arrived. By then I'd been nearly sliced in two, hit by shrapnel that took my horse right out from under me, killing the animal. My men dragged me over to what we referred to as the dying tree—a shady place out of the line of fire where men had been set to bleed out and die."

Carrie's heart squeezed as she imagined the scene.

"Johnston was there and managed to hold my side together. After a time, he placed my right hand over it and encouraged me to press it together. He made me promise not to let go until he returned." Peyton's voice took on a somber tone. "I tried, although I went in and out of consciousness the rest of the afternoon. I came to my senses sometime during the night."

Peyton sat forward and stared into his coffee cup. "Fog had settled over the battlefield, and the cries of thousands of dying men sounded like the biblical account of hell—weeping, wailing, and gnashing of teeth. I'd heard about hell plenty of times from Johnston as well as other preachers, but I experienced it that night. At one point, I actually believed I had died and gone to a godless eternity. I knew I deserved it as I'd been living like the devil."

"Hard to believe."

"But true, and I'm not proud of my past. I cheated on my former fiancée

Lavinia the night before we were to get married. She found out and called off our wedding."

Carrie put his admission together with his prior friendship with Miss Phoebe and knew exactly what kind of a rake the colonel had been. She'd met such men at the Wayfarers Inn. "But you're alive . . . and you're different."

He lifted his gaze and smiled. "Miraculously. When I realized I wasn't dead, I started praying. I asked God to spare my life. I promised that if He did, I would start living right and going to church. I vowed to quit imbibing along with all the other filthy habits accompanying it."

"And God took you up on it." Carrie smiled and realized she'd been holding onto her cup a bit too tightly. She relaxed her grip.

"Indeed He did. The next morning, orderlies found me. The pain was so great when they moved me onto the stretcher that I lost consciousness. It was LaFont who stitched me together. I'm fortunate he was the attending physician. When I awoke, I was in the York Army Hospital with Aunt Ruth sitting at my bedside, reading from her Bible."

"And now you're making good on your promise to God."

"That I am."

Hope and gladness soared through her. "How wonderful that this dark tale has a happy ending." She sank her gaze into her teacup. "I'm thankful you didn't fall at Gettysburg. I'm even more thankful that you turned your life around. However . . ." She paused. How to best phrase her next thoughts? ". . . the cost of this war has been great. So many lives lost."

"No one knows that better than I." The colonel reached across the table and took her hand. "Carrie, you should be proud. You comforted many a soul during his final moments here on earth."

"I'm not proud. I'm . . . I'm . . ." She couldn't even find the words to express her emotion.

His palm pressed hers gently. "You're a very compassionate young lady, Carrie, and you never cease to amaze me. You could have refused to help, as I brought you here against your will. Instead you rolled up your sleeves and went to work, helping LaFont."

She glanced up to see warmth in his golden-brown eyes—and something else. Mischief, perhaps.

"Not that you had a choice in that either." He grinned. "However, I sense the toll it's been taking on you, which is why I've planned for you to leave camp tonight."

Her heart leaped with anticipation. "Tonight?"

"General Sheridan has ordered that the Union line here near Halltown be fortified and defended. Meanwhile the cavalry still has its burning orders. My regiment and I leave on a mission at dawn. I'm not sure when we'll make it back to camp, so I can no longer guarantee your safety. But when I heard of General Sheridan's scouts heading for Winchester, I knew it was a divine opportunity."

"Scouts? You mean you're not taking me to Winchester?" Disappointment fell over her.

"I'm afraid not." Releasing her hand, Peyton sat back in his chair, and Carrie immediately missed the physical connection. "A few of Sheridan's scouts are heading for Winchester within the hour. They'll see you safely to my aunt's home. It's a journey of about eight hours and it's fairly hard riding. Do you think you can manage?"

"Yes." She hoped so, anyway.

"Beneath the cloak of darkness, you won't be spotted leaving the camp. After the scouts clear Charles Town, they'll likely bivouac and get a few hours' sleep."

"Something to look forward to." She stifled a yawn. "And if you feel I'll be safe with the general's scouts, then I trust I will be."

"You will be." Peyton finished his cigar and ground it out on the grass under his chair. "I appreciate your cooperative attitude, Carrie, and I'm sorry to spring the news on you this way. But you see, war, such as the Shenandoah Valley has never seen, is coming. When it does, I want you somewhere safe, not that Winchester would be my first choice for you—or for my aunt."

"What do you mean?"

He took another drink of his coffee. "At the present, the Confederate flag flies in Winchester, but I learned from scouts that Lieutenant Colonel Elijah Kent has recently moved into my aunt's home. Ironically, Eli Kent and I are good friends from our West Point days. Both Virginians. After we joined opposing armies, we vowed to look out for each other's kin if at all possible. His folks reside near Richmond, and while I have never had use of their home, I believe they'd make me comfortable. Therefore, Aunt Ruth makes

Eli's stay in Winchester pleasurable. To make a long story a breath shorter, you will be safe there even though Confederates are in control of the town—*temporarily* in control, I might add."

"Your optimism impresses me. In the past, the Rebs have forced the Union to abandon its occupation of the Valley."

"Not this time."

His tone, soft, but with a saber-sharp edge to it, sent a chill down her spine.

"I'll miss you, Peyton." A heartbeat later, she realized she'd spoken her thoughts. "Oh!" How horrifying! "I beg your pardon. My remark probably sounded quite forward." She stared at the flickering lamplight on the table between them. "I assure you I didn't mean anything by it." She'd never said such things to a man. What was wrong with her?

"Quite all right. You'll be missed as well."

By you? Dr. LaFont and his staff? Other volunteers? Why did she hope that he'd miss her most of all?

"At the same time, I hope I haven't encouraged you in . . . well, in the wrong way."

Her heart took a tumble. "No, you haven't." She didn't need clarification on what the *wrong way* was. She knew exactly what he'd meant. She was a farm girl from Woodstock, a serving girl at the Wayfarers Inn. He was a fine Union officer, a colonel, and a handsome one at that. They couldn't be more ill-suited. "You've been very kind to me." She smiled, deciding to add a bit of humor to cover her inexplicable disappointment. "Even if you did have the gall to arrest me."

He grinned. Moments later, another man entered the tent, capturing Peyton's attention. He immediately pushed to his feet.

"My scouts are saddling up." Removing his hat, the officer glanced Carrie's way. "Is this the young lady we spoke of earlier?"

Carrie stood.

"Yes, sir." Peyton stepped around the table and took her hand. "Miss Carrie Ann Bell, allow me to present Major General Philip Sheridan."

General Sheridan! "A pleasure to make your acquaintance, sir." She'd never met anyone of such importance.

"The pleasure is mine, Miss Bell." He stepped closer, and Carrie was surprised at his small stature. He stood only an inch or two taller than she, although his odd-shaped head looked overly large for his frame. "I have heard of the tender care you administered to our wounded men. You have my sincere gratitude." He gave her a bow.

"I didn't mind helping."

"Good, because you'll likely be called upon again, particularly if you reside with Ruth Collier." His mustache twitched with a smile. "She's a fine nurse, and the Union army has men recovering in both area hospitals. I'm told they've been treated well, but that's largely due to our loyal ladies in Winchester."

"I hope to be considered among them, sir." Carrie meant it too. She liked these men, and after living among them she found herself believing more in the Yankees' cause than she did the Confederates'. Even so, she understood the South's grievance that its states' rights had been violated. For Carrie, it was easier to view men of both blue and gray as human beings. Wasn't that what being independent minded was all about?

"I'm sure you will be an asset," the general said. "Your audacity will get you far in life." He chuckled softly. "One particular tale of your service will remain etched in my memory for a long while."

"Which is that, sir?" Carrie chanced a peek up at Peyton, wondering what General Sheridan had heard—or what she'd done—but she couldn't make out his expression.

"As the story goes, my dear lady, while suturing a gash above Colonel Ackerby's brow, you very unabashedly told him to 'quit whining and take his stitches like a man.'"

She sucked in her next breath. "I meant no disrespect." A blush burst into her cheeks, its heat spreading down her neck. "It's just that there were other men worse off than the colonel."

"Indeed." General Sheridan guffawed and looked at Peyton. "Ackerby is full of complaints, is he not?"

"I'll reserve my comment for a later time, sir." A subtle lilt to Peyton's tone revealed good humor.

"You're a wise man, Collier."

Relief engulfed Carrie. The last thing she wanted was to cause Peyton any embarrassment. Seemed she hadn't.

Another laugh from the army commander, and then he reached for her hand and held it just briefly. "You've got pluck, Miss Bell, and I like that."

"Thank you, General."

He dropped his hat onto his head. "With that, I shall bid you Godspeed."

Carrie dipped her head gratefully.

General Sheridan faced Peyton. "My scouts await. They're cleverly disguised as local farmers. If questioned, Miss Bell will be a sister or cousin. The men will think of something. I don't expect any problems." The general smiled at Carrie. "Everything is in order for your departure from camp."

"Thank you, General."

Peyton extended his arm toward the tent's flap. "Lead the way, sir."

Collecting the cape and cap that Miss Phoebe had scrounged up for her, Carrie followed General Sheridan. Peyton trailed her.

Outside of the mess tent, Major Johnston and Tommy stood by while, in the near distance, two men sat on horseback, waiting. General Sheridan walked off with several of his staff.

"I packed some gear for you, just in case it rains or you get hungry," Tommy said, stepping forward.

"How very thoughtful. Thank you."

"And . . . well, I can tell you look real pretty in that dress."

Carrie was touched. Standing on tiptoe, she placed a sisterly kiss on Tommy's cheek. "You'll make a fine soldier someday."

"Golly." He rubbed the spot on his face that her lips had touched.

Carrie's face flamed as Peyton and Major Johnston's chuckles sailed the distance. She'd never known a male to react to her like Tommy did just now.

"Good-bye, Miss Bell." Johnston doffed his hat and sidestepped around Tommy. "It's been a pleasure meeting you."

"Likewise. I hope to see you again."

"You will. If not on earth, then in the sky when the trumpet sounds the Lord's second coming."

"Nevertheless, Reverend, keep your head low."

He guffawed. "I shall, Miss Bell."

Carrie turned to Peyton. "Will you tell Dr. LaFont good-bye for me?"

"You can tell him yourself."

She gazed in the direction of Peyton's nod and saw the Frenchman leaning against a nearby tree, smoking a cigar. He pushed off the trunk with his shoulder and strode toward her.

"I am not happy about this, *petite*."

Carrie didn't know how to reply. She didn't feel happy about leaving either. What a difference a week made.

"It's not her doing, LaFont," Peyton put in. "It's mine."

"And I told you the same thing, did I not?" Dr. LaFont met Carrie's gaze. "You may volunteer in my hospital any time."

"Thank you." High praise, coming from a man who demanded perfection in the very worst of conditions. Nonetheless, Carrie observed his calm and skill amidst chaos, and aside from the hand of God, Dr. LaFont had most likely saved Peyton's life.

Cupping her elbow, Peyton led her over to the scouts. "Miss Carrie Ann Bell, allow me to introduce your escorts for this evening."

She smiled. He spoke as if they were in attendance at some well-to-do affair.

"Majors Roddy and Brown."

Carrie gave a polite nod to the men before one of them dismounted. His movements struck a chord of familiarity deep inside of her. Seconds later, dread knotted in her belly as she peered into the face of her childhood friend, Joshua Blevens.

CHAPTER 13

"Pleased to make your acquaintance, Miss Bell." Joshua removed his hat and combed his fingers through his shaggy, walnut-colored hair. "Like the colonel said, I'm Major Brown." He spoke the name slowly as if to warn Carrie against revealing his true identity. "If there's anything you need, just let me know."

"What she needs," Peyton said tersely, "is to get to Winchester safely."

"Yes, sir."

Darkness hid his frown, but Carrie heard it in his deep, dark tone. She felt as though she'd forgotten how to breathe.

Peyton untied a saddled sorrel and led the animal over to her. "Tommy selected this horse especially for you."

She gazed across the way at Tommy and smiled, hoping she could convey the gratefulness she felt inside. After all, she was thankful. Scared to death, but thankful. What was Joshua doing here? Was he a Confederate spy, or had he deserted the Confederacy and joined the Union?

"The gelding has a gentle nature—"

Carrie forced herself to pay attention to Peyton.

"—and he's too small to meet cavalry regulations so he's of no use to us. But he'll make you a fine mount."

"Th-thank you." She hoped Joshua hadn't heard the quiver in her voice. She glanced in the scouts' direction before seeing Tommy, Major Johnston, and Dr. LaFont amble off. Nice of them to say farewell.

Looking back at Peyton, she wondered whether to invent some reason why she couldn't ride away with the scouts. Joshua would likely give her a thrashing once they left camp. Like an older brother, he protected her, allowed himself to be cajoled by her, but he had also reprimanded her. He'd wrestled her to the ground for lesser offenses than this one—showing up in a Union camp. But she could hardly use that as an excuse to stay. She'd have to face Joshua sometime. After all, she'd accepted employment from a Union cavalryman in Winchester.

Peyton slid the cape from her grasp and set it around her shoulders. With particular care, he hooked its top clasp. He leaned closer. "I must admit to feeling a bit jealous that Tommy got a kiss and I didn't."

She found the remark amusing.

"I mean it."

A pleasurable blush burst into her face. He wanted a kiss? She'd happily give him one, provided Joshua didn't see.

She flicked a glance over the horse's back and saw him conversing with the other scout. If done quickly, her actions wouldn't be noticed. Then again, if she was already in hot water with Joshua, she may as well make his wrath worth it.

Standing on tiptoes, Carrie placed one hand on Peyton's shoulder and touched her lips to his cheek. Before she realized it she'd brought her fingertips to his chin. His beard felt as soft as she'd guessed.

In that moment, she knew she'd fallen in love with this man. A handsome Yankee colonel who was well above her station in life.

Slowly, reluctantly, she stepped back, wishing she could remain close to him.

Peyton said nothing, his gaze fixed on her.

"Thank you for everything," she whispered. "You've been more than kind and generous to me."

"Entirely my pleasure."

She peeked over the saddle at Joshua. His frowning countenance stared back at her.

The blood drained from her face.

"Is something wrong, Carrie?" Peyton's voice was soft, intended for her ears alone.

She didn't know how to respond. Did she nod? Shake her head? How did she let on that something was very, very wrong? If she wasn't mistaken, the other shabbily dressed scout was Rodingham, the Confederate major she'd met the day she left Woodstock. And, of course, she'd recognize Joshua anywhere and at any distance.

"Carrie?" Peyton held her shoulders. "You need not be frightened. The scouts value their positions with this army far too much to risk harming you."

She opened her mouth, but not a single utterance came out.

"Colonel, that girl won't be any trouble to us, will she?" Joshua asked.

Resting his right elbow on the saddle, Peyton peered across the way. "I thought I made it clear, Major Brown. She won't be any trouble." Irritation oozed from each syllable.

"Just making sure, Colonel."

Carrie dropped her gaze and stared at the toes of her boots. The damp breeze ruffled her skirt. If Joshua kept this up he'd likely give himself away without her saying a word.

"It's your choice, Carrie," Peyton said softly.

"I'll go." She may as well face Joshua now. Besides, she hadn't done anything wrong. Joshua was the one in disguise! But unless he let on, she'd go along with the pretense, especially since she couldn't say for sure which side of this conflict the men were on. She felt safe with Joshua, although she didn't care a whit for his friend.

After tying her bonnet's ribbon beneath her chin, Carrie pulled on her gloves. She stroked the horse's nose. "You and I are going to be friends for a while, all right?" The animal tossed his head as if he nodded in understanding.

Peyton helped her mount.

"Please give Aunt Ruth and Tabitha my regards."

"Yes, I will." She smiled down at him, noting again what a handsome figure he made. "I'll be praying for you—you and your men."

"Likewise, you won't be far from my thoughts." Reaching up, he gently squeezed her gloved hand. "I'll be in touch." He gave the horse's rump a firm pat and Carrie rode over to the men filing into line ahead of Joshua.

This night's journey to Winchester had begun.

—◌ ◌—

"I hope you'll be comfortable, Eli." Ruth placed the pitcher of water beside the basin. "Is there anything else I can get for you before I turn in for the night?"

"No, nothing." The lieutenant colonel produced a little laugh as he removed his gray jacket. "I feel like I'm home again."

Ruth smiled, pleased that she could put him up in her home. Hosting Eli ensured a measure of protection while the Confederates occupied Winchester. "You're always welcome here."

He arched a brow and ran his hand down the length of his rather hedge-like beard. "Even though I'm a Confederate officer?"

"Even though." Ruth sighed. Some men looked better with a beard than others. She'd see that he got a sharp razor. "I'll have you know that you're about the only Confederate officer I can tolerate these days." She paused to mull over her suspicions. "You are a Confederate, aren't you?"

He gave her a quizzical glance. "Aunt Ruth, are you reading those detective novels again?"

"Alas, I must confess to reading *Bleak House* by Mr. Charles Dickens for the umpteenth time. It does make one question system norms." But how interesting that Eli didn't take offense, although he knew her well enough not to.

"It's been a long, nasty war, hasn't it?"

"Indeed." Ruth ambled to the doorway. "At least we agree on that much."

Smiling, Eli sat in the side chair near the window and stretched out his booted legs. "What's Peyt up to these days?"

Ruth turned from the doorway. "Are you asking as a friend or a Confederate officer?"

Eli took a moment to think it over. "Does it matter?"

"Ah . . . well, Peyton is fine. He's a colonel in the United States Army."

"He outranks me, that rascal."

"And he's a Christian man now." A fact Ruth was most proud of. "He turned his life around after Gettysburg."

"No fooling?" Eli's brows went up in surprise and perhaps awe. "Peyt's a Christian? My, but that is a turnaround . . . no offense intended."

"None taken. Peyton's checkered past is no secret, I'm afraid, although he's doing what he can to make up for it."

"Is that why he reenlisted after recovering from his wounds?" Eli gave a wag of his head and several locks of his dark brown hair fell onto his tanned forehead. "For myself I think I would have taken my retirement and settled in upstate New York as our home and property in Richmond are gone now that my father is dead. My mother and sisters moved to a small house in town." He turned momentarily pensive, but then smiled. "Or maybe I'd attempt more filibustering in Cuba."

"Oh, good gracious! It's much too hot in Cuba."

Eli chuckled softly.

Ruth steered the subject back to her beloved nephew. "Peyton is determined to finish what he started, fighting for freedom for all men, women, and children, as well as the integrity of the Union."

"What about state sovereignty? Are you forgetting how our forefathers included states' rights in the American Constitution?"

"I'm not a forgetful woman, Eli. But you and I both know that states' rights is the argument slaveholding Southerners hide behind so they can keep other human beings in bondage. Why? Because the Southern economy demands it. The entire matter all boils down to one word: money."

"I'm glad you have it all figured out, Aunt Ruth." Amusement twitched his whiskers. "Although President Jefferson Davis might disagree with you."

"I'm sure he does, but I don't see Jeff Davis picking cotton in the hot sun. Do you?"

Again Eli ran his hand down his beard before yawning. "Good night, Aunt Ruth."

"Good night, Eli." She smiled, pleased that he'd allow an old woman to win the debate . . . for now, anyway. However, on occasion, Ruth sensed Eli wished he'd signed with the other side—the *right* side.

Leaving the bedroom, Ruth closed the door softly behind her.

_◦ ◦_

"Carrie Ann, you'd better have a good explanation for being at that Yankee camp."

"I got arrested for impersonating an officer." She tethered her sorrel, grateful the men chose to stop for the remainder of the night—make that wee hours of the morning. Confederate pickets surrounded the town of Win-

ANDREA BOESHAAR

chester, and any attempt to enter at this hour would certainly arouse suspicion. "You know I was looking for my sister, Joshua."

"Major John Brown."

"You couldn't think up a more original name than *John Brown*?" A pity he couldn't see her roll her eyes at his lack of imagination.

"Carrie Ann, this ain't games we're playing." Joshua's voice was barely audible, but he may as well have been shouting. "This is war and you've gone and got yourself in the middle of it."

"Well, it's your fault," she hissed, removing her cap and dropping down on to a grassy spot near her mount. She reclined, stretching out her back. Oh, how it ached. It'd been a while since she'd ridden that long astride a horse. Her legs felt like overcooked green beans.

"My fault?" Joshua planted himself beside her while Rodingham bivouacked a short distance farther up the road. "How do you figure?"

"You refused to help me find Sarah Jane and then allowed me to leave Woodstock looking like a Yankee sergeant. I never bothered to look at the shoulder stripes."

"I didn't know you'd gone." A weary-sounding sigh. "I left Woodstock after dinner and you . . . you took off after Sarah Jane even after I told you not to, huh?"

"You gave me the boots."

"I didn't think you'd really wear them."

"I had to find my baby sister."

"And? Did you?"

"No." A fact that continually troubled her. "But Pey—" She dared not call him by his first name in front of Joshua. "Colonel Collier came up with a plan that will help me locate Sarah Jane and provide for Mama and Margaret too. He hired me to be a companion to his aunt who lives in Winchester. The colonel said he'll pay me seven dollars a month."

"Yankee money?"

"Uh-huh." Carrie smiled, sensing Joshua might even be impressed. "What's more, the colonel promised I'll have my own bedroom and a full belly at the end of the day. That's more than I ever got working for Mr. Veyschmidt."

"Seven dollars a month, Yankee money?" Joshua let out a soft, slow whistle. "I might even have taken that job."

137

"I thought you might see it my way." Money very often said more than words ever could.

"What about kissing that colonel good-bye? You didn't imagine I'd see you, but I did."

Carrie had a reply all prepared. "It was a very pristine kiss—and the colonel deserved it. He was exceptionally good to me. In fact, Peyton treated me better than my own family and Mr. Veyschmidt combined."

"*Peyton*, is it?" There was an edge to his voice. "You're on a first-name basis with a Yankee colonel?"

Carrie hadn't rehearsed a response for that slipup. "We're friends."

"Sure you are."

Carrie rolled onto her right side, her back to Joshua.

"But I can understand you getting confused by the first man who comes along and treats you nice. Most of us men in Woodstock think you're just plain crazy."

"That's because most of you are fools. You don't appreciate my intellect. Peyton said I'm brave and tenacious."

"I think a woman ought to be soft and sweet."

"Who said I'm not soft and sweet?" She huffed. "But you'll never find out."

Joshua grunted. "You got it all figured out, don't you, Carrie Ann?"

"As usual." She wished he'd shut his mouth. She wasn't confused at all. However, her punishment would likely be worse if she didn't allow Joshua his say.

"Well, to set matters straight"—his voice lost its mocking tone—"my folks would have helped you after the fire if it weren't for your mama, dare I even call her that. She's truly touched in the head. Truth is my mama and Mathilda Bell have been at daggers drawn since before you and me was born."

"You and I."

"That's what I said."

A rueful sigh escaped her. He'd never learn gentlemen's English.

"And I'm sorry I wasn't around to help out after the fire."

"I'm sorry too." She swallowed hard and blinked away the sudden tears. She'd needed him—she'd needed someone, but no one came to her rescue. It was as if God Himself had turned His back on her—

But she knew that wasn't so. The Bible said that God would never forsake her, and she wouldn't dare call God a liar.

Maybe it was God who'd sent Peyton to rescue her from the Wayfarers Inn and Mr. Veyschmidt's hamlike fist.

"Would have been nice if your papa wasn't off chasing rainbows somewhere when it happened."

Carrie rolled onto her back again. The sky was dark, the air still. Only an occasional rustling of treetops whispered overhead. "Papa is documenting the war. He'll be a famous journalist someday. I know it."

"The way I was raised, supportin' his family comes first in a man's life. Your papa left without giving you a way to reach him so you could tell him about the farm. Worse, he hasn't sent you or your family a nickel."

"I'm sure he'd send money if he could. Maybe he even tried but it was stolen before it reached Woodstock. You know how robberies frequently occur with the mail."

"Did his last letter contain money? Was the seal unbroken when the letter arrived?"

"No and no," Carrie admitted.

"Well, there then. I say shame on him for leaving behind an unbalanced wife and three daughters. He should have stayed home like my pa had the good sense to do."

Carrie's fists clenched by her side. "Mama wasn't unbalanced until the fire."

"She's always been unbalanced. You just got accustomed to the craziness 'cause that's all you knew since you were four months old."

"Since I was four months old?" Her head lolled toward the sound of Joshua's hushed voice. "Is that when Mama first appeared unstable?"

"Carrie Ann." His voice had turned gentle. "That woman ain't your real mama, and I'm sorry to be the one to tell you that." Her breath caught. "Your birth mother, well, she took sick and died while your papa was traveling with her down the pike. He should have told you this."

"That's ridiculous. You're lying! You're angry because I accepted Peyton's bargain to work for his aunt."

"Think whatever you like, Carrie Ann. You always do. Except, when it comes to you, I ain't no liar. We made a pact, remember?"

She remembered. She was about ten years old when she and Joshua pledged never to lie to each other, no matter what the consequences. "But if what you say is true, then why didn't I suspect it all these years?"

"Because you always had your nose in some newspaper or book, that's why. Mostly everyone in Woodstock knows the truth."

She thought over his words. Her stomach cramped like she'd swallowed a plum pit. "And you never told me—my best friend?" She wanted to slug him. She felt like the brunt of a terrible joke. "All this time folks were laughing at me."

"No one was laughing, Carrie Ann. Wasn't your fault—it was your folks' doing."

"Who's my mother?"

"I don't know. You'd have to ask your papa—or my parents."

The young lady Carrie believed herself to be exploded like a fully loaded Napoleon cannon. She wasn't the wild-haired daughter of Charles Andrew and Mathilda Mae Bell. No wonder she never fit into the family. No wonder her mama—make that her stepmother—treated her disdainfully. And her grandfather—step-grandfather—was a crotchety old soul. When he was alive, he'd behaved like Carrie was some unwanted guest on the farm they shared with him. Now she understood why: she wasn't his kin.

"Do both Margaret and Sarah Jane know the truth?" Even after the question passed her lips, Carrie doubted her sisters knew. They would have leaked the information over the years, and Carrie would have learned of it.

"Not sure."

Carrie allowed the information to sink in further. Questions swirled in her mind, but several pieces of her life now made sense. "So that's why my mother—stepmother—was more than happy to send me after Sarah Jane. She probably hoped I'd get myself shot."

Joshua released a long sigh. "I know you're upset—"

"Upset?" Everything she knew and believed about her family was fiction.

"But if it's any consolation, my folks never had a grievance with you. Just Mathilda Mae."

Carrie battled one eddy of bitterness after another.

"My folks were miffed at your papa for marrying her. See, your step-mother was a saloon girl. My mama knew her from grade school, and then saw her around town. Never approved of her working in the saloon."

"So Margaret isn't my sister?"

"Stepsister."

"Sarah Jane?"

"Half sister." Joshua fired off a string of profanity.

"Watch your mouth!"

"Well, I shouldn't have to be the one to say all this. Now you're gonna hate me."

"I don't hate you—or anyone else. I only wish you'd have said something sooner."

"Like I said, your folks should have been the ones to tell you."

Carrie stared up at the inky sky wondering what other truths lay hidden beneath the folds of the universe. Maybe Papa never planned to return to Woodstock.

"So Margaret takes after her mama, huh?" Although whispered, the sarcasm in Carrie's tone came through like a shout.

"Don't be too hard on her, Carrie Ann. Maybe Margaret will run away like Sarah Jane and be all right in the end."

"Well, one thing's for sure: I'll find Sarah Jane, but I'll be hanged if I return her to the Wayfarers Inn. Sarah can attend school in Winchester while I work for Peyton's aunt."

When Joshua didn't reply, Carrie looked in his direction. Had he fallen asleep? "Joshua?"

"It's Major Brown, Miss Bell." His voice suddenly sounded as hard as iron. "Now, it's our turn to bargain."

Carrie grew wary. "What sort of bargain? I mean, if you think I'll marry you, you're as touched as my stepmother." She'd love Peyton Collier till the day she died. She knew it deep down in her soul.

"I don't want to marry you!" He groaned. "That'd be like marrying my own sister."

"Good. At least we agree on that much."

"Listen, I'll keep my eyes open for Sarah Jane if you'll keep my identity a secret."

"I've kept all your secrets."

"Well, this one is more important than all my youthful confidences combined. I'm Major John Brown and you gotta remember that."

"Are you a deserter," she whispered, "or a Confederate spy?"

"I can't tell you that, else I'd have to kill you."

Carrie found the remark amusing. "You'd never kill me."

"I'd have to, Carrie Ann. No matter what. It'd be my sworn duty."

His knife-edged tone sent a shiver up her spine.

"Do we understand each other?"

"Yes." She figured he was a bushwhacker to have sworn such a vow. No matter, he chanced execution, whether bushwhacker, deserter, or spy—or all three, depending on the situation and who apprehended him. "The last thing I want is to see you swing from a rope. Lord knows I've seen enough death in the last couple of weeks, both Yankee and Rebel blood."

"Anyone we know?"

"No . . . but all human beings just the same."

Joshua snorted. "Typical female sensibilities."

"And thank God for us women or there wouldn't be anyone to nurse you men back to health after you attempt to kill off the human race!"

"Quiet over there!" A reprimand from Rodingham. "You havin' problems with that girl, Brown?"

"No. No problems."

"I'd be happy to take her off your hands."

"Nah, we don't want Collier after us. She's not worth the trouble." Joshua jabbed his elbow into her ribs.

Despicable louts! *Definitely bushwhackers.*

Carrie stretched and returned to lying on her side. Sleep beckoned, and her eyes grew heavy.

"Promise me, Carrie Ann," Joshua whispered, leaning over her. "You'll keep my secret."

"I promise. I already told you that."

"Good. Even so, I'll be keeping an eye on you."

His voice came close to her ear and she shivered. Old friend or no, Joshua kept bad company. Rodingham was a scoundrel. But for now she had no alternative except to trust Joshua.

However, she vowed never to be at his mercy again.

CHAPTER 14

"It's awfully quiet without Miss Bell around."

"It's just before dawn, Peyt. She's only been gone a few hours."

"I realize that, but . . ." He glanced at Vern as they prepared for a typical early morning drill. Breakfast would follow it and, by then, details would have taken down tents and packed supply wagons. ". . . it's still awfully quiet without her."

"Rest assured, my friend; the quiet won't last. At any moment we might hear an ear-splitting Rebel yell, and then you'll wish for the quiet again."

"Good point."

Peyton stared at the brightening sky. It was shaping up to be a nice day.

"Although, if you ask me—"

"I didn't."

"—I think you miss her."

"Perhaps I do." He'd admit that much at least. "Her chattering got my mind off the war for a spell. It's just as well she's gone, though. I'd never forgive myself if she got hurt or killed during an attack. Besides, I can't afford any distractions."

"None of us can, but that doesn't stop me from thinking about Meredith and wondering how she's getting along."

And it didn't stop Peyton from thinking about Carrie who, by his calculations, should be settled in at Aunt Ruth's by lunchtime—that is, if those scouts didn't run into trouble.

Lord, protect her.

Peyton recalled her apprehension when she learned those two men would be her escorts into Winchester. But General Sheridan trusted them, and that endorsement was good enough for Peyton.

Recollections of the surprise attack on the north fork of the Shenandoah nearly two weeks ago surfaced. It was the day Peyton found Carrie wedged in that tree. He grinned and a comforting warmth like a swallow of fine brandy spread through him. How was it that Miss Carrie Ann Bell had affected him in such a short time the way no other woman ever had in all his twenty-eight years?

Both Peyton and Vern packed their saddlebags and carried them to where their horses grazed. They strapped their gear to their saddles.

Peyton ran his hand over Brogan's silky neck. "I'll meet you at the drill site. I have to check my orders with General Merritt."

"Yes, sir. I'll make sure the rest of the troops are roused."

"Good." The day had begun.

Peyton swung up into his saddle. Indeed, things were heating up between the Union and the Confederacy. A battle, perhaps as devastating as the one in Gettysburg, could very well result. Or the deciding conflict could come in the form of a string of battles, all as intense as Cold Harbor. Either way, his little journalist would have something to write about.

_____ ᏕᏮ _____

Incessant shaking caused Carrie to open her eyes. Joshua knelt over her. "Wake up."

"But it's not morning yet." Her body cried for an additional hour of rest.

"Carrie Ann, you are the laziest thing on God's footstool. You know that?"

"The Yankees never complained."

"Get up! Major Roddy wants a word with you before we set off."

Joshua pulled her into a sitting position. Carrie groaned. She hadn't felt this sore since the day after her fall off the bridge and into that sycamore.

"Whatever you do," Joshua said, tossing her bonnet at her, "don't let on you're the same serving girl from Woodstock who we saw running wild down Main Street last week."

"Hasn't he recognized me?"

"Nah, you're forgettable—except for that hair color of yours. Just put on your bonnet and watch that sharp tongue of yours."

"You got trouble over there, Brown?"

Joshua stood and walked over to the small campfire where his crony sat, drinking what smelled like coffee. "Some females have rotten dispositions when they first wake up."

The man snickered.

Carrie donned her bonnet and tied it beneath her chin. Clambering to her feet, she stretched, taking her sweet time. She even made a trip into the woods to take care of her personal needs before strolling over to Joshua and Rodingham. Once she reached them, she leaned against a tree trunk and folded her arms.

"Sit down, Miss Bell," Major Rodingham—that is, Roddy—invited.

"No, thank you."

"Sit, Miss Bell." Rodingham stood and his voice took an edge. "Or I will sit you down myself."

But he needn't have bothered. Joshua made good on the threat by grabbing hold of her left arm and yanking. Carrie's backside hit the ground hard. When she tried to backhand him, he caught her left wrist.

"Don't twist it," she begged. "I injured it recently."

Joshua released her with a warning. "Behave yourself or you'll be suffering from more than a sore arm."

"You're a devil." Tears stung, and she massaged her wrist. Was Joshua playacting for the benefit of his comrade? She'd never known him to be so cruel.

"We only want some information from you, Miss Bell." Rodingham was obviously the leader, while Joshua was the muscle. "Approximately how many men do you think comprise General Sheridan's army?"

"Wouldn't you know that better than I?" Carrie couldn't contain her simmering indignation and it bubbled right out of her mouth. "You're supposedly one of the general's scouts."

"Miss Bell . . ." Warning hung on both syllables. "I hate the thought of your tortured, lifeless body lying on the side of the Valley Pike."

"Your job, Major Roddy, is to see me safely to Winchester. Remember?"

"How many men do you suppose Sheridan has, Miss Bell?" Joshua asked in a more mannerly tone.

"I don't know." She'd die before she'd tell these men anything. "I volunteered as a nurse, so most of my time was spent in the field hospital, tending to dying men." She glared at Rodingham and imagined walking away from his battle-beaten body without so much as offering him water.

But, no . . . if it ever came down to it she'd probably, out of a sense of Christian duty, give him at least a sip.

"You must have heard something. It's in your best interest to talk to us, Miss Bell." Rodingham's threat was veiled, but unmistakable.

She released a sigh. "General Sheridan has thousands of men, I presume. How many thousands? That answer I'm afraid I don't know." She'd heard the Army of the Shenandoah was some forty or fifty thousand strong, but she wouldn't give out that figure. After all, her heart belonged to a colonel in that army and she'd never betray him.

"Where's General Grant?" Rodingham asked.

"Outside of Petersburg, or so they say." That information was common knowledge. Newspapers reported from the front there nearly every day.

"What about Sherman?"

"He's eating peaches for breakfast this morning somewhere in Georgia."

"Very amusing," Joshua muttered.

"Well, how do I know where General Sherman is?" Carrie huffed and gazed off toward the pink and gray horizon.

"What's your relationship to Colonel Collier?" Rodingham drained his tin cup. "You ought to know the answer to that."

"As it happens, I do know the answer." She pressed her lips together.

"Miss Bell . . ." Joshua set his arm around her shoulders and then took hold of her left hand. "It's a shame you're injured. But don't you worry. I'm not going to hurt you worse." The tone in his voice said otherwise, although Carrie figured it was a show for Rodingham more than a real threat.

"Colonel Collier values my compassion and nursing abilities, so he hired me to be his elderly aunt's companion. The woman lives in Winchester, and that's where I'm supposed to be headed." She narrowed her gaze at Rodingham. "When the colonel finds out how you mistreated me I'm sure he'll be very displeased."

Rodingham chortled, and Joshua joined in, although his mirth didn't sound genuine.

He released her. "She doesn't know anything. I told you that earlier. I tried getting information out of her last night and arrived at that same conclusion."

"For a young lady who talks so smart," Rodingham said, "you sure are an ignorant creature."

"And you just lost your one sip of water." Carrie stood.

"What's that s'posed to mean?"

Ignoring the question, Carrie stomped over to her sorrel. In the light of day, she saw what a fine animal he was, even if he was too small for cavalry regulations. She stroked his neck and then stared down the road. She could probably gallop away before—

"Don't even think about it." Joshua, speaking softly, came up behind her. "Besides, you wouldn't get far." He moved the stirrup and tightened the cinches. "I loosened the straps last night so your horse could blow."

Carrie folded her arms. "I don't appreciate your companion starting the morning off so rudely." She shot a glance in Rodingham's direction, thankful the man was occupied with saddling his horse.

Joshua faced her. "He is not a nice man, Carrie Ann," he said softly with a wary glance in Rodingham's direction. "He will hurt you if it pleases him, especially since you seem to mean something to that Yankee colonel. I'm tryin' to save your skinny backside. Now get on that horse and do what you're told." Setting his hands around her waist, he lifted her to the saddle.

"Whatever you say, Major Brown." But her sass was only a cover for her rapidly beating heart. Deep down, she knew Joshua's words were true. Rodingham would, indeed, harm her without a second thought—if and when he could get away with it.

CHAPTER 15

After getting stopped and questioned numerous times, Carrie and her escorts finally rode into Winchester as the sun reached its noontime high. The steady *clip-clop* of their horses trotting along the macadamized street echoed between the battle-sore structures, some constructed from wood, others red brick. Carrie took in the clusters of Confederates standing around every corner and was grateful that her couriers were dressed in gray. Women smiled and conversed with the troops. CSA flags were draped over buildings and flapped in the wind on flagpoles. A sense of festivity pervaded the war-torn town . . . and why not? Like Woodstock and other towns in the Valley, Winchester was comprised of largely Confederate supporters, and recently the Rebel army had routed Federal troops. Peyton said it had been a great disappointment for the loyalists, his aunt included.

Lord, I hope she likes me. Her first paying job and Carrie didn't want to fail at it. But if she was completely honest with herself, she'd have to admit her primary desire was to please Peyton. She'd be the best companion his aunt ever knew.

Majors Roddy and Brown slowed to a halt in front of a large, limestone home. Its faded white pillars stood as tall as the shuttered second-story windows. The paint on the home had chipped and peeled, but despite its slight disrepair, the place looked as proud as any Southerner.

"This is it." Rodingham twisted in his saddle and peered at Carrie. "Climb down from that horse and get out of my sight."

Carrie dismounted, although she held the sorrel's reins. This morning she'd decided to call the horse *Charlie*, since Peyton had presented him to her in camp between Halltown and Charles Town, and Charles was Papa's given name. She began tying him to the black iron hitching post.

"You ain't keepin' that horse."

She glared at Rodingham. "He's mine. Colonel Collier gave him to me."

"Get on up to that house, missy. I ain't going to say it twice."

"You're not taking my horse—and I ain't saying it twice."

"Miss Bell," Joshua hissed, "quit your sassing and do what Major Roddy says." Saddle leather creaked as he got down from his mount.

Still, she refused. Surely the man wouldn't harm her here in town and in broad daylight.

Rodingham threw his leg over the saddle and jumped to the ground. He tethered his horse. Carrie watched his every move, but sensed Joshua inch closer behind her. His presence and the fact that she was right gave her the courage to dig in her heels.

"This is my horse." Her heart raced as Rodingham neared. His brows furrowed in a menacing frown. She'd have to fight him to keep the animal, but it was the last thing Peyton had given her. What's more, if she and his aunt didn't get along, Charlie was her only means out of town, other than a long walk.

Besides, it was the principle of the matter.

Rodingham glanced around and then peered down at her. His eyes looked like someone had just spit chews of tobacco into their sockets. "Major Brown, take those reins."

"No. This horse is mine." Carrie held them fast while Charlie nickered as if taking her side of the argument.

"Girl, you are fraying my last nerve."

Joshua reached for the reins and she slapped his hand away.

As Joshua drew back, Rodingham made his move, grabbing Carrie around the waist and covering her mouth with a gloved hand that smelled like dung. He lifted her off the ground while Joshua wrestled Charlie's reins from her fist.

Her gagged protests were unintelligible against his smelly, leathery palm. She squirmed and kicked but she was no match for Rodingham. He hauled her up two flights of steps and set her feet none-too-gently on a brick portico.

His hand still across her mouth, he knocked hard on the door with the other.

Exhaustion and anger ignited and Carrie back-kicked, striking his knee. She jammed her elbow into his ribs. It was enough that Rodingham removed his hand. When he did, she whirled around and shoved him hard. He stepped back and teetered slightly on the edge of the porch step. She gave him another push and down he went, landing on his backside.

Just then the front door opened. Carrie turned to see a slender Negro woman with frosty hair. Spying the white apron covering the black dress, Carrie assumed this was Tabitha, the housekeeper. The woman's dark eyes bounced from Carrie to Rodingham, and then widened in fright. She raised her hands. "Don't shoot, mister! Don't shoot!"

Glancing over her shoulder, Carrie saw the pistol pointed directly at her. "It's me he wants to kill." Turning slowly, she cautiously moved to the left so the woman wouldn't be injured if Rodingham fired.

The barrel of the gun followed her steps. Oddly, Carrie felt unafraid.

"Don't do it, Roddy." Joshua bounded up the first flight of brick steps. "Don't shoot her." He helped Rodingham to his feet. "The last thing we need is that Yankee colonel putting a bounty on our heads."

Rodingham's hand shook slightly and then he lowered his gun.

Carrie released the breath she'd been holding. Her heart banged like drumbeats, as if that body part had come lately to the scene and only now realized she'd been facing imminent death.

Two women now stood at the entryway instead of one.

"What in heaven's name is going on here?" Tall, with a willowy figure and a head of well-styled gray hair, the second woman stepped onto the porch with a dignified air. Carrie presumed she was Peyton's aunt.

"Begging your pardon for the disturbance, ma'am," Carrie said, "but I abhor being manhandled by ruffians." She flicked a look at Rodingham.

"I don't blame you." The older woman peered toward the yard. "Ruffians, eh?"

"And horse thieves."

"Mercy!" Her hand drifted up to her lace collar.

"Now, that ain't quite right, ma'am." Joshua strode to the lower step of the covered porch and politely removed his hat. "Taking this horse was part of our arrangement. Miss Bell, here, must not have understood those terms."

"Miss Bell?" The older woman's hazel eyes widened, and her thin lips curved upward in a pleased-looking grin. "You're the guest we've been expecting." A moment later, she clasped Carrie's right hand. "I'm Miss Ruth Collier, but I insist you call me Aunt Ruth." She leaned close. "And let's not say my nephew sent you for obvious reasons."

"Yes, ma'am. I mean . . . Aunt Ruth."

With a smile at Carrie, she turned to the dark-skinned woman who now fanned herself with her hanky. "And this is Tabitha, my trusted friend and housekeeper."

"Pleased to make your acquaintance," Carrie said.

"Likewise I'm sure—that is, once my heart goes back down into my chest." Carrie shared the feeling.

A man dressed in Confederate gray pushed his way out the front door.

Aunt Ruth put a possessive arm around Carrie's shoulders. "This is my . . . my niece. Miss Carrie Ann Bell, please meet Lieutenant Colonel Elijah Kent."

She knows my first name? Carrie fought to hide her surprise and faced the officer. "A pleasure, Colonel Kent."

"Miss Bell." He gave her a gentlemanly bow. "I am at your service."

"You can start, Colonel Kent," Aunt Ruth said, "by reprimanding those scoundrels on the walk. They manhandled Carrie Ann and are proceeding to steal her horse. Why, that man there was about to shoot her!"

The colonel walked onto the porch. "Sir, sheathe your weapon at once and answer to these charges or I'll have my men arrest you."

As if on cue, four Confederate pickets appeared from the side of the house and converged on Joshua and Rodingham, their guns drawn.

"A misunderstanding, sir." Rodingham holstered his gun.

"Misunderstanding? How dare you threaten any guest or member of this household?"

Carrie glared at Rodingham, forcing her lips not to curl upward in satisfaction.

As the colonel descended the porch steps, Aunt Ruth guided Carrie into the house. Disappointment fell over her. If the majors were about to get a dressing down she wanted to stand gleefully by and watch.

But, alas, duty called. She'd been hired as Aunt Ruth's companion. She wasn't a guest.

Her new employer led her into the parlor, where Carrie removed her hat and cape.

"We've been expecting you. I hope those men didn't hurt you."

"No, I'm unharmed. Colonel Collier wanted me to have safe passage to Winchester. Up until last night, it wasn't possible. The army was getting the last of the injured from Sunday's skirmish to the hospital in Harpers Ferry."

"Yes, we've been hearing of that conflict. Eli told us the Federals were successfully routed and moved farther north."

"It's true."

Aunt Ruth looked dismayed as she placed her right hand over her heart.

"But it was a controlled rout, if you will, not a panicked one. You see, General Sheridan is being very careful of what conflicts he engages in. He's saving his troops for the anticipated bigger battle—and it's coming. Which is why I'm here now. The word around camp is another Gettysburg-like storm is brewing. So you see, it's a tactic, not a defeat."

"I'm so glad you shared that information, my dear. I feel infinitely better . . . I think."

Smiling, Carrie glanced around the sparsely decorated parlor. She counted seven pieces of furniture: a sideboard, standing up against the inside wall; a settee; three armchairs, all arranged in front of the brick hearth; a side table between the chairs; and a grandfather clock which stood on the carpetless, wooden floor. No knickknacks appeared on the mantel. No framed art on the walls. But that wasn't surprising as nary a home in the Valley survived the war this far without loss of property.

"You can trust that I won't breathe a word of what you just told me."

Carrie assumed as much.

"And the men who brought you here? Peyton trusted them?"

"He did, but only because General Sheridan was convinced they were Union scouts. But they're not, and you were correct when you referred to them as scoundrels, although one of them tried to protect me."

"Thank God for him anyway." After peering out the window, Aunt Ruth laughed softly and faced her once more. "But you needn't worry. Eli's taking care of them."

"I'm grateful."

Aunt Ruth turned from the window. "I take it that Peyton told you about Eli?"

Carrie nodded.

"A pity Eli is a Confederate." A long sigh. "Like General Robert E. Lee, who we loyalists wish would have taken our side, Eli is a fine gentleman and would have been a credit to the Union army."

"Yes, ma'am. I'll take your word for it, although I must say Colonel Collier is also a fine gentleman and officer. He saved my life."

"Is that so?" Aunt Ruth sat down and indicated that Carrie should do likewise. "Do tell of the rescue."

"I'm happy to." Carrie thought back on that day. "I was heading down the Valley in search of my runaway sister, Sarah Jane . . ."

_____ ‿ ❧ ‿ _____

She's in love with him—or, at the very least, infatuated. Definitely devoted. Ruth could see it reflected in Miss Carrie Ann Bell's eyes as she spoke about Peyton. And she was very attractive, with her curly hair, the color of glowing embers, braided and pinned. But a serving girl from Woodstock? Originally from a farm?

Ruth quickly reminded herself that this very home was once a farmhouse after the Revolutionary War. Twenty-five years later, and needing money, Pappy sold Granddad's wheat fields and cornfields, upon which neighbors built their homes—including the Monteagues' next door.

"My father is a journalist."

"Oh?" Ruth pulled her attention back to her guest. That was notable employment.

"I'm very proud of him." A particular light, a mix perhaps of pride and awe, filled her blue eyes. "He left Woodstock in '62 alongside General Jackson's troops. He decided to record the hopes, fears, and determination of the Confederate troops first. Papa's last letter was postmarked from Washington, so I presume he's documenting the Union's side of things now. Perhaps he's even met President Abraham Lincoln."

"How impressive." Ruth wouldn't steal the girl's thunder and say she'd met Abraham and Mary Lincoln numerous times. As one of Lincoln's more generous contributors, Ruth received her share of invitations to various Washington social functions.

At least she used to. However, as long as the Confederates maintained control of Winchester and continued destroying railroad tracks to the north, travel to Washington was nearly impossible. Of course Peyton had wanted Ruth to remain in the capitol after his recovery, but she just couldn't leave Tabitha here on her own.

"Did you enjoy your work at the inn?" Ruth held her breath, praying the young lady did not enjoy her days as a serving girl even a little.

"No, ma'am."

She exhaled.

"Mama—that is, my stepmother, my sisters, and I worked there for our room and board after our farm burned down."

Ruth listened to the sad account. Yes, the fear of destruction to their homes and properties was on most everyone's mind these days.

"My ambition is to follow in my father's footsteps and be a journalist too. I ran his newspaper after he left Woodstock. In fact, Colonel Collier actually read one of my articles last year. That's when we first met. I stitched a gash in his arm."

Ruth knew of the incident, as Peyton had spoken of the girl—an aspiring author. "You're the one!" It all made sense now, why he would send Miss Carrie Ann Bell here. "I have seen that scar. Indeed, you made very neat stitches."

"Thank you." Her cheeks pinked and she glanced around the room. Obviously she disliked having the attention on herself, which spoke well of her character. "What would you like me to do first, Miss Collier?"

"Aunt Ruth."

"Aunt Ruth." Another blush.

"And I should call you Carrie Ann. After all, you're supposedly my niece. Do you mind?"

"Not at all."

"Now, to answer your question, what did you mean by . . . do?"

"The colonel hired me to be your companion."

"Companion?" The idea tickled Ruth. "I have no need for a companion, my dear."

A tiny dimple appeared above Carrie Ann's right eyebrow. "But I can't sit around here and do nothing all day and expect you to provide me with room and board. I need to work for it."

She's used to earning her keep. Ruth put the pieces together like a puzzle and concluded that Peyton had hired the young lady to be a companion; she wouldn't have accepted his invitation to come here to Piccadilly Place otherwise. And, of course, Peyton hadn't been able to discuss the matter of a companion with Ruth because he hadn't been home to do so. However, he could have stated something about it in his missive regarding Carrie Ann's arrival. Mercy! Peyton had caught her by surprise.

Ruth noted Carrie Ann's troubled expression. Obviously Peyton wanted the young lady here for a reason, and perhaps the only way to get her here had been to promise her employment.

"I must admit," Ruth began, "my nephew is always thinking of my needs even before I realize I have them. A companion would be most appreciated."

The young lady released a heavy breath and visibly relaxed.

"Let us continue getting to know each other and then I'll put a list together for, um, companion duties."

"Thank you, Miss Collier . . . Aunt Ruth." Another frown. "But I suppose when we're in private I should refer to you as *Miss Collier*. That would be more fitting for my station."

"Nonsense, dear girl, a companion is so much more to me than a mere hireling. A companion, as I see it, is part of the family."

"Thank you. It's nice being included in your family as mine has completely unraveled."

"Oh! Then I'm doubly glad my nephew rescued you."

Splashes of pink appeared on Carrie Ann's cheeks, quickly spreading downward to her neck. There was no question in Ruth's mind as to the young lady's intentions. She obviously had no designs on Peyton's inheritance. She was in love, plain and simple. Goodness, but she was as easy to read as a Waverley novel.

And on that thought . . .

"Do you enjoy books, Carrie Ann?"

"Yes, books and newspapers both."

"Have you read *North and South* by Elizabeth Gaskell?"

"I have, yes." She smiled with what seemed like fond recollection. "Papa always said it's the book that molded me into a humanitarian. That and the Bible, of course."

"Of course. And what is your favorite work of fiction thus far?"

"That's easy. It's *Emma* by Jane Austen."

"I should have guessed it. Most young ladies enjoy Austen novels."

"When I was a little girl, I used to imagine that I was Emma. I practiced talking like she did and walking regally as though I were she. I'd recite various passages, such as"—Carrie Ann stood—"'I may have lost my heart, but not my self-control.'" She lifted her chin and proceeded to act out a particular scene. "'Silly things do cease to be silly if they are done by sensible people in an impudent way.'"

Ruth laughed and applauded. "Brava!"

Carrie Ann made a grand curtsey.

Eli darkened the parlor's doorway just then and set down her haversack. Carrie Ann quickly sat and smoothed the folds of her skirt over her lap as if nothing out of the ordinary had occurred. Ruth, however, couldn't stop smiling. What fun she and Carrie Ann would have!

"Pardon my interruption, ladies." He gave a little bow. "I brought in your belongings, Miss Bell."

"Thank you."

"Come in, Colonel Kent."

He entered, pausing near Carrie Ann's chair. By now the young lady's cheeks had turned cherry red.

"I chided those men for their bad manners, Miss Bell, and refused them your horse."

"Again, my thanks, Colonel Kent."

Eli wore a sheepish grin and Ruth guessed what was coming next.

"Unfortunately, I must confiscate the mount. The Confederate army is in desperate need of horses and yours is a fine animal."

Carrie Ann sprang to her feet. In a heartbeat, she abandoned her chagrin for indignation. "But that horse was given to me . . . selected especially for me." She softened her tone, her blue eyes pleading. "Please? Won't you let me keep him?"

Ruth observed the exchange, ready to intercede if necessary. If Peyton were in Eli's shoes, he wouldn't be able to refuse such a sweet pout. Could Eli?

"Miss Bell, as much as I would like to give in to your request, I can't because of standing orders that come from my superiors."

"From General Ramseur?"

Was she fact-finding? Ruth touched her fingertips to her chin and tilted her head. Carrie Ann would make a delightful Union spy. She appeared so innocent. What soldier wouldn't divulge information and perhaps brag a little on himself in the process?

"The orders came from General Lee himself," Eli said. "As I said, horses are in great demand everywhere in the South."

"I'm aware of that, but—"

"Again, my apologies, but I can't disobey an order so that's the end of it."

"Carrie Ann, take heart." Ruth stood, sensing the end to Eli's patience too. "If one army doesn't take that horse, the other army will—that is, if deserters don't steal it first. You might as well allow the colonel to have him."

"What choice do I have?"

Grinning, Eli took a step closer to her. "I'll tell you what, Miss Bell, once this war is over I will personally see that you get another horse—an even finer one."

She shook her head. "I couldn't accept such a gift."

"Colonel Kent comes from a wealthy Richmond family," Ruth said with a small shrug. "Let him buy you a horse."

"No, thank you, Colonel."

So she's a mite stubborn too. Ruth made a mental note.

"Then allow me, Miss Bell, to make up for this entire unpleasant affair by escorting you this evening to a celebratory party in town."

Ruth stared on. Seemed Peyton had competition. Then again, Eli and Peyton were always rivals, gentlemanly rivals, at least until the war broke out.

"I'm honored by your invitation, Colonel, but I must refuse. I've had a long journey and I'm much too exhausted for a party." She looked at Ruth. "I'll probably fall asleep, standing right here, and won't wake up for days."

"Then I'd best see you to your room."

"Thank you, Aunt Ruth." Carrie Ann turned to Eli. "I hope you understand, Colonel."

"I do, of course." He bowed politely.

Tabitha entered. "Excuse me, Colonel, Miss Ruth . . ." She dutifully played her part of housekeeper well whenever they were occupied by Eli or another Confederate officer. "I made a meal for our guest." Tabitha's dark eyes rested on Carrie Ann. "You must be hungry."

"Famished!" With a parting glance at Eli and then Ruth, Carrie Ann crossed the room and followed Tabitha toward the kitchen.

Eli's gaze lingered in her wake. "She's quite delightful, although"—he turned to Ruth—"she nearly got herself killed, arguing and fussing with those men the way she did."

"You must admit they weren't the most savory of characters."

"Exactly. I'd hate to see something dreadful happen to your niece."

"Thank you, Eli." Ruth reclaimed her seat. "I'll speak with her about the matter."

He grinned. "Seems as though she inherited your pluck."

"Afraid so." Ruth narrowed her gaze. "Now, see here, Eli, I'll not have you trifling with her."

"I wouldn't dream of it."

Ruth nodded in slight satisfaction, although Eli didn't look the least bit deterred. "At any rate, she doesn't have the pedigree that your family desires for your future wife. Her father is a journalist by vocation and a farmer by trade in Woodstock."

"My family comes from a long line of horse breeders and tobacco farmers. The occupations are quite similar, really."

"Except farmers rarely own slaves."

"My father freed his slaves years before the war broke out. Those who chose to stay were compensated." Eli cleared his throat. "But back to the more pleasant subject of Miss Bell—she seems well-spoken and mannerly, and that says much to her having more education than many young ladies." His forehead crinkled and his dark gaze reflected his puzzlement. "She's not Peyton's sister? I understood you had only one brother, Aunt Ruth?"

Oh dear . . . "I should have specified. Yes. Carrie's stepfather is a journalist and farmer." Ruth gave a dramatic sigh as she altered the facts. "Alas, it's no secret that my brother was something of a philanderer." That statement was as true as April rain.

She paused to allow Eli to draw his own conclusions.

"She's Peyton's half sister?"

Ruth's fingertips flitted to her neckline. Mindful of the pesky nervous habit, she clasped her hands and placed them in her lap. "I would appreciate your discretion."

"Of course."

"I only recently learned that she existed, but I've grown fond of her and you can see why."

"Most certainly." Eli smiled and seemed to accept the piece of fiction without further inquiry. "She's obviously both intelligent and brave, although she needs someone to protect her from confronting the wrong man."

"Undoubtedly." Ruth sensed Eli wasn't about to give up thoughts of pursuing Carrie Ann. Rumor had it that unattached females of marrying age were a rare commodity from here all the way to Richmond.

"Is she spoken for? Promised to another?"

"Promised? I'm not sure, but I believe Carrie Ann has given her heart away to another. We were just getting to those details."

"Ah . . ." Eli momentarily pursed his lips. "If she's not betrothed, then I suppose I could still get my foot in the door, so to speak."

"There's always that possibility." Ruth wouldn't discourage him just yet. She would rather let Carrie Ann speak for herself. Besides, all Ruth had to go on at this point was an assumption, although the fact that Carrie Ann so quickly refused Eli's invitation reinforced the hunch that she harbored romantic feelings for Peyton.

"While I would rather entertain your new guest today, I have work to do." With a gentlemanly bow, he backed up toward the parlor's doorway. "I'll see you at supper this evening, Aunt Ruth."

"I look forward to it."

Eli took his leave and Ruth headed for the kitchen. It appeared that, like her horse, Carrie Ann was in high demand.

CHAPTER 16

"This bedroom . . ." Carrie glanced around the pretty, albeit faded papered room. A cherry-finished four-poster bed occupied the far wall, complete with an ivory lace dust ruffle. She ambled to it and ran her hand along the top of the patchwork quilt. Then she noticed the two plump feather pillows resting at the headboard. How she ached to stretch out and sleep. Glancing at her hostess, Carrie felt ashamed to admit that she hadn't slept in a real bed since the farm burned down and, even then, she'd shared the bed with her two sisters. "I'm sure I'll be very comfortable here. Thank you, Aunt Ruth."

"Your room at the inn in Woodstock was nicer, I imagine."

"On the contrary. My mother—rather, stepmother, sisters, and I shared a very small space."

"Seems to me that innkeeper should have, at least, provided adequate rooms for you all."

"At the time of our bargain, I was desperate for lodging. My sisters were young and tired and our mother was ill of mind as a result of the fire. I accepted Mr. Veyschmidt's less-than-fair terms so we'd have a roof over our heads."

"I'm sorry to hear you were put in such a regrettable position."

"Don't pity me. My family and I have fared better than many in the Valley."

"My pity is not easily given, I assure you."

Carrie took the woman's words to heart. "The hardships of so many are the reasons I didn't dare complain to Mr. Veyschmidt about our cramped accommodations." She walked to the small round cherry-finished table with its two matching hard-back chairs. They'd been placed near the window. She could write here, and Carrie felt blessed, indeed. "In any case, I'm very glad to be here."

"Do you plan on returning to Woodstock anytime soon?" Aunt Ruth strode to the large oak wardrobe, standing tall beside a dressing table and mirror.

"No. I can better help my family by working for you."

Everything came into question again. Carrie supposed she was obligated to send back money, despite the fact that her stepmother and Margaret weren't her direct relation. She felt certain Joshua hadn't lied. Why would he? What could he possibly hope to gain by lying? But regardless of whether it was true or not, they were all the family she'd ever known.

"Mr. Veyschmidt doesn't pay us with cash money," she added softly. "Room and board only."

"Hmm . . ."

Aunt Ruth eyed her closely—or was it critically?

"I'm a very hard worker, and capable. You can assign me any duties and I'll prove it."

"My dear, I don't doubt your abilities."

"Forgive me for assuming you did."

"All is forgiven. After all, it's difficult to know whom one can trust these days."

"Yes, ma'am, it surely is."

"But you can trust me." Aunt Ruth's smile was as warm and comforting as the oven-fresh bread and jam she'd eaten only minutes ago. "You should know, however, that I like to pamper and spoil my . . . companions."

"Pamper and spoil?" Those two words were quite foreign to Carrie, especially in reference to herself.

Aunt Ruth opened the closet doors and pulled out the prettiest calico dress of beige and green. "I think this one will complement your hair coloring and complexion, don't you?"

"For me?"

"Yes. And this one also."

Another dress, this one made of a dark blue and brown checkered print.

"It complements your eyes, don't you think?"

"Auth Ruth, I can never repay you for these . . ."

"They're gifts. Besides, Eli believes you're my niece. I can't have my niece wearing—" She crossed the room and lifted the shoulder of the too-large dress that Miss Phoebe had bestowed on her last night. "Just where in the world did you acquire this dreadful garment?"

"Um, well . . ." Carrie felt her face heating to a simmer.

"And, no personal offense, but you reek of cheap perfume."

"Trust me, I smelled infinitely worse before soaking in bubbles last night." But it seemed Joshua had been correct when he said she smelled like a saloon girl. "It's a long story. You see, I was wearing a deserter's uniform when Colonel Collier arrested me."

"Arrested you?" Aunt Ruth's hazel eyes widened. "Good heavens!"

"It was before he knew I was a female."

"Oh, my!"

Carrie clamped her mouth shut. She'd rather remember Peyton's gallantry over her folly. "Again, Aunt Ruth, it's a long, involved tale. But I promise to tell you the specifics when I'm not so tired."

"Very well, I look forward to hearing them, my dear." A spark of mischief entered her gaze. "*All* of them."

"Yes, ma'am." If any sophisticated matron could handle all of them without judging Carrie too harshly, Aunt Ruth probably could.

"I'll leave you to undress. Tabitha is filling a tub of hot water for you, and she'll be in shortly to assist you with your bath."

Carrie waved away the offer. "Thank you, but I don't require assistance."

"Perhaps not, but my pampered niece or companion does."

She didn't dare argue. "Thank you."

With a smile Aunt Ruth walked to the bedroom door, her petticoats rustling with each step. "After your bath, Tabitha will help you into a nightgown in which you can comfortably nap. She'll awaken you before teatime. Eli may be in attendance. I believe he has set his sights on you."

Carrie laughed. Certainly Aunt Ruth made her remark in jest.

"I fail to see what's amusing, my dear." Aunt Ruth paused near the doorway. Her tone wasn't harsh, but merely laden with curiosity. "Enlighten me."

"You mean to say you weren't joking just now?"

"I should say not. Eli asked me if you were promised to another. Clearly he's interested in pursuing you."

Carrie's jaw slacked. "Oh . . ." She stared at the blue draperies gracing the two long windows. How should she respond?

"You're surprised."

"Very. Men usually aren't interested in me unless they're waiting for me to serve their supper."

"Surely Peyton didn't make you wait on him."

"Oh, no, ma'am. But he's different."

Aunt Ruth closed the bedroom door softly. "How so, if you don't mind my asking. I mean . . . well, I guess I need to know if you'd like me to discourage Eli."

"Yes, please do discourage him." Carrie's heart was at least as stubborn as she was, and the only man she'd ever love was Peyton.

But, of course, he was far above her station in life. He'd all but come right out and said so.

"You're promised to another, then?"

"In a manner of speaking." Carrie lowered her chin. "Although I don't expect anything will ever come of it."

"Peyton?"

Carrie's gazed snapped up a little too quickly. She met Aunt Ruth's inquiring expression. A little, knowing smile worked its way across the older woman's thin lips.

"A schoolgirl infatuation, Aunt Ruth." Carrie chose to make light of her feelings. "Your nephew is too charming for his own good."

"How well I know that! Peyton has Tabitha and me wrapped around his little finger—and it's been that way since he was a toddler."

Carrie smiled. Humor felt better than the embarrassment causing her temperature to rise on this already too-warm August day.

"You're sure it's just infatuation?"

"Positive."

"You're hardly a schoolgirl, Carrie Ann."

"All I meant was that I'm not very . . . experienced with matters of the heart. But you must know that Peyton—I mean, the colonel—never said or made me think there was ever anything more between us than a passing friendship. The colonel was always a gentleman to me."

"Except when he arrested you?" Aunt Ruth wore that same mischievous grin that Carrie glimpsed earlier.

"Except then, but only because I was being stubborn."

"I see." Aunt Ruth's grin remained. "Well, perhaps I can shed a bit of light on your situation by confessing that never in my nephew's life has he sent a young lady to our home and asked that I care for her—and she for me. That is, Peyton may have promised you a paying job so you'd come here, Carrie Ann, and he'll pay you whatever wages he's promised, have no doubt. But both Tabitha and I sensed Peyton had an ulterior motive for your visit, and our guess is that he has feelings for you too."

"Alas, I wish it were true, but I must respectfully disagree. I'm here for all the reasons I stated previously." Carrie leaned against one of the bed-posts. "Besides, Peyton concluded that working at the field hospital with the wounded and dying men was taking its toll on me, and maybe it was. You see, when I arrived, Peyton put me to work in the field hospital under Dr. LaFont's supervision."

"Paul-Henri?" Aunt Ruth smiled. "He's a dear friend."

"He saved Peyton's life, as I understand." Carrie realized her mistake. "I meant to say, he saved Colonel Collier's life."

"You've slipped more than once, my dear. So . . . you and my nephew are on a first-name basis?"

"Friends, nothing more."

"Carrie Ann, why would a colonel in the United States Army bother with you or any other young lady whom he apprehended, mistakenly or not, if he didn't have feelings for you? Goodness, but Peyton could have passed you to one of his corporals and instructed him to deposit you at a nearby farm or church and be done with you."

The thought had crossed Carrie's mind. And Aunt Ruth was right. Peyton's debt to her would have been paid had he safely delivered her somewhere else after rescuing her from that tree.

"As for Eli, I will strongly suggest that one of the other unattached ladies in Winchester is a better choice for him." Aunt Ruth sighed dramatically.

"My neighbor's daughter, Lavinia, has her eye on him. Perhaps I'll point out her finer attributes. I'm sure she has them."

"Lavinia?" Carrie knew that name. "Is she Peyton's former fiancée?"

Aunt Ruth arched a brow. "He shared that much with you, did he?"

Carrie blushed.

"Yes, she's the very one."

"Is he still in love with her? He's a changed man. Maybe he wishes he had a second chance . . ."

Before Carrie could finish her sentence, Aunt Ruth was shaking her head. "No, my dear, Peyton never loved Lavinia. She trapped him into proposing marriage and then Peyton felt obligated to go through with it. What a blessed relief when she didn't show up for the wedding."

"I'm not sure I would have either, considering Peyton's actions."

Again, Aunt Ruth arched a stately eyebrow.

Carrie wasn't winning her argument over Peyton's intentions, and yet she refused to foster hopes that he regarded her as anything more than a trusted friend and employee.

"Regardless, Carrie Ann, you make a good point. I'm not excusing my nephew's actions years ago, but Lavinia is not without her flaws. Let's just say that I'm ecstatic she is not my niece by marriage and leave it there."

"Is it cruel to encourage Colonel Kent to pursue her?"

"Hmm . . . well, he is the enemy." Aunt Ruth gave a deliciously wicked little laugh. "Seriously, though—Eli's a grown man, and I'm confident that he can handle himself around the likes of Lavinia."

"Yes, ma'am."

"And to think that now I'll have an ally in you when the Monteague women come to tea. You see, as a Negro, Tabitha isn't acceptable company to my neighbors. I'm grateful Eli doesn't regard her as a slave. Nevertheless, you can understand why I'm glad you're here."

"I think you are awfully blessed to have a good friendship with Tabitha." While she was rough around the edges, Carrie liked the older black woman who had served her lunch. "Papa had a good friend who was a free black man and a sharecropping farmer. Sometimes I'd pass away hours listening to him and my father talk. They'd drink cider and smoke their pipes. And I loved tagging along with Papa when he visited different communities in the Valley to get newsworthy stories for his paper. Papa and I spoke with all manner of people, and in general, I enjoyed keeping company with them all." Carrie caught herself. "But I'm rambling, aren't I?"

"No. And how precious you are." Wearing another warm smile, Aunt Ruth crossed the room and placed her palms on Carrie's upper arms. "I do so look forward to getting to know you. But my suggestion for now, dear, is that you take your bath and have some rest." Her smile vanished and frown lines appeared on her aged and powdered forehead. "Suffice it to say you'll need your wits about you later when the Monteague ladies arrive."

～ の ～

"What are you cryin' about, girl?"

Carrie wasn't crying. She tried to tell that to Tabitha, but no words came out. How could she possibly communicate her feelings as she stared into the oak-framed mirror? The reflection looking back was no one she'd ever seen before. It was someone who looked lovely, someone who, perhaps, Carrie had seen only in her wildest imaginings.

"Hmph!" Tabitha placed her hands on her narrow hips. "You don't like the dress? Then put on a different one."

"The dress is beautiful."

"I wouldn't go that far, but it's passable."

"I've never had anything so fine in my life!" And here Carrie had thought the brown dress Miss Phoebe had acquired for her last night was the finest garment she'd ever worn. It paled in comparison to this beige and green calico. "So, you see . . . these are happy tears."

"Bah! They'll put red blotches on your face just the same as sad 'uns, and then you'll show up downstairs for tea looking like your best friend just got hanged."

Joshua. Carrie grimaced inwardly at the thought of him swinging from a rope. He may no longer qualify as her best friend, but she'd never betray him.

Nor would she hurt or embarrass Peyton or Aunt Ruth.

Carrie swallowed her tears along with her sentiments. She had to look her best at teatime.

"Now, let's see if I can do something with this bird's nest you call hair." Tabitha ran her hands over Carrie's hair. The woman had taken out the braids before Carrie's bath so, in the hours since, Carrie's thick tresses hung in a mass of tangled auburn waves. "C'mon over here and sit down at the dressing table."

Carrie did as Tabitha bid her and sat on the cushioned stool, facing the mirror. A hint of lavender reached her nose as Tabitha smoothed lotion through her curls. Then she expertly pinned them up in a knotted chignon, leaving several tendrils coiling prettily around her face. Carrie marveled at her transformation and wondered if her family would recognize her if they could see her now.

"Run along downstairs, Miss Carrie Ann." Tabitha shooed her toward the door. "Ruth is waiting on you in the parlor."

"Thank you, Tabitha. You're a miracle worker." After giving the woman a quick smile, she left the bedroom and bounded down the steps. As she reached the parlor, Aunt Ruth met her at the doorway.

"My dear girl, one never descends a stairwell so hastily unless one is shouting, 'Fire!' at the same time."

"Yes, ma'am." She'd have to recall more ladylike manners, although she'd not had to use them in some time. "I apologize. I didn't want to keep you waiting."

"You, dear girl," Aunt Ruth said, her gaze falling over her, "look lovely. And I do appreciate your promptness, since our guests will be here soon." Looking pleased, she motioned Carrie into the room and closed the door behind them. "I can see why my nephew is taken with you."

"No, Aunt Ruth . . ." Before Carrie closed her eyes and slept this afternoon, she thought long and hard about the presumption. "The colonel," she said, deliberately, "made it clear that he did not want to encourage me in the 'wrong way.'"

"Well, of course he didn't. Peyton is a gentleman. But I'm sure he means to encourage you in the right way."

Her shoulders sagged ever so slightly. She wouldn't win this argument.

"However, for the sake of Eli and our neighbors, you are Peyton's half sister."

Carrie's eyes widened.

"I've said you're my niece and I only have one older brother." Sadness crept across the older woman's age-lined face and settled in her eyes. She sat on the settee. "Such a tragedy when Philip and his wife, Eleanor, were killed after their carriage tumbled over a steep embankment. They were vacationing in France and Philip was driving an unfamiliar road."

"Yes, the colonel told me." Carrie took a seat in one of the three armchairs. "A terrible shame."

"Yes. I adored my brother, which is why I have always adored Peyton. He was just a boy of twelve years old when his parents were killed—and a hellion to boot. Why, he was nearly the death of poor Tabitha and me."

Carrie could well imagine.

"Finally, I had no other choice but to put him in boarding school. The boy was fairly terrorizing Winchester. A family friend was a senator at the time and wrote the necessary letter of recommendation which earned Peyton entry into West Point Academy. He went on to college there also."

"He mentioned that. You must be very proud of him."

"Indeed I am. And now he's a Christian man." Aunt Ruth sighed. "His salvation was my sincerest hope and prayer, and God answered it."

Carrie enjoyed hearing the story, particularly as she was interested in its topic. Nonetheless, she'd spent the better part of her childhood listening to her elders tell their tales, when she'd accompanied Papa as he collected newsworthy items for the *Bell Tower*.

"But as for our little fib—"

"Yes, about that. What if someone recognizes me? I am, after all, from Woodstock."

"We'll have to deal with that obstacle when it presents itself. For the time being, you're the niece I never knew I had until recently. I will introduce you as such to our neighbors who are coming for tea, Frances and Lavinia Monteague." Aunt Ruth tipped her head. "Will you play along?"

Did she have a choice?

Carrie thought it over, wondering what Papa would say. Of course, journalists frequently disguised themselves in order to get compelling stories. Perhaps she'd write about this experience as well as about nursing wounded men in a Union camp.

Meeting Aunt Ruth's questioning gaze, she smiled. "Yes, I'll play along."

"Oh, thank you, my dear." Aunt Ruth clasped her hands together and pressed them over her heart. "What fun this will be."

"So . . . did I know my father? Your brother? Just in case the subject comes up."

"No, you never knew him. Your mother made a deathbed confession, and you contacted me after you learned Philip was your biological father."

Plausible. "All right."

"You were an innocent victim of circumstance."

Carrie couldn't help but grin. Aunt Ruth should be a writer—a fiction writer.

"I did, however, tell Eli that your stepfather was a journalist in Woodstock."

"Oh . . . well, I suppose that's fine as there were many journalists there before the war writing for the larger newspaper. Papa's *Bell Tower*, a small publication by comparison, covered human interest stories as well as local politics."

"Then the explanation will work?"

"I'd say so." Carrie laughed softly before turning serious once more. "But I'm sure I needn't remind you of what Sir Walter Scott wrote. 'Oh, what a tangled web we weave—'"

"'When first we practice to deceive.' Yes, I know the quotation well."

"I supposed as much."

"But here in Winchester, we women—loyalists and secessionists alike—have had to tell many fibs to ensure our very existence. Now, let me tell you about the Monteagues."

As Aunt Ruth filled her in on the neighbors, Carrie wondered about her new friend. She had never met any woman like Ruth Collier—independent, intelligent, even a tad mischievous. She couldn't help but like her. But could she trust her?

That remained to be seen.

Chapter 17

A more excruciating tea Carrie had never attended, and primarily painful because she had to gaze at the most beautiful woman she'd ever seen. Peyton's former fiancée. Carrie could well understand why he, or any man, would be attracted to her. Having a perfectly heart-shaped face—the kind Carrie had only read about in fiction—and almond-brown eyes, Miss Lavinia Monteague seemed to embody the whole of femininity as Carrie knew it. What's more, a woman like her would possess far too much dignity to reside, even temporarily, with Union soldiers, no matter what the circumstances.

Lavinia sat in the chair next to her mother and smoothed down the skirt of her sapphire-blue gown. The color accentuated Miss Monteague's lily-white skin and curvy figure, causing Carrie to feel decidedly insignificant.

But then Miss Monteague opened her mouth and spoke, complaining first about her horrid, week-long journey to Winchester, and next, how utterly boring this town was compared to Staunton, where she'd attended numerous parties.

Did she not realize that a war was going on?

Lavinia prattled on about an incident at a party, ending a long-winded story with, "So I said to Veronica Lewis . . ." Miss Monteague turned to her mother. "You remember Veronica. Her father is an attorney at the prestigious law firm Lewis, Cardwell, and Blinkman."

"Oh, yes, of course." Her mother sipped from the porcelain teacup.

"So I said to Veronica, 'You must be joking.'" Miss Monteague released a peal of laughter.

Her mother chuckled merrily.

Was that remark amusing? Carrie glanced at Aunt Ruth, who twiddled her thumbs.

"What a witty comeback, Lavinia." Turning slightly toward Carrie, the older woman hurled a glance upward.

At last Carrie had a reason to smile.

"So, Miss Collier . . . my, but it feels strange to be sitting here speaking to Peyton's half sister." Miss Monteague gave Carrie a speculative glance.

"It feels strange to be sitting here and speaking with you, Miss Monteague. Even stranger to be referred to as *Miss Collier*. You see, that's incorrect." A fib was one thing, but denying her identity, her very self, was quite a different matter.

"She's a Collier by birth," came Aunt Ruth's speedy explanation. "However, her adoptive father's last name is Bell."

"Carrie Ann Bell. My, my . . ." Mrs. Monteague smiled. "Your name even has a ring to it." She laughed. "Like your last name. Bell."

Her daughter's countenance lit up as if the pun had just resonated with her too. "Oh, yes . . . Bell. Ring to it."

The two Monteague women twittered together like a couple of chickadees on the back fence.

Carrie sighed at their attempted humor and wondered how long this gathering would last.

"So what do you do with yourself, Miss Bell?" Mrs. Monteague set her teacup and saucer on the small table beside her chair. "Were you away at boarding school or are you employed somewhere? A scullery maid, perhaps?"

"It must not have been good whatever it was, Mama," Miss Monteague said as if Carrie were no longer in the room. "She's here living with her auntie whom she never knew until recently."

"That's true, Lavinia, my pet."

Both women stared at Carrie, wide-eyed, as if they expected refutation.

They'd get none. Their rudeness didn't warrant one. Scullery maid, indeed! Although, the work Carrie had done at the Wayfarers Inn was equally lowly.

Bringing her teacup to her lips, Carrie sipped the brew. Mmm . . . rich black tea from the Orient. "Aunt Ruth, where did you get this wonderful tea?" she asked.

"We're fortunate, dear, that Colonel Kent and his men are . . . guests in our home," Aunt Ruth said. "You see, they procured Federal currency and purchased foodstuff that we wouldn't have had otherwise . . . like black tea."

"I read somewhere," Carrie said, "that General Ramseur was lamenting the fallen Confederate currency but stated that he and his men could buy almost anything for their table in Southern towns with Yankee money."

"Indeed." Aunt Ruth peered across the room at her neighbors. "Carrie Ann is studying to be a journalist, like her adoptive father. What's more, she's been a volunteer, nursing wounded men on the battlefield."

Miss Monteague's upper lip curled. "How dreadful, the nursing part. As for your interest in journalism . . ." She produced a dainty guffaw. "That's a man's world, Miss Bell."

"Nursing is what Ruth and Miss Bell have in common, Lavinia." Again, Mrs. Monteague behaved as though neither woman sat in the room. "Ruth was a nurse during that dreadful conflict almost twenty years ago. You were too young to remember."

"The Mexican-American War?" Impressed, Carrie glanced at her hostess. Oh, how she'd love to write an article based upon Aunt Ruth's experience.

"I tried to talk her out of going, but she insisted." Mrs. Monteague brushed crumbs off the skirt of her dark brown dress. "But, bear in mind, Ruth didn't have a husband or children to care for like I did."

Carrie felt the jab. Would Aunt Ruth be insulted? Hurt?

"A choice I freely made, dear Frances. I had my offers of marriage, as you well know."

"Swimming upstream, Harm used to say." A sentimental look softened Mrs. Monteague's features. "Ruth is always swimming upstream, against the current of social propriety."

Any offenses were forgotten as Aunt Ruth seemed to share in the nostalgia. "Yes, Harm told me the same thing many times. And he was correct."

The air of animosity—which had fairly crackled in the room only moments before—vanished, and the two older women suddenly behaved like long-lost friends.

"Oh, but didn't we have good times, Ruth?"

"Yes, we certainly did."

Miss Monteague yawned, unabashed. "So has anyone heard from that scoundrel Peyton?"

Aunt Ruth snapped from her walk down memory lane. "Oh, well, I believe Carrie Ann was the last to see him, weren't you, dear?"

"Um . . ." She thought that was supposed to be secret. "Yes."

"Carrie Ann heard of that recent skirmish near Charles Town," Aunt Ruth said, "and she went there straightaway to see if she could be of some help. Amazingly, she had a chance to visit with Peyton."

Miss Monteague's dark eyes fixed on her. "Is that so?"

"Yes, and he's in good spirits and good health." Carrie wasn't sure what more to say.

"Edward said the Confederates routed the Federals," Mrs. Monteague said, "and the Union army retreated northward where those nasty invaders belong."

Carrie brought her fingertips up to nervously brush the side of her neck. She didn't want to say too much. Best to let Aunt Ruth make the replies.

"We're anxious to hear news of this young lady with whom Peyton has been corresponding," Mrs. Monteague said. "Do you know anything about her?"

"Yes, Carrie Ann knows all about her."

She did? Carrie stared at Aunt Ruth.

"Her name is . . . Lois, isn't it?"

Feeling awkward, Carrie half shrugged and half nodded.

"And Peyton is quite smitten, I'm afraid."

"Lois?" Miss Monteague's features contorted and she looked as though she'd been smacked in the face with a wet dishrag. "I've always disliked that name for some odd reason. And now I'm being told that Peyton is serious about a young lady by the name of Lois? It's almost too much for me to take in."

"What do you know of her, Ruth?" Mrs. Monteague asked. "What does Lois's father do?"

Carrie mirrored Aunt Ruth's raised eyebrows. "He's a . . . surgeon," Carrie blurted.

"Yes, that's it. I couldn't recall for a moment, but you're correct, Carrie Ann. He's a surgeon."

"I suppose Peyton met Lois while he was convalescing last year in Washington."

"You're correct." Aunt Ruth smiled before politely sipping her tea.

"I hope you know that I plan to put an end to this affinity Peyton has for this woman." Miss Monteague's eyes flashed. "He made a promise to me and I intend to see that he keeps it." She stood abruptly and thumped her teacup down.

Aunt Ruth rose in less haste. "It's too late, Lavinia."

"Hardly, if he's just now corresponding with . . . Lois."

"No, what I mean is . . ." She drew in a breath. "I'm afraid I made up Lois to protect Peyton's real love interest." Aunt Ruth peered at Carrie then back at Miss Monteague. "There is no Lois. But, you see, Peyton is . . . married."

Carrie felt the blood ebbing from her face as she feared what would come next. "No, Aunt Ruth, please . . ." She pushed to her feet and shook her head.

"Carrie Ann is not his half sister. We merely thought she'd be safer if we lied and said she was."

"I've always said you aren't a good liar, Ruth."

"How right you are, Frances."

"He's married to . . . her?" Miss Monteague shrieked and pointed at Carrie. "But . . . look at her. She's as thin as a reed." She pouted. "Pretty enough, I suppose, but her father is a journalist from Woodstock. Peyton has married far beneath his social standing. All our friends will reject him for this poor decision."

Carrie's gut cinched.

"I highly doubt that." Aunt Ruth's voice sounded smooth as velvet.

Carrie's mind began to swim. If she played this game of pretense, that would mean she was a Union officer's wife in Confederate Winchester. She was in more danger here than she was among the Yankee cavalrymen.

"Aunt Ruth, word of this cannot be spread. The Confederate authorities might jail me—or worse."

"Not to worry, dear." Aunt Ruth looked at the Monteague women. "I trust you won't divulge this news."

Miss Monteague huffed and pursed her lips.

"Whatever are you doing in Winchester, Mrs. Collier?" The last to stand,

Mrs. Monteague slowly got to her feet. "Shouldn't you be in Washington where you'd be safe among your . . . own kind?"

"Yes." Carrie glanced at Aunt Ruth. "I probably need to leave immediately."

"Nonsense, dear." Aunt Ruth took Carrie's hand between both of hers. "The Monteagues will keep our secret. Heaven knows I've kept plenty of theirs."

In all the exchanges of glances, Carrie could tell that it was so. But what would Peyton say?

"Now, let's all sit like civilized women." Aunt Ruth motioned for her guests to take their places.

"I'm sure Colonel Kent will overlook the fact that you're the enemy's wife," Aunt Ruth said. "After all, he and your husband were the best of friends at West Point."

"It was a delightful summer the year Colonel Kent visited Winchester." Miss Monteague smiled dreamily then affixed Carrie with a hard stare. "Before the war."

"So I assumed." Carrie turned to Aunt Ruth. "Still, I don't think this was a wise plan."

"Oh, stop fretting, Mrs. Collier. It's most unbecoming." Miss Monteague sipped her tea. "Your secret is perfectly safe with us."

"Pray, what secret is that?"

Carrie swung her gaze toward the smooth male voice, and found Colonel Kent darkening the parlor's doorway. The teacup and saucer clattered as her hand shook until Aunt Ruth took it and offered a refill.

"Why, Colonel Kent." Aunt Ruth gave a tenuous smile. "Please come in and join us. May I pour a cup of tea for you?"

"Thank you, but no. It's much too hot for tea—unless it's served over a block of ice."

"I'm sure that can be arranged—come November."

Smiling at the jest, the colonel strode into the room.

Aunt Ruth nodded toward her guests. "You, of course, know Miss Lavinia Monteague and her mother, Mrs. Harmon Monteague."

"I do, indeed." The colonel gave the ladies a polite bow. His ebony hair and suntanned face seemed accentuated by his faded, butternut frock. Then his deep brown eyes landed on Carrie. "And Miss Bell and I met earlier. In fact, I had a lengthy conversation with a mutual friend of ours."

"Oh?" Carrie's heart hammered. She thought it might leap into her throat. "And who would that be?"

"A man who, like you, hails from Woodstock." The corners of the colonel's lips twitched slightly but gave no real indication as to whether he was angry or amused.

Instinctively, Carrie knew who he meant. Her insides caved.

"Major Joshua Blevens."

CHAPTER 18

To say that Lieutenant Colonel Elijah Kent had a commanding presence was putting it mildly. He made an imposing yet charming figure, and Carrie thought his aura filled the entire parlor. However, she didn't get the impression that he was interested romantically in her as Aunt Ruth claimed.

"You do remember Major Blevens, don't you, Miss Bell? He escorted you here."

"How could I forget him, Colonel? I've known him all my life."

"And I'm told that you're aware of his . . . duties to the Confederate army."

"I am, and I believe he and I have an understanding regarding his . . . duties." The colonel obviously wanted to be sure she kept Joshua's dual identity to herself. And she would. After all, she'd promised.

Glancing across the room at the neighbors, Carrie couldn't say she trusted them to keep quiet about Aunt Ruth's blunder. Their gazes were bouncing between Carrie and the colonel as if they watched a shuttlecock match.

"What duties are you speaking about?" Miss Monteague finally inquired, batting her lashes ever so innocently.

To his credit, Colonel Kent wasn't persuaded to answer. "My apologies, ladies, but Miss Bell and I have business to discuss. Won't you please excuse us?"

His dark eyes moved from the Monteagues to Carrie, their depths, deep and somewhat fathomless. Fear nipped at Carrie, but she refused to allow it to take hold.

"Oh, but her name isn't Miss Bell," Mrs. Monteague spouted, wide-eyed. "This is Peyton's wife."

"His . . . wife?" The colonel appeared dumbstruck and Carrie almost grinned.

Almost. Until she realized what a terrible fix she was in. How could Peyton's aunt do this to her? She sent an annoyed glance at the older woman.

Aunt Ruth rose and strode to the parlor doors, sliding them closed. "This news must not leave this parlor." She turned and stared imploringly at Colonel Kent. "Please. We were going to tell you, but—"

"I don't believe it." His dark brown eyes fixed on Carrie's. "Everyone in this room knows that Miss Bell is not Peyton's . . . how do I put this delicately? She's not his type." He sent a glance toward Miss Monteague. "I mean that with all due respect, of course."

"Of course, and I agree." She focused on Carrie. "She's not at all Peyton's type."

"I told you before that Peyton's a changed man," Aunt Ruth said, each word spoken with a clipped tone. "His wife will attest to it."

That much Carrie felt comfortable attesting to. She gave a nod.

Colonel Kent, on the other hand, didn't appear convinced in the least. He turned to Aunt Ruth's guests. "Miss Lavinia, Mrs. Monteague, I'm afraid I must ask you both to leave. I have pressing business here." His eyes locked on the younger of the two. "However, I trust I will see you later at the celebratory party, Miss Lavinia."

"You will indeed, Colonel Kent." Suddenly Miss Monteague appeared in her element. She glided across the parlor. "Come, Mama. We have to find something for me to wear tonight."

"Of course, pet." The older woman dutifully followed.

Aunt Ruth opened the parlor doors and called for Tabitha, who showed the two neighbor ladies out. When only the three of them remained in the parlor, Aunt Ruth slid the doors closed once more.

"Oh, Eli, I intended to tell you later, but I was so overjoyed with the match that I blurted out the news of Peyton's marriage to the Monteagues and gave Carrie Ann away. However, I'm sure they'll keep it quiet."

"I think you may have overestimated their abilities in that regard, Aunt Ruth." The Confederate colonel gave her a hard stare then strode over to

Carrie, who still sat on the settee. She supposed he was handsome, but she disliked his intimidating manner. Amusingly, it brought out the rebel in Carrie.

But for Peyton's sake, she studied a point across the room. She pondered the idea of telling Colonel Kent the truth—that Aunt Ruth did, indeed, blurt out the news, except it was a lie. If Joshua found out that she posed as a Union colonel's wife, he'd likely strangle her—that is, if Peyton didn't do it first. Then again, Peyton adored his aunt. How could Carrie betray him by exposing her as a talebearer?

"Well, Miss Bell—or should I say, *Mrs. Collier*? What do you have to say about all of this? Is it true? You married Peyton?"

Carrie hesitated.

"It was a battlefield wedding," Aunt Ruth said. "Eventually they'll have a traditional ceremony, and if the war is over, you, of course, will be invited."

"That's enough, Aunt Ruth," the colonel said, irritation thick in his tone. "I don't know what kind of scheme you've concocted, but I'm interested in the truth."

Something darker than his gaze passed between them. Aunt Ruth gave a little huff and sat in one of the vacated armchairs.

Carrie knew right then what she'd do. She would go along with this "scheme"—at least for now. Then, later, she'd leave and continue doing what needed to be done: looking for Sarah Jane—and maybe finding Papa too.

"You want the truth, Colonel, then I shall tell you." Carrie stood, pretending she had as much tenacity as Jane Austen's Emma. "I fell in love with Peyton last year in April when he and his cavalrymen came through Woodstock. Peyton was wounded and I sutured his forearm. Months later I heard from another soldier that he fell at Gettysburg. I was deeply saddened." Carrie stepped toward the empty hearth. "Recently, however, I learned the Union cavalry was in the Valley again, and I left Woodstock under the guise of finding my runaway sister."

"To find Peyton? But you thought he was dead."

"I always wondered if it was hearsay, but I couldn't very well check in the newspapers because he's a Northerner." She faced Colonel Kent. "The only time I got my hands on a Yankee paper was if one was left behind at the inn. But no Federal troops have been in Woodstock for some time." That was the truth. "I love him. I told Joshua that, but he doesn't know all the particulars, although he saw me kiss Peyton good-bye. Up until the day I left Woodstock, I hadn't seen Joshua since the war began."

"I find your story compelling, but highly suspect." Colonel Kent folded his arms. "On the other hand, as a serving girl, I imagine Peyton's inheritance was more temptation than you could handle."

Carrie lost her verbal footing and frowned at Aunt Ruth. *Inheritance?*

"Honestly, Eli, must you be so boorish?"

Slowly, he turned. "One more word from you, Aunt Ruth, and I will arrest both of you on suspicion of spying."

She parted her lips then wisely pressed them together. But the threat didn't stop her from sending Carrie an apologetic look.

"Colonel Kent, I'm not aware of any inheritance. The reason I fell in love with Peyton is because—" Indignation bubbled up in Carrie and flamed in her face. "On second thought, it's none of your business. Go ahead and arrest me." She held out her wrists.

"Don't tempt me, Miss Bell."

"I wouldn't dream of it," she replied tartly. She lowered her arms back to her sides and walked toward him, her chin held high. Oh, but she longed to slap his handsomely arrogant face. "And it's *Mrs. Collier* to you."

He blinked and Aunt Ruth produced a little cough, but neither reaction was enough to halt her as she headed to the doorway. Colonel Kent didn't try to restrain her when she pushed the doors open. All Carrie knew was that she couldn't stay here, feeling trapped, any longer. She needed a plan.

A plan of escape!

※

"Oh, now you've done it, Eli." Ruth stood and went after Carrie. She reached the stairway in time to see the young lady ascend with a flash of petticoat and black stockings. "Oh, my . . ."

Behind her, Eli chuckled. "Why does Shakespeare's *Taming of the Shrew* suddenly come to mind?"

"This is no time for jokes."

"Come now, Aunt Ruth. Surely that's the reason Peyt sent her to you, to groom her in the ways of dignified social etiquette."

"Well . . ." Ruth wished she'd thought of that. It made perfect sense.

"And, rest assured, Aunt Ruth, I believe her." Eli's dark eyes moved from the now-empty stairway to Ruth. "That is, I believe she loves Peyt and that she knew nothing of his inheritance until moments ago. I saw it in her face and I could tell she wasn't lying."

"She is easy to read, isn't she?"

"I know from our years of friendship that Peyt always wanted a woman who loved him regardless of the trust his parents left him." His brows pinched, causing deep lines to form above the bridge of his nose. "But a serving girl?"

"Eli, she had no choice but to move into that *inn*. Her father is a journalist, who has been away for two years, and her stepmother took ill after their farm burned to the ground. Carrie had to find a place where her family could get room and board."

"Yes, well, I guess that can be overlooked, particularly since I've already heard as much from Major Blevens. Still, allowing her to come here wasn't wise—unless, of course, Peyt feels confident that the Union army will triumph in the Valley." Eli gave a wag of his head. "But they won't. Just like in the past, the Confederates will defeat those Yankee invaders."

"I sense a lack of enthusiasm on your part, Eli."

"On the contrary. I'm very much enthused. Nonetheless, I can't promise how long your new niece or you will be safe here in Winchester."

"We shall take our chances."

"I had a feeling you would say something like that."

Ruth smiled. "Now, if you'll excuse me, I'd best see to Carrie Ann. No doubt she's upset."

"Then I look forward to seeing you both at dinner tonight." Eli gave her a parting bow.

As Ruth made her way upstairs, she prayed for guidance. She'd been a veritable old windbag. She couldn't blame Carrie Ann if she was angry. Ruth hoped she wouldn't want to leave. How could she allow it? Somehow Ruth knew that Peyton would never forgive her if Carrie left. However, she couldn't very well hold Carrie here against her will.

Her usual confidence shaken, Ruth's hand trembled as she knocked on the bedroom door. "It's Aunt Ruth, dear . . . may I come in?" She knocked again.

Carrie swung open the door. "It's your house. You may do whatever you please."

"Oh, now, Carrie Ann . . . don't be angry with me."

"Pretending to be your niece was one thing, but pretending to be Peyton's wife is quite another and I won't do it."

"Shhh!" Ruth quickly closed the door. Leaning her shoulders against it for several long moments, Ruth felt any remaining fight drain out of her. Slowly, she crossed the room and sat down in one of the two chairs near the window. "I can't argue, Carrie Ann, especially after I voiced such an outrageous idea. I don't know what possessed me to blurt out such a thing. I only wanted to protect you."

"Protect me?" Carrie Ann shook her head, setting loose several curls. "Thanks to you, my life is now in greater danger than when I was traveling in the Yankees' rear."

Carrie Ann's voice stung Ruth like a dozen bees. "You're in no danger. I'll see to it. The Monteagues will keep our secret and so will Eli. He just said so. Despite this terrible war, he and Peyton have remained friends. Eli will make certain that, as Peyton's wife, you're safe."

"There is no secret, Aunt Ruth, because there is no wife!" Carrie Ann dropped several dollar bills down on the bed. "This is payment for the dress I'm wearing."

"I'm not taking your money. As I told you, the dresses were gifts."

Carrie Ann moved toward the door.

Ruth stood and quickly stepped into her path. "Please? Can't we discuss this?" She noted the stubborn set to the younger woman's jaw and tried not to grin. Mercy, but she reminded Ruth of herself in younger days. "Now, Carrie Ann, you can't just up and leave. It will be dark in a few hours. There are guerrilla fighters in the area that aren't attached to any particular army. They've been terrorizing residents, particularly farmers. Union and Confederate generals alike have tried to apprehend and stop these marauders, but they've been unsuccessful. It's best you remain here—at least until morning."

Folding her arms, Carrie Ann appeared to consider the idea.

"And about this afternoon . . ."

"I will not pretend to be Peyton's wife. He will be apoplectic when he learns of it, and should his commanders hear the news, it could harm his military career." Carrie Ann lowered her chin and stared at the toe of one of her black leather boots. "I'm not exactly the kind of woman whom a refined, sophisticated man like Peyton would choose." When her head came up, the evidence of her pain and disappointment pooled in her eyes.

Ruth alone was to blame for it.

"You heard Colonel Kent mock me. I'm a serving girl at the Wayfarers Inn, and that's hardly a position to brag about."

"He wasn't mocking you. Besides, I explained why you were forced into such an occupation, but your, um, friend Major Blevens had already told him. Eli understands."

"And what am I now, other than Colonel Collier's pretend wife? Thanks to Joshua and your tall tales, I don't know who I am anymore."

Ruth saw Carrie Ann's blue eyes tear up. "Oh, my dear girl, you're a woman who is seeking to help her family by finding her sister and father. You're courageous, working to support them any respectable way you can."

Carrie Ann didn't argue, and Ruth knew that she'd presented her story honestly and that her heart was pure. True, she barely knew her, but Ruth hadn't reached the ripe old age of fifty-five without knowing a thing or two about people. She could practically sniff out the superficially sweet, the swindlers, and the connivers as well as the fortune hunters who merely wanted to drain her nephew's trust fund.

But Carrie Ann was none of those. She had an innocence about her that was refreshing. She was well-read, well-spoken, straightforward, and protective of those she loved.

Including Peyton.

Ruth wanted to giggle. Mercy, but it was so obvious! Even now, Carrie Ann stood up in his defense, not hers.

She was perfect. The wife Peyton needed and the niece for whom Ruth had longed. And with the stipulations of Peyton's trust met, Ruth and Tabitha would have the funds they so desperately needed.

Ruth would visit her attorney first thing in the morning.

And then she'd write a message to Peyton . . .

"Don't worry about my nephew and his reputation. And the Monteagues won't tell anyone. Better still, the news of your marriage to Peyton will discourage both Lavinia and Eli, which was its intended purpose. And you said yourself, you have nowhere else to go. Therefore, you must stay here where you have a room to yourself and a soft bed to sleep in. You'll be fed . . . and paid, just as Peyton promised. You'll be helping your family too."

Carrie Ann's expression softened. "I must admit, you're right on all points."

"Of course I am." Peace enveloped Ruth. "So, you see, while the ruse was an absolute blunder on my part, one which I admit and promise to take full responsibility for, it works together for the greater good."

The greater good of all of us.

New York Times

September 5, 1864

Five telegraphic words—"Gen. SHERMAN has taken Atlanta," on Saturday, thrilled the nation with a joy . . .

Four months of constant and vigorous campaigning, a contested march of full two hundred miles, ten pitched battles, and two score of lesser engagements by night and day, make up the price we paid for Atlanta. It is worth them all . . .

The Daily Dispatch

Richmond, Virginia
September 5, 1864

On Saturday evening a rumor was in circulation that "Atlanta had gone up"; but the vague nature of the accounts previously received made it all a matter of conjecture, and no one seemed to be possessed of sufficient information to explain the true situation of affairs. The report, as usual, gathered proportions as it progressed, and by nightfall the croakers were brooding over the most exaggerated statements and false representations.

The Daily Dispatch

September 7, 1864

General Hood formed a junction with General Hardee at Lovejoy's station at one o'clock Saturday, and the whole army is now concentrated at that point. As a matter of course, the fall of Atlanta is regretted; but neither the army nor the people are at all discouraged. All was quiet at last accounts. Our army was re-organizing, and taking the rest so much required.

CHAPTER 19

September 7, 1864

"It's been two weeks." With rain in his eyes, Peyton glanced at Vern before swinging out of his sodden saddle. "Those scouts who took Carrie to my aunt's in Winchester had explicit orders from General Sheridan. They should have returned by now." He handed off Brogan's reins to Tommy.

After reconnoitering all day, they'd discovered nothing new. Neither army had moved since yesterday. But while in the saddle, Peyton had found time to speculate with Vern about who those scouts had been and whether they were trustworthy.

They determined they were not.

Adding to Peyton's worry was the fact that he'd received no mail from Winchester since Carrie left camp, although Vern reminded him that Winchester was under Confederate authority and mail from loyalists to Union soldiers was likely prohibited. Either way, Peyton had no way of knowing whether Carrie had arrived safely at Piccadilly Place.

Tommy patted Brogan's neck. He was as drenched as Peyton and Vern. "Glad you're alive and well, Colonel. Major." The boy's shaggy brown hair partially covered his eyes and dripped with rain. As Tommy pushed it back off his forehead, Peyton glimpsed his expression of relief.

"Every time I make it safely back to camp," Peyton said, "I thank God."

"Me too." Tommy spoke over the downpour. "I keep thinking of Anderson's attack on General Crook's men at Berryville, sir. Word is the final count of the Union dead is a couple hundred."

"More like three hundred." Vern handed his mount's reins to Tommy also. "Anderson lost at least that many troops as well, but neither side was victorious."

"And it didn't involve my brigade, Tommy."

Peyton bestowed the best reassuring smile he could muster on the boy, although, personally, he would have liked to fight those Rebs alongside Crook's troops four days ago. He and his men expected to meet the enemy sooner or later—Peyton would prefer sooner. But just as Early's Army of the Valley hadn't marched an inch, neither had Sheridan's Army of the Shenandoah. Instead the Union dug in, and now its entrenchments stretched eight miles long.

The men, including Peyton, were getting antsy.

One enlisted man referred to this campaign as merely "mimicking war." Peyton feared his men would become complacent if this cat-and-mouse game continued any longer. His troops were ready for battle now.

"Don't take our horses too far, Tommy," Peyton instructed. "We may need them in a hurry. Early's men are bivouacked right across the Opequon."

"No foolin'?" There was a note of awe in Tommy's voice.

"No fooling." Peyton had a good mind to smuggle that young man to Winchester where he'd be safe from the fighting . . .

And he could check on Carrie at the same time.

Giving Vern a side-glance, an idea formed. A grin tugged at the corners of his mouth. It would take some planning and, of course, General Merritt would have to agree to it—that is, whatever plan Peyton cooked up. But it was already hot on the fire. He just needed several volunteers.

"Vern, let's go find some supper. I'm famished."

"Good idea."

"I was hoping you'd say that." He clamped one hand on his friend's shoulder as they strode toward the officers' mess tent.

—◦ ◦—

It took a good three days, but finally Peyton received approval from Generals Merritt and Sheridan for his brilliant albeit risky plan to scout the area. The Union army hadn't moved in days and neither had Early's troops. The two enemies were kept apart only by the rapidly rising Opequon Creek due to the continued storms. He had approval for Tommy and Vern and three others to accompany him on the journey. Tommy hadn't stopped grumbling about going to Winchester, however, and Vern, normally an optimist, predicted one catastrophic scenario after another. It was enough to make Peyton wish he'd gone ahead with his mission alone. Meanwhile the rain didn't let up, adding to the usual discomforts of morning and evening drills and general camp life, spoiling even the best of temperaments.

"You're insane." Vern's whispered voice reached Peyton's ears as their horses plodded through the soggy underbrush. "You know that, right?" He paused a moment before adding, "Sir."

Only Vern could get away with a retort like that and avoid a court-martial. However, Peyton was beginning to think that he might have, indeed, lost his mind. Sneaking past Confederate pickets and vedettes wouldn't be easy, although Sherman's daring in Georgia and the Federal victory there emboldened Peyton.

Nonetheless, he had good reasons for this covert quest—at least that's what Peyton told himself.

"Neither army has moved since that skirmish near Berryville, Vern. But unless the Confederate army decides to surrender soon, a full-scale battle will be under way shortly. You know that as well as I."

"Can't argue there."

"Good." Peyton kept his voice as low as possible. "And as I've said, I don't want Tommy's life endangered."

The boy rode closely behind them. "I can handle myself, sir."

Peyton cast a brief glance over his shoulder. "Of your capability, Tommy, I have no question, but I'm not willing to test it just yet."

Tommy muttered something under his breath. He'd been sulking since they left camp.

"Let me remind you that your instructions are to look after my aunt and Miss Bell. But seeing as more than two weeks have passed without word, I'll look in on Miss Bell before returning to camp. After that, Tommy, you may be on your own, fighting the Rebel Army with sheer wit."

"I'd rather fight with a gun in my hand, Colonel."

"You have a gun." He'd given the boy his Colt Sidehammer and told him where he'd hidden the Repeater in the house. "You're going to be the Army of the Shenandoah's eyes and ears in Winchester and the defender of the ladies of Piccadilly Place. Just remember what I told you."

"I know. I know. I have to say I'm fifteen so the Rebs don't force me to fight in their army." Tommy groaned. "But jumpin' jackals, sir. I've been waiting to turn seventeen for almost a whole year now just so I can sign up with all you men."

"Tommy, you're an important part of my brigade. If you can prove to me you're ready for the cavalry by succeeding at this assignment, I'll see that you get an immediate promotion once you're officially enlisted."

"Yes, sir." He replied in a hushed tone, but Peyton still heard the boy's enthusiasm. "I can do that, sir."

"I know you can." Another glance back and Peyton thought Tommy sat taller in his saddle.

Under the veil of darkness, Peyton reined in Brogan as they reached the banks of the Opequon. He'd forded the creek at this particular spot dozens of times when he was a boy. Turning in his saddle, he waited for Tommy and Vern to catch up. Several days ago he'd taken four trusted and skilled subordinates along with him, Vern being the first to volunteer, albeit reluctantly. After meeting together, they arrived at a plan which included dressing as Quaker farmers. Then he received approval from the higher-ranking brass for this unofficial scouting expedition. All Peyton had to do was wait for the right time.

And now was that time.

Peyton removed his field glasses from his coat pocket and scanned the area for enemy movement. Just as he suspected, there was none. After rechecking his sidearm and his Spencer repeating rifle, he signaled his companions onward and they crossed the swollen creek. On the other side, they dismounted and walked their horses up an incline. The muddy banks of the Opequon could be treacherous, especially after all the rain. Another reason Sheridan chose not to order his army to ford the creek and attack. Doing so would hand over an advantage to the enemy.

Careful to remain hidden by the clumps of trees, Peyton reached the top of the hill. Spotting pickets, he motioned his men back into the shadows, praying the horses would keep quiet. Buzzing insects taunted him, but he dared not even lift a hand to swat at them lest he disrupt the brush. Perspiration trickled down the sides of his face and back of his neck.

The guards rode slowly past. Peyton breathed easier.

He stepped forward and glanced around for more vedettes. He spied none, although a good mile off, the enemy's campfires were scattered across a meadow, looking like fallen stars.

He motioned his men forward.

Stealthily, they led their mounts along the tree line. As soon as their boots touched on the gravel road, Peyton gave the signal and they swung up into their saddles. Then they rode like the wind into town.

The next difficulty came in avoiding soldiers patrolling the streets. Even though they were disguised as farmers, the threat of being detained and ultimately captured lurked. Peyton knew his men would rather fight than waste away in a Confederate prison. On the other hand, if everything went according to Peyton's plan, they wouldn't have to fire a single shot and Rebel troops wouldn't suspect a thing.

General Sheridan received word that the Confederates in Winchester considered themselves victorious in what was largely an indecisive battle at Berryville. Nonetheless, Early's men had held their line, except they hadn't attacked the next morning. The Rebs accurately guessed they were outnumbered. So they'd crossed the Opequon and camped—and they hadn't moved for the last few days. They only marched around and around as if circling the walls of Jericho.

And tonight, being Saturday, celebratory parties were being held around town. Peyton relied on his assumption that most officers, like Eli Kent, were out enjoying themselves. Only ragtag enlisted men guarded the town. Armed with bottles of whiskey, tobacco, and Federal currency, Peyton and his men could easily bribe whoever stopped them. Reportedly, some CSA soldiers hadn't been paid in months. Their families were hungry. The Confederate dollar worth very little. But, God willing, Peyton and his men wouldn't attract unwanted attention.

Splitting up, three of his men rode slowly down Piccadilly Street. Meanwhile, shrouded by the blessed development of low-lying fog, Peyton, Vern, and Tommy rode down the alleyway that led to the back of Aunt Ruth's house. Music and laughter wafted from the Monteagues' home and muffled their horses' hooves as they clapped against the cobblestone pavement. Peyton whispered a prayer that his aunt and Carrie weren't attending their neighbors' party. He needed to find them both at home. Safe.

Reaching his aunt's wide back yard, Peyton left Vern and the horses hidden in the fieldstone wreckage of what had once been a spacious barn and stable. The terrible memories of what took place there still haunted Peyton. Those murdering thugs! To convey their message of anti-abolitionism, several slaveholding Confederates hanged Samuel, Tabitha's brother. The black man had been a loyal, faithful friend of the Collier family and had done nothing to deserve brutality.

Peyton signaled Tommy to follow him across the yard. They kept low and hidden in the shadows of tall firs, pines, and Aunt Ruth's fragrant eucalyptus. The trees stood along a narrow ravine that divided the Colliers' property from the Monteagues' place. Despite the natural partition, the faint but rich smell of cigar smoke made its way from the celebration, accompanied by the hum of men's voices and strains from the musical ensemble inside the buildings.

They reached Aunt Ruth's back porch and slipped into the house. Tabitha's quarters were off the kitchen, and Peyton decided he'd best make his presence known to her first, lest she kick up a fuss and alert soldiers.

He crept into her sitting room. Evidence of fried foods lingered in the air and caused Peyton to long for a home-cooked meal. He grinned, seeing the older woman rocking in a favorite chair while darning a garment. Silently removing his riding gloves, he put his hand over her mouth, muting her gasp.

"Don't scream, Tabitha. It is I," he whispered, as though he recited Shakespeare, "your dear boy."

She slapped his hand away. After kissing her cheek, Peyton chuckled softly.

"What you doing here? Trying to get yourself killed?"

He removed his hat. "I'm attempting to check on Miss Bell's welfare. Is she all right?"

"Yes, although . . ." Tabitha stood and faced him. Beneath the dim lamplight, she looked no worse for wear despite the Confederate invasion of their home. "You'd best talk to Ruth about her."

"Why?" Peyton narrowed his gaze, feeling a niggling of concern. "Something wrong?"

"It ain't for me to say." Tabitha huffed and folded her arms. "And I won't either."

He expelled a sigh. Apparently Carrie and Aunt Ruth weren't getting along. Odd. He'd been so sure they'd like each other.

He'd investigate the matter momentarily. "I've got another guest for you. A young man named Tommy." He quickly explained the circumstances. Tabitha could be trusted. "Come on out and meet him."

"And feed him, I suppose. You too?"

"No, but thank you." Peyton strode toward the door. "Where are Miss Bell and Aunt Ruth now?"

"Up in their rooms, I imagine."

"Is Eli about?"

She wagged her head of downy-white curls. "He be gone next door for the Monteagues' victory party." She gave a derisive snort. "His men too, except for a couple of guards, and one of them is usually lurking about."

"Hmm . . . interesting." He and Tommy hadn't run into any guard. He hoped Vern wouldn't happen upon them while alone. "I'll be careful."

"You'd better be," Tabitha said. "Your aunt's got papers that need signing."

"Papers?"

"Don't ask me." Tabitha raised her hands in surrender. "I ain't saying no more."

Peyton's curiosity was now sorely piqued. Nonetheless, he introduced Tommy and told him to keep watch on the first floor. Next Peyton quietly ascended the stairs. He glanced at the closed paneled door of the room in which he suspected Carrie stayed, then eyed his aunt's closed door. He decided to surprise Carrie first. She'd tell him of any problem existing between her and Aunt Ruth while his aunt would be more likely to hedge so she didn't worry him.

But he was worried.

He rapped lightly against the door.

"Come in, Aunt Ruth."

Sounded friendly enough. Peyton turned the knob, opened the door, and quickly stepped in. He found Carrie sitting at a round table near the windows. She turned. Seeing him, her smile vanished and her eyes grew wide.

She gasped and sprang to her feet.

"Shhh . . ." He held his forefinger to his lips as he closed the door behind him.

"Peyton!" Her wide eyes took in his attire. "Have you deserted?"

He grinned. "Hardly. Several of my men and I snuck into Winchester so I could check on you. I've been concerned." His fears seemed ungrounded. Carrie looked well and quite pretty in that calico dress. Her hair was swept up and curly tendrils fell alongside her face. "The scouts never returned. I suspect they were Confederate spies."

"Oh, my." Her voice was feather soft.

"You seemed upset when you saw them. Did you know that they were spies before you left camp that night?"

"I-I wasn't sure," she stammered. "Remember, I've seen scores of soldiers come through the Wayfarers Inn."

"True enough." Peyton stepped closer to her and caught a whiff of lavender. "Did they mistreat you?"

"Other than a little manhandling and trying to steal my horse, no." As she stared up at him, her pretty pink lips parted slightly. "Colonel Kent intervened on my behalf, but then confiscated the gelding."

Peyton moved toward her. "The Rebel army is desperate."

"Right now, they don't act like it." She took a step closer.

Peyton marveled at his powerful reaction to their nearness. It was more than a mere attraction. He'd never felt this way about a woman before, and he sensed she felt the same. "Carrie, you're lovely."

She blushed and lowered her gaze. "Thank you." When she glanced up at him again, she had a twinkle in her eyes. "But I'm afraid I'm growing more spoiled with each passing day."

"You deserve a little spoiling." There certainly didn't appear to be any problem. "How are you and my aunt getting along?"

"Wonderfully, I think." A glow seemed to cover her being. "Oh, Peyton, Aunt Ruth has been more like a mother to me than my own mother, or stepmother, ever was."

When he frowned, his confusion obviously apparent, she explained the latest developments about her mother. It was likely her stepmother and stepsister whom she left in Woodstock.

"I won't bore you with the details. I'm sure you don't have a lot of time."

"No, I don't." Although he wished he had all the time in the world. "But nothing is amiss between you and my aunt?"

"No, not that I'm aware. Aunt Ruth has coached me on certain social proprieties." She arched a delicate brow and wagged a finger at him. "But you didn't warn me about the tea parties."

"My apologies." Smiling, he gave her a gallant bow.

"Accepted."

Peyton felt all the more drawn to her. He took another step closer.

"Aunt Ruth has also helped me write letters to officials in neighboring counties as well as Baltimore and Washington, expressing my desire to find Sarah Jane." A determined glint entered Carrie's eyes. "Aunt Ruth is certain we'll find her—and my father too."

"I believe you will."

He felt warmth penetrating his suede jacket before noticing the small fire glowing in the hearth. His gaze slid to the bedside table where a stack of four or five volumes lay. Then he saw the numerous newspaper pages spread across the table at which Carrie had been sitting when he'd entered her room. She appeared in her element.

He cleared his throat. "You do have cozy quarters, Miss Bell," he teased. "Little wonder you deserted my brigade."

"Deserted? How dare you, sir." She lifted her chin in a demure but dismissive way.

He chuckled. Sassy as ever. "Ah, yes . . . I see the fruits of my aunt's coaching already."

Her eyes sparked at his retort, but it was her smile that turned his heart inside out.

She took another step toward him. "You may be interested to know that Aunt Ruth and I were invited to tea at a well-known secessionist woman's home."

"Oh?"

"Yes. Mrs. Tavish."

Peyton knew the busybody quite well.

"She felt the need to try to convert us to the Confederacy."

"I'm sure that was amusing."

"Quite. But, interestingly enough, Mrs. Tavish confided in me when she learned I hailed from Woodstock. Perhaps she concluded that I was a Confederate at heart."

"Did you learn anything noteworthy?"

"As a matter of fact, I did." She beamed. "Mrs. Tavish said that General Lomax was—or is—Colonel Mosby's commanding officer. They have plenty of scouts who are trained to tap telegraph lines among other things. Evidently, General Lomax stated that the Valley is impenetrable to Union forces. He's got General Early convinced of it. Therefore, Early is considering sending Anderson's troops back to Lee so they can help fight General Grant at Petersburg."

Peyton kneaded his whiskered jaw as he considered the information. If Early did such a thing, the Union army could break through his forces with little problem. "To be clear, you said Mrs. Tavish heard this directly from Lomax?"

"Yes. He and his staff stayed in her home for two nights."

"Hmm . . . Generals Merritt and Sheridan will be pleased to hear it."

"Good." She leaned forward as if his presence drew her too. "Then putting up with Mrs. Tavish's babbling for an entire afternoon was worth it."

Another of her smiles charmed Peyton nearly out of his senses. No doubt Eli noticed her. Did Carrie enjoy his company or that of another man? Surely she didn't want for male attention. "I hope Colonel Kent has been nothing short of a gentleman."

She blinked at his abrupt change of subject. "He has, except . . ."

"Except?" He frowned. Was that the problem Tabitha hinted at? "Except . . . what?"

She moistened her lips. "Colonel Kent showed interest in me, but I didn't share it. At the same time, Miss Monteague—"

"Lavinia?" Peyton stifled a groan. "Is she back in Winchester?"

"Yes, and she's still very unattached. She—" Carrie's voice fell and so did her gaze. "She was quite disappointed to hear that you're . . . well, that you got—" She pressed her lips together.

"That I'm . . . what?" Cupping Carrie's chin, Peyton urged her gaze to meet his. What could be so awful that she had trouble speaking her mind?

At last she lifted her eyes, but they were filled with remorse.

"You can tell me anything, Carrie."

"On my very first day here, Aunt Ruth began explaining who I was to the Monteague ladies. She couldn't tell the truth for obvious reasons."

Peyton began suspecting one of Aunt Ruth's tales went horribly awry.

"So she fibbed with the hopes of sufficiently discouraging both Miss Monteague and Colonel Kent."

"So just who did Aunt Ruth say you are?"

That familiar tiny pucker appeared above Carrie's right eyebrow, and Peyton's gut tightened.

"She said I'm your . . . your wife."

Chapter 20

"My *what*?"

"I'm sorry, Peyton. I wanted to fix the slipup, but couldn't think of how to talk my way around it without casting a bad light on Aunt Ruth."

Carrie squeezed her eyes shut. Perhaps she shouldn't have gone along with the hoax. Poor Peyton looked like he'd gone into shock.

Either that or he was so angry he couldn't speak.

"I can leave Winchester," Carrie offered, praying Peyton wouldn't agree. "Aunt Ruth can blame it all on me. Then you can reconcile with Miss Monteague or any other suitable young lady."

"Lavinia? I have no intentions of reconciling with her." He gave his head a shake as if clearing it. "And I have no plans to pursue any other young ladies."

"You don't?" Carrie brightened. Still, she had to tell Peyton the entire truth. "Miss Monteague seemed saddened to hear you're married—but, of course, you're not." She blew out a breath, wishing Aunt Ruth were here to explain. It was her blunder, after all.

"I don't give a whit about how Lavinia may or may not feel. I'm more concerned with your safety." He paced the small area in front of her. "A Union officer's wife here in Confederate-controlled Winchester?" Peyton shook his head again.

"There are other loyalist women here in town whose husbands are officers. As for Colonel Kent, he has pledged his cooperation to ensure my protection and has one of his men following Aunt Ruth and me."

"To monitor your activities."

"Yes, but it also serves as protection." The way Peyton pursed his lips and rubbed his knuckles along his bearded chin told Carrie he was, at least, considering what she said. "I've been able to attend various luncheons and teas with Aunt Ruth, and today I volunteered at the orphanage, all unaccosted." The sad faces of the many parentless children had been etched into her memory. "Oh, Peyton, you should see these little ones. Their parents are dead, their homes are gone."

"Begging your pardon, Carrie, but I don't have time to hear about your work at the orphanage, as admirable as it sounds. I'd best find my aunt and settle this trouble of . . . of our marriage."

Her chest constricted and Carrie wondered why her feelings were hurt. Of course he couldn't stay and chitchat. And, of course, he'd want to solve the problem of Aunt Ruth's unfortunate gaffe.

"You could take me with you, Peyton. That would be a solution."

"Out of the question."

"But I can assist Dr. LaFont like I did after you arrested me, and I promise I won't become squeamish or dispirited again." She prayed she could keep such a promise.

He reached out and cupped her cheek. She put her hand on top of his, leaning into his touch. Maybe he wasn't as angry as she'd imagined.

"Believe me, I would like nothing better than to take you with me. However, you're safer here, which doesn't say a lot, but it is enough. In fact, I brought Tommy here too. While I'm away, it will bring me a measure of comfort to know that you four are out of the line of fire."

"It's coming, isn't it? Another large battle?" She didn't want to think about all the loss of life and how she fretted over Peyton's safety. "Everyone in Winchester is still abuzz over the fall of Atlanta."

"That win has encouraged the Union army greatly." He took her hand and she felt its roughness as his thumb brushed over her knuckles.

"I think the Union can and must win in the Shenandoah Valley. The victory would be a means to ending this dreadful war."

"Carrie, let's not talk of the war anymore." Peyton pressed a kiss on her cheek, slowly, deliberately.

Her eyes fluttered closed as she relished his nearness. His musky scent mingled with woodsmoke and leather. "What would you rather talk about?" She fought to keep her composure in spite of her heart's sudden hammering.

Without another word, he gathered her in his arms and slid his lips to her mouth. Carrie's world began to spin. Her legs threatened to give way. The fire crackled in the hearth, but even its flames couldn't rival the newly sparked feelings for Peyton. They burned deeply inside of her as she returned his kisses.

After several delicious moments, his lips brushed the bridge of her nose. "Now, what did you ask before I so rudely interrupted?"

"I can't remember." She heard his husky chuckle as he kissed her jaw, her neck . . .

The door to her bedroom swung open.

She froze.

"Carrie Ann, I heard noises—"

The door closed again.

Peyton released her.

"Oh, good gracious!" Aunt Ruth stepped forward. Her gray hair was braided and fell over one shoulder. Clad only in her nightgown and wrapper, she clutched a rifle in her hands. "Peyton, is that you? What on earth are you doing here? I heard a man's voice, and I thought Carrie Ann was in trouble." Aunt Ruth arched a brow. "Perhaps she is, although I won't shoot my own nephew."

"I'm much obliged." Peyton crossed the room. He took the rifle from Aunt Ruth's hands. "I understand you've married me off."

Discomfort quickly replaced passion inside of Carrie.

"I reckon I did at that. The words just flew out of my mouth."

"Well, how 'bout that." He set the safety on the gun. "And you're pleased with the match?"

"Extremely."

"Ah, your approval at long last." He handed the weapon back to his aunt.

"No need for sarcasm, my dear boy." The older woman's expression brightened as her gaze lit on Carrie. "But I do adore this precious girl you sent here." She tipped her head to one side. "But perhaps you wanted my approval, eh?"

Peyton let go of a long sigh.

"So I went ahead and I had our attorney, Horatio Finch—you remember him, don't you, Peyton?"

"Of course."

"Yes, well, I asked him to draw up the appropriate papers, as I told him that you and Carrie Ann had a battlefield ceremony minus the legalities."

"I see." Peyton folded his arms.

"What are you talking about?" Carrie asked.

Peyton turned to her. "I believe my aunt is declaring that she would like us to marry. You see, I have a trust fund that I cannot have access to until I am married. If something should happen to me—"

"Oh, my dear girl, I'm sorry to hurry things along like this," Aunt Ruth said, "but desperate times call for desperate measures."

"Aunt Ruth, what am I going to do with you?" Peyton hung his head back and released another sigh, this one born from obvious exasperation. Then he gazed at Carrie again and apologies filled his eyes. "I would never want to blemish your reputation or hinder your future plans, Carrie."

"You never would." Her mind was still reeling from what they were implying. Marriage to Peyton—for real?

"Would you find marriage to me abhorrent?" He stroked her cheek with the backs of his fingers. "Of course, I could be killed in battle and then you would be a very rich widow."

"Don't say such a thing!"

"I'll get the papers." Aunt Ruth left the room.

Peyton watched her go. After she'd closed the door behind her, he looked back at Carrie. "You don't have to go along with this . . . insanity."

"You don't either."

His gaze narrowed as he considered her reply and, perhaps, his options. "Once it's done it may be hard to undo. There is the option of annulment, I suppose, but if it's discovered that you were married, despite the circumstances and outcome, it could haunt you for the rest of your life."

"I'm not the least bit concerned. To be honest, marriage to you, even premature and dangerous, is more acceptable to me than a so-called 'safe' marriage to someone else I don't love and never will."

"You say that now, but—"

"My mind's made up."

"I see." He folded his arms and stared down at her. "Have you considered the possibility of someone recognizing you as having lived in Woodstock? Being a

Union officer's wife makes you a traitor now in parts of Virginia and throughout the Confederacy. It's just fortunate that Eli is behaving so graciously."

Carrie inclined her head. "I've considered the consequences, yes."

"If guerrillas capture you, it could develop into a terrible hostage situation."

"Pity the guerrillas who capture me," Carrie quipped, hoping to lighten the atmosphere.

Peyton didn't appear amused.

She forced her smile to disappear.

"Listen to me." Peyton held her by the shoulders. "I don't want you going anywhere by yourself. Don't trust your protection to Eli. Take Tommy with you, even if you're simply going for a stroll up the block." His steady gaze and solemn expression said he meant each word. "Promise me."

"I promise."

Peyton inhaled deeply through his nose, released her, and appeared thoughtful again.

"We've discussed me, but what about you and your future goals?" It had been one of Carrie's more troubling thoughts, although Peyton seemed to enjoy kissing her moments ago. Perhaps Aunt Ruth was right and he did have feelings for her.

Even so . . .

"I'm a serving girl from Woodstock, Peyton, and everyone's been saying how I'm not like any of your 'usual women.'"

"Feel complimented. As for your position at the Wayfarers Inn, I know what it entailed and the reasons surrounding your employment. This war has pushed people into positions they wouldn't normally deem suitable."

"But would my past damage your future in the military?"

"I highly doubt it." He shook his head. "Carrie, your background and my career are about the furthest things from my mind. Your safety and happiness are paramount."

"I'm safe . . . and I'm very happy here." She adored Aunt Ruth, but the notion that she'd been a pawn in the older woman's grand scheme was disconcerting, if not insulting. Regardless, Carrie was certain of her love for Peyton. "You're the finest, most honorable man I've ever met. So, in short, if you want me to go along with this ruse, I will."

"A ruse . . . yes, of course, that's all this is."

Why did he appear hurt?

Aunt Ruth returned with an envelope and handed it to Peyton. He opened it and unfolded the papers requiring his signature.

"I don't have time to read between the lines of all the legal jargon, Aunt Ruth." He scanned the documents. "I will trust everything is in order."

"I've read them over three times. They're in order."

Carrie stood by, feeling more like an observer than a bride.

Peyton took the proffered pen from his aunt.

"Once I provide the papers to Mr. Finch," Aunt Ruth added, "he'll take care of the rest. Within weeks, the bank will release the money in your trust. What a blessing it will be to Carrie, Tabitha, and me. However, I think it's best to keep the funds in Washington for now or the Confederacy will confiscate them."

"Agreed."

"And Carrie Ann will become the legal heiress to the Collier estate." Aunt Ruth smiled at her.

"Me? But shouldn't you be the heiress, Aunt Ruth?"

"My dear girl, I'm no spring chicken."

Peyton glanced at Carrie, but then lowered his gaze to the papers in front of him as if he'd decided against a retort.

He finished scribbling his signature on the numerous pages before looking at Carrie again. "I know this is all so hurried, but do you mind? In the event of my untimely demise, will you manage the details of my trust?"

"The subject is one I'd rather not think about. I can't bear the thought of anything happening to you."

"I'm not saying it will happen, but if it does, will you promise me that you'll always take care of Aunt Ruth and Tabitha?"

"I will. I promise." She didn't have to consider it.

"As for this marriage ruse, Carrie, you and I will discuss it further at a later date."

"Aunt Ruth . . ." He kissed the older woman's cheek. "Behave yourself, if you can."

She clucked her tongue at him.

Carrie followed Peyton to the bedroom door. How she wished their marriage wasn't a farce.

His hand found hers and he brought her fingertips to his lips. "Thank you, my dear wife."

Carrie did her best to hide her disappointment. She wished they were alone so she could send her new husband off with a proper good-bye. But, of course, their marriage was in name only. A legal agreement between them. She'd uttered a single vow and it had nothing to do with their union.

"Farewell, ladies."

"Godspeed. I will continue praying for you every day."

"I covet those prayers." Leaning forward, Peyton pressed a kiss on her cheek. Then he donned a floppy brown hat. "I will see myself out."

With that, he took his leave.

─◦ ◦─

"So let me get this through my thick head," Vern said once they'd skirted Confederate guards and crossed the Opequon. "You did what exactly?"

"I got married."

Up ahead, dwindling firelight flickered from the Union camp, and Peyton's three additional cavalrymen galloped toward it. Peyton slowed his mount so he and Vern could talk and wouldn't be overheard by patrolling vedettes.

"Married? As in you and Miss Bell?"

"Yes, but we're only sort of married."

"Excuse me? You're either married or you're not—it's like either you're dead or you're not."

"An uplifting analogy, Reverend." He chuckled.

"You know what I mean, Peyt."

He explained the situation in short. "So I signed all the legal documents. I must admit, marriage to Carrie solves a lot of problems. Money, for one thing. The conditions of the release of my trust are that I reach the age of twenty-five, which I accomplished three years ago, and that I'm married. As of tonight, both requirements are filled. Secondly, I now have peace of mind that Aunt Ruth and Tabitha will be looked after in the event of my death."

"And if you survive? You're a married man now."

"I realize that." Peyton had no regrets. None.

Vern was silent the rest of the way into camp. After dismounting, they deposited their saddles and gear in their respective quarters, and then met back outside. After finding a pot of coffee, they filled their tin cups just as rain began to fall. They ducked into the officers' mess tent.

"About this marriage business," Vern said. "Have you prayed about any of it?"

"Maybe, but not in words exactly." The feeling was difficult to express. "Have you ever done something, Vern, that's seemingly on a whim, but then it becomes evident that you made the right choice because you can feel it down in your soul?"

"I'm sure I have, although I can't think of a particular instance." Several moments of silence ticked by. "It's quite obvious that Miss Bell has feelings for you, Peyt. While marrying her might have seemed to solve immediate troubles, what happens at the war's end? Will she be a suitable helpmeet to you?"

"Of course," Peyton countered. The more he thought about it, the more sure of it he felt.

"Then you'd best make this thing right by God and have a ceremony, take your vows."

"You're right."

Peyton had been considering little else since leaving Winchester. He hated the thought of his arrangement with Carrie ending. He couldn't imagine her going off on her own, unprotected and vulnerable. What's more, the idea of another man holding Carrie in his arms, kissing her . . .

Peyton felt a vein begin to throb in his neck.

Unacceptable!

Peyton tossed his coffee. The stuff had been on the campfire far too long. "Vern, the truth is I'm in love with Carrie."

"I observed as much, but I wanted to hear you admit it." He chuckled.

"You're an exasperating friend, Vern Johnston."

"I've been called worse."

Peyton grinned. "You'll be pleased to know that I'm willing to formally ask for Carrie's hand in marriage if she finds her father. At this point, she can't even be certain that he's alive, although she hopes he is, of course."

Vern took a swallow of coffee. "I wish I could do the honors, but I'm not a licensed minister in Virginia."

"Will you stand as a witness?"

"I'd be honored."

Peyton would let Aunt Ruth take care of finding a preacher. "On that favorable note, I shall bid you good night." He stretched. "Now that I'm a married man, I'm going to write and propose to my wife."

"I hope she says yes."

A grunt of amusement, and then Peyton jogged to his quarters in the pouring rain.

CHAPTER 21

September 17, 1864

"Ooh! Ooh!" Tabitha's excited voice reached the parlor before even her shadow did. "You won't believe what happened to me in town today."

Alarm rang through Carrie as she exchanged concerned glances with Aunt Ruth.

"Carrie Ann and I are in here, Tabitha dear."

The housekeeper entered and closed the sliding paneled doors behind her. "You won't believe what happened!"

"Do tell, Tabitha, before you keel over from apoplexy."

"It's a letter from our boy." She pushed an envelope into Aunt Ruth's hands.

Peyton!

Aunt Ruth mouthed his name for Carrie's benefit, although the silence wasn't necessary. The only other person in the house was Tommy. Earlier this morning, the Rebel army had moved out, leaving behind fear and disappointment from secessionists and garnering speculation from loyalists. Last night Union troops burned mills along Opequon Creek. Tommy had cheered the Yankees, and not before Carrie could hush him up. She expected Colonel Kent to issue a reprisal as he overheard the exclamation, but none came.

Turning her gaze to the missive in Aunt Ruth's hands, Carrie guessed Peyton wrote of his misgivings regarding their marriage charade. It had been an entire week since Peyton stole into her room like some gallant knight, looking in on her welfare. He'd kissed her so thoroughly yet exquisitely that the memory of it still caused her limbs to feel like jelly and sent her heart beating in double time.

But even knights eventually came to their senses.

"Well, what does it say, Miss Ruth? Rip open that envelope. What you waiting for?"

"Give me a moment, Tabitha, and I shall tell you."

Carrie hid a grin at the older women's squabbles. While they parried verbally, neither was ever mean or vicious. What a difference from the home in which Carrie had grown up. Mama never parried; she used words to assault and maim, and poor Papa had been the most wounded of them all.

Aunt Ruth extracted three sealed envelopes. "A note for each one of us."

Tabitha quickly unfolded her note and scanned it. "Our boy wants his favorite pies waiting for him when he comes home. He asks that we pray for peace and a swift end to this war." She paused. "Amen to that!"

"No doubt Peyton is anxious to spend time with his new wife." Aunt Ruth grinned.

A smile broke out across Tabitha's face, and her dark eyes twinkled as she looked at Aunt Ruth. "Glory, but our boy's probably gone and invited General Sheridan and General Merritt to dinner when the time comes. Maybe General Custer too. I'd best get to planning the menu."

And Tabitha has a renewed sense of purpose. Carrie smiled.

"Don't you smile, Carrie Ann. You're washing windows right next to me so this house is spic-and-span when them Union officers arrive."

"Yes, ma'am." She glanced down at her boots so Tabitha wouldn't see any remaining mirth.

Aunt Ruth opened her letter and several dollar bills fell out. "Oh, praise be to God! I wondered how we'd purchase supplies now that Eli and his troops have marched off. I must admit that in spite of the Confederate invasion of our home, we were all treated respectfully and ate well. Eli saw to it."

Carrie couldn't argue either, although a couple of days after Peyton's clandestine visit, one of Colonel Kent's subordinates rummaged through her bedroom and made a horrible mess. Thank God that she'd hidden her journal and the other personal items she'd acquired under a loose floorboard just as Aunt Ruth directed.

"Peyton writes that he hopes we're all well and that he looks forward to seeing us soon. He asks for prayer for the army."

Aunt Ruth gave a sigh that sounded like a mix of wistfulness and distress. At last her hazel eyes lit on Carrie. "What does your note say, my dear?"

"It says . . ." Carrie unfolded it. "My dear wife." She giggled at the jest, the same one he'd used before he left a week ago. "I have contemplated my impulsive actions and humbly apologize for them . . ."

Carrie stopped reading and refolded the epistle. She knew what was coming. Rejection. And why not? As Peyton had written, it was an impulsive decision on his part. He'd had little more than five minutes to think about marriage to her. Carrie, on the other hand, was afforded nearly two weeks in which to playact the role of his wife—a role that oddly came quite naturally to her.

"I think I'll read the rest upstairs." She slipped the note into her skirt's pocket. She wasn't about to let Aunt Ruth and Tabitha see her cry. "Please excuse me."

Aunt Ruth halted her and Carrie blinked back the tears already threatening. "You may have assumptions about Peyton's opening remarks and apology, but I urge you not to discard his letter before reading its entirety."

"I'll read it."

"And then tell us what it says." Tabitha put her fists on her hips and peered down at her. "Ain't right that our boy writes you a whole book, but we only got three sentences."

"Mercy, Tabitha! Peyton has a lot to say to his new wife," Aunt Ruth chided, "and that letter is Carrie Ann's personal business."

"We shared ours. It's only fair that she shares hers."

Carrie left the parlor and hurried up the steps. In the privacy of her room, she extracted Peyton's letter with shaky fingers. Then she closed her eyes and lifted her face upward, whispering a quick prayer for . . . fortitude.

She opened the letter and skimmed what she'd already read before continuing.

You deserve better than my hasty signature. You deserve a ceremony with ribbons, cake, champagne, and a houseful of wedding guests. I would like the chance to give you that—and more.

Had she read those sentences correctly? Pleasantly surprised, Carrie moved to the table and sat down then reread the letter from the top before moving on.

We have not known each other long, barely a month. Half of that time I spent in the presence of my regiment rather than in your delightful company. Nevertheless, I have come to admire your wit, bravery, and honesty, the latter of which I deem a rare and precious commodity. Let it always be so—that we are perfectly honest with one another despite this war and societal pressures. Please allow me to begin in such straightforward sincerity and declare my true self.

After the intimate moment we shared last week

A pleasurable heat worked its way up Carrie's neck, blossoming in her face as she recalled their kiss.

—I realized that I hold you in the highest possible regard. When I close my eyes to sleep, it is your lovely blue eyes I see shining in the darkness. It is your smile that lights my way. These words come from the innermost workings of my heart—a heart which you have completely won and only awaits your claim. I will be the happiest man in all of Virginia—and the world—if our "ruse" can become reality.

Eternally Yours,
Colonel P. B. Collier
Cavalry Division, Army of the Shenandoah

Carrie folded the letter as her mind swam. Could this really be happening? She felt like jumping out of her chair and shouting for joy, although she was certain it wasn't proper behavior for a lady. However, it didn't stop the little giggle from bubbling out.

She hadn't been prepared for a real marriage proposal, for their ruse to become a reality. Of course, it's what she'd been dreaming of and praying for, but—

What would Papa say? Sobering, Carrie ran her finger along the crease of the letter. Papa would like Peyton. She felt sure of it. Her gaze fell on Peyton's missive. All her life she'd wished for a love letter. Today she'd received it.

A knock at the door gave her a start. She stood and stuffed Peyton's letter into her pocket. "Come in."

"Carrie Ann?" Aunt Ruth looked cautious as she stepped into the room. "Are you all right? You didn't receive bad news, did you?"

"No." But this happy moment still had a surreal feel to it. "It wasn't bad news. Peyton simply reiterated his plan for us to further discuss the matter of our . . . wedding ruse."

"Hmm . . ." Aunt Ruth seemed to digest the information. "I see. Then all is well?"

"Quite well. Thank you." Could it be her hero loved her as much as she loved him? Truth to tell, such good things just didn't happen to a girl like Carrie Ann Bell.

But perhaps they happened to Carrie Ann Collier.

‌⸺ꙮ ꙮ⸺

Two days later, Ruth awoke with a start. She sat up in bed, her room dark in the predawn hours. Moments later a shell exploded nearby, shaking the glass panes on her windows. Was that what awakened her? Cannonading?

"Mercy!" They had to take cover.

Her body stiff with age, Ruth forced herself out from beneath her warm bedcovers and pulled on her wrapper. She left her room and strode down the hallway. "Carrie Ann?" She knocked on her door. "Carrie Ann, wake up." She proceeded toward the stairs and stopped by Tommy's room. Giving a few knocks, she called his name. "Wake up, Tommy."

He was in the hallway before Carrie Ann, and surprisingly he was already dressed in baggy blue trousers and a wrinkled cambric shirt. "I think fighting has commenced nearby," he said. "It started about a half hour ago."

"Then we must stay clear of the outer walls." Ruth willed her arthritic knees to bend with each stair. "Will you see that Carrie Ann is awake while I rouse Tabitha?"

"Yes, ma'am."

"We'll meet in the dining room."

Another shell exploded some distance away, but close enough that it rattled the pans hanging in the kitchen. Yet, in spite of its percussion, Ruth guessed the cannon were miles away. But which army fired them?

"Tabitha! Wake up, dear. Winchester may be under another attack." It amazed Ruth that, while still sleepy, she felt more exhilarated than afraid. "I suspect the Union army is firing on the Confederates, but I don't know for sure."

Lord, command Your angels concerning Peyton and us. Ruth kept knocking until Tabitha opened the door to her quarters.

"You're liable to wake the dead and not just this household." She yawned.

"We'd best make plans. We may have to retreat to the cellar."

"Now, Ruth, calm yourself. War ain't no stranger to this town."

"I know, but—"

"I'll dress and be out in a few minutes." The door closed in Ruth's face.

"Well! Some folks certainly are testy in the morning." Ruth didn't bother to lower her voice, but she prepared a pot of coffee and set it on the stove to boil. Tabitha would appreciate that.

Then she headed for the stairway. About halfway up, Ruth heard the front door close and then Carrie Ann's voice sailed down from over the railing above her.

"Tommy just left to see what he could find out."

"Very good." Satisfied that everything had been set in motion, Ruth walked to her room and dressed.

Three hours later, Tommy returned, his face flushed, his breathing heavy. Standing in the parlor, he pulled his hat off his head, revealing a head of damp brown hair. "The Army of the Shenandoah finally attacked Early's troops, except their wagons got backed up on the Berryville Pike." He wore a wide grin that stretched nearly from ear to ear. "And you should have heard the words coming out of General Sheridan's mouth."

"No need to repeat them," Ruth warned. "I'm sure we'd be scandalized if you did."

"Yes, ma'am." A more sober expression darkened the young man's features. "Anderson's men were well on their way to rejoin Lee at Petersburg when the cannonading began. We boxed in Early's men near Stephenson's Depot with no escape going south." Another smile broke.

"What exciting news!" Even so, Ruth wondered if the United States Army would be victorious in the Valley at long last. The Union army had come so close in the past, only to be overtaken again by the Rebels.

"I gotta do something." Tommy slammed his right fist into the hat he held with his left hand. He gazed at Carrie Ann, hope glimmering in his eyes. "I'll leave the colonel's pistol for you ladies and I'll take the Repeater with me."

"No." Carrie Ann stepped forward, looking determined. "Colonel Collier wouldn't want that. Besides, we need you here to protect us."

"You know how to shoot a gun, Miss Carrie Ann. I've seen you do it."

This was news to Ruth. With renewed interest, she glanced at her new niece. "You're capable with a pistol?"

"More than capable." Tommy looked proud. "She hardly missed a single empty can of beans on the fence rail when we were practicing one afternoon in camp."

Carrie Ann seemed to ignore the compliment, such as it was. "Tommy, you should stay here with us."

"What if I don't volunteer to fight? Instead I'll find the colonel and ask how I can help. Maybe he'll want me to deliver messages up and down the line. I've done that before."

Carrie Ann stood her ground for a time, but finally relented. Tommy ran out of the house, eager to join the men he so obviously loved like brethren.

The gunfire and shelling continued but still a safe distance away, so an hour later Carrie cautiously ventured out with hopes of discovering if the army was heading into Winchester and whether they should seek refuge in the cellar. Ruth worried about her, but Carrie returned just after the grandfather clock in the parlor chimed eleven, saying that General Ramseur's line had given way and that scores of wounded men, many in ambulances, had begun arriving in town.

"One officer told me that those who can make it will be taken to Staunton." Carrie Ann dropped her shawl on a nearby chair, then untied the ribbon beneath her chin and removed her cap. "But it looked to me like the majority of wounded won't survive the journey. They're lying on the street from the corner of Piccadilly all the way down Market, but I couldn't get through the chaos to see clearly."

Ruth nodded. "Quite all right, dear. You've brought a lot of news."

"Oh, but there's more."

"I was afraid of that." Ruth sat in her favorite place on the settee.

"It was an amazing sight. Confederate soldiers are running through town, away from the battle. A handful of secessionist ladies are standing in the street, arm in arm, begging them to turn around and fight like men, but they kept on running."

"Good news for our side."

"I suppose it is." A dimple formed above her right eyebrow. "The sight of all those wounded is upsetting, to say the least, and we may soon have company if they get down this far west."

"We need to prepare." Ruth got right to work, collecting her laudanum bottle and gathering all the linens she could spare. Returning to the parlor, she instructed Carrie Ann and Tabitha to begin tearing bed sheets into strips, some wide, some narrow, which could be used for bandages.

Getting comfortable on the settee, Ruth joined in the task. No sooner had she torn several pieces of cloth when a knock sounded at the front door. Tabitha stood to answer it, but Frances and Lavinia rushed in unannounced.

"Ruth? Ruth?"

"In the parlor, Frances."

Both women appeared at the doorway. "Yankees are attacking Winchester, and I'm sure you're as pleased as punch about it!" Frances's voice shook with unmistakable outrage and obvious fear. "How dare they! Doesn't Sheridan know he can't win?"

"Apparently not." Ruth smiled at Carrie Ann.

Lavinia lifted her eyes upward as if muttering an oath loud enough for all to hear. "If I so much as get one ash on this new gown, I'll sue the Yankee army."

Ruth's gaze fell over the dress, a lovely peach creation that complemented Lavinia's dark hair. She glanced again at Carrie, who sat nearby wearing a simple brown calico and tore bandages quite expertly. There was no question as to whom Ruth preferred. The dress certainly did not make the woman!

Still, she'd made that loathsome promise to Harm . . .

"You're welcome to join us here, ladies." Ruth held out her right arm, welcoming her neighbors. "Please, make yourselves comfortable."

"I think we should go down into your pappy's secret cellar." Frances hugged herself and rubbed her arms. "I'd feel safer down there."

"But then we won't know what's happening." Carrie Ann's gaze fixed on Ruth. "Tommy might return with news from Peyton. Wounded soldiers might need our help." She shook her head and several auburn curls broke free from their pins and dropped alongside her face. "I'll stay up here if you all prefer to go down."

Poor Carrie Ann. The dear girl worried over Peyton's safety as much as Ruth and Tabitha did. A smile pulled at the corner of Ruth's mouth. How precious Carrie Ann had become. Truly, Ruth's blunder had proved a blessing.

"I believe we're all safe enough here in the parlor for now." Ruth met Frances's anxious gaze, then Lavinia's seemingly perturbed one. "You ladies are welcome to keep us company as we work. We recently heard that wounded men are coming into town."

"I want no part of tending to wounded soldiers." Frances wrinkled her nose.

"Nor do I." Lavinia shuddered.

"We're much too sensitive for the job, Ruth dear," Frances explained.

"Yes, as you've made it known in the past." Ruth wrestled with indignation. Why, Frances couldn't tend to her dying husband even a little by sitting at his side and reading to him.

Tabitha gave a derisive snort.

Frances glared at the black woman. "Are you going to offer us some tea? That would be the proper thing to do."

"Getting these bandages ready is the proper thing to do," Tabitha sassed. "Besides, it ain't teatime."

"Really, Ruth, you must instill manners into this slave of yours."

Carrie Ann looked ready to speak in Tabitha's defense, but Ruth caught her attention by a wag of her head before a single, and likely regrettable, word rolled off her new niece's tongue. While Ruth admired Carrie Ann's intellect and opinions, squabbling with the Monteagues wasn't wise. If provoked, Frances and Lavinia might divulge secrets—secrets that could result in Piccadilly Place getting burned to the ground, Tabitha being harmed, or worse!

"Ladies, let's just keep tearing these linens and rolling them into bandages," Ruth said. "And praying. Let's keep praying."

⟋ ♋ ♋ ⟍

It was just before three o'clock when the noise of war increased. Ruth rushed to the window. Seeing only several plain-clothed horsemen ride by, a strange mix of disappointment and relief assailed her. "The action must be taking place east of here."

"I'll go take a look."

Carrie Ann was out the front door before Ruth could stop her. Seconds later, a projectile whistled over the house and exploded close enough to shake the floor on which she stood.

For the first time today, Ruth felt fear—fear of harm coming to Carrie Ann. Why, Peyton would be heartbroken if something happened to her . . .

And so would Ruth.

She rushed to the front door, relieved to see Carrie Ann hurrying up the porch stairs. Deep frown lines were etched on her forehead, and the little mar above her eyebrow looked more pronounced. All the while smoke billowed in the unnaturally darkened sky, and gunfire cracked in her wake.

"Aunt Ruth," she said, panting as she entered the house, "I believe it's time for us to take shelter in the cellar."

CHAPTER 22

Aunt Ruth slid aside a giant section of bookshelf in the library, revealing a paneled door. Lamp in one hand, Tabitha opened it with the other, and then led the way down the darkened stairwell. The Monteague ladies followed closely behind her. Carrie walked down ahead of Aunt Ruth, holding onto her arm in case the older woman had a misstep. Behind them, the bookshelf slammed shut on a spring mechanism and the stairwell grew dark, save for the little bit of lamplight farther down.

"Be careful of your footing, Aunt Ruth."

"My dear girl, I could walk down these stairs in my sleep—and, in fact, I have." Her laughter had a merry sound to it which seemed odd considering the dire situation. "Winchester has endured two previous attacks, the last being in '63, when General Ewell's troops defeated General Milroy and captured Winchester." She sighed. "I hated to see General Milroy and his wife leave town."

"He was a brute, Ruth." Mrs. Monteague's voice came from several steps below.

"Only to the secessionists," Aunt Ruth said. "Personally, I found the Milroys to be quite amiable."

"You're able to find commanders on both sides amiable, Ruth. How do you do it?"

"By charm and sheer wit, my dear Frances."

"And my cookin' don't hurt either," Tabitha drawled.

Smiling at the debate, Carrie Ann made certain that Aunt Ruth's foot landed square on the dirt floor before releasing her arm. Cool air enveloped Carrie. Then, beneath the lamplight, she strained to survey the large basement. Half of it was set up like a sitting room and had more furniture than did the parlor upstairs. The other half was filled with paintings wrapped in brown paper and other unidentifiable items.

"This is our secret cellar where we keep everything we don't want the Rebel army to get its greedy hands on," Aunt Ruth said as if reading Carrie's thoughts.

"Oh, now, Ruth," Mrs. Monteague scolded, "you know the Yankees are just as greedy."

"I suppose some are, yes. I can't argue with you there."

Confusion descended on Carrie. "Here I thought we were going into the same cellar where the canned foodstuff is kept."

"That's on the other side of the brick wall there." Aunt Ruth pointed to the far end of the basement. "As you know, that cellar can be accessed from outside the kitchen and it's raided frequently by both armies as well as deserters and guerrillas. I wouldn't hide any of my valuables in that cellar."

Carrie agreed. They wouldn't be safe there.

"When he built the house, my father dug out this basement then fortified this room with brick. He possessed the forethought to hide his valuables and his family from British soldiers if the need arose."

Carrie was still familiarizing herself with her surroundings. "What if the house starts on fire? How will we escape?"

"Through this here," Tabitha said, patting the paneled doorway behind her. "These stairs lead to an opening beneath the back porch, although one of you young ladies will have to crawl on your belly and then push out the latticework so the rest of us can get out."

"I hope you won't expect me to do any crawling today." Lavinia Monteague sank into one of the two settees.

"Of course not." Carrie knew that left her to accomplish the task. She sat in an armchair. "I'll crawl out if the need arises."

"But there might be snakes under the porch. Aren't you frightened?"

"No, they'll hear me coming, Miss Monteague." Carrie felt sure she'd met more frightening vipers, the human kind, at the Wayfarers Inn. "Besides, I'm more concerned about Peyton's welfare than my own right now."

"Of course you are, my dear girl." Aunt Ruth reached for her hand.

"Peyton should be the least of your worries," Lavinia said above the rustling of her skirts as she shifted her sitting position. "My brother Edward and that handsome Colonel Kent are fighting for the Confederacy, for real freedom, and you don't see a single one of my nerves frayed."

Carrie's mind had parked on the words *for real freedom*. Was she serious? It would seem so, judging from her comment. Nonetheless, Carrie couldn't bring herself to challenge Lavinia's statement and scrambled to find a safe topic. "Are you . . . romantically interested in Colonel Kent?"

"Every unattached female in Winchester is romantically interested in the man." Lavinia raised her chin. "However, I do think he's particularly fond of me. I told him I'd write to him every day."

"Marvelous. Then why don't we set aside our political differences and pray for the fighting men on our hearts today." Aunt Ruth was never one to lack diplomacy. "Let's pray for all the soldiers, blue and gray."

Aunt Ruth looked at Carrie as if knowing Peyton was in the forefront of her mind.

Everyone bowed her head as Aunt Ruth began petitioning the Lord.

"Heavenly Father, blessed Savior, faithful Friend, we come boldly before Your throne of grace, asking for mercy for our sinful selves, but also for our men fighting today, each battling for freedom as they see it. We bathe our loved ones in the same promise that You gave King David so long ago. A thousand shall fall at their sides and ten thousand at their right hands, but no harm will come to them. Command Your angels all around them, Lord."

Carrie prayed along, adding her own pleas for Peyton's safety. Then she remembered Joshua and others whom she'd grown up with in Woodstock who had enlisted in the Confederate army. She asked for protection and provision for her family and thanked God for Aunt Ruth and the living arrangements here in Winchester. And she prayed for her marriage. Whether a ruse or reality, Carrie prayed it would soon be an acceptable union in God's sight.

—◦◦ ◦◦—

For the rest of the afternoon, Carrie got in plenty of practice at patience. Time passed at a turtle's pace. Finally, she didn't think she could abide another moment of the Monteagues' discussions about fashion and the parties which they may or may not be invited to in November. Did they not realize they might not live through this day?

"It's been quiet for some time now." Carrie stood. "I think I'll have a look outside. Perhaps the fighting has stopped."

"Do you think that's wise, dear?" Aunt Ruth pushed to her feet and walked alongside her to the stairwell.

"If Tommy returns with news, he won't know where we are."

"I suppose that's true enough."

"Besides," Carrie added, "one of us will have to check at some point." She lowered her voice to a whisper. "And I'm rather certain it won't be either of the Monteague ladies."

"Agreed. Do you have the pistol with you, the one Tommy left us?"

"Yes." Carrie patted her dress's pocket.

After instructing her on how to open the door at the top of the cellar steps, Aunt Ruth hugged her. "Do be careful."

"I will. I promise."

Carrie had little problem manipulating the door. She waited until the bookcase slid back into place behind her and then tiptoed into the library. All was quiet—perhaps too quiet.

Outside, the smell of war hung heavy in the evening air. Down the next block she saw several wagons roll by at breakneck speed, and then heard a collection of men's and women's voices. The din of a crowd grew louder the farther she ventured from Aunt Ruth's home.

Rounding the corner, Carrie continued walking on Loudoun Street. She could almost ignore the buildings that stood in ruins from previous battles.

What lay in rubble this time?

No sooner did the question flit through her mind than Union horsemen and ambulances hurried past. Less than a minute later, she stood in the midst of unfolding chaos.

Men rushed in and out of the Taylor Hotel, many carrying stretchers containing the injured. Many of the walking wounded straggled down the street. Some had fallen before even reaching the steps of the makeshift hospital and lay moaning where they dropped.

A boy wearing a Confederate gray cap paused in front of her. "Have you heard? General Robert Rodes is dead." He wiped dirty fingers over his eyes. "It's a sad day." He ran off to tell the next bystanders before Carrie could ask which side was victorious.

A few minutes later, she got her answer when she saw a large United States flag being draped from the second floor balcony of the red brick courthouse. It hung to the structure's front entrance. A band struck up a victory song as Yankee soldiers marched into town. One tavern burst with merrymakers, and all the while, ambulances brought in more wounded from the battlefield. On certain areas of Loudoun Street, groans and cries from the injured drowned out the sound of drums. Women scurried about, tending to wounds and asking after loved ones, only increasing Carrie's fears for Peyton's safety. Had he survived? What about Joshua—had he been involved in the fight today? How about others she'd known from Woodstock?

Dazed by the sickening sights and anguished sounds around her, Carrie wandered the streets, searching for familiar faces.

Meanwhile the wounded kept coming. Vacant buildings, churches, and several houses were quickly overtaken by Union troops and converted into hospitals. But those accommodations weren't enough. Men, some horribly disfigured, some with mangled and missing limbs, were set down on street curbs, one after another, until they formed a queue that went on for blocks.

Carrie pushed up her sleeves. She couldn't stand by and watch a moment longer. As grotesque as the sight was to behold, she had to do something to help these poor souls.

In spite of her good intentions, it took Carrie less than five minutes to determine that she was not prepared for this. She remembered the bandages and other supplies back at home. She should collect them and return. The situation desperately required more nurses and helping hands. What's more, Carrie had left the four ladies in the cellar, blissfully unaware of all the bedlam. She needed to go back and tell them the fighting had stopped, the Union won Winchester, and now the consequences of the battle filled the city's streets.

—◦つ ◦ა—

"I'll get busy makin' sandwiches." Tabitha headed straight for the kitchen after coming upstairs from the cellar. "Those men'll be powerful hungry."

Carrie wasn't sure how hungry they were. The fact was, they were starving for medical care.

Aunt Ruth set her hand on Carrie's forearm. "Any news about Peyton?"

Carrie shook her head. "None. The men I saw weren't in any condition to answer questions."

"Then we'd best collect medical paraphernalia."

"Did you ask over Edward?" Mrs. Monteague said, dusting herself off.

"I didn't get a chance."

Her gaze darkened. "Well, then, Lavinia and I will leave you ladies to your gruesome tasks."

"Yes, and bring us any news of Edward." Miss Monteague followed her mother out of the library.

"Well!" Aunt Ruth folded her arms and watched her neighbors leave. "That's gratitude for you. Not even a thank you for providing them a safe haven this afternoon."

"Thank you." Carrie placed a kiss on Aunt Ruth's cheek.

"Oh, my dear girl, I wasn't referring to you."

"I know, but I am grateful. Now how about we find those medical supplies?"

"Good idea."

Carrie trailed Aunt Ruth from the library and together they gathered items they might need to care for the wounded. Then they walked through the breezeway onto hallowed ground—Tabitha's kitchen and adjacent living quarters.

Tabitha turned, and seeing Aunt Ruth and Carrie, her eyes grew round. "What are you doing in here? Go on. Out with you."

"Now, Tabitha," Aunt Ruth said, "many hands make light work."

The rumbling of hooves in the backyard stole Carrie's attention. "Soldiers!"

"Yankee or Confederate?" Tabitha looked poised and ready with a butter knife in her right hand.

"I wonder . . ." Aunt Ruth's hand fluttered to her dress's unadorned neckline. "Did we leave the cellar too early?"

"I don't think so. After all, I saw the Union flag hanging over the courthouse." Carrie rushed to the window and moved the crisp yellow curtain aside. Riders wearing blue and gold uniforms filled the yard. "They're Union. And . . ." She scanned the men's rugged faces, spotting one so dear to her.

"It's Peyton!" Carrie's knees threatened to buckle as tears of joy welled in her eyes. Peyton was alive and unharmed! Her hand trembled as she held back the curtain. "He's got Major Johnston and several others with him. And Tommy!" Smiling, she whirled around. "I'll wager they're hungry too, Tabitha."

"I'll bring these here sandwiches out to 'em then, and make more later."

Carrie was already pulling open the back door. As she stepped onto the small covered porch, she saw Peyton dismount. She passed Tabitha's wicker rocker before hurrying down the brick steps. Peyton swept off his hat just as she reached him and jumped into his arms.

"I'm so glad you're alive!" Was she laughing or crying? Carrie wasn't even sure.

She heard his chuckle as he swung her around in a circle before setting her feet back on the ground.

"I'm very much alive." Barely any dirt or soot smudged his face, and his eyes sparked with unmistakable elation. "The Army of the Shenandoah has won Winchester."

"Congratulations." Carrie smiled as Peyton embraced Aunt Ruth, and then Tabitha.

"And now I have some people for you to meet." Placing his arm across Carrie's shoulders, Peyton led her toward a man sitting high in his saddle. He looked familiar, and doffed his dark blue hat as she approached.

"Carrie Ann, you remember General Philip Sheridan."

"Yes." She stepped forward and extended her hand. "Congratulations on your victory today, sir. The United States' flag can already be seen in the town square."

"I won't ask how you know that," Peyton muttered.

Good. She wouldn't have to confess to venturing out on her own.

The commanding general's dark mustache twitched when he smiled. Then he removed his right gauntlet, leaned forward in his saddle, and took Carrie's hand. "Thank you, Mrs. Collier. I was surprised to learn of your marriage and insulted that I was not invited."

She felt bad until he chuckled.

"I'll have you know that you aren't the first woman who disguised herself as a soldier in order to be near her husband."

"I hope you won't hold it against me, sir." Carrie glanced at Peyton and the general released her hand. Was that the tale Peyton had told to explain her visit to their camp?

"No hard feelings, Mrs. Collier. I understand your worry over your runaway sister also." The humor vanished from the general's tone. "Have you found her?"

"Not yet, sir." She looked up at him again. His face was darkly tanned from months beneath the summer sun. "But I hope to hear word soon, especially now that the Union will take control of Winchester. I happily anticipate regular mail, but I especially hope for an end to this war."

"You and everyone else."

"President Lincoln included."

"Long live our president and the Union!" General Sheridan stated the words loud enough to bring cheers from his men. Then he leaned forward in his saddle. "Tell me, Mrs. Collier, has there been much trouble in town that I should know of?"

"Well . . ." Carrie thought a moment. "The newspaper reported the increase of guerrilla activity."

"I will pass that bit of news on to my pickets and vedettes. Thank you."

"Anytime, sir."

"And I trust I will see you both later at my headquarters?" The general affixed his hat on his large head and glanced at Peyton for a reply.

"You will, sir. Thank you for the invitation."

"Very good."

Tabitha handed him a sandwich.

"Much obliged, madam."

"Oh, you're welcome, General." A rare smile shone from her dark face. "If I'd baked a dozen cakes that wouldn't be award enough for what you done."

Aunt Ruth offered him coffee or lemonade.

"Thank you, but no. I had best take my leave. I will, however, enjoy each bite of this sandwich." He touched the rim of his hat. "Until this evening, ladies."

As the general rode off with his staff, Carrie turned to Peyton, curious about the Union commander's parting words. But Peyton had already begun introducing her to another general, followed by several officers.

At last they came to Major Johnston, who sported an impressive black eye.

"You're injured!" Concerned, Carrie stepped toward him. He still sat astride his chestnut mount.

"Not to worry. I'm fine, Mrs. Collier." He spoke her new name with a smile in his voice. "However, I do think we need to discuss a proper ceremony," he said softly, "one that's pleasing to God."

Carrie's heart raced. She looked up at Peyton. "Truly?"

"Truly, and the sooner the better as far as I'm concerned." Peyton reached for her hand.

"I'd like that too." She longed to throw herself into his arms a second time.

"Peyton?" a singsong voice called. "Oh, Peyton Collier?"

Carrie peered around Major Johnston's horse and glimpsed Lavinia gliding out of the thicket of trees like some ethereal nymph. As the woman neared, Johnston's horse jerked his head as if the animal knew something Carrie only suspected.

"Easy, boy." Johnston patted the roan's neck.

"Peyton!" Lavinia smiled and strode closer in a courtly manner. "I hoped I'd find you among all these Yankees." She held out her hands.

Instead of taking them, Peyton removed his hat and gave a slight bow. "Miss Monteague."

She quickly lowered her arms and glared at him. "I was stunned by the news of your marriage." Her gaze flitted to Carrie and remained there briefly, and then it returned to Peyton. "You needn't have hid the fact. Mama and I kept your secret, although it was probably a lapse in judgment on your part, allowing her to come to Winchester. Most Union officers' wives prefer residing in safe Yankee cities."

"Then, as you're aware, Miss Monteague, my wife is unlike most Union officers' wives."

"That she is." Lavinia seemed to have to put much effort into producing a smile. The expression in her eyes belied the one that curved her ruby lips.

"Well, then . . ." After replacing his hat, Peyton rubbed his palms together and looked at Johnston. "The three of us have much to discuss, and I'm looking forward to eating something substantial, as is my staff." He gave Lavinia a bow. "If you'll excuse us, Miss Monteague." He put his arm around Carrie's waist and moved in the direction of the house.

"Just a moment, please . . ."

Peyton halted.

Lavinia's expression softened. "Have you heard anything from Edward?"

"I'm sure I have if he was one of the Rebels shooting at me today."

"He probably was, but he's been your neighbor, as have I, for longer than there's been a war."

"That's true and I have nothing personal against him." Peyton took another few steps toward the house.

"I have never sided with either army," Lavinia stated.

Peyton replied with a dismissive nod. He took Carrie's hand, and this time, they managed to get across the yard and into the house. A glance back revealed the other men lingering behind, to give them a moment of privacy. Major Johnston, meanwhile, spoke with Lavinia.

"Perhaps you should go back out."

"You're worried about Major Johnston?" Peyton laughed softly before kissing the side of Carrie's head. "Vern's a big boy." Hands on her shoulders, he turned Carrie so she faced him. "You should have seen him repelling the enemy today. Most men surrendered before he could even raise his saber." Peyton gathered her in his arms.

"And you?" Carrie toyed with the gold trim on his shell jacket before looking up into his face. "I'm sure you fought bravely."

"Amazingly so, thank God, and with such ease. The cavalry as a whole performed well, but my regiment in particular. Carrie, if you had witnessed it, you'd be in awe of their skill and dash."

"I'm sure I would have been very proud to see them . . . and you. I'm proud of you, and so very relieved that you're alive and uninjured."

Looking pleased, he touched the tip of his nose to hers.

"I hope I didn't cause you embarrassment by my rather enthusiastic greeting. When I saw you I lost all sense of dignity."

"Hardly." His eyes smoldered, and his hold around her tightened. "Carrie, I am now the envy of an entire brigade." On that pronouncement, he kissed her soundly.

September 21

The signal victory in the Shenandoah Valley on Monday is one of that class which permits no cavil either as to its scope or its completeness. . . . The attack was made by our cavalry under AVERILL by gray daylight on Monday. . . . Our forces, by a series of stubborn and sanguinary engagements which lasted until 5 o'clock in the afternoon, compelled the rebels to fall back, completely defeated Early's main army, and drove it from one defended line of works to another, until what remained of the routed force, as General STEVENSON tells us, was "sent whirling through Winchester;" all their dead, most of their wounded, and two thousand five hundred prisoners being left on our hands. The wounded in Winchester alone are found to number three thousand and if the dead are counted in, the rebel loss will be found to exceed six thousand, or about one-fourth of the entire army under EARLY.

—ᘒ ᘓ—

Cleveland Morning Leader

September 26, 1864

To Major General Dix: The following official dispatch has just been received from General Sheridan, detailing some of the particulars of the battle and victory at Fisher's Hill.

HEADQUARTERS OF MIDDLE MILITARY DIVISION, Woodstock, Sept. 23

To Lieutenant Gen. Grant, City Point

I cannot yet give any definite account of the result of the battle yesterday. Our loss will be light. General Crook struck the left flank of the enemy, doubled it up, advancing down along their line. . . . The rebels threw down their arms and fled in the greatest confusion, abandoning most of their artillery. . . . I pursued on after the enemy during the night to this point . . . and have stopped here to rest the men and issue rations.

CHAPTER 23

October 1, 1864

Peyton drank his morning coffee and listened to Carrie read selections from the various newspapers he'd scrounged up for her. Aunt Ruth and Tabitha were upstairs cleaning, Vern had gone to fetch Meredith at the train depot in Martinsburg, and the rest of Peyton's staff were on duty. This was a rare moment alone with Carrie and Peyton relished it.

She glanced at him. "Did you get as far as Woodstock?"

"Yes, but we weren't able to stop in town. My regiment went up the Luray, hoping to find Early. We did, in fact, capture several of his scattered troops. Then some of my men and I searched a cavern. I have a hunch Mosby is hiding out in one of them." Peyton took another swallow of coffee. "But, of course, those caves are treacherous and we didn't have adequate lighting, so we ended up calling it a night and making camp."

Sadness entered Carrie's eyes. "Won't General Sheridan stop the burning? The Union won the Opequon battle."

"He's following Grant's orders. The idea is to make sure the Confederate army can't return and to let the people in the Shenandoah Valley know they can no longer support the enemy."

"I know, but . . . I overhead one soldier say that there's so much burning going on in the Valley, with barns, factories, and mills going up in flames, that it looks like hellfire."

"It does, and General Grant won't stop until he gets his—"

"Unconditional surrender," Carrie finished for him. "U. S. Grant . . . Unconditional Surrender Grant."

Peyton sat back and folded his arms. "Whose side are you on?"

"Your side."

The blue of her eyes deepened, making Peyton long for their private ceremony tonight at which their vows were to be taken. With each passing day, he fell more deeply in love with her—and that made having separate sleeping quarters difficult if not awkward. It had just been fortunate that none of his staff had the need to awaken him in the middle of the night, or they would have discovered that he and his bride slept apart.

But that would change after tonight.

"While you were away, I wrote Margaret a different letter, so I'm glad you weren't able to deliver the one I wrote in camp."

"Letter?"

"Don't you remember? I gave it to you after you first offered me employment."

"Ah, yes . . ." Arching a brow, he considered his bride-to-be and noted the twinkle in her eyes.

"And to think I've earned my way to the position of your wife in such a short time."

He grinned at her teasing. "I'll make you work for it, don't worry."

"Oh, I'm not."

Sassy little thing. "So, tell me . . ." Peyton sat back in his chair. "Did you tell your family of your promotion?"

"Of course." She feigned indignation, glaring at him then lifting her chin and looking away.

Peyton folded his arms. "Keep this up, Mrs. Collier, and I may have to kiss you."

"Not until this evening, although I suppose it doesn't really matter." Her voice fell into a whisper. "It's not like it'll be our first kiss. Even so, I still say it's bad luck for the groom to see the bride before they speak their vows."

"Only in arranged marriages," Peyton whispered back, "in which the groom is likely to renege if he sees his bride and decides she's hopelessly ugly."

"Or vice versa." Carrie's voice returned to normal amplification.

Peyton inclined his head in deference. "Either way, that hardly describes our circumstances. I'm aware of your feelings for me, and you have my word that I won't renege. I adore you and I am your humble servant."

She giggled at his theatrical attempt.

"You laugh, madam? I'm crushed."

She pressed her lips together and he watched amusedly as she tamped down her amusement. But she wasn't successful and they both ended up laughing.

He caught her hand. "All humor aside, I love you, Carrie." He sent her a bold wink and basked in the blush flooding her cheeks.

"The feeling is mutual, Colonel."

The clock in the parlor chimed loud enough for Peyton to catch the time. The day was getting away from him.

He expelled a sigh. "Carrie, as much as I regret it, I need to be on my way." He pushed back his chair and stood. "I'm meeting with Colonel Edwards within the hour. We're discussing the best way to restore law and order to Winchester. As you're aware, it's been something of a challenge, what with those Rebel renegades, likely Mosby's men, raiding loyalists' homes and Union wagon trains."

"I understand." She pushed to her feet. "Aunt Ruth and Tabitha have asked for my help with putting the final touches on our wing of the house, and I've probably kept them waiting long enough."

"It's hardly a wing, Carrie." Her description of the upper hallway with its two bedrooms, one large enough to have a sitting area, amused him. His grandfather had built on the addition after marrying his grandmother. Later, it was inhabited by Peyton and his parents whenever they visited Piccadilly Place. After his parents died, Aunt Ruth moved his bedroom to the one in which Tommy now resided. However, during the last few years, officers, including Eli, along with a host of guests, had made use of it. "After this war is over, I'll take you to England where we'll tour castles and estates so you can see my interpretation of a *wing*."

"Really? To England?" Her blue eyes sparkled with obvious delight. "I've always dreamed of a journey to England."

"Then we must go." Peyton pulled her close. Her head tipped back slightly as she gazed up at him. Her pink lips parted. "On second thought, I think I will kiss you after all."

Aunt Ruth and Tabitha both fussed over Carrie as she dressed for the private ceremony and celebration to follow. Somehow the conversation shifted from the gorgeous ivory silk gown to the cracks in the plaster of the eggshell-colored walls.

"I'm sure you'll want to have this entire addition repaired and redecorated to suit your tastes," Aunt Ruth said. "When the time comes, I'll help you select paint colors and we'll hire one of the Quakers to do the work. They're about the only men left in town." She strode to an armchair. "You'll want to have all the furniture reupholstered also."

"Whatever you think is best, Aunt Ruth."

Carrie was quickly learning her place in this family. She would go along with whatever the older woman wanted. Her marriage to Peyton depended on it. After all, he adored his aunt and she adored him right back. Far be it for Carrie to come between them. Yet, Carrie believed Aunt Ruth was genuinely fond of her. They got along well, and that pleased Peyton. However, Carrie learned when this war began that people's affections changed quickly. Those who were long-standing friends became instant enemies over politics. Peyton loved her now, but God forbid Carrie ever compromised it by disagreeing with Aunt Ruth.

How she longed to rest in Peyton's devotion and Aunt Ruth's kindness, but there was a niggling deep within her. Would Peyton soon come to his senses and see her for what she really was—a farmer-turned-journalist's daughter who became a serving girl at the Wayfarers Inn? Peyton might begin to care the minute she stepped into a room filled with well-bred women. What if she embarrassed him somehow? What if he grew bored with her and regretted marrying her? And Aunt Ruth—she was happy and relieved that Carrie and Peyton's union ensured the release of his trust, but once the money was in the Colliers' possession, they might discover they had no need for Carrie anymore. And if her worst fears were realized, it might be to her advantage to be on Aunt Ruth's good side.

"Now hold yourself still," Tabitha scolded while brushing Carrie's thick hair. "You are the wiggliest young lady I ever did know!"

"It's impossible for me to be still. I'm nervous."

"That's perfectly natural," Aunt Ruth assured her. "Of course, I don't know that from experience, but every one of my friends admitted to me that they contracted a horrible case of nerves before reciting their vows."

Carrie released a pent-up sigh. If she didn't love Peyton so much, she'd be tempted to run for the foothills of Massanutten and hide out for the rest of the war. Maybe the chance at happiness wasn't worth the possible heartache.

"Ouch!" Carrie put her hand to the back of her head. She was sure Tabitha had just pulled out half her hair.

"I wouldn't have pulled if you woulda been sittin' still."

"Oh, I'm sorry, Tabitha. I can't help it."

"Now, Carrie Ann, stop frowning so hard." Aunt Ruth gathered Carrie's left hand in both of her warm palms. "You'll give yourself premature winkles. Why, Tabitha is living proof of that."

"Hmph!"

Carrie did her best to suppress a smile.

"That's better, my dear girl. This is a happy day."

"It surely is," Tabitha said.

"Yes," Carrie repeated, "it's a happy day."

She mentally recited those words over and over. In fact, they saw her out of the bedroom, down the stairs, and into the parlor where the Johnstons and Reverend Bidwell waited. One glance at Peyton, who looked dashing in his dark blue Union frock coat with its red sash encircling his waist, and Carrie knew she'd never love or want to marry any other man. She felt the tension inside of her melt away. Peyton was worth any amount of emotional risk, should her fears come to fruition.

Oh, God, please don't allow that to happen.

"I think we're ready to begin," Reverend Bidwell said in his aged and raspy voice. Standing near the hearth, he made last-moment adjustments to his billowing black robe. "Please take your places, everyone."

Aunt Ruth approached Carrie with rosy cheeks from all the excitement. She wrapped Carrie in a quick but snug embrace. "You'll make Peyton a fine wife, my dear girl." She spoke softly, close to Carrie's ear. "And, my, my, but you look so beautiful."

"Thank you." Truth be known, for the first time in her life, Carrie felt beautiful. After Aunt Ruth released her, she nervously smoothed her hands over her gown. The dress was on loan from another loyalist woman whose husband was a state senator. A good friend of Aunt Ruth, the woman insisted Carrie wear it for good luck.

Aunt Ruth fussed with last-minute decorations. Her excitement was obvious, if not a tad contagious. Under her direction yesterday, and with Major Johnston's help, Peyton carried up rugs and furniture along with various artifacts from the secret cellar. Now Piccadilly Place looked tastefully festive. Aunt Ruth's friends would talk about this affair for weeks. Maybe even months. Even so, Carrie knew the display of her fondest possessions was no small sacrifice on Aunt Ruth's part. As had occurred in the past, the Union army could, at any time, be pushed out of Winchester and the Rebel army could move in. Aunt Ruth could lose all her prized possessions if her home was invaded by the enemy and inhabited by an officer who wasn't as considerate as Eli Kent. Worse was the threat of a guerrilla raid. But Aunt Ruth casually disregarded Carrie's concerns, insisting this wedding celebration was worth the gamble.

Everyone took their places. Vern Johnston planted himself beside Peyton, and his wife, Meredith, stood next to Carrie. Despite her long, arduous journey from Germantown, Meredith's green eyes were bright and her smile, wide and genuine. Her soft brown hair seemed haloed by the golden glow of the candlelit room.

"Thank you for acting as my witness," Carrie whispered.

"I'm honored."

Tabitha closed the parlor doors, and Peyton offered his arm to Carrie. Mesmerized by his amorous expression, she threaded her hand around his elbow. Could this really be happening? Was she actually marrying the man she loved with all her heart?

Within minutes they'd recited their vows and the reverend challenged them from the Scriptures to be the kind of husband and wife that God expected.

Then Peyton presented Carrie with a delicate rose-gold ring adorned with tiny sapphires and diamonds. "It belonged to my mother," he murmured as he slipped it onto her finger.

Tears sprang into her eyes. Such a precious gift! "I will treasure it always,

Peyton." A tad too large for her finger, but over the many years to come she'd most likely grow into it.

Reverend Bidwell cleared his throat. "I now pronounce you man and wife. Colonel Collier, you may kiss your wife."

Giving Carrie a gentle smile, Peyton lowered his lips to hers in a beautifully tender kiss, yet polite enough so as not to embarrass the small assembly. As applause erupted, Peyton's amber gaze reflected the flames in the hearth and promised all the love and passion for which Carrie yearned. She thought her chest would explode from the joy swelling inside of her.

By the time she accepted hugs from Aunt Ruth, Meredith, and Tabitha and congratulations from the gentlemen who then shook Peyton's hand enthusiastically, the small ensemble in the music room had begun to play a lively melody. They signed the marriage certificate, although Peyton had signed other legal documents over a month ago.

They traversed into the foyer where three men in black jackets and stiff white collars carried trays of food to the dining room.

And all this for her—for them—in celebration of their marriage. Carrie wished her family could be here. But, then again, they wouldn't care for all the blue-clad soldiers milling about.

More guests arrived.

"Carrie, my sweet, you look more shell-shocked than happy," Peyton whispered. "How about putting a smile on that lovely face of yours?"

She obliged him. "I'm in awe of all the goings-on. I've never attended such a lavish party. And to think it's in our honor makes me dizzy."

"Good. I hoped and prayed this evening would be memorable."

"I'll never forget it." She smiled, this one filled with all the joy she felt. "Thank you."

Peyton shook his head. "It is I who should be thanking you."

Their conversation halted then as guests greeted them. Some of the women Carrie had already met, but some she'd never seen before. Aunt Ruth stood nearby, making introductions when need be and then whisking her friends into the music room.

And then Miss Monteague arrived, looking more stunning than ever in her emerald-green gown. Every man's gaze lingered on the beautiful Lavinia. Carrie watched Peyton closely. Did his?

"So glad you could make it, Miss Monteague," he said politely, taking her hand for only a second or two.

"I wouldn't have missed it." She turned to her bearded escort. "Allow me to introduce Sergeant Enoch Strothers."

The handsome, dark-haired soldier gave a bow. "A pleasure to meet you, ma'am."

Peyton shook Strothers's hand. "I believe, Sergeant, that you and I have met, although it's nice to see you off the battlefield."

"Yes, sir. I agree." The man smiled, causing his high cheekbones to become more pronounced. He appeared every bit as charming as Lavinia was lovely. Carrie wondered if the man was equally simpleminded.

The queue inched forward. The sergeant politely stepped out of line, but Miss Monteague remained and brazenly clutched Peyton's hand.

"I'll be sure to save a dance for you, Peyton," she whispered loud enough for Carrie to overhear. "It'll be like old times."

Before Carrie could hear Peyton's response, an older, distinguished-looking gentleman with bushy gray whiskers claimed her attention. She forced a smile and politely gave him her hand, but all the while her insides churned. Would Lavinia make trouble tonight?

She closed her eyes ever so briefly. *Oh, Lord, please don't allow that woman to ruin my wedding celebration.*

When the line of incoming guests ended, Peyton put his arm around Carrie's waist. She looked enchanting tonight with her reddish-brown tresses pulled back off her face save for the ringlets that brushed against her bare shoulders. Her skin glowed with softness, and Peyton longed to kiss his way down her neck and across her collarbone.

But he'd wait until he had Carrie all to himself.

"Miss Monteague's presence seems to have troubled you," he said close to her ear. "While we were once engaged to be married, she never owned my heart. It's you I love and adore, Carrie."

"I know." She turned her head and her blue eyes held him captive.

"I will never love anyone else."

Happiness shimmered in her eyes. "I love only you, too, Peyton."

He believed every word.

Yes, he adored this woman, and he couldn't help but kiss her right here in the foyer. She didn't push him away or scold him for crushing her crinoline. When their lips parted, her cheeks turned a pretty pink and her gaze brightened.

And then, success! She smiled.

"All right, you two!"

Peyton knew that voice. It caused his earlobes to throb with memories of his younger days. Releasing Carrie, he turned to face Tabitha's frowning countenance. It was almost startling to see her in something other than her dark work dress and stained white apron. The gold satin dress she wore complemented her rich skin tone.

"Get on in the music room and be sociable. I didn't polish that floor for no reason."

"How can I refuse such a request when it comes from someone so lovely?" Peyton gave her a bow. "We shall make our way to the music room straightaway."

"And don't you try to charm me." She lifted her chin. "*Hmph!* I knowed you since you were knee high to a bear cub."

Tabitha stomped off with a rustling of her skirts. Peyton chuckled in her wake.

"I believe you did manage to charm her." Carrie leaned against his arm as she spoke.

"I always could."

With his hand at the small of her back, Peyton guided his bride into the music room. Within that very minute, Vern whisked her off for a waltz while Peyton danced with Meredith. He changed partners every couple of minutes—

And then Lavinia was in his arms. Her imported perfume caused a dull throb in Peyton's temples. He'd never found her Paris cologne appealing. Nor did her shiny dark hair, now gleaming beneath the lamplight, allure him in the least.

Lavinia brought her chin up, her ruby lips forming a perfectly annoying pout. "Just like old times, isn't it, Peyton?"

In more ways than you know. He glanced over her head, pleased to see smiles on his guests' faces. "One thing, however, is very different, Lavinia. I'm a married man now."

"And I'm still available. You might want to remember that if you get bored."

"Why would I get bored?" Peyton watched the suggestive grin slip from Lavinia's face. There was no doubt she'd enjoy seeing him fall from grace. However, when it came to Lavinia Monteague, Peyton's self-control was stronger than the Union and Confederate armies combined. "Carrie and I love each other."

"And she has good reason to love you or say she loves you, namely your inheritance, which, I might add, should be mine!"

Peyton resisted the urge to reply to her hissed accusation. Instead, he searched the room for his bride, but didn't see her anywhere. He spotted Tabitha, Aunt Ruth, Meredith, Vern, and even Reverend Bidwell. A deep unsettling began gnawing at his gut.

As Lavinia prattled on, Peyton waved over a young lieutenant, who gallantly accepted the handoff. Peyton caught Lavinia's scowl before heading for the doorway. Had Carrie seen him dance with Lavinia and jumped to incorrect conclusions? Was she in the library? The parlor? Or had she retreated to her room to rest? In any case, something didn't feel right.

Peyton set off to locate his bride.

CHAPTER 24

"Tell me this is some joke, Carrie Ann, and that you didn't really marry a Yankee colonel."

"Let go of me!" Carrie had stepped outside for a breath of fresh air, only to be rudely accosted by Joshua. Dressed in ragged attire, he resembled one of the poor local farmers.

What a night for him to turn up on the Colliers' doorstep!

Carrie jerked her arm in an attempt to free it, but Joshua held fast as he walked her briskly across the back yard. "Peyton is going to wonder where I am."

"I doubt it. He's dancing with every pretty lady in the room, and probably flirting with them too."

"How dare you say that? You don't know Peyton."

"I know of him." Joshua gave her arm a painful yank. "The man's a scoundrel, Carrie Ann."

"A reformed scoundrel . . . and you're hurting me!"

"Carrie Ann, men like that don't ever change."

She tried prying open his hold. "Let me go!"

Joshua ignored her demand and half dragged her through the tree line and toward the wooden footbridge that spanned a narrow ravine.

"You're going to ruin my dress."

"What a sorry shame that would be. Your family and friends in Wood-stock might be starving, but you're worried about your dress."

"Let go!" she cried again. What a simpleton she'd been to think she knew him—that he was still her friend. He even looked like a different man with that beard covering the lower half of his face.

At last he stopped. "I have a good mind to take you home right now, Carrie Ann, and put you on public display. The town will stone you. You're a traitor. Unfortunately, it ain't possible to make the trip at the present time. Do you have any idea what's happening in the upper Valley near Woodstock? Sheridan and his men are burning everything, robbing citizens of their livestock, and ravishing the womenfolk."

"That's a lie." Part of it, anyway.

"Yankees are killing every man over sixteen and taking boys off to jail."

Carrie hadn't heard that before. "If I were back home, Joshua, what would I do? Would I be able to save anyone's farm from General Grant's orders?"

He didn't seem to have an answer to that.

"So you've given up on us in the Valley, eh? The people you once loved, the country you were born and raised in? You've swallowed all those Yankee lies, right along with all that rich food you're eating." He squeezed her upper arm. "You're looking downright plump, Carrie Ann."

She slapped his hand away. "So what if I am?"

"So what?" He gave her a shake. "So what?" The words sounded as though they came through a clenched jaw. "Look at you, all dressed up in that pretty gown while your sister lies ill in a tumbledown tavern. Have you no shame?"

"What are you talking about?"

"Sarah Jane, that's what I'm talking about. You asked me to keep an eye out for her, remember? Or is it just yourself you think about these days?"

"You know that's not true. I risked my life to find her."

"You're not the only one. Why do you think I'd be such a fool as to walk in under Collier's nose tonight? It was the fastest way to get the news to you."

"Joshua, tell me. Where is she?"

"She's in a town twenty miles north of here called Martinsburg. She's being cared for at a place called the Sundowner Tavern. Sarah Jane turned up there about a week ago, beaten and suffering with a fever. She was mumbling nonsense, like she was out of her head."

A flash of memory surfaced. Her mother—stepmother—uttering gibberish after the farm burned.

"I left some money to help pay for her keep, but it won't last long. Carrie Ann, you'll need to fetch her soon."

"I will." She felt like sprinting to Martinsburg this minute. "I promise."

"Good." Joshua gave a nod and put his hands on his hips. "Hurry and change your clothes. I'll wait."

"I can't leave right this minute, although I'd like to for Sarah Jane's sake. It's my wedding day."

"Oh, don't tell me you gotta wait until your honeymoon is over—"

"I need to speak with Peyton."

"And you think that he'll approve?" Joshua's sugary-sweet tone had a vinegar edge to it. "So tell me, Carrie Ann, why did you marry the enemy? Money?"

"Peyton is not my enemy. I have always been independent minded, remember? Like my papa." Sheer defiance propelled her on; she wouldn't allow Joshua to cow her. She lifted her chin. "Besides, I love Peyton. That's the plain truth and all the reason you need to know."

"Love?" Joshua guffawed. "What do you know about love? You up and married the first man who showed you some interest."

"Peyton loves me too."

Joshua gripped her chin in a painful hold. "Don't come crying to me when that Yankee breaks your heart. You hear?"

He released her forcibly and Carrie stumbled back a few paces. Tears sprang to her eyes. "I hate you!"

The venomous words flew out of her mouth before she could think better of them. She regretted them instantly, but maybe she did hate him—for being a Confederate spy or worse, for doing Rodingham's bidding and treating her roughly. Yes, for that Carrie despised him!

God forgive me . . .

Joshua fell silent. The only sound was the faint rustle of the leafy treetops as the wind blew through them.

"I never thought I'd hear such a thing from you, Carrie Ann. Not ever."

"I never thought you'd hurt me."

"You mean just now?"

Carrie's fingertips touched the bruised places on her face. "Yes."

Joshua chuckled. "I've done worse to you, and you about licked me nearly a half-dozen times in the past."

"I'm no longer a child and a tomboy."

"So I noticed." Silence passed between them. "But you're not my friend anymore either, are you?"

Carrie shivered. "I'm cold. I want to go back to the house."

"I'll always think of you as my little sister, Carrie Ann." Joshua continued to block her way. "But I didn't get an invitation to your wedding celebration."

"For obvious reasons. You, sir, are my husband's enemy."

"What about your enemy, Carrie Ann? Are we still friends?" His tone had softened. "Tell me. Do you truly hate me or are we friends?"

"I don't know. You confuse me. You're kind and then you're cruel. Are you a Confederate spy? A bushwhacker? Or are you a Union scout?"

"I'm Major John Brown. That's all you have to know, and I'm holding you to your promise that you'll keep quiet about my true identity."

"Well, know this: I will never lie to Peyton." Her whole body stiffened with determination.

"I'm not asking you to lie. Just keep your mouth shut."

She tried to step around him.

He matched her stride. "I found Sarah Jane, just like you asked. Now you owe me."

"I already gave you my word."

"You'll keep quiet?"

"Yes, yes, for finding my sister, I will . . . now let me pass or I'll tell my husband what a rogue you are, Major John Brown."

Somewhere behind Joshua, leaves crunched beneath heavy footfalls. He quickly slipped around Carrie, standing behind her as if she were a human shield.

"How very unchivalrous of you."

"A safety precaution is all." He jabbed the barrel of his pistol into her ribs.

A heartbeat later, Peyton came into view. The cocking of weaponry cracked across the ravine, indicating Peyton wasn't alone.

"Carrie, are you all right?" Peyton halted on the edge of the ravine.

She nodded, not trusting her voice.

The pressure from the barrel of Joshua's gun disappeared, and she heard him holster his weapon. Carrie breathed easier.

Peyton held out one hand. Joshua had no hold on her now, so she ran to her new husband. Enveloped in Peyton's embrace, Carrie lost her resolve and buried her face in his coat and sobbed.

"You're safe now, my love," Peyton whispered.

She shuttered at the very thought of what might have occurred tonight. Clinging to Peyton, she peeked at her childhood friend. He stood with his hands in surrender while two Federal vedettes searched him.

Peyton's hold tightened around her. "How dare you force my wife to stand in the night air without her shawl, Major Brown? And to take her to a secluded place against her will? This is an outrage!"

"My apologies, sir." Joshua didn't sound a bit shaken—or contrite, for that matter. "I merely wanted to explain to Mrs. Collier why I wasn't able to return to the Union camp as you instructed."

"Your explanation should have been made to me directly. My wife had nothing to do with the orders I gave you." With a protective arm around Carrie, he waved an armed picket forward. "Sergeant, arrest this man and charge him with attempting to kidnap an officer's wife."

"Yes, sir," came the vedette's enthusiastic reply.

The soldier moved toward Joshua just as another guard stepped out of the shadows. Both men trained the barrels of their guns on Joshua.

"Peyton, don't let any harm come to Major Brown." Joshua had found Sarah Jane for her, after all. She'd keep his identity a secret but she had to tell Peyton about her youngest sister's whereabouts. "Please, Peyton?"

He gently pushed her back, his face near hers. "You want me to show leniency to a man who stole you away from our wedding celebration and frightened you? Just look how you're shaking."

As if to prove the foolishness of her request, Carrie shuddered. "I c-can explain. Later. Much later. We have guests waiting."

"Of course. Let's get you into the house and in front of a fire."

She welcomed his snug hold around her shoulders as he guided her toward the house.

"Are you sure you're not hurt?"

"Yes." Contrary to her reply, she massaged her injured forearm.

"You are hurt. Why didn't you tell me?" After pausing on the back porch, Peyton gently inspected the wrist that she'd hurt in August.

"It's nothing, really."

He cupped her face with one hand, gliding his thumb across her cheek. Carrie preferred his tenderness over Joshua's gruffness.

"I searched the house for you, but you'd vanished." He kissed her forehead before pulling her into an embrace. "Fortunately, Tommy was tending to our guests' horses and overheard your protests. He came and got me right away."

She wrapped her arms around his midsection and placed her ear on his chest. She heard his heartbeats, strong and steady. Ironically, it used to be Joshua coming to her rescue when they were children. But now it seemed her childhood friend was now her enemy.

"Why didn't you scream for help?"

"It didn't occur to me. I suppose I've grown accustomed to handling confrontations on my own."

"I suppose you have." Peyton's calm soothed her jangled nerves. "Your courage is one of the things I admire about you, although it puts a scare into me at the same time."

She wondered why.

"Are you sure you're all right, Carrie?" Holding her at arm's length, he peered into her face. "If you'd like to rest, I can explain your absence to our guests."

"No, I'm fine. A bit shaken, but unharmed."

"Good, because I'd like a dance with my bride."

Pushing aside all the unpleasantness, she smiled. "And I would very much enjoy dancing with my husband."

Carrie quelled the desire to travel to Martinsburg and collect Sarah Jane. The news about her sister could wait until morning. Joshua said she was getting the care she needed. And this, after all, was her wedding night.

Ruth had checked the parlor, the dining room, the music room, and the library, but Frances was nowhere to be found. She'd been sure her irksome neighbor would have stayed until all the food and champagne were gone. How odd that she'd only stayed for the better part of an hour. Something was wrong.

Back in the music room, Ruth spotted Lavinia in her glory with four officers in attendance. "Excuse me, Miss Monteague, may I have a word?" She relished the formality, grateful Carrie Ann was her niece by marriage.

Oh, my, how close we came . . .

Lavinia tore herself away from her admirers. "Yes, what is it?"

"Is your mother ill?"

"Mama?" Lavinia waved a hand. "Her health is fine, thank you." She turned toward the officers, but Ruth halted her.

"She left the party so quickly. Is something amiss next door?"

A dramatic sigh. "Oh, I suppose you'll find out soon enough." She lifted her fan so as not to be overheard. "Edward died tonight. He was wounded in that last Winchester battle."

"What terrible news!" And it was news, all right. Ruth's hand fluttered to her neckline. Edward, that spoiled, pampered brat who had participated in Samuel's death and the burning of their barn and stables had been killed. "Tragic."

"Horribly. But I'm grateful that a couple of Edward's faithful comrades brought him home when it was clear he would not recover." A shadow crept across Lavinia's face and an uncharacteristic sorrow filled her dark eyes. "We hid the men in our home because no sooner did they bring us Edward when our entire downstairs filled with invaders and their wounded."

Ruth gasped. "You harbored Rebels in your home?"

"The same way you've harbored Yankees in yours over the years. I trust you'll keep our secret as we've kept yours."

She gave a curt nod. "I'll say nothing."

"Good." Lavinia kept her voice above a whisper. "To answer your initial question, Mama left the party so she'd be home when the undertaker arrived."

"Please accept my condolences."

"Thank you." Lavinia glanced at the officers who were now chatting with several young ladies. Her expression fell at her missed opportunity. And then something else glimmered in her eyes. Was it fear or perhaps desperation?

Ruth couldn't blame Lavinia for feeling insecure and frightened. Peyton's marriage combined with Edward's death must have caused Lavinia to realize her precarious position in life. If the South lost the war, her remaining brother would be bankrupt—and Lavinia, unmarried and vulnerable, might be left destitute.

Ruth knew the feeling all too well. In '62 when General Jackson routed the Union army from the Valley, it looked as if the CSA might prevail. And then this past summer . . . so many lives lost as General Grant pressed on with his Overland Campaign. Nearly forty thousand men dead after The Wilderness and Spotsylvania Courthouse battles with no decisive winner. And then the loss at Cold Harbor . . .

Yes, all did seem lost back then.

"Lavinia dear, I'll see to it that food is brought over for you and your mother and any mourners who might stop in." It was the least Ruth could do.

"The last thing we want is a loyalist's pity."

"You'll get none of that, I assure you."

Again, Lavinia glanced over her shoulder at the mingling officers. It appeared she had one particular blond lieutenant in her sight.

"His name is Luther Heffinger," Ruth offered.

"I have learned his name, thank you anyway."

"His father is German and owns a shoe factory in Chicago."

"A shoe factory? Imagine that." Interest sparked in Lavinia's dark gaze. "Is he rich?"

"Unfortunately, no. With the economy such as it is, the factory contracted with the federal government, and it is manufacturing boots for the troops instead of fashionable shoes."

A groan from Ruth's young neighbor. "Wouldn't it just figure?"

"Now, Lavinia, take heart. Who's to say the factory won't rally after the war?" Ruth arched a brow. "I encourage you to look to the future, my dear."

"Is that what you do?"

Before she could reply, movement in the center of the music room drew Ruth's attention. Peyton gathered Carrie Ann in his arms and the couple began to waltz. What a fine sight they made, Carrie gazing adoringly up into Peyton's smiling face. He held her gently yet possessively, as if she were a rare treasure, which indeed she was. And then . . . mercy! The rascal kissed her right on the mouth.

Lifting a lacy gloved hand to her lips, Ruth laughed softly. "Yes, Lavinia, I focus on the future." It looked bright indeed.

Ruth's gaze traveled around the room. Some older women fanned themselves, aghast at Peyton's actions. Many of the men chuckled. A few officers even had the audacity to applaud. Soon other couples joined the bride and groom, and the room became a sea of colorful hooped skirts and dark blue uniforms.

Sensing a presence to her left, Ruth turned to find Tabitha watching on. They exchanged smiles.

"Our boy married the right one, that's for sure."

"Yes, he did." Ruth willed herself not to glance at Lavinia.

"We knew it right from the start, when we got Peyt's letter. You remember?"

"I do." Ruth's smile grew.

"I don't think I ever saw him so happy as right now."

"Oh, shut up, both of you!" In a swirl of emerald silk, Lavinia stormed from the room, pushing rudely past several officers as she left.

Ruth pretended she didn't hear or see anything out of the ordinary. Of course, it was rather typical of Lavinia to throw a fit over something or another.

"That girl's as green as her dress." Tabitha snorted a small laugh.

"Normally, I'd agree, but tonight Lavinia is genuinely distraught." Ruth lowered her voice to a whisper. "Edward died this evening—wounded a couple of weeks ago. His comrades brought him home where he breathed his last."

Tabitha's jaw slacked slightly open. Recovering, she wagged her head. "It may sound heartless of me, but now my brother's soul and I can rest easier. One of his killers is standing before King Jesus."

Ruth agreed. It certainly was difficult to feel sad over the loss of one of the enemy, even if he had been Harm's son. "Frances is upset, of course."

"I imagine so. But that don't excuse Miss Lavinia's bad manners. She shouldn't have come here tonight." Tabitha clucked her tongue. "It's disrespectful to her dead brother." Tabitha paused to watch the dancers. "I have to admit, I didn't see much of Miss Frances tonight."

"She kept to herself."

"She shouldn't have come here tonight either."

Ruth kept her eyes on the dancers as she conversed, lest she arouse suspicions.

"Tommy said one of them fellas who saw Carrie Ann here from the Union camp was outside only minutes ago. From what I gather the scoundrel accosted our girl."

Ruth inhaled sharply. "Not the same man who threatened to kill her—and you?"

"No. The other one."

"What on earth was he doing here, Tabitha?" Ruth put the pieces together. "Oh, my stars! You don't suppose—" Ruth finished the idea silently. The Confederate comrade who brought Edward home to die—a spy? No doubt they were one and the same. She'd have to let Peyton know as soon as possible.

Ruth drew in a breath. "And to think a Confederate informer is lurking about right under the pickets' noses!"

"Not anymore. Tommy said our boy rescued Carrie Ann and ordered the Rebel off to jail."

"Well, that's a relief." More importantly, God had protected her new niece of whom Ruth was so very fond. Oh, she supposed she initially had used the young lady, and perhaps that was shameful. But they were all better off for it—including Carrie Ann. Why, just to look at her one could see she was the epitome of the joyous bride. Peyton, too, was happy, so what was so wrong about Ruth's forcing the matter? Now their financial woes were over. Piccadilly Place would return to its original glory. She and Tabitha would be taken care of and so would Carrie Ann. It had all worked out perfectly.

The ensemble began to play a lively tune and the bandleader called for guests to dance the Patty-Cake Polka. Couples formed a circle and began a hop-step-hop to the music, then stopped, faced their partners, and made patty-cake before clapping. Taking hands, they side-skipped before changing partners and beginning another hop-step-hop around the room.

Ruth smiled as she watched Carrie, whose gaze often strayed to Peyton. Likewise, his eyes didn't often leave his bride even while he patty-caked with old Mrs. Hightower.

Weightlessness enveloped Ruth, and even the idea of a threat against her family couldn't curtail her joy at this moment.

A man's shout caused the ensemble to cease their playing.

"Colonel Collier! Message for Colonel Collier!" The messenger waved a slip of paper in his hands.

Peyton led Carrie Ann out of the circle of dancers. He whispered something to her, and Carrie glanced across the room at Ruth and Tabitha. After a nod to Peyton, she strode toward them while he discussed matters with the messenger.

Ruth watched him reading the note and saw Peyton's expression darken.

"Oh dear. There's trouble." Ruth reached for Tabitha's hand. "I can see it on Peyton's expression."

He called to Major Johnston and waved him over.

"I wonder if the army got wind of the goings-on next door," Tabitha said. "Frances should've knowed that the Union army has its spies too."

Ruth clutched Tabitha's hand tighter. Their friend Frances would likely pay a high price for not reporting Edward's presence and death to authorities, not to mention harboring Confederates. Unless Frances could weave a believable tale or Lavinia could turn on her considerable charms, the Monteagues would pay a high price indeed.

CHAPTER 25

"Carrie, I have to go. I have my orders."

Her chin tilted downward. "Can't you send your men to take care of the matter?"

"I'm afraid not." Standing in the darkly paneled study, Peyton slid his saber into his scabbard. "General Crooke requested my regiment and me by name." That was puzzling. Peyton had been under the impression that Colonel Thoburn's brigades occupied the area around Cedar Creek. Why hadn't Crooke selected those troops to quell the uprising? They were closer. He heaved a rueful sigh. "But, not to worry, Colonel Edwards and his men are about town. Winchester won't be left unprotected."

"Is that supposed to comfort me? I'd rather Colonel Edwards and his men take care of the uprising."

"Carrie . . ." Peyton arched a brow. He wanted no argument. He had his duties and they took precedence over all else, including his wedding celebration, as much as he hated to leave.

"I know. You have your orders."

With a little grin at her mild sass, he half cocked his Colt .44 and inspected each cylinder. Certain each was loaded, he uncocked the weapon. "I shouldn't be too long." He placed the revolver into its holster.

"I'll be waiting."

Carrie peered into the hallway and waved good-bye to the last of the departing guests. Did she blame him for their ruined wedding celebration?

"I'm sorry, Carrie." He didn't know what else to say.

"No need to apologize." She turned and smiled, but the disappointment in her eyes was evident. "The important part of our celebration is complete and that's all that matters to me. Besides, I'm just being selfish."

"How so?"

"I don't want to share you with the Union army. I want you all to myself."

And he wanted nothing more than to give himself completely to her. "Carrie, when I return, we'll have time to ourselves. I promise."

"I'm going to hold you to that." She stepped toward him, her blue eyes shining.

Peyton's heart swelled with varying emotions. Amusement, love, joy—curiosity. How did she do that? How did she make him feel ten feet tall and invincible just by staring up at him so adoringly? How blessed he was to have married a woman who loved him more than his trust fund.

Tearing his gaze away, he draped his dress frock over the back of the desk chair and shrugged into his shell jacket.

"Oh, by the way, Peyton, your attorney Mr. Finch sent his regrets. Apparently he and his wife weren't able to attend the reception tonight because she just gave birth to a baby."

"How nice. I'm sure Horatio is thrilled."

"Did you know this little one is number six for them?"

Peyton chuckled softly. "Mr. Finch will soon have his own company of Union troops."

Carrie moved closer to him, her skirts rustling with each step. "Did I forget to tell you that I hope and pray we have as many children . . . or even more?"

"Oh?" Peyton buttoned up his jacket. "You may have forgotten to communicate that small detail." Not that it mattered to him. If God blessed them with a brood, he would consider his quiver full indeed. If not, he and Carrie would still find happiness together.

"You do like children"—her right eyebrow dimpled—"don't you?"

"I eat them for breakfast." He chuckled at her wide-eyed expression. "If you'd known that, would you still have married me?"

"Yes." She lifted her chin rather defiantly. "I will just keep the urchins away from you in the morning."

His smile grew, but then activity at the doorway stole his focus. Vern stepped into the room.

"We're ready whenever you are, Colonel."

"Good. I'll be along momentarily."

Peyton's attention returned to Carrie. Her smile had vanished and a frown reappeared.

"I'll be back soon." Pulling her against him, he dipped his head and nudged her with the tip of his nose so she'd meet his gaze. "My men and I are more than able to put out a little uprising in no time, so don't fret, all right?"

After she nodded, he kissed her slowly, longingly. He wanted to savor the sweetness of it until he returned. She clung to the front of his jacket and her equally passionate response only increased his determination to settle the disturbance across town and get back home.

Their lips parted. "And if you want an entire flock of children, my sweet, I shall be happy to do my part."

"Thank you." The reply came out rather dreamily. But then she blinked and sucked in a breath. "Oh!" Crimson flooded her cheeks. "No, I didn't mean—"

"You didn't?" Swallowing his mirth, Peyton narrowed his eyes. "I meant every word, Carrie."

Her mouth moved, but not a sound tumbled out. How fun she was to tease.

"Seriously, I understand what you're telling me, and when I get back we'll discuss the matter at great length." After one last kiss, he released her and strode from the study, deciding to leave her with the anticipation of his return.

―◌ ◌―

After the house emptied of visitors, Carrie helped Aunt Ruth fold tablecloths while Meredith and Tabitha collected plates and glassware and put the items onto the dining room table. The hired help transferred the dishware to the kitchen where they washed, dried, and stored it away.

Carrie wouldn't have minded if the guests had stayed. It might have helped to pass the time. But when the men took their leave, the ladies grew anxious and chose to depart as well. Aunt Ruth explained that, in the past, when the Union army took control of Winchester—and the Valley—it was eventually pushed out by Rebel forces. Once the town was again in Confederate possession, loyalists suffered dire consequences. Houses were burned and free people of color were often murdered.

"Do you think that will happen again?" Meredith looked as concerned as Carrie felt.

"I doubt it." With the tidying finished and the hired help dismissed, Aunt Ruth dropped into an armchair. "The Rebel army was demoralized during that last battle."

Carrie admired the older woman's confidence. "Peyton didn't appear too worried about the Union army being pushed out of town before he left either."

"Nor did Vern," Meredith said from the armchair closest to the hearth.

Eyeing their Baltimorean guest, Carrie wondered how she coped with Major Johnston's absences. "Meredith, have you gotten used to your husband leaving you at a moment's notice?"

"No, and I'm afraid I'll never get used to it."

"I don't believe I will either." Sitting alone on the settee, Carrie wished Peyton sat beside her.

Meredith's smile was sympathetic. "Take heart, you're not the only bride whose husband got whisked away by the Union army on her wedding day."

Carrie didn't say, but it was hardly consolation. "Should we pack away your collectables again, Aunt Ruth?"

"I don't see the need for it. Union pickets are patrolling the streets."

Tabitha walked into the parlor beside Tommy, who carried a tray containing a teapot and four porcelain cups and saucers. The young man set it on the sideboard. No doubt Tommy wished he rode off with Peyton's regiment tonight.

"Nice to have you around, Tommy." Tabitha bestowed a rare smile on him. "Saves my tired, old arms from breaking off."

"Yes, ma'am." He loosened the tie around his neck and tugged on his dress jacket, obviously uncomfortable in the restrictive clothing. In spite of it, he'd looked dapper tonight in his dark suit and sporting a new haircut. He behaved like a true gentleman, and he'd even taken a turn around the dance floor with a young lady.

Carrie made a mental note to tell him later how proud of him she was.

Glass smashed somewhere in the back of the house, drawing Carrie's attention.

"Sounds like it came from the back porch door." Aunt Ruth stood.

"Probably one of them boys from the neighborhood," Tabitha muttered, handing Meredith a teacup.

"I'll go take a look." Aunt Ruth strode from the room.

Not more than a minute later, Carrie heard her cry out, followed by shuffling of feet. The others heard it too, and Tommy set off to investigate.

Carrie stood.

Aunt Ruth returned unharmed—but in the clutches of a man wearing dark clothing. His arm encircled the older woman's neck, and he held a gun to her head.

"Don't nobody move."

Rodingham. Carrie recognized him at once. She whirled to run for help, but crashed into another man as she reached the foyer. "Joshua!"

His blue eyes darkened. She'd forgotten to use his pseudonym. He grabbed her arm and roughly hauled her back into the parlor.

At that moment, Tommy made a dash for the front door. Rodingham pointed his pistol at the boy.

"No!" Carrie's scream was drowned by an explosive shot.

Tommy stumbled forward, a hole in his left shoulder oozing crimson red. He collapsed on the foyer floor and lay there, unmoving.

"Tommy!" Carrie cried.

Meredith began to pray aloud and Rodingham backhanded her, keeping the gun still pointed at Aunt Ruth. Meredith fell to her knees.

"Stop it, you madman!" Carrie tried desperately to twist out of Joshua's grasp so she could tend to Tommy.

"And you, Mrs. Collier, need to learn some respect." Rodingham's gaze shifted to Joshua. "Tie up these women while I teach that girl some manners."

"I can teach her just as good as you." Joshua jabbed the barrel of his gun into Carrie's ribs.

She winced. "I thought Peyton's men arrested you and put you behind bars."

"Funny thing about that, Mrs. Collier," Rodingham answered, sounding wickedly amused. "Those two men weren't much up to a fight. I easily overpowered them." He puffed out his chest. "Single-handedly. So Major Brown here owes me a little favor." His dark, beady eyes moved to her captor. "Now tie up these women like I said."

"Sure thing."

Carrie's pulse quickened. Joshua wouldn't really allow her to suffer at the hands of Rodingham, would he? "You're both despicable excuses for—"

"Shut up." Joshua's leathery palm clamped over her mouth. "Roddy, if you'll find me something to tie 'em up with, I'll do your bidding and make short work of it."

Rodingham's gaze roamed the room and settled at the front windows. He strode toward them.

"When I loosen my hold on you, Carrie Ann," Joshua whispered, "you take my gun and run." Joshua's breath was warm against her neck and she pulled away. "Roddy will follow you. Just do what I taught you."

Part of her wanted to refuse, but another part of her saw it as her only hope to escape so she could help the others.

Tommy lay so still. Was he still breathing?

God in heaven, Savior of the world . . . Carrie squeezed her eyes closed, but didn't have time to even finish her prayer before Rodingham's voice intruded.

"You sayin' something to that girl, Brown?"

"Told her to settle down."

A crooked grin slinked across Rodingham's clean-shaven face. "Don't forget she's mine first."

"I ain't forgot."

Meredith had scooted over to Aunt Ruth. Her light brown hair had come undone from its pins and fell in waves to her waist. Aunt Ruth and Tabitha eyed the gunmen while Rodingham yanked off the two heavy cords holding the draperies in place, his back momentarily turned away from Carrie.

Joshua's hold slackened, and Carrie broke free. He slid his hand behind his back and she grabbed the pistol's barrel and ran.

Rodingham turned and shouted at Joshua. "Brown, you idiot, stop her!"

"You want her first, you get her!"

The raised voices wafted to her ears as Carrie dashed down the hallway.

"She ain't going far. Go get her while I tie up these women."

Carrie ducked into the library. Her heart thudded so loudly it echoed in her ears. But then footfalls pounded down the hallway, coming nearer.

Keep calm. Breathe.

Carrie stood with her back against a shelf of books. Her hand trembled as she cocked the gun, trusting it was loaded and ready to fire.

Seconds later, Rodingham burst into the room. Carrie took aim, and just as he pivoted toward her, she squeezed the trigger. The explosion in the carpetless room was deafening. Acrid smoke rose from her weapon, but her shot had met its mark. Holding his neck, Rodingham stared at her in utter surprise before crumpling to the floor like a gray bag of rocks. Blood spurted from his wound.

Several heartbeats later, the miscreant and his stunned expression faded into eternity where he'd meet his Maker.

Thank you, Lord, for protecting me. Carrie slumped against the tall shelves behind her.

Joshua rushed in and skidded to a halt. He stared at his fallen comrade. "Nicely done, Carrie Ann." He retrieved his pistol from her shaking hand. "I'd wager he didn't even suffer."

"Why didn't you just kill him for me?" She felt a sob coming on.

"Because he would have killed me first."

Was he joking?

"Carrie Ann, I knew a long time ago Rodingham was an evil man, but I was ordered to work with him. So I tried to play his game while limiting the damage as much as possible. Tonight he went too far, and I can't say I'm sorry to see him gone."

"Neither am I sorry, although"—she gulped—"I never killed a man before." Her gaze bounced from Rodingham's lifeless form to Joshua.

"You thinkin' you'd like to see me dead too, Carrie Ann?"

"I didn't say that."

"Well, you might hate me for fighting the Yanks, and that includes your husband, but I'll always be your friend. And you will always be the same as my little sister. Nothing will change that." He steered her out of the library ahead of him. "Now, you go see about that injured boy and those other women while I get out of here."

Carrie felt numb, dazed, as if this were all a bad dream. She made her way to the foyer, where she found Aunt Ruth comforting Meredith while Tabitha fanned herself and muttered up a prayer.

"Oh, my dear girl . . . are you all right?"

Was she? "Yes, I think so."

Aunt Ruth embraced her with one arm but held on to Meredith with the other.

Tommy!

Carrie inched her way forward. She stared at the blood where the young man had fallen.

Tommy was gone.

CHAPTER 26

Something didn't feel right. It was too quiet, the air too still. Certainly, Peyton was aware of horses' hooves, plodding along on the dirt road as he and his men traveled farther outside of town. Bridles and weaponry jangled and clanked. Around them, the night was alive with trills from tree frogs and the chirp of crickets. But no sounds of an uprising. Only the eerie sound of silence before an ambush.

Peyton held up a hand and halted his men.

Vern pulled up beside him. "What are you thinking, sir?"

"Nothing good." He pointed straight ahead. Mottles of moonlight fell over the pike. "We're coming up to Hanson's Woods—at least that's what Aunt Ruth called it when I was a boy. I have this strange sensation that the Rebs might be lying in wait for our arrival."

"The same thought occurred to me, sir."

Affirmation. "Then we'll disappoint the enemy tonight, Major. Order your men to return to Winchester. The uprising proved false."

"Yes, sir."

Peyton turned his horse around. While he wasn't afraid of a fight, he refused to sacrifice good soldiers simply because the area was dark and unfamiliar to most of them. But he especially wouldn't engage if it was, indeed, an ambush. For all he knew the enemy outnumbered and outgunned him. Peyton would much rather meet the foe on his terms.

A shout signaled a rider's approach. Murmurs of "hold your fire" and

"Tommy to see the colonel" soon reached Peyton. He dismounted while questions swirled around his head.

"Sir, sir . . ." Tommy sounded winded.

"What is it?" Peyton took hold of the bay's bridle strap, wondering why the lad slouched so far forward. "Tommy?"

He straightened, and moonlight illuminated the bloody wound below his left shoulder.

"Dear God . . . what happened?"

"Shot, sir."

A little moan, and then Tommy slid sideways. Peyton caught him and lowered him to the ground.

"I need some light!" Peyton ordered. "Keep a lookout, men, for the enemy."

A soldier handed Petyon a folding pocket lantern. Once the candles were lit, several officers gathered closer to hide the glow if the enemy should be in close proximity. Peyton tore open the front of Tommy's shirt and inspected the wound. Blood leaked out with every heartbeat. Peyton removed his handkerchief, placed it over the wound, and applied pressure. Tommy had likely used every ounce of energy he possessed to ride hard and catch up to Peyton's regiment.

"Shot in the back. It came straight through me."

Sure enough. Peyton felt the wet, sticky hole beneath the boy's left shoulder blade. Tommy was losing blood quickly. "Who did this?" He would see that the perpetrator was brought to justice.

"Roddy."

The name was familiar.

"There was trouble . . . I went for . . . the pistol." Tommy labored to inhale. "Roddy shot me. I played possum and heard him go after Miss Carrie Ann next . . . Not sure how it happened, sir . . . but I believe Miss Carrie Ann killed him . . . she shot Roddy . . ." Tommy wheezed. "The other man fled alone."

Peyton got the picture. "Johnston!" He tried not to let his panic show in his tone.

"Sir?"

"Take some of your men, return to my home, and investigate."

"On my way, sir."

"Are the ladies all right, Tommy?"

"Yeah, I think . . . "

"And get a doctor," Peyton added.

"Yes, sir." Vern clamped a hand on Peyton's shoulder. "Sounds like God protected them."

Peyton prayed it was so.

Vern called orders to his men. Within seconds, horses and riders galloped down the pike.

Looking back at Tommy, Peyton implored him to relax. The more excited he became, the more blood spurted from his wound. At this rate, he'd bleed out. "Easy, now."

Two privates approached. They claimed to have medical experience, so Peyton inched away. One medic gave the boy sips of water from a canteen while the other held pressure on his wound in hopes of slowing the bleeding. They arrived at the conclusion that there wasn't much they could do without supplies.

"You're going to be just fine, Tommy." While Peyton hoped so with all his heart, he feared the opposite was true.

"Sir . . . please listen to me."

"Of course." Peyton sat back on his haunches.

Tommy took another labored breath. "The second man . . . Major Brown."

"Brown? No, it couldn't have been him. I sent him to jail for accosting Carrie. Remember? You were the one who told me and identified him."

"It was him, sir . . . except . . . Miss Carrie Ann . . . she called him Joshua."

Joshua! Carrie's friend from Woodstock. Could they be one and the same man? Had to be. No wonder Carrie begged for leniency on his behalf. Anger simmered inside of him.

"I'll see that we find him."

Tommy made choking sounds, and blood trickled out of the side of his mouth. The volunteer medics held him upright.

"He needs a doctor," Peyton said. "A surgeon." *Please, God, not Tommy. He's too young to die.*

"He won't make the trip, sir," the medic on Peyton's left said. "He's dying."

They were words Peyton didn't want to hear. But it was true.

"I'm proud of you, Tommy." Peyton leaned forward and grasped the young man's right hand. "The Union army is proud of you, and because of your bravery, loyalty, and excellent horsemanship, I'm granting your request to enlist. Furthermore, I'm recommending that you be immediately promoted to the rank of corporal. I am confident our commanders will agree."

Each of the medics congratulated the boy.

Tommy attempted a smile and looked fondly at Peyton. The kid didn't even have a last name. He'd been orphaned as a newborn and passed from one orphanage to another. But he'd found a family among the United States cavalrymen.

Peyton affectionately squeezed Tommy's hand. The boy tried to speak but couldn't manage it. Then his body went limp, his head dropped back, and that familiar vacancy seeped into Tommy's eyes.

Peyton momentarily bowed his head. The urge to weep nearly choked him.

"That was a nice thing you done, Colonel," said the private on Peyton's left. "It's just what Tommy wanted."

Peyton didn't trust his voice to reply. He'd worked hard to keep Tommy out of the army so he could protect the kid.

"May you rest in peace, Tommy-boy," the other medic said. "You were a good kid."

The other private crossed himself and mumbled up a prayer.

Peyton stared at Tommy's lifeless form. His chest muscles constricted until he winced, and with a heavy heart, he ordered his men to tie his young friend's body to the horse on which he'd ridden out here. Peyton would take Tommy back to Piccadilly Place and see that he had a decent burial—and with the Collier name since he didn't have one of his own.

As for Major Brown—Joshua—that man was as good as dead!

—◌◌—

Carrie couldn't stop shaking. She'd never killed a man, and now the reality of it was sinking in. *Thou shalt not kill . . . oh, God, forgive me.* Except she couldn't see how she had any other choice.

Standing near the hearth in the parlor, she listened as Aunt Ruth, Tabitha, and Meredith relayed the events to Major Johnston. He made notes in a record book while behind him soldiers carried off Rodingham's body.

Carrie's shuddering intensified.

"It wasn't a robbery or a raid. It was a plot to harm Carrie Ann," Aunt Ruth declared.

"A downright wicked man," Tabitha huffed. "He was the same one who wanted to steal Miss Carrie Ann's horse when she first come here. She had some words with him and he wanted to shoot her then and there, but Colonel Kent stepped in."

"So what you're telling me is that the deceased—this man, Roddy—had reasons for revenge."

"He sure did," Tabitha replied.

"Clearly, Vern," Meredith said, "it was self-defense."

"I believe you and Mrs. Collier, without question. Even so, I'll have to make out a report, which is the reason for my inquiries."

Alone on the settee, Meredith arranged her skirts. "Be sure to take down my account."

Major Johnston nodded at his wife. "Go ahead."

"I watched in horror as that Roddy fellow went after Carrie Ann. But God saw fit to put mercy into Major Brown's heart. He slipped her his weapon. That's what she used to kill that devil Roddy."

"Is this true, Mrs. Collier?"

"Y-yes."

Johnston made a note. "I will relay this information to the colonel as soon as he arrives."

"When will that be?" Carrie hoped soon. Peyton's presence always calmed her.

"I expect him anytime." Johnston gave her a sympathetic grin.

"Do you suppose Peyton took Tommy to the hospital?" Worry lines formed on Aunt Ruth's forehead. "After all, he did require medical attention."

"Tommy . . . of course." Carrie cupped her face with her hands. She had been replaying tonight's tragic events in her mind when she ought to have been praying for Tommy. "I hope he's all right."

"The poor brave boy." Aunt Ruth's eyes were round and sad. "He was determined to find you, Major Johnston, and Peyton, even with a bullet in his shoulder."

"He succeeded, although I must be honest, ladies, Tommy was feeling poorly by the time he reached us."

Major Johnston suggested they pray together, and Carrie was more than happy to agree to it. The mere thought of prayer quelled her trembling.

Taking hands, they bowed their heads and petitioned the God of the universe on Tommy's behalf. Major Johnston concluded with, "Not our will be done tonight, Lord Jesus, but Thine. For Thine is the kingdom, and the power, and the glory forever and ever."

After a collective "amen," Tabitha made her way to the parlor door. "If you all will excuse me, I'll go and fix us some hot tea."

"Thank you, Tabitha dear. A cup of tea is always soothing." Aunt Ruth placed her arm around Carrie's shoulders. "Perhaps you'd like to change into your nightclothes. I know I would. Then let's us ladies meet in my chamber with our tea. That way Major Johnston won't have any interruptions when he gives his report to Peyton."

Carrie liked the idea and nodded. "I'd rather not be alone right now anyway."

After bidding Major Johnston good night, Carrie took to the stairs. She walked down the hallway and opened the door to her new quarters. Just inside the darkened corridor, she struck a match and lit the wall sconce, followed by a table lamp. The latter in hand, she walked the rest of the way into her new bedroom, complete with its own sitting room.

Aunt Ruth wasn't far behind, and offered to unfasten Carrie's borrowed wedding gown. Carrie gratefully accepted. Afterward, Aunt Ruth headed off to her own bedroom and Carrie finished undressing. She suddenly felt physically drained, as if she'd spent the day climbing Massanutten Mountain. Trembling, her mind numb, she decided against joining Aunt Ruth and Meredith for tea. Instead, she'd thaw her thoughts and attempt to make sense out of what happened tonight.

If only Peyton would return.

Carrie padded to the window and opened it a crack. The mild October breeze sailed in, carrying with it a remnant of sweet honeysuckle from the vine that grew alongside the window. Horses nickered somewhere below.

Carrie pulled on her wrapper and headed toward the door, but Peyton entered the room before she reached it.

"I'm so glad to see you." She ran to him and didn't stop until her body collided with his, and her arms held him fast. She pressed her cheek against his rough wool jacket. How safe and protected she felt within his embrace.

Peyton kissed the top of her head. "Are you all right?"

"Shaken, but unharmed."

"Good." He placed a kiss on her forehead. "Carrie, we have to talk." He pushed the door closed with the toe of his boot.

"I killed a man, Peyton. I didn't want to, but I felt sure he'd hurt me if I didn't."

"I know, and I believe you did the only thing you could." He held her at arm's length and peered into her face. His expression was solemn. "But now I need you to tell me the truth. Is Major John Brown's real first name Joshua?"

She blinked. *He knew.* Well, she wasn't going to lie and she told Joshua that. "Yes, it is." Her breathing came more quickly. She obviously had some explaining to do, but, like she'd told Joshua, she wouldn't lie to Peyton.

"Is he the same Joshua who was your childhood playmate?"

"Yes."

Peyton released her and hung his head back. "You've been protecting him all this time?"

"No, not protecting him. Please, let me explain."

"You lied to me, Carrie."

"No . . ."

"You deceived me!"

"Not intentionally." When Peyton didn't reply, she hurried on. "The night I left camp I reasoned that Joshua had deserted the Confederacy and worked for General Sheridan. He made me promise not to reveal his identity then, and I agreed, thinking it was for the good of his mission. I didn't think I'd see him again . . . and I didn't, until tonight."

"But you still didn't say anything, even after he accosted you on the footbridge."

"I wanted to, but . . . I had given my word not to expose him. Peyton, he'd been like my older brother all my life." She exhaled. "Now, I suppose he's my enemy. He's a Confederate spy, isn't he?"

"I suspect so. Yes."

"But he did save my life tonight by handing off his pistol to me so I could protect myself against Rodingham. I suppose that's something." If Peyton knew that, perhaps Joshua wouldn't be hanged.

"Did it ever occur to you, Carrie, that had you been honest with me from the start, tonight's tragedy could have been avoided?"

Tragedy? Is that how he saw Rodingham's death?

"No, of course you didn't. All you cared about was protecting your friend."

She winced at his raised voice. "That's not true, Peyton."

He began to pace, his hands now clasped behind his back. "Did you give him any information?"

"No. I would never do anything of the sort, and Joshua knew better than to ask."

"How did he get out of jail?"

"Rodingham bragged about overpowering the two soldiers who accompanied Joshua."

"Hmm . . ."

Why did Carrie feel as though she was the perpetrator? "I didn't think by merely shutting my mouth I'd commit any wrongdoing." Usually the opposite got her in trouble.

Peyton halted and stared at her. "Tommy's dead, Carrie."

"No!" She pulled her calico wrapper more tightly around herself. "No, he can't be dead! He got up from the foyer, and—"

"He's dead, Carrie. I was there when he passed." Peyton's voice sounded strangled. "Worse, his death was senseless."

Her breath caught at the implication. *It's my fault.*

Peyton walked to the door.

"Peyton, please wait."

He paused, his back to her.

"I'm so sorry . . ." A sudden knot in her throat threatened to choke her. Tears clouded her vision.

Without another word, Peyton yanked open the door and left, slamming it behind him.

CHAPTER 27

How long Carrie paced the empty bedroom, she couldn't say. It seemed like days though it had only been hours since Peyton stormed out. And he hadn't returned, which left Carrie's imagination to run unchecked. Had Peyton gone after Joshua? He'd likely kill him if he caught him—unless Joshua killed him first.

Please, God, protect him. She paused, then added, *both of them.* Somehow she couldn't bring herself to condemn Joshua.

Shouts outside drew Carrie's attention. Crossing the room, she pushed back the draperies and flung open the long window. The night was dark, but the air sailing into the room felt cool—cool and smoky.

Smoky?

"What's going on, soldier?" she called to a Union guard below.

"Sorry to alarm you, ma'am. The house next door is on fire, but you're in no danger."

Carrie wasn't worried about herself. "Are the Monteague ladies all right?"

"Yes, ma'am. No one's been injured."

Carrie wondered if that explained Peyton's absence. Of course he would help extinguish the blaze.

She turned from the window. Still wearing her wrapper, Carrie ran from the room. At the top of the stairs, she paused, seeing Aunt Ruth and Tabitha below, deep in conversation.

"You heard Peyton. The orders to burn the Monteagues' home came directly from General Sheridan," Aunt Ruth said. "The general won't tolerate any threats to his troops, directly or indirectly, and the Monteagues harbored Confederate spies—including the one who intended to harm Carrie Ann."

"It's the least them Monteagues deserve," Tabitha groused.

Aunt Ruth muttered something Carrie couldn't hear, then said, "Peyton said the burning will be an example to Winchester's secessionists."

"Frances and Lavinia ain't stayin' here, I hope."

"No, of course not. Union soldiers packed a wagon and are forcing Frances and Lavinia to leave town as we speak. I expect they'll go live with Anthony in Richmond, where he will continue to try to penetrate Union blockades. I'm sure they'll be fine, but still I think . . ."

Carrie couldn't hear the rest of what was said, but the slight edge in Aunt Ruth's tone was evident.

"I ain't sad to see them go," Tabitha muttered. "And don't you be feeling sorry for them either. Burning their house ain't no more than what the Rebels done when they controlled the town. Lots of loyalists lost their homes."

"You're right, Tabitha dear. We're very blessed that Piccadilly Place is still standing. Even so, I hate to see Frances and Lavinia homeless. And traveling up that rutted pike in the dark. How frightening!" Aunt Ruth's voice was laced with both sadness and concern. "In my opinion the Monteagues' punishment is too harsh, especially since Carrie Ann's friend is just as guilty as the dead Confederate spy she shot in our library. And to think she kept silent about their identities."

Standing in the shadows, Carrie felt wretched. Obviously, Aunt Ruth blamed her for what happened tonight. For Tommy's death and now losing her friend, Frances Monteague.

Her heart shattered.

Turning silently, Carrie made her way back to her quarters. Smoke wafted in through the window that she'd left open. The acrid smell of burning wood and upholstery mixed with the sounds of breaking glass and loud voices caused her to vividly remember the fire on the farm in Woodstock. A moment later, she was there, reliving each painful second—Mama, out of her mind, and no one to help. No house. A cold night. Nowhere to go.

These past weeks Carrie had wanted to forget her life in Woodstock and begin anew without the burden of her family. Joshua had been correct: she was selfish.

If so, then losing everything tonight was her just deserts.

Blinking back tears, Carrie closed the window then began to dress. She knew what she had to do. She needed to remember the reason she left Woodstock in the first place . . .

To find Sarah Jane!

—☙ ❧—

Peyton blinked. He couldn't have read this letter from Carrie correctly.

He reread it, particularly the first two lines. *Because of tonight's tragedy, you will, no doubt, want to annul our nuptials. It may surprise you to learn that I concur, considering I am entirely to blame . . .*

With a weary groan, Peyton dropped into the armchair in their bedroom. He combed his fingers through his hair, then massaged his now-throbbing temples. How in the world had she arrived at the conclusion that he'd want to annul their marriage? Certainly she bore some responsibility for what happened, but it was, as she penned, a tragedy. Peyton didn't blame her. No one did. And he certainly didn't want an annulment.

He scanned the remainder of Carrie's letter, which largely consisted of a list of the items she'd taken and her promise to pay back the sum of their worth once she found employment in Martinsburg. She was heading there to find Sarah Jane, who was being cared for at a tavern called the Sundowner.

Employment? At a tavern? Surely Carrie didn't want that kind of a lifestyle. Not again. And when did she discover the whereabouts of her sister?

On a long sigh, Peyton let his head fall back against the top of the chair. Staring at the ceiling, he noted it needed a new coat of white paint. At least that much was clear to him. He'd come up here, carrying a tray of coffee and two plates of breakfast for his new bride and himself. He'd hoped to make up for lost time. And this is what met his efforts—a cold room, an empty bed, and a note from his beloved stating that she'd left him.

She left me. Those three words bruised him more than exchanging saber clashes with Rebels, although his mind wasn't yet willing to accept them. There were too many questions that required answers.

Sitting forward, he turned Carrie's letter in his hands and critically picked apart the situation. She had interpreted his intentions wrongly. But if her stepmother wouldn't forgive her for Sarah Jane's rebellious actions, Peyton supposed he could understand how Carrie applied the same twisted logic to their situation. Yes, he'd been angry that she'd kept silent about the enemy's identity. But he believed her explanation—and forgave her. The only reason he hadn't returned to their room last night was because of the issues next door with the Monteagues. Mercy, but those ladies were problems—problems now on their way south to Staunton, guarded by several troops who would stay with them as long as safely possible. It was dawn before all the commotion died down. He could understand how Carrie might jump to conclusions when he didn't return last night.

But it didn't excuse her running off the way she did.

Peyton drew in a long breath and slowly released it. His mind sought a plan of action. One thing was certain: he had to find Carrie, not only because he loved her but because she was likely to get herself killed!

CHAPTER 28

It hadn't been difficult to skirt around pickets and vedettes in the dark of night. Wearing her black woolen cloak pulled over her head, Carrie managed to blend in with the shadows. The only time she nearly met guards was as she neared the Valley Pike, but she'd quickly ducked into a farmer's buckwheat field, and while going terribly out of her way, she managed to evade the soldiers.

Carrying a small valise, it wasn't long before Carrie felt sure she'd drop from exhaustion. But then as the sun popped over the horizon, an old Negro man came by in his rickety wagon and offered her a ride to Martinsburg.

"I's goin' that way anyhow."

The next Union guards rode by and paid them no mind.

"I always gots my pass with me so I reckon they know you got yours."

Carrie had forgotten that important detail. A pass was needed to leave town . . . and she didn't have one. "I- I'm afraid I forgot mine."

"Name's Jeremiah Fry. What's yours?"

"Carrie Ann Collier." Too late, she wondered if she should have used her maiden name.

"Pleased to meet you, ma'am. We'll just pray we don't get stopped. Like I said, most of these fellas know me already. They say, 'There's ol' black Jeremiah and his po' old mules, going for Missus Tate's supplies again.' You see, I travel on Sunday so I steer clear of trouble that otherwise might get in my way. I stay overnight at my cousin Hester's home, pick up the order on

Monday, and make it back to Winchester before any wickedness figures out I ever left."

"Who's Mrs. Tate?"

"The woman that owns me. Oh, but don't frown so hard, Miz Carrie Ann. I'm treated all right. Couldn't do better on my own, I figure. Not at my age for sure. And Missus Tate needs someone to look after her since her husband passed on."

Bells clanged in the distance, and as they passed travelers on their way to church, Carrie Ann felt ashamed. She'd forgotten today was the Sabbath. *God, forgive me.* Maybe she should have made a plan before leaving Piccadilly Place.

By early afternoon, as Martinsburg came into view, Carrie felt certain she'd made a terrible mistake. The hymns Mr. Fry sang at the top of his lungs only confirmed her wretched feelings. But as she bounced along on the wagon bench, she knew there was no looking back.

They rode through town, whose main thoroughfare was largely deserted. Respectable businesses were closed on Sunday. Even the livery looked vacated. The Sundowner Tavern, on the other hand, appeared to be a lively place. Piano music from an untuned instrument wafted to their ears, and several rough-looking men stood outside, smoking cheroots and clinging to whisky bottles.

"I think we best keep on moving, Miss Carrie Ann."

"No, please." She placed her gloved hand on the slave's forearm. She'd told him that she was looking for her youngest sister who, according to Joshua, was gravely ill and being cared for in the tavern. "I've got to get Sarah Jane out of that place."

"We-ll. I guess I can wait here for you."

"That's not necessary, and I wouldn't want to cause you any trouble."

"No trouble, ma'am, and you might need a wagon to transport that sister o' yours. Don't sound to me like she's in a condition to walk anywheres."

He was correct, of course. "Thank you, Mr. Fry. Hopefully, the hotel will be able to put us up tonight."

"Yes, ma'am." Mr. Fry jumped down and helped Carrie alight from the wagon's bench. She gave Peyton's Sidehammer a pat. It was well concealed in her dress pocket. Her courage bolstered, she glanced over at the men. Their clothes were sweat stained and tattered. One man was barefoot and swayed slightly as he stared at her. Another spit a wad of chew onto the ground and then wiped his mouth with his dirty sleeve.

"I won't dally. You can be sure of it." She turned to Mr. Fry. "But if you feel your safety is in jeopardy, don't wait. Keep going. I'd feel horrible if I brought any harm to you." *Like I did to Tommy.*

"You ain't bringing harm to me. Jus' hurry up, and if'n you're right and it's your sister in there, get her out quick. We'll put her in the wagon bed."

After a nod of agreement, Carrie made her way toward the tavern. Upon closer inspection, she concluded the structure was in far worse shape than the Wayfarers Inn. Constructed with thin, rough wooden plank walls, it was a wonder the place withstood strong winds.

She reached the men. They surprised her by removing their hats and nodding politely.

"Excuse me, but I'm looking for my sister. I received word that she's here . . . Would you know where I can find her?"

"'Fraid not, little honey. But ask Abby Enders inside. She'll know." The tobacco chewer smiled, revealing several missing teeth, and pulled open the door. "Go on in."

Carrie murmured a word of thanks and walked inside the dimly lit tavern. She waited a moment for her eyes to adjust before glancing around. The only light came from a few lamps hanging on nails above the bar.

"Thar she is. That's Abby over yonder, holdin' a pitcher of beer." The man had followed her in, and now spoke close to Carrie's ear, sending prickles of apprehension down her spine.

Carrie moved off to the side, waiting for a moment when Miss Enders wouldn't be occupied. As she watched the matronly server at work, she wondered what would become of Sarah and her. She'd have to find employment until she could transport Sarah Jane home to Woodstock. Would she find a respectable position somewhere, or would she be stuck working here?

Carrie's eyes began to sting from the smoky haze, and she grew increasingly aware of men's glances at her—and at her reticule. It dangled from her right wrist. She wished she had remembered to tuck it out of sight. She'd brought her allowance to pay for Sarah Jane's keep. While Peyton had been generous, giving her an allotted monthly sum, it wouldn't last long if she had to support the two of them.

She swallowed hard. Was she glimpsing her own fate as she gazed at the harried server, arms now laden with a tray containing a whiskey bottle and four short glasses?

Maybe she could return to Winchester and throw herself at Peyton's mercy. Then, again, no! She clenched her gloved hands. She loved Peyton, but she wasn't about to grovel.

Miss Enders emptied her burden onto the middle of a table surrounded by men playing cards. Hoping to catch her before she took care of another customer, Carrie stepped forward.

The woman noticed her and tugged up on her bodice in what seemed to be an act of self-consciousness.

"Miss Enders?"

Her eyes narrowed. "Who're you?"

"My name is Carrie Ann. I was told my sister is very ill and here in the tavern."

"Your sister?" Understanding washed over her face just before deep lines set in on her forehead. "She was here, Miss."

"She left?"

"In a manner of speaking." Miss Enders took her elbow. "I'd best show you. Come with me."

Miss Enders led her to the back of the tavern and then down a narrow hall. The soles of Carrie Ann's boots stuck to the grimy floor with each step. At last they exited the side doorway and walked into the yard behind the tavern.

"There. She's over there."

Carrie's gaze followed in the direction that Miss Enders pointed. "I see a meadow, maybe a stream beyond it, but I don't see Sarah Jane anywhere."

"The cemetery, Miss. She's in the cemetery."

The wind left Carrie's lungs. She staggered forward. Miss Enders steadied her.

"I know it's a shock, Miss. But I did all what I could for her. Even called Doc Parker, who examined her and prescribed her several treatments. Nothing worked."

"Sarah's . . . dead?" No! It couldn't be true!

"Yes, Miss. I'm real sorry 'bout it too."

"Surely you're mistaken."

"No, Miss, I ain't. The girl passed a day after that dark-headed fellow left. And if you'll be wanting a refund of his money, I'll be straight with you, I ain't got it anymore."

"I-I don't care about the money." Feeling dazed, Carrie walked to the gravesite.

Miss Enders followed. "The girl was bad off when that fellow left her here. She never woke up."

"How did it happen?"

"The man who brung her said some peddler beat her up and left her for dead. She developed a fever soon afterward that wouldn't leave her. Then the fellow said—"

"Joshua—or perhaps you know him as Major Brown?"

"That's him." Miss Enders inclined her head. "Told me he found the girl, said she was like family to him. The hospital's been full up with wounded men for weeks, so he asked me to take care of her and he promised to inform the girl's older sister—must be you."

"He kept his word." Reaching her sister's grave, Carrie dropped to her knees. Tears flowed freely. "Oh, Sarah Jane, I'm so sorry . . ."

Why couldn't she have found her baby sister before it was too late? Maybe if she had escaped the Union camp instead of falling in love with Peyton, she could have rescued Sarah Jane from that no-account peddler.

The sound of horses' hooves drifted toward them.

"Yankees is here." Miss Enders heaved a sigh. "I'd best get back inside. Those men probably got a powerful thirst."

Carrie remained at the gravesite. Around her the long dry grass blew in the October wind. There was nothing more she or anyone else could do for Sarah Jane. She was with Jesus, meeting Him either as her Savior or her Judge. Carrie longed to believe Sarah met Him as her King of kings, and that she'd see her youngest sister again someday in heaven.

Slowly, Carrie got to her feet. Her head swam. When had she last eaten? A few bites at last night's party? The dizziness passed but left a heaviness in its place. She trudged back toward the front of the tavern. Mr. Fry stood near his wagon, kindly waiting for her.

Seconds later, a blue-jacketed soldier rounded the corner of the tavern, pistol drawn.

Carrie halted. But in her present state she didn't much care if he shot her.

The soldier lowered his weapon at once, and removed his cap, revealing a head of unkempt brown hair.

Recognition set in. "Sergeant Kramer?"

Kramer holstered his gun and looked to his right. "Colonel Collier," he hollered. "I done found your wife."

At that moment, Carrie's legs threatened to give way. She hadn't believed Peyton would follow her. After all, he didn't seek out Miss Monteague when she didn't show up for their wedding years ago.

Carrie's mouth went dry at the thought of facing him. He must be terribly angry if he trailed her all the way to Martinsburg.

A heartbeat later, she crumpled to the ground. Kramer rushed forward. Mr. Fry hollered her name. Carrie struggled to stay conscious. The weight of her limbs wouldn't allow her to get back on her feet. She glimpsed the top of Mr. Fry's peppery head as he bent over her, and then a wall of blue before Peyton gathered her into his arms.

"I've got you, Carrie." His lips touched her ear, and his voice held that same low, sturdy-soft timbre that always made her feel so safe.

Eyes closed, she gave in to the overpowering sea of nothingness.

CHAPTER 29

"I'm fine."

"You're not fine, and we're staying here until you're well enough to travel back to Winchester." Peyton turned from the drapery-lined hotel window and faced Carrie. He didn't care one bit for her pale complexion. It was an alarming match to the downy pillows behind her. "You need to rest. You're exhausted."

She didn't reply, but picked at a multicolored quilt that covered her. He worried over her mournful expression about as much as her ashen face.

Peyton stepped toward the bed. "I'm sorry for your loss. I know you hoped to find Sarah Jane alive."

"I did." Her voice sounded strangled. "I pictured locating Sarah Jane in many different situations, but I never dreamed I'd discover that she'd died before I reached her."

"I've sent a telegram to your stepmother and Margaret in Woodstock, letting them know of Sarah Jane's death." He knelt beside the bed and stroked her hair. "If you'd like, we can have a proper ceremony for her and move her body to—"

"No. Let her rest in peace."

Peyton wondered if Carrie would change her mind once she felt better. He'd broach the subject again at a later time.

"How and when did you discover that she was here in Martinsburg?"

Carrie still didn't look at him. "Joshua told me. Last night on the footbridge. That's why he came."

"Ah . . ." Peyton clenched his fist then forced himself to relax. "That explains a lot." He rose from the bed and paced the room. Perhaps the man had some good in him. Still, Peyton was more than certain that her childhood friend would like nothing better than to tear him and Carrie apart and see him, a Union colonel, dead. They were, after all, enemies. "Did Joshua help you leave Winchester last night?"

"No. I left of my own free will—and alone."

Her reply pained him.

"Now that I found . . . Sarah Jane—" Her voice cracked. "I have to find Papa." Finally, she turned toward him. "But I'm grateful for your thoughtfulness, Peyton."

"I'm not being *thoughtful*. I'm being your *husband!*" His renewed aggravation would not be stemmed. In fact, his anger and determination had been what kept Brogan galloping nearly the entire way to Martinsburg. "As for that love letter you left me, it's in the hearth where all rubbish belongs. What's more, you can search for your father—but from Piccadilly Place where I don't have to worry about you."

"Oh . . ." Carrie covered her face with her hands, but not before he caught a glimpse of her teary eyes. Immediately he regretted his harsh words. Years spent at West Point and in the army didn't foster a man's sensitive nature, that was most certain. He rubbed his whiskered jaw and vowed to work on it. Carrie wasn't one of his enlisted men.

He softened his tone. "We made vows to each other, Carrie. Vows I take very seriously."

She removed her hands from her tear-streaked face. "I know, but—"

"We love each other and we belong together. You said so yourself."

She nodded.

"There will be no annulment. I wish you had waited and told me that you located your sister instead of running off and endangering your life."

Carrie's tears leaked from her eyes and coursed down her cheeks. Her narrow shoulders shook with a sob. "I should have told you a number of things, Peyton."

"I won't argue."

Peyton sat down on the edge of the bed and retrieved his handkerchief, pressing it into Carrie's palm. She dried her eyes and gathered her composure.

"What made you believe that I am so unforgiving?"

"I can hardly forgive myself for contributing to Tommy's death. How can you ever forgive me?"

"I love you. I forgive you freely."

"Even though I lied and deceived you?" Her blue eyes shined through the moisture filling them.

"You explained the reasons for keeping your friend's identity secret, and I believe you. I also trust you won't keep secrets from me again."

"I won't." She dried her eyes and met his gaze.

He smiled gently at her, and relief crossed her pale face.

"However, we do need to discuss a few additional matters."

She nodded.

"About Tommy . . . I know you cared a great deal for him. I apologize for being so cross with you last night."

"You had good reason to be cross." She stared into his handkerchief. "You cared about Tommy too. I still can't believe he's . . . gone."

Peyton had seen too much death to question it. "Tommy died a Union soldier, with valor and honor. That's all he wanted."

After several moments lapsed, Carrie looked up at him. "How did you find out about Joshua?"

"Before he died, Tommy told me that you called Major Brown *Joshua*. I guessed the rest quickly. I was livid, and regrettably, I acted on my emotion."

"I would have been angry too, if I were you."

"But you're not me, Carrie." Peyton spoke softly. "You can't assume my thoughts. You need to talk with me instead of jumping to conclusions and running away."

Carrie dropped the handkerchief and covered her face, but Peyton pried away one of her small hands and enfolded it in his much larger ones.

"I have so many regrets, Peyton."

"Like marrying me? You were rather coerced into it."

"No! I don't regret marrying you for a moment. The love I feel for you is real. What I regret is keeping Joshua's secret." Her eyebrow dipped with a heavy frown. "I never imagined anyone would get hurt or die because I said nothing. It was a naïve and foolish belief. I know that now. Now that it's too late for Tommy." Her shoulders sagged as she expelled a rueful sigh. "And then there's Sarah Jane . . . I regret not finding her in time to save her life."

"There are some things that are beyond our control. Life and death are among them. We do what we can for the sick and dying, but ultimately God's will prevails."

"True enough." She seemed to consider the matter further for several moments. "My next regret is losing Aunt Ruth's respect."

Peyton narrowed his gaze. "Aunt Ruth?"

"The Monteagues' home would still be standing if it weren't for me."

"More rubbish. Mrs. Monteague and Lavinia harbored spies—"

"Joshua and Rodingham?"

"Correct. And both ladies were unapologetic about it when confronted, after which Mrs. Monteague charged one of my sergeants with a fireplace poker."

Carrie's jaw dropped slightly.

"Had it been just me in the room with no witnesses, I might have overlooked Mrs. Monteague's aggression. Her son Edward had just died. However, I had a number of officers with me, and the burning orders came from General Sheridan himself. I had no choice but to see them carried out. Aunt Ruth knows all of that. She doesn't blame you in the least. Furthermore, she wanted me to round up the entire Union cavalry and search for you." Peyton grinned. "I selected a somewhat smaller group of enlisted men to accompany me."

Hope shone in Carrie's teary eyes.

"Aunt Ruth loves you, my sweet. You haven't lost her respect—nor mine. And please know this—I'm not like your stepmother or anyone else from your past who has refused to forgive you."

"I should have known that," she whispered.

"And now you do."

"Now I do," she echoed.

She brushed one finger over an ages-old scar on the back of his right hand, a permanent reminder of some skirmish years ago.

"Oh, Peyton . . ." Carrie rolled forward onto her knees. "I beg your forgiveness. I love you and I swear I will never keep a single secret from you again."

He pulled her onto his lap and wrapped her in an embrace. "All is forgiven, Carrie."

He kissed her, and then his lips moved from hers and glided across her cheek. She snuggled into the place betwixt his neck and shoulder. He rested his chin against her forehead and stroked her soft, curly hair. "I've lost far too many people in my life, people for whom I cared deeply. I watched friends die on the battlefield. I've seen good men cut down like saplings. When I look back on my life, it's like peering out a window on a gloomy, rainy day. After Christ saved me, the world became brighter, but I still had this small dark void deep inside. It was as God said, it's not good that a man should be alone. Then I found love in a sycamore." Peyton would never forget that day.

Leaning back and smiling, Carrie put her hands on either side of his face and touched her lips to his in the sweetest of kisses. He tasted remnants of her salty sadness when they parted.

"You brought sunshine to my dreary existence, Carrie. I can't bear the thought of losing you."

"You won't." Again she kissed him, dousing the last smidgen of his concern. "I'll never leave you again."

She whispered the promise against his mouth, and at her words, a deep, abiding love burned inside him, a love that would weather life's storms. Peyton had no doubt that God created Carrie especially for him to love, cherish, and protect—and to make him a better man.

"And no matter what," he promised in return, "I'll love you till the day I die."

TOO DEEP
for
WORDS

Book Two

coming November 2016

CHAPTER 1

October 6, 1864

"Well, I'll be hanged. The Yankee Cavalry is ridin' into Woodstock."

Margaret Jean Bell paused in midstroke and dropped the rag she'd been using to clean the sticky bar. She looked toward the entrance of the Wayfarers Inn where a raggedy-dressed old man stood staring out to the street. "More Yankees in town?"

"That's what I jest said, girl." The old man swayed slightly and kneaded his bristly jaw. "Judging by the black smoke over yonder, them blue bellies is burning ever'thing in sight too!"

Margaret clutched her midsection as if the panic crimping her insides was visible to the few male patrons around her. Questions tumbled through her mind. Would one of the Yankee soldiers recognize her and, if so, did he have an inkling of her trickery?

Instinct screamed, *run!* Her breath came and went in quick repetitions, as if she'd already cantered a mile up Main Street.

Breathe. Breathe.

Her light-headedness slowly abated. Logic soon returned.

Wasn't she accustomed to soldiers, Yanks and Rebs alike? She was, sure as the sun set in the west. She'd learned men were men, bluecoats or gray, and she could handle herself in their presence. Should one of the soldiers insist on getting his money back for services that were promised but never rendered, Margaret would simply tell the truth. Mr. Veyschmidt snatched her ill-gotten gains. Therefore she could provide him with no refund. Afterward, she'd accept the beating likely to follow.

Oh, God, if only I could get out of this place!

How lucky her oldest sister Carrie Ann was to escape by marrying a blue-belly. Her younger sister, Sarah Jane, managed to get away by running off with a peddler, except she got herself killed in the process. Sad as it was, death seemed preferable to life here at the Wayfarers Inn. Mama, too, was gone now, died at the end of September, leaving Margaret in the care of a temperamental, tyrannical innkeeper who enjoyed reminding her of the debt she owed. He insisted on federal currency no less. He paid her nothing for the daily chores, nothing for serving plates of food and ale to customers. Many times she worked until the wee hours of the morning. Each week the sum she owed grew larger, not smaller. Margaret, in all her life, would never be able to repay him, so this was a life's sentence.

Yes, death was preferable to this wretched existence.

She set down two bottles of Mr. Veyschmidt's backroom concoction, which he called *ale*, on the bar. Then she waited. Soldiers usually had a powerful thirst when they walked in. She glanced over at the portly innkeeper. He stared out the window and nervously chewed a fingernail. The swine. What a blessing it would be if the man got shot dead by a Yankee bullet.

Within minutes, a tall, bearded, blue-clad officer crossed over the threshold. His spurs chinked against the plank floorboards with each step he took. He squinted as his eyes adjusted to his dimly lit and smoky surroundings. The gold trim ornamenting his uniform bespoke an upper rank. Odd. Men like him usually didn't wander in to the Wayfarers Inn.

Two additional Yanks followed him inside. They made such an ominous threesome that the few remaining men loitering about in the saloon scattered like roaches after a match strike.

The first officer made his way to the bar. He removed his wide-brimmed hat.

"Care for a drink? The innkeeper says it's on the house." Margaret poured a glass of ale and pushed it toward him.

"I said no such thing," Veyschmidt growled. Then he seemed to reconsider, just as Margaret expected him to. "Well, all right. Just one's free."

"No, thanks. I'm looking for Miss Margaret Bell."

Her heart stumbled over its next beat.

"That's her." Mr. Veyschmidt pointed a thick finger. "Right there she stands."

No help or hope of protection from him—as usual.

Margaret set her hands on her hips. "Listen, mister, I don't give refunds, so—"

"Are you Miss Bell?"

She nodded and lifted her chin, fully expecting to feel the explosion of pain after his fist connected with her face. If he was like all the others, she'd swindled him. She prayed he'd knock her senseless. Maybe she'd never regain consciousness.

"My wife would like two jugs of the innkeeper's ale."

Margaret blinked, the tense muscles in her body relaxed, and she released an audible sigh of relief.

"My wife claims the ale aids in the healing of wounds. In fact, I'm living proof it does." The Yankee cracked a grin and arched a brow before his gaze slid to Mr. Veyschmidt. "She also insists the stuff makes an amazing metal polisher. Wonder of wonders."

"Metal polisher?" Margaret tipped her head. The only person who touted Mr. Veyschmidt's ale as good for something other than sheer inebriation was . . .

Margaret sucked in a breath. Could this be her oldest sister's Yankee husband?

She looked him over again. Not a chance. This man was large and handsome with a head of thick blond hair and neatly trimmed whiskers. His upper rank and sophisticated demeanor suggested he was too refined for a poor, skinny, pie-in-the-sky dreamer like Carrie Ann. More likely a customer heard of the ale's supposed benefits and spread the word. Medicine was scarce, what with wounded men pouring into towns up and down the Valley, so every sort of home remedy was in high demand.

Margaret fetched two stoneware jugs and set them on the bar. The officer slapped a couple of bills into Veyschmidt's wide, outstretched palm. Next the colonel retrieved an envelope from his coat's inner breast pocket and extended it in Margaret's direction.

"May I speak with you in private, Miss Bell?"

Before a single utterance passed her lips, Mr. Veyschmidt stepped in front of her as if she'd suddenly become a precious commodity. "Afraid not. You want a private appointment, shall we say, then you'll have to pay for it like everyone else."

The blond officer narrowed his gaze. "I suggest you shut your mouth and get out of my way."

Veyschmidt eyed the man, then his comrades, and relented. "Make it quick," he muttered to Margaret. "And you owe me every coin you get out of him."

She squeezed her eyes shut. If hating a man was indeed the same as murder like the reverend preached, then she was guilty a thousand times over.

The colonel moved several steps away from Mr. Veyschmidt. Margaret trailed him, wondering what he wanted with her.

She didn't have to wait long to find out. "Allow me to introduce myself, Miss Bell," the brass-buttoned officer stated. "I'm Colonel Peyton Collier, Cavalry Division of the Army of the Shenandoah."

Collier. Margaret frowned. Wasn't that . . . ?

"I'm Carrie Ann's husband."

Margaret blinked. "Truly?" So this was him. How had Carrie Ann snagged such a fine gentleman?

"Well, well . . ." Veyschmidt overheard the introduction and puffed out his barrel-like chest. "What a coincidence. Your, eh, wife, left quite a large tab here what needs to be paid."

Colonel Collier's face reddened and his eyes narrowed to angry slits. "My wife owes you nothing, so spare me more of your lies."

Margaret saw the emotion blazing in his eyes as he defended Carrie Ann.

"Destroying your inn would be within my orders," he stated in the darkest of tones, "but it's because of my wife's request to leave this place intact for her family's sake that I hesitate, should Mrs. and Miss Bell decide to remain here." He glanced at Margaret before peering down at Veyschmidt again. "I am well aware of your abuse of the Bell sisters and their mother over the past two years. I know you habitually overcharged them for room and board, effectively enslaving them. You worked them hard and fed them little. Worse, you left my wife and her family unprotected and vulnerable to every kind of evil." The shake of his head was slight. "You are a despicable worm in my estimation and had it been up to me—"

Margaret strained to hear his words, but gauging by the fear gathering in Mr. Veyschmidt's beady eyes, the colonel's threat rang loud and clear.

She worked to hide a grin. She liked her new brother-in-law already.

"It would give me great pleasure," he added, "to watch this sorry place go up in flames. You inflicted suffering on the Bells. For that reason, you've earned a black mark against you."

Mr. Veyschmidt wisely held his tongue, although he chewed his thick lower lip and worked his hands anxiously.

"Pardon the interruption, sir," one of the other Yankees said. He stood even taller and broader shouldered than the colonel. He, too, had removed his hat and an abundance of shaggy brown hair framed his face. "This establishment has most likely been a Rebel meeting place and gave sustenance to the enemy. Could be Rebels are recovering in rooms upstairs as we speak."

"No, no . . . there ain't no soldiers here," Mr. Veyschmidt insisted. "I refused all the wounded. Don't want the mess. You know . . . blood and all." He waved a meaty hand and shuddered.

The colonel's eyes met Margaret's and she gave a slight nod. Confederate soldiers had met here only days ago. Several injured lay in rooms upstairs as the major suspected.

"Gather your men and search the premises, Major Johnston."

"Yes, sir."

Within minutes, a small army of Yankees crowded into the Wayfarers Inn. Mr. Veyschmidt grew increasingly anxious as the soldiers disbursed to search. He fell to his knees in a pathetic, theatrical display.

"Please don't burn my inn," he begged. "This business is all I have left of my dearly departed mother who worked her fingers to the bone to make this a respectable place for one to lay his weary head."

Such lies. Margaret rolled her eyes and just barely kept from snorting aloud. And respectable? How utterly laughable.

"Miss Bell?" The colonel's brown eyes fixed on her. "I am allowed to show mercy where it's warranted. What do you think I should do?"

"Me? You're asking me?"

"Don't bother with the girl," Veyschmidt groused. "She's nothing. Customers often complain about her poor service. She's brazen and rude."

"Quiet, you scoundrel!" After a simmering glare at Mr. Veyschmidt, the colonel's gaze returned to Margaret. The hard lines around his eyes vanished. "Miss Bell?"

"I have no place to go." Despite her best efforts, her bottom lip quivered. It wasn't the answer she longed to give.

"My wife wishes for you and your mother to live with us in Winchester. While she asked me to relay the invitation, she was fairly certain your mother, in particular, wouldn't accept."

"Mama's dead." Surely Carrie Ann would rescind her offer with that change of circumstance. They'd quarreled a lot during their growing-up years, but that didn't stop Margaret from missing Carrie's bravery when she stood up to Mr. Veyschmidt, sparing Margaret a beating. And she could use one of Carrie Ann's harebrained schemes right about now. Margaret often imagined implementing Carrie's daring escape from the Wayfarers Inn, and dreamed of it almost as many times as she envisioned Mr. Veyschmidt's delicious demise.

"Please accept my condolences." The colonel sounded sincere. He reached across the scuffed wooden bar and pressed the sealed envelope into Margaret's hand.

She inspected it, impressed by the expensive parchment. Her name had been penned across the front, and she recognized Carrie Ann's handwriting. She closed her eyes. To her left, Mr. Veyschmidt's pleas for mercy grated on her nerves.

"Carrie addressed this letter to you because she presumed your mother would never forgive her or want to see her again because of Sarah Jane's death."

Margaret conceded his point with a nod. What he said was true. "I received the telegram about Carrie Ann's marriage and about Sarah Jane's death, but Mama had passed by the time the news arrived."

"You've lived through quite an ordeal, Miss Bell. I urge you to come to Winchester. You'll travel with a group of contraband and dunkers—freed slaves and German Baptists who are following the army down the Valley. Because of the war, they've been forced to leave their homes for some reason or another. My guess is, you'll be safer in the army's wake than here with

Veyschmidt." The colonel walked around the bar. Standing directly in front of Margaret, he tapped the envelope in her hand. "Regardless of what's happened in the past, I'm confident Carrie's invitation still stands."

"How can you be sure?"

"Because I know my wife and her kind, generous heart." He smiled, emitting a dizzying dose of charm. No wonder Carrie Ann married the man, and almost instantaneously too, it would seem. "Carrie volunteers at an orphanage in Winchester. She thought you might help out there also."

"Oh, I would. I love children."

"Sounds like you'll do very well in Winchester then."

Margaret watched him, noticing his confident manner, his commanding presence. But she couldn't help wondering if she'd seen him before.

The colonel's troops finished their search and he conversed with them in undertones. Minutes later, they filed out of the inn, and he refocused his attention on Margaret. "I'm afraid I must have your decision now, Miss Bell."

She only needed to glimpse Mr. Veyschmidt's rotund, pleading form. His beefy hands were clasped as if in prayer—the same hands that shamelessly groped and beat Margaret and her sisters, each to varying degrees. And Mama too. He'd killed Mama the same as if he'd strangled the life right out of her.

Oh, how Margaret despised the man!

"I accept my sister's invitation. Thank you." She tasted sweet freedom in the air. "But please, I beseech you"—now it was her turn to beg—"light your Yankee torches and burn this den of iniquity down to the devil where it belongs!"